Birds, Booze and Bulldozers

a novel

by Peter Styles

small world media

SMALL WORLD PUBLISHING
Knocknaquirk
Magheramore
County Wicklow
Ireland
www.smallworldmedia.ie

First published by SMALL FICTION, November 2007

Trade enquiries to
00 353 [0]87 955 1504 (Ireland, Europe)

info@smallworldmedia.ie

© Peter Styles

ISBNs: 978 0 9554634 5 7 [hardback]
978 0 9554634 3 3 [trade paperback]

A CIP record for this book is available from the British Library

Cover and book design, typesetting: SMALL WORLD BOOK SERVICES

Cover artwork: Polyp

Printed by La Grafica Nuova S.C.R.L., Torino

This novel is dedicated to anyone who has ever:–

climbed up, ran at, sat on, locked-on to, obstructed, lit, built,
organised, attended, barricaded, chopped, pedalled, licked, folded,
done jail for, donated, sabotaged, 'stolen', sung, commissioned
or proofread

anything

to make planet earth more sustainable.

It is also for all who have

wrestled; argued the toss with, thwarted, been arrested by,
leafleted, phoned, picketed, camped with, supported, boycotted,
defended, observed, catered for, pied, slept with and even voted for

anyone

in order to stand up for what we stand upon.

You know who you are.

Peter Styles, August 2007

Acknowledgements

The following people should be singled out for being great in various ways that have nothing to do with lentilism: Ed Cancela, Sandor Dus, Tammi Dallaston Wood, Kairen Hancock, Sue Hendra, Brian Kemp, Oz Mansions, David & Ashlene Millard, Paul Linnet, Mike Yeoman, Chris Yianni and my family.

These folks deserve special mention for remembering specific hippy-type stuff: Helen B, Roger Geffen, Jim Hindle, Becca Lush, Alex Plows, Paul Monaghan, Quartermaster Nick, Jason Torrance, Paul Williamson and Chris Woodford.

This lot helped magnificently in physically getting the book together: Robert Allen, Anne Addicott, Paul Fitzgerald, Allan Robinson and Gemma Sayers.

And finally thanks for all those who've managed to make progress on the issues covered in this novel since the mad old days 'ended'. You know, little things like the shelving of the roads programme and the self-determination of East Timor.

P.S. A 2006 survey found the Desmoulins whorl snail to be extinct in the Newbury area.

PART ONE:

CRIME

CHAPTER 1

SUMMER 1993

'Can you draw cartoons?'

'No.'

'Do you have a reputation in the world of comic writing?'

'Umm ... no. Got me there, but I've got some great ideas, like Placenta Playcentre.'

'Go on.'

'Well, it's about an old woman who keeps her mouldy afterbirth to turn into a children's playground. She applies for funding and all sorts.'

'Where is this Viz comic based?'

'Newcastle.'

'Fancy moving up there?'

'No.'

Here I am, in Worthing Job Club being interrogated. Ken Bierce is his name – ruining my summer is his game. Only graduated five minutes ago and the bastard wants me to think about what I want to do next. I'd like to say 'Have a fucking rest after jumping through grade-shaped hoops since I was five.' Three glorious years in Manchester is a fast fading memory as I'm cooped up with this prick. He may be wearing loafers on his feet but part of the Slacker Generation he is certainly not.

Freedom – that's what I'm after. That lofty concept which covers everything from having an extra chocolate biscuit with your tea to not getting your bollocks electrocuted in a Turkish prison. Doing precisely what I want for a while. Going to work for some smelly fucker who's older than my dad isn't on that list.

I know Worthing's a shit hole – they hold the World Bowls Championships here every year – probably cos nowhere else can be bothered. Don't worry – I'll do something big, soon. No fucking idea what, when or indeed why. But like I said, no biggie.

Oh, how very rude of me. Lester Stype's the name, pleased to meet you. Twenty-two going on six, and up for a summer of absolutely fuck all.

'Look, I just want some time to find myself,' I say to him. Find myself a big fat beer garden and swig my way through the afternoon more like.

'In my day ...' Oh here we go.

'... we didn't have that luxury. Had my first job just before I was sixteen – fishmonger's boy, up at five to meet the boats. Anyway – that's the best way of "finding yourself" as you call it – good honest work.'

'I've been sweating on my finals like a dog with four ... legs.' I was going to say 'cocks' but this is a guy who thinks listening to Van Morrison is risqué.

'Look, you may not want a career just yet, but there are other options,' he says. I'm looking out of the window, there's a grey squirrel chasing another one. Is a fight on? Potential shag? If so, is it consensual or against her little squirrel will?

'Hmm,' any enthusiasm in my response is stillborn. It's harassment – pure and simple.

'Have you considered voluntary work? Lots of organisations could use a hand from a bright lad like you.'

'S'pose they could.' I've put the A3 piece of paper stating I'm a bright lad in a cheap frame on my parents' wall.

'How about working with the elderly, or a youth group? Have you ever had much contact with the disabled?'

Appetising as a cup of cold sick stirred by a turd. The turd has a beard and is called Ken. I shake my head. The bigger squirrel has the other trapped on a twig. Whatever it wants – looks like it's gonna get it – and for better or worse I've got a ringside seat.

'What do you think then, something voluntary? You'd get some really good experience, eh?'

Make it stop – please. There were better ways of spending a July afternoon than this. A whole world out there – women, beer, laughs – the whole early twenties shebang. And yet here I am chewing the fat with a man who's not a woman, beer or even a laugh. Time for evasive action. Come on brain say something.

'Well – I am a member of the Green Party.' Where the fuck did that come from? I know I did join but surely 'I've got AIDS' or 'I love you' would have done just as well.

My brother's partner dropped a kid on the day the Berlin Wall fell. I kind of looked down at the cute little gurgling fella and thought – the planet'll be fucked when he's my age.

'Excellent,' sniffs Ken, chalking up another victory against sloth.

'Give them a ring, I'm sure they'll have something for you.' What a wanker. On the plus side, I've never seen squirrels do that before. Tick in the box.

'Hello Green Party, can I help you?'
'Er, yeah. I've just graduated and I'm interested in doing some voluntary work.' The voice on the other end of the phone is warm, friendly and female. Maybe a summer doing something worthy might not be such a pain in the arse after all. At least not for me – I'm not sure what I meant by that but it had nothing to do with bum touching – men's bum touching.
'A lot of our work is organised on a regional basis. Whereabouts do you live?'
I say Worthing dejectedly. Phonetically it even sounds sadder than Manchester.
'I can put you in touch with a local contact if you like. Isn't there a proposed new road scheme going on down that way?' This bird knows her stuff. Wonder if she's as impressive in the flesh?
I show off my hippy knowledge with 'Yeah, the A27 bypass and shit.'
'Well, the contact is ...' I can hear the tapping of a keyboard. 'Stewart Johnson. Do you have a pen handy?'
Why can't I have her phone number? The Green Party 0898 Line. Still, better try ringing this Johnson bloke – but later. Life's too short to bust balls on a lovely sunny day like this. Besides, this Job Club phone booth smells of doleys. Have you read 'Trainspotting' yet? 'kin great – if only I could understand what they say. Perhaps they'll make a film of it some day.
I suppose voluntary work could kill some time. For the last couple of years I've given my £8 a year membership to the Green Party – to keep my conscience clear, you know. Fuck knows what they do with it to save the planet? Up till now it's been an S.E.P – someone else's problem – the best kind. What am I letting myself in for? Looks like I've really stuck my cock in the good ideas machine – and shafted it.

'Hello, is that Stewart Johnson? ... well, err ... you don't know me, my name's Lester Stype and I'm into helping out.'
'With what?'
'Well ... you know.'
'What?'
'Um ... green stuff, the environment.'
'Ok ...' Stewart's probably thinking – and not without justification – that the people from Care in the Community have passed on his number to some Joey. You remember? Joey Deacon who was on Blue Peter that year.

'I've just left uni and I want to help.'

'Well, as you may know we're trying to stop the bypass from being built at the moment. We need research done for the public enquiry. The next meeting is on Wednesday. Fancy coming?'

I nervously knock on the door of the mid-terrace house where the meeting is – a few streets up from the sea – it's opened by a woman around my age, who's pretty skinny in a pretty, skinny kind of way.

'Hi, I'm Nikki, come in,' she says. The nose-ring is a passion killer but if she was a Top Trumps card she'd score reasonably well in most categories. Mid-length hair and cute slightly upturned nose. I've definitely seen worse.

'Thanks – Lester.' I shake her hand and am led into the hallway, leaning my bike against some others presumably belonging to the hippies. A dozen or so scruffs of varying ages litter the front room. A map and various documents I can't make any sense of are laid out on the floor.

'Would you like a drink?' Nikki asks.

'Tea please – one of each.'

'Pardon?'

'One milk – one sugar.'

'Oh – I'm afraid I've only got herbal. There's lots to choose from. Camomile? Lemon and ginger?'

'I'm good thanks – I err ... had some earlier,' I say defensively.

'Stewart?' Nikki signals over to some bloke his early fifties. Looks like he used to be cool and thinks he still is.

'Don't tell me – Lester. Nice to meet you. How local are you?'

'Sompting.'

'Up near the Downs?'

'Yeah – a couple of minutes' walk.' Those hills were my playground as a kid. Making dens. Chopping up pregnant slow worms. I even tried smoking aged thirteen – tasted like shit – and my mum found out. I really don't want four lanes of tarmac banged through it all. Again I try to show I can talk the talk.

'I can't believe they want to mess up Cissbury Ring. It's the second oldest Iron Age hillfort in the country.' This much I know. Me and my mates have done some brilliant camping up there. Real Lord of the Flies stuff. Eating hash cake, taking acid and getting mad vertigo up a tree.

In short – the Downs has been like a huge security blanket for the people of Sussex for centuries, and this is no time to start ripping it up.

'D'you know something Stewart?' I say, 'The South Downs is the closest thing to ... how would you put it ... a green and pleasant land I've ever experienced. It's been the backdrop to my childhood and no one should take that away.'

'We'll see what we can do at the public enquiry, eh?' he replies. Too fucking right.

There's a strange smell in the air. I don't want to seem rude and ask but what is it? Smells like rancid coconut or incense or something. It's the unmistakeable smell of hippies – get used to it.

'So what's with this public enquiry?' Stewart's next to this bird in her forties with massive tits. She's a bit mutton-as-lamb, wearing a T-shirt with a picture of John Paul II blowing smoke out of the corner of his mouth and underneath the words, I Like The Pope – The Pope Smokes Dope.

'Well,' she says. 'As far as I can gather all major planning decisions go through this bullshit. You get some boring old fart – maybe a civil servant close to retirement – to sit there and seem like he's listening to all the evidence. Then he just rubber-stamps the decision. It's just a political trick of the light and it sucks.'

'Shit,' I say.

'That's why some of us want to go a bit further than Green Party activity.' She hands me a leaflet from a group called Earth First! It's actually got an exclamation mark at the end.

Unusually for me there's no opportunity to talk about the Premiership or indie bands or finals or boozing. Don't know if this is a good thing or not.

Then Nikki says: 'Would anyone like to watch this new NVDA video?'

I haven't got an earthly what NVDA is, so I ask Wendy with a whisper. This means I can also have a sly peek at her jugs. Although she's old they're quite impressive.

'It stands for non–violent direct action. You'll soon get the idea if you haven't already.'

Ok. There's been green stuff on the TV but most of it is how to make a pencil holder from an empty washing-up bottle or whether non-biological toilet cleaner really does the business under the rim. The video starts. NVDA is anything but this.

The footage is rough – and certainly isn't going to challenge Merchant Ivory for cinematography awards – but refreshingly honest. It shows protest from around the world. Africans defending their homelands against an oil company. Indians getting hot under the collar about a dam or something. Americans blocking logging roads in the middle of nowhere. Brits in canoes preventing a ship full of mahogany from docking.

The space between the freighter and the dock is the just more than the width of a canoe, with all three virtually touching. A thin line of human defence – skin, bone and fibreglass versus hundreds of tonnes of engine room-powered metal. One woman – wearing an Earth First! T-shirt – has to take evasive action and jumps out just before the canoe is crushed. I'm shitting it on her behalf.

'This lot are really going for it eh?' Nikki replies with a glance, grin and nod. Whoops and cheers ring around the Worthing sitting room as the ship is forced to turn around.

'Woah! Looks like a right rush. Have any of you lot done stuff like that?' I say to Stewart.

'Err ... not exactly. It's early days.' He looks slightly embarrassed at the admission. 'But I certainly gave the police what for at Grosvenor Square back in '68.'

Direct action didn't even look that hard to do. Apart from it being dangerous, the primary skill was being able to sit – and have the courage to do so in one place (in front of a huge cargo ship in a canoe) rather than another, (in a house in front of a video). Maybe something could be done about the bypass after all.

'I want to join Earth First! Where do I sign?' I ask the group.

'You don't so much join EF! as just be. Welcome aboard,' says Alan, a forty-plus cyclist-cum-printer who seems to hate the car with a vengeance.

Unfortunately, like many new graduates my initiation into the 'real world' has meant going back to live at my parents'. Most days I cycle over to Nikki's and a strategy for the public enquiry starts to form. It's not long before I have a plan for getting hold of resources. Running a campaign requires a lot of phone time, photocopying and postage. After an initial discussion of what to do each morning I go over to the Job Club and use theirs.

There's not a great deal of method to the madness. Just trying to use my initiative to build up evidence, allies and arguments against the road. To be honest, some days it feels like I haven't got a fucking clue what I'm doing.

To a casual observer it seems like I'm busting a gut to get a job. I'm like Mother Nature's special agent – though there's been a lack of exotic women and fancy gadgets thus far. With my short back and sides and reasonably tidy appearance I appear to be a career-hungry graduate. In fact I'm usually on the phone to vicars, badger experts, other campaigners, archaeologists, lawyers, journalists, politicians, historians, and just about anyone who Nikki and I can think of to help in the run–up to the public enquiry.

I'm over at hers and she's reading the Guardian.

'That's fucking outrageous,' she says. 'Our beloved Roads Minister, Robert Key, was speaking at an Auto Express dinner last night. D'you wanna know what he said?'

'He ... loves to rear end his Jag?'

'Nearly ... and I quote,' then apeing a public school accent she adds, 'I love cars. I loved my father's cars and my mother's cars.

I loved my first car. I adored and worshipped my MGB. I even polished the copper pipes on the engine. I love cars of all shapes and sizes.'

'How blatant is that? He's not even trying to be even–handed. And the decision for the bypass is ultimately his. Wanker.'

'Yeah – apparently he even said trains were environmentally unfriendly.'

'Nikki, do you think we'll stop the road?'

She pauses, give the question genuine thought then replies, 'Fuck knows. As voluntary organisations go we're not even in the same league as Meals On Wheels.'

I lean over to read the article. 'Urgh ... he looks like Billy Bunter's paedophile uncle.'

'Thanks for that mental image.'

'How about this one?' I pick my nose and wipe green-grey smeg across the MP's face.

'Just ... just be off with you. Haven't you got to write that letter to the Herald?'

'Ok, ok. I don't know why we even bother with them anyway.'

'Public opinion's important.'

'Yeah – but most people who read the Herald are only interested in who won the begonia competition at the Town Hall. Besides, it's obvious the editor is pro-bypass.'

'They do print our side every now and again,' says Nikki as she carries the snot-addled paper to the recycling. 'It must be your natural charm that wins them over.'

Stewart's lent me this big fuck-off book called Autogeddon by some weirdy-beardy called Heathcote Williams. Judging by the photo on the front he looks pissed off – in this instance with cars – and he doesn't let it lie. Like – did you know more Americans die on roads every year than they lost in Vietnam? Don't know if that's a blessing or a curse, but it's a shame. Globally, cars kill over a million people every year. I kinda knew the Nazis' preferred choice of gas was carbon monoxide but not that Hitler kept a signed portrait of Henry Ford on his desk. Also, cars only harness about 20% of the potential energy in fuel. On the plus side the level of fumes inside a car are higher than on the street. I agree with H.G. Wells who once said, 'When I see an adult on a bicycle, I have hope for the human race.' Good on him – let's hope it's the shape of things to come.

'We need an awareness-raising exercise,' says Stewart at our next meeting. I am warming to him – he knows what he's talking about and though he's the most experienced campaigner he listens. 'It needs to be – dare I say it – very fluffy.'

'Keep it spiky,' jokes Gip – who beneath his short green Mohawk haircut and multiple piercings – is a lovely bloke once you get to know him. Even these days someone looking like Gip can get a good kicking walking up the wrong street on the wrong Friday night.

I suggest a family day of activities on the Downs. My Downs. Lancing. And – bugger me – people seem to like it.

Stewart's off on one now. 'We need a name for it. Lancing Downs ... L.D. How about S.O.L.D. as an acronym? That way we could paint a big 'Sold' sign and put it across the hills.'

'How about Save Our Lancing Downs?' says Nikki.

'Perfect. When?'

'Well, the public enquiry's at the end of September. How about then?' offers Wendy.

'Yeah – leaves us about a month get something concrete together.'

'Concrete's the last thing we want on those downs,' says Gip. Not funny, but nice one for trying.

'Are you sure we've been invited to this party?'

Dave's an old mate from school days. We're walking through the badlands of East Worthing, not far from the chimneys of the local pharmaceutical factory – to his new girlfriend's eighteenth birthday.

'Yeah, Penny won't mind. She's a good bird.'

'But you've only been seeing her five minutes.'

'Bollocks, man. She needs to meet my compadres.'

'Are you sure? I'm alright – but how about Sean?'

Sean's so drunk he shuts one eye to focus. 'What about me?'

I say to him. 'You're a fucking disgrace sometimes. Like when you smeared mayonnaise over Sharon's head as she slept.'

'That was dead funny.'

'She thought you'd wanked on her head.'

'Well at least I'm not a fucking hippy.'

'Do you see long hair? Tie-dye? Fuck yourself.' I say waving my arms around me demonstratively.

'Anyway, do you think she'll mind us bringing these?' I hold the beer bongs aloft. Consisting of a funnel and a metre of brewing pipe they've been the beer–drinking method of choice this summer. The general idea is to pour the beer into the funnel, put pipe to mouth, lift funnel and let gravity do the rest. Half a dozen cans of Tennants Super strain a thin carrier bag in my other hand.

'Have more faith, my friend, she'll love it,' says Dave.

'Yaaaaaaaaa,' belches Sean.

I open my eyes and am a bit freaked. I see an unfamiliar living room and sofa. A blue-check blanket has been draped over me. However, I'm comforted by routine sight of Sean and Dave passed out nearby

– the former in an armchair, the other covered over with a three-quarter length coat on the floor.

'Geezer, where are we?'

Dave turns over, snorts then methodically spits on the laminated floor, wiping it up on his sleeve. 'Oooooh ... Don't you remember? It was carnage.' The look on his face doesn't bode well. 'Soon after we arrived you were organising beer bong races between us and Penny's dad and uncles.'

'That sounds ok.'

'You got through to the final.'

'Result.'

'Sean tried to pull Penny's little sister. She's only fifteen.'

'Honest mistake.'

'Then you fell into the flower bed, rolled around a lot, threw up several times then passed out. '

'Oops.'

'Look below you.'

I crane my neck towards the floor and see a large casserole dish half full of sick.

'And ...' Dave rubs the bridge of his nose and points at me. A cross-eyed examination reveals much dried blood.

'It was when you were chundering. You were that wankered. Basically, the blokes wanted to string us up. The good news is that Penny's mum was a star and took pity on us ... on the other hand, I've been dumped.'

'Sorry geezer. We'd better get Sean out of here before he wakes up and tries to find the sister's bedroom.' I'd like to say we make our excuses and leave. But we just leave.

Back in the Job Club phone booths it's time to spread the message. 'Hi, is that Leicester Earth First!? You don't know me but funnily enough my name's Lester and I'm calling from the Worthing group. I've got a great blag for you.'

I'm trying to keep my voice low enough to keep out of Bierce's earshot yet not sound like a sex case. I swear he tries to lip-read what I'm saying sometimes.

I've decided it's a good thing for the planet that I tell the other EF! groups about using the Job Club. The largest groups are in places like Manchester. I bet they get up to all sorts of exciting shit. Come to think of it ... Manchester. I do miss the place. Some of the old gang from uni are thinking of moving back.

Preparations for the SOLD family day continue. We've got fliers – computerised wording with a hand–drawn Celtic knot border. I've done my first radio interview. I was a bit all over the shop but the finished edit sounded ok. Worthing Green Party have requested a mailshot to all members. I'd wager the in-tray of a certain organisation for those without work will be heavy with envelopes this afternoon.

The next day Bierce comes up to me. 'Could we have a private chat in my office?' he says. Oh shit. Is it the phone calls? Has he lost patience and signed me up as a fruit picker in Kent? I look over and on his desk and see several of the mail-shot envelopes, ripped open and looking very sorry for themselves.

I suppose it's like the scene in Quadrophenia when Jimmy gets called into the office and tells his boss to stick the franking machine right up his arse. However, this is no time for mod heroics. I take a seat and look meekly at the floor.

'Did you seriously think this was a proper use of our resources? How much of this stuff have you put through our franking machine?'

How did he know I was thinking of that? I feel a strong desire to laugh but stifle it the best I can. This is no time for smiling, smirking, gurning, grinning or indeed chortling.

'Ok, I'm sorry. It was stupid and was the first time – and the last. Besides, West Sussex Green Party are considering taking on more staff.' I don't even know if they employ anyone.

'That's neither here nor there. You use this place to apply directly for positions, not do your apprenticeship for them using our budgets. Do you know how tight our budgets are?'

A respectful silence replaces the 'No, and I don't give a flying fuck' inside my head.

'I'm sorry, it was all for a good cause.'

'That may or may not be the case. Whether I agree with your opinion about the road is irrelevant. You cannot use the Job Club to further your personal political beliefs. You know I could contact the police?'

'Yes, I suppose you could. I'm sorry ok? We all make mistakes.' I feign a sob. At my age I can still act like a child and just about get away with it.

'Well, I'll overlook it this time, but if I discover anything like this again ...' Bierce says, holding a few of the envelopes aloft in his clenched fist. '... you won't know what hit you. Understand?'

Result. A theft charge three months after graduation wouldn't be the best way to enter adult life.

I sheepishly leave, unlock my bike and go to break the news to Nikki. Her reaction – a mixture of concern, laughter and a certain lack of surprise – is a tonic.

'It was really only a matter of time, especially with stunts like the mail-out,' she says.

'What are we going to do now?' I ask. She looks me square in the eye.

'Well, there's always Gip. He's on the dole and could go and use Job Club.'

'Yeah – those three nose rings don't exactly shout trainee recruitment consultant to me. Bierce'll be all over him like the FBI at Waco.'

Following the loss of the prime movers and shakers in the campaign – i.e. the photocopier, telephone and franking machine – me and Nikki have worked extra hard. Perhaps it's a blessing in disguise. She's good company – and between you and me – I wouldn't kick her out of bed for eating crisps.

It is Friday afternoon and we're trying to cover as many bases as possible for the SOLD event. Buying stuff like facepaints, producing signage and making sure as many people as possible know it's happening as well as continuing our research for the public enquiry.

'Time we called it a day I think.' It's seven-thirty and I go in search of the kettle.

'Shall I put something on the stereo? What do you fancy?' she says.

'Hmm ... have you got Modern Life Is Rubbish?'

'Who's that by?'

'It's only the best album of the year – by a mile – philistine.'

'Sorry I haven't heard of that band.'

'Ha ha. Laugh it up. I'm too knackered to humour you.' I bring back two mugs of lemon and ginger tea – yes I have been converted on that score – and plonked myself next to her on the futon. I sense the moment is right and act on several weeks of unspoken sexual tension. 'I tell you what I fancy as well as listening to Blur. You.' She's a decent kisser and we start having a bit of a roll around, passionate clinch, heavy petting – whatever you want to call it.

'Hold on. How about our working relationship?' She's in the process of lifting my long-sleeved Wedding Present T-shirt over my head.

'Look – the way society's gone these days – if people were barred from getting off with workmates ... well, you get it. Besides, we're not on anyone's payroll.'

'I'll be honest – with all that's gone on lately – it's been a while.' I could have said exactly the same thing myself and am happy to oblige. Though not buxom there's sufficient breast to muster the brain-to-penis synapses. I'm not shallow – it's just part of my wiring I suppose. I slowly slide her knickers to the floor and begin gently kissing her inner thighs.

She collapses the futon and pushes me down onto it, then rifles in a drawer for a condom. As she rolls it on I ask her if the rubber was from a sustainable source.

'Shut up and fuck me hard.'

I respond in an Alabama-type accent 'Yes ma'am – don't whoop me ma'am. I is gonna fuck you good'. Amid various moans, groans and giggles it's thirty minutes before a coital 'Jesus' is the next actual word said. Like I'm not saying I'm porn star of the century, but for my age and experience I think I can cover the basics in pleasing a lady. Oh yes.

After a leisurely sex-and-breakfast filled morning I cycle back to my parents with severe knobache and a self-satisfied grin.

The Downs is mostly lazily rolling, arable land. The odd clump of trees, the river Adur and Lancing College add variation – relaxing, inspiring, a haven and source of contemplation for even the most devout non–believer.

To most it's the backdrop to the existing dual carriageway – but for dog walkers, joggers and the odd underage courting couple it has other utility value. I – like most – take it for granted a lot of the time. But today – Save Our Lancing Downs day – is a chance for me to repay those gentle slopes for happy memories.

The weather's been good to us. The sun – streaking through light cloud – bathes sections of the hills in come-hither heat. On a hill overlooking Lancing – with the distant foliage looking like pieces of green painted sponge glued onto a model railway – we stake four large painted sheets into the ground. One has a large 'S' on it, the next an 'O' and so on.

'They're bloody beautiful, aren't they?' Stewart says with pride at his handiwork. I agree before busying myself with setting up a welly whanging arena and a rudimentary football pitch.

'How did you get into all this?' I ask him.

'I don't know really. I think I saw some footage of Dylan singing Subterranean Homesick Blues and he seemed the coolest man on earth. I wanted to find my own way of being like him,' he says with a nostalgic sigh.

Stewart is full of beans and very pleased about recent developments. He's been involved in social change stuff in one form or another since the anti-Vietnam protests of the '60s. An engineer of thirty years' standing, he's been fighting the Worthing bypass since I was at first school. It's ten o'clock, about an hour till people should start turning up. I start to get paranoid. Will people actually take time out on a Sunday morning to show they care?

'Have faith man, don't worry. By the way, how are you getting on with Nikki these days?'

I tell him it's been a bit pressured sometimes with the forthcoming enquiry. I don't tell him that my commitment phobia has risen to the surface and I haven't seen her since we fucked each others' brains out last week.

Soon after Nikki arrives with face-painting kit and a ready smile. 'Hi guys,' she hugs us both but reserves a pinch on the buttock for me. The car park slowly begins to fill and people walk up from the village. All normal, local people, some of whom I've known all his life. Picnic blankets are unfurled. Sausage rolls, sandwiches and pieces of cake appear from Tupperware containers.

A primitive division of labour helps the afternoon go with a swing. Stewart mans the information stall, Gip overcomes the initial suspicions of the locals and co-ordinates the welly-whanging wonderfully. By the time Nikki runs out of paints, the children of Sompting have been facially transformed into various endangered species. Meanwhile I gather together a band of a dozen or so eager footballers.

Stewart comes over to the match just as I trap the ball underfoot and lay it off to a youngster. 'Lester, I just wanted to say this has been great. The campaign's had a bit more zest since you came on board.'

'Nonsense mate. It's a team game. Mike ... man on, lay it off back door. Sorry where was I? Yeah, I've loved it, really.'

'I'll catch you after the match for a proper talk.'

'Sure thing. Lee – triangles – give and go. Yes ... yes! Great goal mate.'

After the match – which we lose by virtue of the hotly disputed 'last goal wins' rule – it's time for a well–earned glass of wine with the others. Alan offers me a couple of squares of organic chocolate. Surprisingly it actually tastes like the real thing.

The afternoon's winding down – most goodbyes have been said and Wendy's conducting a radio interview and dealing with the final farewells.

Stewart beams. 'You know. If all the bullshit of life and mortgages are scraped and heaped aside for a moment and today was a straight fight between whether people cared or not – they do.'

'Yeah – that's fair enough but I didn't see the enquiry Inspector here,' says Gip.

'Ah ... he might have been. You don't know what he looks like,' says Stewart.

I say, 'Mate, you've been sucking milk from the tit of human kindness too long today. You need winding to bring you to your senses.'

'I've had one glass of wine. I'm driving,' he replies.

'How did the interview go?' Nikki asks the approaching Wendy.

'The BBC man thoroughly enjoyed himself and was totally on board in his commentary. He asked me how many were here. I reckon there was what, 200, but I said 350 and he bought it.'

'Nicely done,' I reply. 'If it's good enough for Peter Mandelson.'

'Who?' Wendy's is just one among several blank faces.

'Some TV bloke the Labour Party have brought in to get us to like them. There was a profile of him in the Independent.'

As we pack everything into the car Nikki sidles over and says: 'You've hardly said a word to me all day. Do you fancy coming over tonight?'

'Look – Nikki, the other night was cool and that, but.'

'But you don't fancy me.'

'Well – I do.'

'Go on.'

'Look – we've got the first day of the enquiry soon – we need to keep our wits about us.'

She slaps me heartily across the face. 'Not alert enough to see that were you?' Before the sound of the clout peters out she's stormed off to Stewart's passenger door. I shrug in faux astonishment to the rest of the guys.

Three months of living with my folks is proving to be a gargantuan balls ache. I'm trying to chill listening to Together Alone, the new Crowded House album when my mum pipes up. 'No one's going to earn a living for you, get off your backside and look for a job.'

The peace I derive from the Maori harmonies of the title track are shattered. 'Look, I've never been busier. You've seen how hard I've been working lately.'

'But for whose benefit? What are you getting out of it?'

'But I've got to do it. It's important.'

'Important my hat. And what about the state of your room?'

'Oh not that again.'

'And you coming in at all hours, forgetting your key. Coming in drunk.'

'Yeah – well, yeah. I'd like to get my own place. Don't think I like it here with these fucking dogs. Yappy little cunts. Pets are a pathetic life substitute for sad wankers.'

'There's something wrong with people who don't like animals. And don't swear at me.'

'Oh bollocks to you.'

Seething, I bomb down the stairs, slam the front door, leap on my bike and am soon pedalling furiously through winding downland roads.

On the uphill parts of the ten-mile route I can blow off some steam, and on the sections where gravity is on my side I can enjoy the nag–free scenery. Both are accompanied by Rage Against the Machine's eponymous album.

As the chorus of Bullet In The Head kicks in, I imagine shooting Jimmy, my mum's pomeranian, stone dead with a single cap in its arse. Take The Power Back suddenly isn't a rallying cry for ghetto insurrection – it's direct advice to me about my circumstances.

By the time I sweatily apply the brakes next to my parents' front gate I've decided to settle for nothing less than a move back to Manchester.

It's the opening day of the bypass enquiry. Pro and anti-bypass groups stake out territory as close to the entrance to Worthing Assembly Hall as possible. I've only been in the building once before – to see All Mod Cons, a tribute band to the Jam. Just as then, people are wearing Farah Sta-Press today, but they belong to those clutching a 'Give way to the bypass' placard with a politically blue-rinsed wife in tow. I know I'm biased, but they really do look like a sad bunch of fucks. Don't suppose to the neutral we look a lot cooler.

We're decked out in pollution masks, as well as our best suits and dresses. The scruffiest thing on show is a dog-eared banner or two. Gip's even worn a trilby to cover his hair. We hand leaflets to shoppers – trying to get our arguments across to anyone who'll give us more than two seconds' attention.

Stewart gathers everyone for a pep talk shortly before the off. 'So – we're good with the plan, eh? Have you made up a group you're going to represent?' His theory is that many made-up organisational names might give the appearance of more opposition.

'I've come up with several.' I say, 'There's the Federation Against Road Transport, the Society of Hills Instead of Traffic, and the Cyclists Raging Against Pollution. Geddit?'

'Thank you Lester.'

'Well, anyone's welcome to those. Personally I'm going to be chair of Cissbury Untouched, Never Touched.'

'Prick,' says Nikki.

'No ... cunt.'

Stewart's keen to restore order. 'Ok, scrap that idea. What's got into you two? Now, have we got our questions sorted?' Good. Remember Archway but don't go too far.'

There's a role model for us to look up to. During the Archway enquiry in London in the '70s, a man called George Stern had excelled in not taking any nonsense. Nearing eighty himself and still a fearsome orator, he'd do things like dressing up as a Nazi and goose-stepping up and down the aisles tormenting the Inspector.

The Worthing enquiry begins in more formal fashion. The Inspector, a Peter Liversedge, takes his seat at the apex of the triangular table at the head of the hall, sat on either side of him are two QCs, one for the Department of Transport and one for those representing the route across the Downs.

'They're on about a hundred quid an hour,' Stewart says to Gip.

'Bugger me. That's more than two weeks' giro. Where's the barrister who's against the road?'

'There isn't one.'

Down table are miscellaneous clerks, rubber stampers and civic officials looking like they care for little other than the next expenses claim.

I say to Alan – my buddy for the action, 'I'm going to enjoy this. You rarely get a slanging match in this town apart from down Montague Street on a Saturday night.' We're paired up and dotted around the hall.

'Could I have the first question please?' says Liversedge. Wendy's first on. She's wearing an exceedingly short skirt and T-shirt with Grooovy emblazoned on her ample cleavage.

There's a ten-second delay while a man with a microphone reaches her. 'I was wondering about obtaining transcripts of the proceedings? Many people, like myself, work during the week and therefore it is impossible to keep up with what's going on without them.'

Liversedge has a typical civil servant's clipped tones. 'Thank you for your question – it has been noted and we will look into it.'

'Was that a yes or a no?'

'Your question has been noted and we will look into the practicality and expense of such an exercise. I understand your concerns but that's all I can say at this juncture.' It's obvious the Inspector has been selected as a very safe pair of hands.

'Ten quid he's wearing musical boxer shorts,' I whisper to Alan.

'What would they play?'

'Up The Junction.'

Some pro-roader asks a question about relieving congestion on the existing A27. A couple of boos ring out. The genteel veneer of the occasion is beginning to peel away.

'Excuse me, I must insist questions and opinions are treated with respect,' says the Inspector. Polite applause filters through the hall.

Alan takes the microphone next, relishing the chance. 'I would like this enquiry to look into the destructive effects of road building, and the consequences in terms of the number of deaths and injuries the road will cause.'

'This is an important matter, and you can be assured it will be dealt with in the fullness of time,' Liversedge, like many middle-aged, middle class white men has a knack of saying quite a lot without really saying anything.

'Sir,' I say with an air of sarcasm when I finally get the chance, 'I'd like to draw your attention to the fact that no proper environmental impact assessment has been carried out on this proposed route, and consequently European Union law will be breached if this road goes through.'

The parry is quick, fluent bullshit. 'The article you refer to actually didn't receive ratification until after the submissions for the route were drawn up. Therefore, there will be no breach of the letter of the law. However, I thank you for your point.'

'But what about the impact assessments?' The microphone's gone and I'm forced to shout.

'Sir, there are lots of people to get through this morning. Would you please desist from shouting?'

I silently mouth some words my mum wouldn't approve of, like a centre forward on Match of the Day who's just blazed an easy chance over the bar.

Nikki's turn now. She's taken out her nose stud for the day. If she'd have done that before I might have fucked her again. 'Isn't it true that this bypass is not for the residents of Worthing, but is part of the trans-European highway stretching from Cornwall to Kent? Isn't it also true that this road is being built mainly for the purpose of transporting heavy freight, and is therefore primarily for the interests of business?'

Some bloke from the local Chamber of Commerce shakes his head, making noises similar to what is heard in the House of Commons when they're being rowdy, childish, or indeed both. Yet again the inspector fudges a reply.

I deliver the next question thus, holding a spine-bound report aloft. 'Mr Inspector, evidence from the Institute of Transport at Lancaster University and others clearly shows that more roads means trouble for the next generation. Not least, is the number of cases of asthma and possible links to some forms of childhood cancer caused by emissions.'

I decide to up the emotive stakes. 'It's all in here if you can be bothered to read it. The suffering of innocents will be on your hands if you rubber-stamp this foolish scheme.'

It's worked. A few old ladies are out of their seats.

This is outside Liversedge's comfort zone. He responds. 'The overall impact and possible benefits of the road are what this enquiry is about. The issues you have raised will be a factor in this.'

There was no thank you this time.

It's time to push it a bit more. Ok, it's un-English, definitely un-Worthing–like. But Britain stands in post-Empire, post-Thatcherite decline, near the bottom of developed nation league table for anything other than teenage pregnancies. It's questionable if doing things the English way has done any good lately.

'Oh come on Pete', I add refusing to sit down or give up the microphone. 'That's all complete waffle and you know it. Why can't you talk to us properly, say what you mean? I tell you what, come out for a beer with us one night and we'll have a proper chat. I'll even get them in.' This is met with garrumphs, shouts and laughter.

'I am afraid ... whatever your name is ... I could not possibly accept your offer. I am an impartial arbiter of this enquiry and fraternisation is strictly forbidden.'

'Now Pete mate. Tell us the truth. Do you care about these kids? I put it that you don't. To paraphrase John Major – 'Sir, you are a bastard'.'

Earlier in the week the Prime Minister had been quoted as to what he really thought of some of his cabinet colleagues. You can feel the disgust and delight in the air.

'I must remind you where you are,' says Liversedge. 'Your behaviour at present is unacceptable, and if you persist I will have to ask you to leave. Cut his microphone,' prompting a huge cheer from most of the pro-road audience.

It's time to limit my input and let the others take up the slack. Not easy though, as adrenaline is shooting up and down my spine. Thrill-wise it's not on the same level as a parachute jump, but not far off. Like gym junkies who can't get enough exercise, I can see this kind of thing could get addictive.

The two-hour mark for the meeting is celebrated by Gip starting and conducting a chorus of 'bypass my arse'. Only after a full two minutes of gavel banging and suited persuasion is order restored.

'Hello Pete,' Wendy's piss-take quotient is now undisguised and acute. 'You have already implied we will not be receiving transcripts of the proceedings. Well, that's a shame, but may I remind you we're part of Europe. We are trying to liase with MEPs and the EU Environmental Commissioner, a Mr Pallossis, who is Portuguese. I would humbly request if you won't give us transcripts in English could you – as your duty as a European – agree for them to be produced in Portuguese, or indeed Italian or even Welsh?'

'I think that's enough questions for now,' says Liversedge. 'We will adjourn after lunch, when I will assume there will more respect for this enquiry or the police will be called. Thank you.' Clearly rattled, he gets up and disappears into the wings of the Assembly Hall.

'You should be ashamed of yourself,' says a sixty–something woman to me near the exit. I offer only a middle finger in response.

Us 'unwashed elements' – as we've been called a couple of times this morning – decamp to a local café.

'I know it wasn't exactly facing down a freighter with a canoe, but I reckon that counts as my first action,' I say with some pride.

'Did you enjoy it?' asked Alan.

'It was great. Like playing for Brighton against Liverpool away, scoring two and getting an assist.'

Alan's reply of 'What's an assist?' forces me to atheistically look to the heavens.

'Anyway – I think we all did well there. We got our points over and showed it up for the bloody shambles it is. Here's to more of the same over the next few months.' Stewart raises his teacup in triumph.

All cups except mine chink in unison. 'Come on Lester, what's up?'

'Er ... guys. I've got some news.'

'Yeah?'

'I've decided to move back to Manchester.'

'Oh. When?'

'Next weekend. But I'll be around. Sometimes.'

'Absolutely. Of course we'll be sorry to lose you but I'm sure we'll see you before we know it. A new toast – all the best of luck to Lester in the next chapter of his life.' Nikki's cup joins the others and we share conciliatory smiles.

'Thanks guys. It's been really great. Good luck.'

CHAPTER 2

AUTUMN 1993

'This is us pissed up at the Washington Monument ... oh, and this one's a classic. That's Mat, someone we travelled with, being sick in the Nevada desert.'

Neil, my best mate from uni, has just got back from a summer in America with holiday snaps – a mixture of landmarks, landscapes and laddishness. We decide to put a few beers between us and immediate concerns in Jabez Clegg, next to the political science faculty, just off Oxford Road.

'So mate – we'd best start looking for a house this week. And jobs,' he says. We've both been sofa surfing and living out of rucksacks since returning to the north-west.

'I was gonna talk to you about that,' I say reluctantly.

'You're not still going to crack on with that activism stuff are you? It's not going to buy you many sharking tokens when we go out Friday nights.'

'I've found something I really love doing.'

'Well you do what you want. I'll have to go down the careers centre tomorrow to see if they've got anything.' Neil's pretty much resigned to a life of nine-to-five looming large on the horizon.

'Bugger that, there's other ways of using your skills, you've just got to look for them, chance your arm a bit.'

'We haven't all got that luxury. I'd love to bum around for a year or two, but I've been doing that all summer. My credit card bill is enough to make you want to reach for the razor blades. And student loans, and the overdraft and ...'

'And ... I get the point,' I reply, 'but most of that debt can be deferred and if you're lucky you can sort of disappear. Simple really.'

'So let's get this straight, for the sake of a couple of thousand quid you vanish like Lord Lucan. It's a bit drastic isn't it?'

'Maybe, but we shouldn't have to pay the fucking things back in the first place.'

'That little rant doesn't solve the fact I need a job.'

'Rather you than me. Besides, if I get pissed off with it, I can still go and do the graduate thing. Go through the ... what's it called? Where we went to those seminars by the likes of Proctor and Gamble and got fed cream cakes and beer?'

'The milk round.'

'That's the one. I could do that. No worries.'

'So – have you met any of these 'lentils' yet?' He bunny ears the penultimate word.

'No, but I'm going to a meeting in Rusholme tomorrow night.'

'What do you think they'll be like?'

'I dunno, wild-eyed baby-eating anarchists obsessed with eco-stuff and nothing else, I s'pose.' Truth is – I fear this indeed will be the case.

At the meeting, deep in the student heartland of Fallowfield – as with Worthing, it's mostly young, slightly hippyish sorts who seem otherwise perfectly 'normal' and 'nice'. I'm not alone in having short hair, but am in the minority.

A lanky guy, maybe mid-twenties with impeccably tidy dreadlocks approaches me with an outstretched hand. 'Dom, and you're ...?'

'Lester. We spoke on the phone. You look familiar somehow.'

'Why?'

'Well, I've lived here for the last three years. I suppose that's it.'

'So you wanna get involved?'

'Yeah, I've some experience with a bypass campaign down south – Worthing – but nothing as hardcore as you guys I'm sure.'

We're suddenly disturbed by someone at least six inches shorter than myself. A small face framed by ginger hair and goatee sneers, 'Oi, you look like a copper. How do we know to trust you?'

'Tango. Shut the fuck up. Sorry about him. Too paranoid by half.' I can tell it isn't the first time Dom has said this.

'No, it's ok. Well ... Tango ... um ... do you want to test me? I can quote you the Worthing EF! phone number and address. Don't know quite what else to say.'

Someone else is coming over. She looks friendly enough, no oil painting but can't be any worse than this ginger twat.

She says. 'Don't worry. If it was down to him to get recruitment going, they'd only be him and the pygmies of West Papua saving the planet. Helen by the way, pleased to meet you.' I agree.

'You leave the Irian Jayans out of this. And for the millionth time don't call them pygmies.'

'Now you've got him started on the fucking pygmies. Jeez,' says an exasperated Dom.

'Have I come through the vetting process, comrades?' I ask. Neither Glasnost nor Perestroika have done anything for my

Russian accent, but I've at least changed the subject.

'Sure you have,' says Dom who proffers a high-five then leans over to whisper, 'You look saner than Tango anyway. You know, he's never even been to West Papua.'

'Hang on, I know where I've seen you and ... er ... Helen. On a Twyford video.' Twyford Down, near Winchester had seen the first anti-road direct actions in 1992. Although the road's well on the way to being built the name has taken on mythic status in activist circles.

'We're waiting to see if we're going to get compensation from all that. The police got an injunction to ban us from the site and we're suing the bastards. Anyway, let me introduce you to our lovely bunch of fuck-ups.'

'Thanks. It's great to meet a real digger diver. You were throwing yourself at those bulldozers like nobody's business on that footage.'

'Oh please. You'll be doing it with your eyes shut before long. Right – this is Jane.'

The brain-to-penis synapses spring straight into action. Six foot tall with gently waving dark chocolate hair, screen idol features and all the correct in-and-out proportions, Jane's about the most attractive woman I've ever seen in the flesh. No really.

'Hi, pleased to meet you,' she extends a hand.

'Oh yes – it's great – to meet you I mean.' Her demeanour suggests she really doesn't know how gorgeous she is. Bingo. Dom leads me away with a knowing arched eyebrow raised in my direction.

'There's a few folks who aren't here tonight. You'll meet Phil, Rachel and a couple of others soon enough no doubt. Oh, this is the phone tree – I'll add your name to it during the week.'

'A what?' I look at the piece of paper which looks more like a Blockbusters board than anything else.

'It's a way of spreading information without one person having to make all the calls. You ring a person next to you on the grid and they do the same in turn. Simple.' He turns away to address the whole group. 'Shall we get this meeting started then?'

Jane's first to speak. 'There's an action next week if anyone fancies it. It's this new thing called ethical shoplifting. Basically, as you probably know, mahogany is illegally logged from the rain-forests in Brazil, and a lot of it ends up in the shops over here. So we go in, get the wood out of the shop, take it to the police and report it as stolen property.'

Sounds like a mad idea. I don't know all the reasons why felling mahogany trees is a bad thing, but it's obviously wrong – and I'm more than willing to let her talk me into it. She continues in her lovely dulcet tones produced by that gorgeous, gorgeous mouth. I'm highly distracted.

'According to research by Norwich EF! quite a few chain stores sell the wood despite all the lobbying over the years. Probably the biggest and most accessible to us is Texas DIY. There are several of their stores around Manchester, so location won't be a problem. They're known as CRISP-O actions, which stands for,' she looks down at the briefing paper by her flawless, toned knees. 'Citizens Recovery of Indigenous People's Stolen Property. Not sure where the O comes in.'

Tango, sat next to Jane, jumps in with, 'Why don't we do more than one store on a day? That'll really freak them.'

'That's a fantastic idea, you gorgeous genius,' she pulls him close and kisses him passionately on the lips. I whimper and am sure it's audible.

'Less of that guys. We've got new people here,' says an exasperated Helen.

I thought I should at least mug up about the mahogany trade if I'm gonna carry out direct action against it. According to a Friends of the Earth briefing sheet I borrowed, 1,450 square metres of forest is destroyed by felling each tree, and logging results in the deaths of many indigenous Indians. Britain's a major importer of the stuff. Something's got to be done – and besides – the thought of nicking something then going to the police and reporting the property as 'stolen' by someone else is going to be a laugh.

On the day of the CRISP-O action a motley collection of props and banners are assembled at the meeting point. There's thirty or so of us, a cardboard chainsaw with red paint splattered on the blade, and a couple of obligatory banners including one splattered in fake blood that reads TEXAS CHAIN STORE MASSACRE.

The plan is to start at the Texas branch in Trafford then do the Ancoats store in the afternoon. Trafford can only be described as a joyless industrial armpit. Factories, warehouses and tall, discoloured chimneys mingled with a huge modern retail park. Booming enterprise zone or an ecocidal nightmare – take your pick.

Dom leads me towards this bloke with piercing blue eyes, short light brown hair, perma-stubble and – I can sense it – the cocky self-assured air of an ex-public schoolboy.

'Phil, this is Lester, he's come on – what did you call it? – a free transfer from Worthing. Bond motherfuckers – bond,' and with that Dom races off to another task, leaving us to get acquainted.

'Nice to meet you mate. Don't worry – Dom's cool – he's just trying too hard and stressed.'

Helen asks for quiet to address the assembled CRISP-O officers. 'Has everyone who's going to take wood written out a statement for the police?'

'We'll, I'm sure we'll catch up properly before long. Best shut up before matron canes us,' says Phil, confirming my suspicions.

Various scrappy bits of paper are scribbled on and copied from. Each says something vague about the person's abhorrence to the trade and state they have no intention of permanently depriving the store of the item. Everyone due to take a banister rail, bathroom fitting, or other piece of fashioned timber – the 'nickers' – are to have a designated observers with them to make sure they're ok if arrested.

It's the start of the academic year and many here are students on their first action. I suppose I qualify as a token fresher.

'Has anyone got a D-lock with them?' Three or four grunt back at Dom. They are the shock troops of the operation, the ones to lock themselves by the neck to display stands.

I've got my lock, but it's for securing my bike. Although 'locking-on' looks cool in videos it seems whacked out and a more than a tad dangerous. This D-lock really doesn't look wide enough to go around my neck. Helen assures me it will – albeit snugly.

'Alright, I will lock on.' The words come forth with adrenaline-fuelled enthusiasm. With my consent – though against my better judgement – Helen's lock is big enough to secure both her bike and mine. Another couple of people also volunteer to lock-on, including Rachel, who's not unattractive for a redhead. At least there'll be something to look at other than kitchen units.

Helen continues the briefing. 'Though it'll be bad for their PR there's a chance people will be arrested. Has everyone got the solicitor's number written on their arms? Good. Remember if you are nicked you only have to give your name, address and confirm that you're over eighteen. Ok let's roll in five minutes. Best of luck.'

It wouldn't need an anthropologist to work out that, though there are no leaders, the group take their cues from Helen and Dom.

Some stay outside the store leafleting shoppers and to my dismay there's going to be some street theatre involving the chain-saw. If anyone asks me to get involved in shit like that they're going to get a D-lock wrapped round their head. Banners are tethered to the front of the store. Dom's gone to the police station in sweet-talk mode to try and convince them we aren't actually stealing the wood. The nickers, the observers and lockers go inside, along with Tango and Jane who are to do 'trolley runs' – filling up their shopping carts with as many items as possible only to leave them at the checkout.

As everyone piles in we're not exactly inconspicuous. We're not beer-bellied guys searching for creosote or some four-by-two to finish that DIY project middle-aged men tend to tackle when they reach 'that age'. Instead there's loads of smirking hippies roaming about. Before long Rachel, myself and an ethnic-trousered fresher called Lorraine find the mahogany racks.

'Hang on,' Rachel says, 'if we lock on before anyone takes some wood, it'll raise too much suspicion.'

'I'll go and give them a nudge,' says Lorraine finding the nickers and signals with a wink for them to get a move on.

Three, four, five people all take a plank, fitting or fixture and then swiftly leave. D–locks are removed from under coats, keys applied, and legal observers are soon in position. Plastic-coated steel is hooked around necks and the observers help them to latch and lock on to the shelving displays. Seemingly immovable and with banner strategically in place, Rachel then begins to chant 'Texas Homecare doesn't care'. I suddenly wish I was anywhere else, and Lorraine looks far more attractive than she did a couple of minutes ago.

An old lady stares at us as we lie on the ground attached to the rails. Lorraine bids her a friendly 'Good morning' met with a response not easy to decipher, but is a compound of confusion, surprise and a desire to visit the paintbrush aisle.

For a man of ample padding the manager is on the scene very quickly. 'What the sodding 'ell is all this about? Terrorising my store.'

Rachel stops her chant to be as polite as possible. 'This is a peaceful protest about your company selling tropical hardwoods, especially mahogany. We'd like you to contact Head Office as soon as possible and register our disgust.'

Phil, in his capacity as legal observer hands him a leaflet.

'I'll do no such thing. You're trespassing and if you don't leave now I'll call the bloody cops. Get out you wankers!'

A store minion with gelled hair and clipboard is summoned over and ordered to contact the police.

'I think you'll find some of the mahogany has gone walkies as well.' This contribution of mine, although truthful, has only fuelled the manager's increasing fury.

'Well, then you'll be charged with theft. That's the kind of thing I'd expect from people like you. Anyway, if you don't like the wood, why try and nick it? Isn't that going against your views?'

Without pausing for too long on this poor logic I say, 'We didn't steal ... nick any of it, but ...' Rachel butts in to stop me putting my foot in it. '... the trade is so despicable we should have done, isn't that right Lester?' I nod.

Within ten minutes three police officers are at the scene.

'Basically,' the manager says to them, 'I want these buggers out. Don't care what it takes. They're really starting to wind me up.'

'What a fat twat,' I say.

'Don't use that word,' replies Rachel.

'Alright, he's a cunt then.' No doubt this is going to be the only occasion I'm getting wood with Rachel.

The veins rise in the manager's temples and his face turns a deeper red than the fallen leaves in the car park.

It's Lorraine's turn to get stuck in. 'Don't you care about biodiversity, or the rainforests, or the people who died for this wood to get here? Do you care about anything? Have you got any kids? How about them?' The tone of her voice, sincere with a rising tone of anger, is strangely intriguing, and affirms my growing notion I should get to know her better.

'Yeah, I've got kids, but this job pays for a roof over their heads. What we sell in the store comes through Head Office. Do you think I have any say in it? Do you? Now are you going to shift or am I going to fucking do it?'

Rachel is defiant. 'You could at least contact your bosses. Frankly, until you do, I'm not moving.'

'That goes for me double.' I'm starting to enjoy this even more. However, quite what we're going to do if the manager doesn't call Head Office isn't clear. Unlock and look slightly foolish is the probable answer.

'Right that's it. I've bloody well had enough.' His face is redder than ever, and sends his minion away for a hacksaw.

Everyday certainties suddenly aren't so rock steady. I call to the police. 'You're not going to just stand there? This is going to be an assault. What if he slips and lops my head off?'

The manager rips the cardboard and plastic wrapping off of the saw and approaches me. Real fear is twinned with excitement. The locking-on bit hasn't been uncomfortable thus far, but the latest development has every chance of dramatically changing that. The police stand chuckling quietly.

The manager begins to saw. At first I try to laugh off the proximity of the blade. 'Look, I know the mahogany trade has a bloody history – but not once it's been made into a cupboard door for Christ's sake.'

As he starts sawing Rachel screams at the bloke to stop. I'm not far off doing the same.

I've no idea of the lock's strength – at least, not enough to entrust my life to it. I move my eyes in such a way to signal for Phil to unlock me – which he does after the manager retreats two paces and mops his brow.

Unshackled, I stand to my full height and go for it. 'I can't believe you just did that. What sort of animal are you? You fucking excuse for a human being. I hope you get bowel cancer you cunt!'

This time, the boys in blue are quick to respond. 'I'll have to remind you, young man, that this is a public place, and that you should mind your language.'

'I don't believe it. This wanker tries to cut my head off and you have a go at me for swearing. That's ... effing rich.'

'Sir, if you do not refrain from this behaviour I will have no choice than to arrest you under the Public Order Act.'

My anger is suddenly tempered by the look on Lorraine's face. She seems to be crying, but a second, calmer examination reveals she's convulsing with laughter.

'Look everyone,' she says pointing at the manager's backside. His exertions have resulted in a five inch split in his trousers, revealing saggy brown pants and a semblance of spotty white buttocks.

She adds. 'It's alright everyone – we've found a source of sustainable logging. Why didn't you tell us about it? We mightn't have come.' Even the police seem amused by his plight.

'Get them out of here pronto,' is the only response he can muster.

Receiving a police escort out of the store, I spot Tango at the checkout with a huge trolley full of all sorts of DIY equipment, including, doubtless, a can of creosote and some two-by-four. The last of the goods are run through the bar code scanner and as I pass hear the shop assistant say. 'That's two hundred and sixty-two pounds thirty-seven pence. How would you like to pay, cash, cheque or Switch?'

'I wouldn't!' is Tango's reply as he casually walks past the check-out following me onto the forecourt.

Rachel approaches three activists catching some Indian summer sun. The street theatre has thankfully ended and they've run out of leaflets.

'How do it go out here?'

'Yeah ok. The guys have just gone down the station with the wood. You have fun?'

'Deffo,' I say, rubbing my neck reassuredly. 'We hit on a rich seam of humour.'

It's time to collect the bikes and ride off to Ancoats. A convoy of twenty bikes gives an enhanced feeling of security – of which many of us – including myself – are experiencing for the first time. Any anxiety at being knocked down is replaced by laughter – and there's sufficient time en route to recount the morning's events. Before long, the Great Ancoats Industrial Park looms large, and it's time to regroup, take stock, write a statement for the police or possibly swap roles with someone else. After the hacksaw incident, I think it best to leave the locking-on to someone else this time.

'Bwaa bwuck-bwuck-bwuck,' Tango gestures to me with small circular arm motions.

'Listen, mate, I'm no chicken. I just don't think I should jeopardise the operation with being too high profile. Besides, I'd like my neck not to change its shape or proximity to my body for the rest of the day.' I take on the role of one of the legal observers in a team with Helen and Jane.

A similar modus operandi is played out; the unusual customers, the knowing grins, the slight confusion over timing, though this time less muddled. We fight off the smirks and head toward the rails of reddish hard wood. Helen's brightly coloured woolly shoulder bag – akin to those possessed by trainee social workers – is opened. A toilet seat is placed within and she calmly wanders off to the exit.

'Candy from a baby,' says Jane with a wide, slightly wild grin and I feel a fizzy sensation surging down my spine. As the two of us head towards the entrance, a plan rapidly forms.

I whisper to her. 'If they can't find the stock, we don't have to steal it.'

'But won't they order more?'

'Not if the sales don't go through the barcode reader.'

'Ok – good plan.'

Any remaining mahogany pieces we see are taken and subtly hidden around the store, in recesses, inside other goods and kicked under shelving units. We try to use the most obscure, dustiest areas, which we guess haven't seen the light of day in years.

'Let's go, eh? That's just about all of it,' says Jane.

'Yeah, but let's get through the checkout first.' As cover, I pick up a Twix bar and pay for it before we walk out of the store.

'Do you buy it to give us a legitimate reason to be here?'

'No – I'm starving. Want some?'

'I'm vegan.'

'So you're seeing Tango then?'

She blushes – having the dual effect of highlighting her complete lack of make-up and heightening the flawless whites of her eyes. 'Yeah – we've such a connection. It's been three months now and I've never been so happy. How about you?'

'No, I don't fancy him.'

I receive a playful shove. 'Any special young lady at the moment?'

'I've got my eye on one or two – but I've only just got back here.'

'Well – good luck. Hope you find someone as fantastic as I have.'

Yeah right.

On the way to the police station to meet with the others the guilty buzz of shoplifting mingles with the belief we're doing something good. However, upon our arrival there's no sign of Helen and the others.

At the reception area Dom approaches the desk sergeant. 'Excuse me, some friends of mine were in earlier to hand in stolen property.'

The desk sergeant blows out his cheeks in an exasperated fashion. 'Oh them? They're downstairs. They've been nicked,' he says with a condescending smile.

Within a minute the police station is the scene of an impromptu sit-in.

Dom is defiant. 'Aren't you going to lock up the manager for selling this stuff? It's illegally taken from Brazil, yeah? I was on this action too, so if you're going to arrest them, then why not me as well? I'm as guilty as they are.'

The sergeant is nonplussed. Most police work round here involves scallies and petty criminals trying to evade the clutches of the cops. I'm guessing that openly asking to be arrested for theft is not in the training manual.

'Look,' he says. 'These people have broken the law by taking goods that they haven't paid for, and the store has asked us to investigate. Now if you'll let me get on and do this paperwork, everyone will be out of here quicker, including me. My shift ends in an hour, so if you'll excuse me.'

'It's completely outrageous. Out of order, that's what it is. What sort of fucking police state do we live in?' Rachel is powerless, angry and still slightly annoying.

'Do you want to join them?' the sergeant asks and waits for a reply. 'No. Then I'd suggest you keep your comments to yourself. Let's get a few things straight. They're downstairs. The lawyer's been called. I'm filling in the charge sheets and there's nothing you can do to prevent that. I'd suggest you go home and wait for them. And ... if you don't all get out of my station in five minutes you're all nicked for wasting police time.'

A group huddle is hastily called.

'We need consensus on this, but we need it fast. He's right. There's no point in us all getting arrested. Not for this,' the last of Dom's words are obscured by a yawn. 'It's been a long day and our beef isn't with him, it's with Texas,'

'Agreed,' says Tango. 'Besides, I've gotta get back and feed Kropotkin.' Tango's Jack Russell is named after a nineteenth-century Russian anarchist thinker.

Jane reaches into her bag. 'It's ok. You guys go, I'll be fine. I'm halfway through Middlemarch,' I can't work out if she's exceptionally kind or has submissive tendencies but would love to find out. However, Rachel also offers to stay thus scuppering any tiny chances of sharking.

As the police station clears, phone numbers and opinions on the criminal justice system are exchanged. I cycle back to my temporary home in a sulk, the earlier euphoria of the day completely gone.

Late one morning I visit my old friend Tessa in her new house in Fallowfield.

'I can't believe you've put those fucking Take That posters up in the hall,' I say entering the lounge. A voice whose owner I cannot yet see replies, 'Amen to that. I thought I got joint voting rights when we moved in.'

A woman I've never met before is sprawled on the sofa. Despite her baggy dungarees – and her eyes being on Richard and Judy – any lingering thoughts of Jane are well on the way to being erased.

'Have you met Debbie before?' says Tessa.

'No, how's it hanging? I mean, hiya.'

'Have a seat, Fred's just about to do the weather and it's looking slippery underfoot.' Though not as tall or objectively attractive as Jane – something – surely it's too early to be love – must be plain old caveman lust – is taking hold of me by the second. As she moves to make room for me, I desperately try to stare at the TV rather than anything else.

'How is it I haven't run into you before? I'm sure I would've remembered,' I ask with a hint of flirtation.

'He's full of it, eh? I was doing paper science with her.'

'I do have a name.'

'Oh yeah, I forgot you did such a fascinating degree – Tess.'

Debbie and I high-five on the couch. There's immediate chemistry. She says. 'But less of your cheek. People will always need paper – at least that's what my dad told me when I filled out my UCCA form.'

'And are you guys out there changing the face of bog roll as we know it? No, 'cos I bet you're sick of the sight of the stuff.'

'Well you're not exactly employee of the month,' says Tess.

'I work bloody hard – and for nothing.'

'At what?' asks Debbie.

'Lester's an eco warrior.'

'Sit on that, mate,' raising a middle finger. 'I'm a campaigner.'

Debbie turns square to face me. 'A man with a passion – tell me more.'

Neil had recently told me the best tactic with women is to leave them wanting. 'I'd love to – there's a lot to tell but – shit ... What's the time?'

'Half-twelve.'

'I've got to be somewhere in fifteen. Let's do it over a pint soon, eh?'

At the front door, Tessa kisses me goodbye. 'You can't fool me. You just want to get Debs out for a pint to try and get her pants off.'

In a medieval style I kiss her on the hand. 'Will you help me in my quest, fair maid?'

'Oh go on then. Laters,' she says as I bow retreating backwards up the front path.

The Texas Five – as they've become known – have been charged. Chris Binns, the solicitor Manchester EF! uses on a regular basis, is pretty hopeful the case will be dropped. He suggests it'd be a good idea to do another action to show we haven't been intimidated by these strong-arm tactics. A couple of days later we do CRISP-O actions in Stockport and Worsley, which go off without further arrests.

It's the day of the plea hearing at the Magistrates Court case and I sense I've slept through the alarm. Me and Neil were out on the town last night. I've little recollection of events but can sense the feeling on my tongue is no ordinary carpet-mouth. Then vague memories of sucking several pints of Guinness through cigarettes enter my cluttered mind. It's 12.15pm and I've missed the hearing.

'Arrggghhhh, fuck. Can't believe you can be such an arsehole,' I say to myself as I struggle towards the phone, then try to punch in the number with the shakes.

'Dom. Sorry I missed it. I'm feeling rougher than a sandpaper cock. What went down at the court?'

'Thanks for that. You're lucky to have caught me in. I'm feeding Kropotkin for Tango before we go out to celebrate. They dropped the charges. Isn't that great?'

'They did what? Fucking get in! Why?'

'I s'pose at the end of the day both the police and Texas didn't think it was worth the hassle. Besides, would've have been a disaster for their PR.'

'We've got 'em on the run. Let's discuss it at the next meeting. Speak to you soon. Gotta dash.'

'Are you coming down the pub?' Dom asks but the receiver has already been replaced.

Trying my best to be triumphant I punch the air en route to the bathroom and unceremoniously throw up the remaining booze, vegetarian kebab and fragments of stomach lining. As I take my head out of the toilet, the manufacturer's name catches my eye. It reminds me of the funniest ever advert in Viz:- a man urinating above the slogan – You can't miss with Armitage Shanks.

'My fucking back's killing me, how much further is this bloody place? I need a bastard Sherpa.' Tango neatly sums up everyone's thoughts.

'Shut up moaning and keep walking. There's no pleasing some

people – and when is it suddenly ok to exploit the Nepalese? I thought you stood up for indigenous peoples?' Jane and her man have hit a rocky patch and are bickering like an old married couple.

The latest Earth First! gathering is taking place in Todmorden near Leeds. Snow is thick and the hill steep.

'Piece of shit minibus. If we'd have had a four-by-four we could have done that no trouble.' I'm thinking more of my aching legs than the biosphere.

Gatherings are the closest thing EF! comes to a party conference. Previous get-togethers have approved the 'policies' of non-violence and neither condoning nor condemning damage to property. However, the 'organisation' has a simple, minimal structure like a piece of honeycomb. Keynote speeches, ten-minute standing ovations and toeing the party line are not required. Anyone can attend the gathering if they wish, though the head of Special Branch may not have been as welcome as most.

Much expletive-filled exhalation powers a dozen of us toward the farmhouse-cum-community centre clutching sleeping bags and beshouldered with rucksacks.

'I'm so cold it's untrue,' says Rachel.

'Chill. Geddit?' As usual she finds me about as funny as contracting ebola.

'Where shall we put our tat, guys?' says Helen to two blokes just inside the main door. Tat is the colloquial word for stuff that generally involves some rucksack-and-tent combination.

'Anywhere. The priority right now is for you to give me a hug,' says the considerably taller of the two.

'Everyone, this is Nick and Steve,' as Helen hugs each in turn. 'Though you may not believe it but they're brothers,' she says to the rest. Indeed they don't look an iota alike.

'That's because I was conceived properly, whereas with laughing boy over here the milkman wanked on mum's legs and the flies did the rest,' Steve shoots a love-you-hate-you grin at his brother in response.

'Doesn't sound like you're behaving yourself, my dear. Guests remember?' a rangy short-haired woman comes over and puts her arm round Nick.

'This is Claire, my probation officer,' he says kissing her tenderly on the lips.

As we unpack our tat, the Leeds gang are frantically running around getting organised. Large pieces of paper are BluTacked to the walls, marker pens tested and a box of flapjacks next to a donation tin is the pick of a veritable hippy food mountain.

There's about a hundred people at the introductory meeting. As Neil said would happen, the gathering begins according to stereotype with everyone sat in a circle. An icebreaker involving everyone forming a dancing train is supposed to help us bond with complete strangers – too touchy-feely for my liking.

I get an overpowering whiff of the rancid coconut and incense smell and wander over to ask Phil. 'Mate – I'm not being funny but I thought you'd be able to tell me straight without offence – what's that smell?' I try to describe it.

'It's patchouli oil – can't stand the stuff myself but it's all the rage.'

The first workshop of the day is direct action training. Two women in their fifties wearing CND badges address the group. The one with considerable upholstering speaks first.

'Hi I'm Linda. You're probably wondering why Brenda and myself have got some teeth missing.'

'Well,' says Brenda, 'it isn't anything to do with not brushing twice a day. It is due to the military police – and the ordinary police – over the years. My front teeth went at Greenham in '84.'

An aura of respect for them quickly builds. More experienced instructors in the art of non-violence would be difficult to come across, short of digging up Gandhi. It seems this pair have had more run-ins with the cops than Robert Thompson and Jon Venables have recently acquired enemies.

The first workshop is to put everyone in a mock action situation. Those participating are split up into groups, then sub-divided into the roles of protesters, police and security guards. Three mock demos take place simultaneously, with people linking together to avoid being dragged away, and some posing as police clearly relishing the task as they drag and manhandle hippies into make-believe cells. I'm not sure whether this is a worrying sign or it's just part of the workshop's realism.

One guy is resisting rather less than passively. 'Stop!' says Linda. 'Would you have acted like that in a real life situation?'

'Well ...'. It's clear he doesn't really know.

'If you'd have done that on an action, you'd have definitely been arrested for assault of a police officer. The police will use anything like that against you. I'm not condemning self-defence, but just be aware, ok? Now, let's continue.' Gradually, amid much screaming, shouting and giggling all the protestors are shifted from one end of the hall to the 'vans', a row of upturned chairs and tables.

This workshop is a salutary lesson for many. As a rule, English people aren't used to being pulled and pushed around unless they play rugby or are still young enough for playground antics. It dawned on me during the exercise that – to carry a person away, even if they are completely passive – takes two people. If, like me, you're six foot tall and quite well built, it could even take three or four. To properly control an action, there'd be need for more police and security than there are activists. It doesn't take a genius to calculate this could prove expensive for the opposition.

It's soon time for a well-earned cuppa, some food and a chance to mingle. I chat to Shelly and Michael, two Twyford veterans with plenty of tales to tell.

'... and there was the time when this solicitor from Winchester came up to see us. Someone spiked his tea with magic mushrooms and before long he was dancing naked on top of St Catherine's Hill.' It's all I can do to prevent my mouthful of tea coming out my nose.

'It's nice to know the spirit in the camps is kept high out of hours,' I say once I regain control.

'That's nothing,' says Shelly. 'Michael has to tell you the one about waking to find a goat shitting on his head.'

'Indeed I could, but Twyford wasn't all fun and games. There were so many assaults – so many times it was just us and the security. No solicitors, no media, no protection. We were sitting ducks most of the time – amazing we lasted as long as we did.'

Suddenly Linda and Brenda come in through the main doors. Brenda shouts, 'Right you lot! This is a raid! We have certain information that Claire Evans has been involved in sabotaging machinery, and we are taking her in for questioning in one minute from now!'

It's pretty clear this is an exercise to see how we cope under pressure. Almost immediately, Nick and a few others rush over to Claire and form a protective cordon. Others think it's a good idea to form a human barrier between her and the 'cops'. Before long the path between hunters and quarry is a mass of bodies – mostly all linked to each other – which is almost impossible to negotiate without injuring someone. Claire is smuggled out the other doorway.

'Well done. It seems like this morning's lessons have sunk in. Looks like we've got a good new crop of activists to take over the mantle from us, ay Linda?' Brenda smiles toothlessly from ear to ear.

During the break I'm introduced to the rest of the Leeds bunch. There's Mark, who, despite the long hair, proudly sports a Leeds United shirt. It's nice to have a fellow football fan among us but his choice of team leaves something to be desired. His partner in crime seems to be Lindsey, with her impossibly curly hair. Quiet but steady and determined by all accounts, she's been one of the mainstays in putting the weekend together.

Next is a legal workshop with Patrick, a London-based lawyer who works for Bindmans, which seems to be the best law firm to be represented by. Everyone receives a handout containing information about a person's rights on arrest.

He says. 'Being arrested, especially for the first time, can be a
quite distressing experience. Police cells aren't the nicest places in
the world and the treatment you receive at the hands of the authorities isn't always the best. Fortunately, like with most things, arrest
is something you get used to and even your technique of dealing
with it improves with practice.' There are guffaws and chuckles
around the room

'However, it's not advisable to get too used to getting arrested.
With each one the chances of losing your liberty start to increase,
as well as the size of fine you're likely to incur.' People share their
experiences of arrest. There's a lot to take in so I take as much
literature to read later.

The evening is set aside for the serious task of getting pissed.
Three litre bottles of cider are very much in evidence, and by midnight the typical walk to the toilets is indirect and incoherent, as is
much of the conversation. I see Tango and Jane making up in the
corner – lucky bastard. Most of these hippies are good fun and over
the two days I have a great time – which included doing a workshop
on knots and treehouse building. It could have been even better –
during lunch on the second day I was sharking a woman called
Charlotte over by the couscous but she had an affliction starting
with 'b' and ending in 'oyfriend'.

As we pack up to leave I go over to Linda and Brenda and thank
them for their encouragement and advice. 'It's you lot we should be
thanking, you're the ones who've got all the hard work ahead. Ours
is nearly done,' says Linda with a look of regret tinged with relief.
Although sounding a bit like a deathbed scene from a Dickens
novel, the message is clear and sincere. I hug them both and
accompany the rest of the Manchester posse to the minibus.

Debbie carries two pints over to the table in the Red Lion in
Withington.

'Cheers. Here's to our new lives – wherever – whatever – to
freedom.' I raise my glass to her.

'To freedom,' she says. Do I detect a slight wink accompanying
her reply? 'So how's the activism going? Saved the planet yet?'

'We're ... doing ok. I'm still learning the ropes to be honest.'

'It's a great thing to do. Don't think I could myself but you have
my support.'

'Uh – it's not hard. Maybe you should try it?'

'Maybe I'll get a job first.'

Two rounds each later and I'm now sat next to her rather than
across the table. I drape my arm across the bench when she goes
to the ladies and when she sits down doesn't ask for it to be
removed. I'm in! She's the most interesting woman – in all the

important respects – I've met in a good long while.

'So,' I down the rest of my pint. 'Do you want any help sabotaging that Take That poster? I've had experience.'

'Well, we could go back to mine and carry out a feasibility study.' My arm goes down towards her bum as I draw in to kiss her. Her body feels even better than it looks. Shapely without being fat; well-defined but 100% feminine. A wonderful feeling of not wanting to be with anyone else on the planet overwhelms me.

'Come on you.' As her hand reaches for mine there's a deliberate brush against my crotch.

It's a ten-minute walk back to hers – one which we perform in thirty due to a couple of essential snog-stops. The late November night means it would be impolite to expose too much of her flesh on the way home but this makes the anticipation all the more delicious.

On her doorstep she says: 'Tess is in tonight. We'll have to be quiet.' I say a silent atheistic prayer to the random factors which have resulted in me having a nailed-on shag with this wonderful woman. And at nearly 24 – a whole year older than me – a woman indeed she is. Over the next couple of hours we explore each other's bodies. Maybe it's my imagination but she's more ergonomic in bed than any woman I've ever slept with. As she rides me I learn more about pressure, friction, movement and angles than I ever did in physics.

Don't appear too eager – the watchwords of a successful man with the ladies. When I wake up the next morning and see her in all her naked magnificence and reflect on the wonderful night before I fail in this basic test. No matter what label you attach to feelings at such an early stage in a relationship – for me right now they are all pervasive – I'm not yet sure but she seems be at a similar level in her feelings for me. What with that and the new place in Withington me and Neil have moved into things are definitely looking up.

The Earth First! Action Update is a four–page publication, which does exactly what its title implies. With a nod to production values on one hand and cost on the other, it's a mixture of news, previews and contact details. The lead story in December's issue is the eviction of treehouses built in a large chestnut tree in Wanstead, on the route of the proposed M11 extension in east London. The opening paragraph, below the EF! masthead of a wrench and a hammer and the strapline RESIST MUCH, OBEY LITTLE, reads: 'Against strong local resistance, the construction of the disastrous M11 Link is continuing at a snail's pace with serious cost to the authorities. This tree and 350 houses will be destroyed by a half-mile slab of tarmac. Part of Epping Forest and Hackney

Marshes are also under threat, but there is a long way to go. Since early November there has been a constant vigil, and on 6th December the fence around George Green is torn down in scenes resembling the Peasant's Revolt.'

The piece describes the eviction of the 250-year-old tree by 300 police and security. Hundreds of local people tried and protect the chestnut, but were 'punched in the face, kneed in the groin, pulled by the ears and pressure-pointed – pensioners and children were not excluded.'

This campaign seems to be gaining a lot of momentum and will be one to watch – and visit – in the New Year. Christmas is coming up fast and activities tend to wind down as the university term draws to a close. It's regrettable but true that despite efforts to reach out into the 'general' population, there are not many non-students involved. I've been told activism in Manchester tends to operate in cycles around the academic calendar. Things start up in October and go very quiet around May, with quite lengthy breaks around Christmas and Easter. Quite how the general population can be persuaded to get hooked on locking on is not clear. A day before the Christmas break recruitment dilemmas are temporarily forgotten when Phil rings me with some news.

'I suppose you haven't heard. I got a fax through this morning from Texas Head Office. They've decided to stop buying mahogany products.'

'What, in Manchester?'

'No, nationally! They're just going to sell their remaining stocks and then that's it, no more. We've won, we've bloody well won!'

There's a pause, a silent realisation of the kind accompanying really good or bad news.

'That's amazing. Well, it's not amazing, but ... oh you know what I mean. I think a celebratory beer or four might be in order this evening.'

'Indeed, I'll get onto the phone tree straight away. See you at the Welcome, seven-thirty?'

We commandeer the biggest table in the pub and before long it's full of glasses, crisp packets, cigarette paper packets and all manner of hostelry paraphernalia. Though the victory has been won by lots of pressure groups around the country there's much mutual back–slapping. It wasn't just Texas who'd buckled but Great Mills, B&Q, Sainsbury's Homebase and Do-It-All as well.

'I can't believe we've won!' says Helen with a hug. 'This is fantastic. It's not just banging on at people's attitudes, you know.'

'Here's to many more victories,' Phil stands and raises his glass and a couple of pints worth of beer is spilled as twenty or so glasses jostle to join the toast.

For some reason best known to herself a rather tiddly Helen begins to sing I Will Survive. Before long it's a competition to find the silliest paraphrasing of the lines to tell the story of the Texas Five.

Lorraine's version of the opening lines is a decent early entry.

Felling giant trees
it's a heinous crime
And so I took some stuff from Texas
now I'm doing time

Even Tango manages to contribute to the beginning of the chorus.

No more
Can you buy doors
Made of mahog'ny
In sev'ral well known UK stores

We get midway through completing the song before the topic gets washed away on a tide of Greenall's Original. The massed ranks of Manchester EF! drinking the night away with spirits higher than a tropical canopy is a lovely sight. I haven't known these folks long but in a short time I've bonded with them on an individual and group basis. The taste of success is sweet and addictive, and I want to be part of it when more occur. This sentiment remains unchanged after a few spliffs after the pub at Phil's – and continues to be so as I travel south on the train to Sussex and a family Christmas the next day.

CHAPTER 3

WINTER 1993/4

'I'm driving to the Twyford rally just after New Year. I might as well take as many as I can in the car. How about it?' Stewart's plan as we talk on the phone is most welcome. I've read of this commemorative event in the Action Update and am eager to go.

'Ok, that'd be great. On the 3rd and 4th isn't it? It'll give me a chance to get over New Year's Eve.'

The landscape of Sussex gives way to Hampshire's, frost decorating the grass, pavements, and unfortunately, the roads. There's an air of anticipation in the car as we near Twyford. The place has taken on a special significance for anti-roaders – it's like Haight-Ashbury to the hippy generation, or EuroDisney to Sun readers.

'Do you think it'll be like visiting the Somme?' I ask Nikki. If she's feeling any lingering resentment toward me it's not showing, though I don't think mentioning Debbie is a good move right now.

'Come on, get a grip, it wasn't a war.'

'Yes,' said Stewart, 'but there's a lot of similarities too – comradeship, hardship, a shared objective and a common enemy.'

'Could be that seventy years from now you'll have a few doddery old fucks marking the event,' I say.

'And they'll probably have jet-powered wheelchairs to get there by then,' adds Gip with a grin.

'Did you hear about the appeal against the Twyford injunction a couple of months ago?' asks Stewart.

'I'm afraid I used the court pages of the Times to line the rabbit hutch that day.' I say sarcastically.

Stewart ignores me. 'The judge said civil disobedience on the grounds of conscience was part of an honourable tradition and the activists would be vindicated by history. And they got compensation.'

'Why didn't you fast-forward to the interesting part in the first place?' says Gip. Stewart falls into a disappointed silence.

On our arrival the camp seems to be deserted. Only two tents stand on the frozen ground. One has its door flaps wide open and there's clearly no one at home. Nikki knocks on the canvas of the other and extends a verbal greeting to whatever is inside. A hairy head pokes out after half a minute or so. Parts of the head aren't hairy at all, but only just enough to prevent the owner looking like a Mexican wolf boy.

'Morning,' it says.

'Alright then, how's it going?' she takes the route of easy conversation.

'Not bad at all. Fuckin' wicked trip last night.'

'Nice to meet you, My name's Nikki, this is Stewart, Gip, and Lester. Who else was up here last night?'

'Oh, well I'm Cosmo. I was up here on me own on liquid acid. Sat on the hill all night and saw lights in the distance. Thought it was aliens coming to suck my brains out my ears.'

'And? What were the lights?'

'After about three hours I worked out it was Winchester.'

More people arrive as the afternoon grows accustomed to itself. The camping area is pretty full – and parents – some of whom I assume used to be digger divers – play with their kids in the mini-maze cut into the turf nearby. One of these is Michael, who I remember from the gathering. 'Do you like the maze? We cut it our-selves on slack days. Can't believe it's still here.'

He points over to the cutting – a huge white scar on the green landscape half a mile away which dominates all the view. 'That's where the rally'll be tomorrow. We'll get there, don't worry. Besides, the contractors shouldn't be working, it's holiday time.'

He asks if we'd like a closer look and within fifteen minutes we reach the edge of the cutting – only by gazing at the wider panorama can you deduce how beautiful the site would have been.

'All this for Southampton commuters to save seven minutes in the morning,' Michael shakes his head. 'All the tricks they pulled for seven bleedin' minutes.'

'Such as?'

'Like the detective agency the government paid to infiltrate the group. Quarter of a million that cost alone.'

'Did you spot who they were?'

''Bout half and half. Some of them were hopeless, others were like best mates.'

Back at the camp the evening's knees–up consists of fires, guitars and dogs narrowly avoiding incineration and is gilt-edged with reminiscence for many. In a frying pan a woman with dread-locks cooks some white foodstuff I can't identify. I go over and enquire.

'They're 'frasers, self-raising flour and water. It was what we ate if there was nothing else.' Although largely cooked for nostalgia pur-poses on this occasion, Cosmo goes on to devour several. Various folks tell us of how the campaign grew from its inception through to Yellow Wednesday when hundreds of security guards raided the camp before dawn.

Later, the combined forces of over 200 police and private security guards moved in and surrounded the Dongas with razor wire before trashing the area with the many assaults and hospitalisations. 'They surrounded us with razor wire then trashed everything – punches, kicks, the works. My mate Meg was strangled by a cop and it took 45 minutes for an ambulance to arrive.'

'Fucking hell.'

'It was so scary – especially for those with kids – after that it just wasn't the same and a few of us wanted to move away. We had a stroke of luck when Kevin – this farmer in Wales – offered us Dongas some land. He's so lovely.'

'Dongas?'

'We took our name from the tribe that defended these hills a thousand years ago.'

'Oh. Right.'

About ten o'clock I go to Dom and say. 'Surely there's some way we can make getting into the compound easier tomorrow?'

He goes off to his tent and returns with a couple of pairs of wirecutters.

The two of us set off into the darkness. We've a small torch but it's only to be used when really needed. There's been some talk today of 'monkey wrenching' – the deliberate sabotage of machinery – but this strictly speaking isn't wrenching as we're only going for the fence. It's still exciting and I'm loving it.

There's quite a lot of hedge cover to obscure us from secret snoopers and within ten minutes we reach the nearest piece of accessible fence.

'Well, how about here? It'll save people a walk tomorrow morning,' Dom smiles as he turns on the torch, eager not to let its beam extend too far. 'You start at the top, I'll go from the bottom and we'll meet halfway, try and go sort of straight.'

The cutters are designed for a right-handed person and I struggle. Like many left-handers, I believe the world's tool and implement industry conspires against me. However, for this task accuracy isn't required and within a couple of minutes, though it seems far longer, the fence is two-thirds done.

'Wait – what's that?' Dom utters in a loud whisper. We both fall silent. There's the faint but growing sound of an engine. 'Shit ... come on, go!'

The torch is turned off, and we run for all we're worth along the track in the opposite direction from the mystery noise. I look behind to see headlight beams coming around the corner. The shape of the vehicle is now visible. It's a Land Rover belonging to Group 4. We've been spotted. Excitement turns into full-blown fear. Suddenly it's like being one of those cartoon characters whose heart beats a foot out of their chest. We dive over a gravel bank and disappear into the woods independently.

Oh shit. Alone in the woods, with security and maybe police on my tail, having just committed criminal damage on a high profile site and I still have the offending object in my pocket. Panic starts to set in. I lay low in some ferns for what seems to be about a quarter of an hour and try to work out a strategy. It's a full five minutes before I can no longer hear my breathing.

Whilst on the lookout for guards I gingerly make it back to the tampered section of fence. I don't think anyone's touched it since we ran and there's no sound of an engine. The night is dark, for though the sky is clear the moon is at its newest. With just enough illumination to see to the rest of the fence, I yank the section away from its original position as a dry run for tomorrow, replace it, then tie a couple of links back into place. As long as no one takes a close look at it everything'll be fine.

I hurry back to the camp, eager to see if Dom's made it back ok.

He's sitting by the fire, can of cider in hand, a blanket across his shoulders, staring into the flames. As I approach he looks up and grins.

'Result mate! What a fucking result, I thought we were done for. Where the hell did you get to?' I manoeuvre past a dozen or so folks and put my hand up for a high-five, expecting a reciprocal movement.

'I don't know what you're on about. I've been here at the camp all evening. I just went back to my tent for a lie-down.'

This is news to me. 'No, mate, you're pulling my pisser. The fence? Eh?'

'Lester, I think the fire's going down a bit. Fancy coming to get some more wood with us?' The fire is blazingly hot. Several are trying to hold their trousers away from their legs to dissipate some of the heat. Looks like Dom wants a chat in private.

'Er ... ok,' I reply, sounding a bit like Beavis or Butthead.

We walk into a clearing then Dom turns sharply to me. 'I know you haven't been doing this sort of thing very long, but there's no excuse for what you just did. This isn't some sort of fucking game. There are millions of pounds at stake on this contract.'

'I ...'

'Me and loads of other people have been named on an injunction for this site. I shouldn't even be here this weekend, and then you come back shouting your mouth off about the fence. What are you trying to do, get us all busted?"

'I'm sorry mate, I didn't think. I let the excitement go to my head.

It is bloody good though, eh?' At this, there's a slight break in Dom's stern expression.

'Look, here are some ground rules I thought you already knew about, but obviously not. One – only talk to people about stuff like this, any action in fact, on a need-to-know basis. Two – even people you think you know really well could be an infiltrator. I could be – you could be. How can we tell?'

'But ...'

'But nothing. In the States there were a couple of EF!ers – Judi Bari and Daryl Cherney. Heard of them?'

'No.'

'They were trying to stop logging roads. One day the car they were driving blew up.'

'Well, that's terrible, but I'm struggling to see the relevance.'

'Bari's partner for two years was FBI, that's what. She never suspected a thing until it was too late. The authorities said it was their bomb. She's been in a wheelchair since and Cherney was really fucked up by it all.'

'Right ... I see.' I pause for thought and effect. 'You're right. I'm sorry, mate. I'll be more careful.'

'Ok, sorry to get angry and that, but I have to be blunt. Now do you want to do that high-five?'

'Too right. I finished the fence by the way. That's need-to-know isn't it? So you don't have to go back and check.'

'Yes it is. Lecture over – let's get back to the fire and get pissed.'

Dom lets out several loud 'yips'. I've encountered 'yipping' before. High pitched and distinct, it's the universal EF! gesture. A warning, a hello, a cry of triumph, a show of unity – it has many uses. Like the vocal equivalent of a Swiss Army Knife – though you can't open a tin of beans with a yip. As we yelp in unison, I feel I've experienced another rite of passage into the movement. We head back to the camp, where I tout around for a spare tent space. I'm in luck – if you count sharing with a fitful and flatulent Cosmo lucky.

Morning comes soon enough, bringing with it a fair share of thick heads and shivering bodies. Each brain cell destroyed in defence of Mother Earth. The sacrifices some people have made are really quite admirable.

About mid-morning the crowds gather for the walk from St Catherine's Hill, half a mile away from the camp, back towards the main cutting. We're each handed a wooden stave-and-rag combination to serve as a torch later on. The hundreds of people who've come from all round the country are a varied bunch – radical anarchists in black hooded tops and balaclavas, jugglers, a fire breather or two, middle-aged ramblers, grannies, locals, full-timers and first-timers. There's no one way to categorise all these people other than a shared belief that the road shouldn't have been built.

One couple even turn up on a tandem, but the route from the hill to the cutting necessitates it having to be left behind at camp. Michael asks a few volunteers to carry a sack of coal. According to the old New Year's custom of first-footing it's traditional to visit a neighbour's property with a piece. The plan is form a black spot on the chalk to symbolise the many accidents the new road will inevitably cause.

The procession sets off to yips, cheers and whistles and drumming. There are many journalists – of the TV, radio and print variety. It can be difficult persuading them to come to actions or indeed cover them, but for one with this level of significance there is no problem.

Those at the head of the march reach the doctored stretch of fence. I've already told Cosmo 'the pixies' have done something to it. This of course doesn't mean a brilliant US indie guitar band have come over and wrecked it. The crude ties are undone, the fence parts and much to the amusement of the marchers, we filter through the hole and make our way down the semi-steep bank to a path that leads to the bottom of the cutting. Group 4 vehicles can be seen moving up the valley at some speed. The massed ranks of security – who've been waiting by the site gates – haven't anticipated this.

I say to Cosmo. 'Christ, they really are as stupid as everyone says.' He nods casually.

'Er … newsflash. That's no big news. They may have the numbers but we have the … what's the word … ingenuity.' It's still a bit early for him, bless.

Down in the cutting it's possible to get a sense of scale. The hole is about 100 metres wide, nearly as deep and as long as … a motorway. It's hard to imagine where there's another hole big enough to put all the chalk. A cement company has probably bought it all, so perhaps some of the chalk will come back as part of the road. There's perhaps five or six hundred of us in all forming a huge circle. The coal is heaped in the middle of the circle and the festivities begin. The interface of boots, winter and chalk whiten the former and darken the latter as people move around. There is music, dancing, and songs including, I'm told, an old Donga favourite.

You can't kill the Spirit
She is like a mountain
Old and strong
She goes on an on and on

And it does. On and on and on and on. Far too hippy for my tastes, I can tell you.

There are a few speeches from direct action veterans as well as one from the Twyford Down Association, a 'respectable' group who opposed the road through conventional means only later to form strong ties with the Dongas and EF!ers once the destruction began.

The security and police keep a low profile, apart from a few verbal exchanges between them and us. After all that's gone before – such as people being run over by diggers, guards pulling the clothes off women and all the unnecessary and vindictive arrests – a bit of swearing and goading is fair enough. The rally ends with a few fireworks, much cheering and of course a chorus of yips.

'How does it feel being a hardcore anarchist?' Debbie is teasing, playing with my chest hair as we lie in bed.

'Anarchism gets a very bad name. It's actually a highly coherent way of running a society. Better than anything we've got at the moment. Anyway, I'm an environmentalist, nothing more, nothing less.' It feels like a strange thing to say whilst naked.

'Oh come on, given the chance wouldn't you like to storm parliament, D-lock in one hand and copy of the Action Update in the other?'

'I'm just trying to protect the future for my nephews and their generation. Maybe our own one day, who knows?'

'Easy, tiger,' she reaches over for a snog. 'Who says I'm going to let you impregnate me?'

She looks straight at me. Her eye colour – a green-grey-brown hybrid – is almost identical to my own. We also both have a freckle in our right eye. I think it's a sign. In reality it's just a mutual over-accumulation of pigment in the iris.

'Besides, who says I want any mewling kids?' I say, but with her genes alone they'd be adorable.

I roll on top, pinning her down. 'Anyway, I'll have my way with you anytime I like, how's that for anarchy?'

We play out some kind of master-and-maid scenario – more through current context than any need to spice things up with role–play. As we lie back – don't worry she's on the pill – she says. 'Just be careful, that's all. Don't get in too much trouble. You're always seeing people getting sent down for this and that in the papers.'

'I've got no intention of going to prison, I haven't even been arrested yet. Even if it did get to that, I hope I'd have the good sense to chill it all out before I got sent down. Anyway, wouldn't I be more mysterious, more alluring on the inside?'

There's no response.

Tails are high after the Texas victory and delicious anticipation of what'll be the next Big Thing. I check the EF! ansaphone in the University campaigns office. There's a message from John, an Oxford activist. 'I'm coming up to Manchester for a few days, any chance of crashing your meeting?' I return the call.

'Sounds good. Why?'

'Had a call from an old friend at the Hulme Community Project. Apparently there's a pond behind the University that's to be turned into a science park. I don't know much more, but he reckons it's something we could do something about.'

'So, let's get this straight, the whole planet is going down the toilet, and suddenly we're going to drop everything to save a couple of ducks and a few weeds. I'm sorry but ...'

'That's where you've got it all wrong. We need to think globally and act locally. This pond could be just the kind of campaign you need to get real locals on board, especially in a place like this.' He tells me that Hulme, backing onto the University district, is synonymous with urban decay, poverty and fantastically bad '60s housing schemes. The area's bad reputation is comparable to Moss Side. I agree in principle but remain unconvinced. 'Good, I'll see you in a couple of days.'

John, true to his word, arrives two lunchtimes later. I'm still sceptical about the plan. 'Well, we can't decide anything until we know what this pond is like. It could be a piddly mud puddle for all we know.'

Helen, John and myself meet up with Barry Hines of Hulme Community Project. He looks and sounds beaten. 'I'm beaten,' he says. 'It's time to hand the problem over to someone else. Tell you what, I'll show you the pond right now.'

We go to inspect the site. Although the only wildlife habitat of its kind in the city centre, Abbey Pond is about the size of two football pitches and strewn with litter. 'Well, it's a bit of a state, but that suggests a sign of use.' Barry's an optimist despite everything. 'The local kids do come here. Some catch baby newts and take them home to their parents. It's about the only contact with nature they get.'

It's decided to run the idea through the group. An EF! meeting is hastily called. Phil rings Polly, the head of the local Wildlife Trust and she's up for coming along.

In the meeting John's gone into Hollywood screenwriter pitch mode, trying to sell the idea of the campaign just as fervently as a newly trained door–to–door salesman.

'If people start to hold a bit of this pond in their hearts, we might just win. It's definitely winnable.' He's in full flow.

'It's also dead close to the office so it'll be really convenient,' Phil says pragmatically.

A campaign to save the pond gains support in the group, especially once Polly has her say. 'There are forty-four species in it, some of which you won't find elsewhere for miles around. We tried to get the pond listed as a wildlife area, and it should have qualified. The council refused it because they knew this planning application was pending.'

'Basically,' she adds, 'direct action is the only method left open. And no-one's going to do it except us, so let's get the ball rolling.'

Despite it being mid-January, we decide the most effective method is to set up a permanent encampment and things-to-do lists are hastily compiled.

The camp is to begin next Tuesday night at 10pm – we have six days to get it all together. Allied to frenzied preparation, a tree dressing event for local school children is also hastily arranged for the Monday, so the kids could say goodbye to the pond. To the authorities, it will seem as if nothing is afoot. The appearance of Manchester Wildlife helping ten-year-olds put pieces of material onto branches won't reek of subversive activity.

That night I tell Neil about the plan when he gets in from work. He's decided to become an accountant and do the year's conversion course to turn a politics and history degree into a valued qualification. Though I don't dwell on it much I did the same course as him.

'Do what? You're going to camp out in the middle of Hulme? Next to a pond? Are you fucking mad? How long for?'

'Which one of those five questions do you want me to answer first?'

'Well, good luck, but how about when there's a match on the telly?' he says. 'Have you seen the weather forecast? There's snow due. You'll catch hypothermia. Tell you what, get Debbie to bring you a food parcel and a carry-out every now and again. Or maybe this is a job for Oxfam?'

'Ho fucking ho. Look, it's only three miles away. I'll try and get back most days for a bath. No worries about that.'

'I know you're being sincere, but I really think those bloody lentils have brainwashed you,' he says to my back as I wearily climb the stairs.

'Where did you hear about the drug trial?' asks the doctor. She's Scottish and quite fit but I'm spoken for. I've decided to keep penury at bay – and to further medical science – by taking anti-depressants.

'It was on a noticeboard in the student union.'

'Ok,' she says as she takes off the blood pressure cuff, 'once you've signed the consent forms we get started.'

I'll be able to take Debs out for a couple of meals. Can't do any harm, eh?

It's Tuesday night and vehicles begin to congregate around the entrance to the pond. Shadowy figures can be seen shifting equipment from vans onto the watery wasteland. Overnight, 'someone' turns the pond into a community of eight tents and a 'bender'. One Hulme resident who's recently got involved with us is called Bender Del. This nickname isn't because he's gay – it's due to his ability to make semi-permanent living spaces from tarpaulins, willow poles and string.

Press releases about the camp have been faxed out. The next morning a clutch of journalists turn up to interview the new residents of the pond. A kitchen area is set up, as well as a semi-circular communal bender, the shape of which allows smoke from the campfire to escape. There's many rounds of tea made amid much mutual congratulation.

I down my antidepressants with a lukewarm cuppa. 'Urrggh ... what's this tea made with?'

'Soya milk? Why?'

'Tastes like the devil's spunk,' I say as I pour the tea on the floor. Despite this upset I soon nod off in front of the fire.

Being the only one who can afford it, Phil's hired a mobile phone-for the camp so an alarm can be raised in a hurry. Even though the site is literally a couple of minutes' walk from the University we're quite exposed right in the city centre. However, as the days go on the camp becomes somewhat remote. Those on site tend not to venture out. We're becoming a tribe. I know this sounds like I've gone mad, but sleeping here most nights has a genuine connection tothe land.

There's a group of local kids who now know each other because of the pond. There's a growing sense of community and I've met loads of people. Most of the time I wear three T-shirts, two sweatshirts and two coats; I get to shower and shave every four days or so and frankly it's starting to tell. I miss home comforts such as toast that isn't covered in ash. Debbie visits at the weekend bringing food but no beer. I can tell she's not happy with the way things are. It's obvious she's feeling neglected but there's not much I can do other than abandon the camp. Avoiding the issue is cowardly but the easiest option right now.

The kitchen receives donations from many sources and the stalwart of the whole operation is Polly. Despite being at least in her late forties and having two teenagers to look after, she's at the camp as much as anyone else. God knows where she gets her energy from.

As well as the everyday routine of living on site there's also the campaigning to take care of. Getting mass support for something outdoors in the middle of winter isn't easy. A candlelit vigil is arranged for the Sunday night. I decide to take matters in hand.

I show Rachel a carrier bag containing a couple of hundred little candles.

'Well done. Where did all they come from?' she asks.

'Holy Name Church.'

'I didn't know the local priest was onside.'

'Err ... I don't know if he is. I sort of borrowed them. After all the crap religion's put us through over the last few thousand years I thought it was time for them to support something decent.'

We attempt to set up talks with the people who run the science park, the University Vice Chancellor and Hulme Regeneration – the driving force behind the development – but no-one wants to listen. Graham Lee, leader of Manchester's Labour council, has called us 'undemocratic extremists' on local radio.

One afternoon, with snow thick on the ground, bailiffs accompanied by police arrive and put up eviction notices. The forces of 'progress' are coming. The only question is when.

Events pass with alarmingly vague rapidity. I don't know whether this is caused by the experimental drugs surging through my system, or the weirdness of life at the moment. There's been a couple of times when I should have gone to the clinic to do the tests necessary for the trial to end, but I've been too busy at the camp. As a consequence I have kept taking the tablets, have still received no money for taking them, am going out of my tiny mind, and to top it all I daren't tell Debbie about it as she'll either kill or chuck me.

The campaign at the pond has reached the barricading stage. I 'borrow' a large wheely bin from Abduls, thought by most students to be the best kebab shop in the north-west and use it as a haulage vehicle. A bit a scavenging around Hulme with the kids reveals a disused children's playground, which has been dug up. Some of this is transported in the bin to the site. We decorate the circular top of a slide and hoist it up a tree. It is to be the alarm gong for when the eviction comes. A curved steel ladder, once part of a climbing frame is cemented into the ground as a lock-on. Best of the helpers is Jezzer, a boy of fourteen who is virtually as strong as me.

'Christ, you've obviously been eating your Shredded Wheat,' I say as he mixes another load of concrete.

'Ay, don't talk crap, I'm just made of steel. Dead 'ard me.' He rolls up his sleeve to flex a bicep.

Conditions are spartan but fun. Don't know why but I've found the life kind of addictive, and have slept only once at home since the camp began. It's now day fourteen and conditions have started to take a toll on my health, and probably my relationship too. I am smelly most of the time. The eviction is not far off, and, after all the time and effort I've put in so far, I'm not gonna miss that for anything.

There's a renewed sense of urgency. Tree houses are hastily constructed. It's remarkable how quickly wood, nails and rope can be transformed into something tangible. We also make a six-foot mascot – a newt called Isaac – out of papier mâché and bin bags one long afternoon. Steel arm tubes are obtained and made into what we think are state-of-the-art lock-on devices. This is of course dependent on budget, and some of our 'impenetrable' lock-ons are made of concrete-filled plastic barrels.

I hear on the grapevine that Hulme Regeneration has double-crossed us – saying they will reconsider the plans but actually have no intention. This coincides with two workers from the local brewery coming to the pond with a couple of crates of tinnies in the evening. We all sit around the fire getting very pissed. I find that I need to have a poo, and, perhaps it's the antidepressants, I decide to take my revenge on Hulme Regen by going round to their offices and park the remains of my vegan supper through the letter box. Not sure if 'poo posting' is a popular tactic around the country, but it made me feel better in more than one sense.

One afternoon, I take another autonomous decision – to go into the science park to see the director. I'm not exactly looking my best, and as soon as the secretary and security guard see me know why I'm there.

'Good morning,' I say approaching the receptionist. 'I've come to see Dr Henry please? It's about the pond?'

'I'm afraid he's very busy right now. He couldn't possibly see you. If you'd like, you can make an appointment for next week?'

'But that's no bloody good, the pond will be a mud pile by then. I've got to see him now.'

'That's impossible. Now either make an appointment or kindly leave the premises.'

'You fucking bitch! You couldn't give a toss, could you? Earth rapist!' I think I can put that little outburst down to the pills.

The security guard ceases to be genial. 'Now then, you little shitbag, there's no need for that. This is a fine, decent woman. You've no right to call her things like that. Get the fuck out of here.'

I bawl as I'm hauled and mauled off the premises. 'Get off me, you fucker, I can walk out of this shit pit by myself.' In mid-rant I turn and see that the secretary is in tears. I laugh out loud and give her the finger. 'Stitch that, you slag, and you too, you old cunt!' I run off to the pond to tell everyone of my latest adventure.

'You did what!' Phil isn't pleased. I can sense it. 'We're trying to carry out delicate talks with these people and then you go in all gung ho. Are you out of your mind?' The pharmaceutical cocktail swimming around head means this is a reasonably valid question.

Polly joins in the cross-examination. 'How about that poor

woman? What has she ever done to you? I think it's a disgrace. Aren't you going to apologise?'

'She deserved it. And if you think I'm going to say sorry to the old cow then you've got another think coming, and another, and another.' As you can probably guess I'm none too popular at the moment.

Three and a half weeks have passed since the formation of the camp, and Phil's received a tip-off that the eviction could well be tomorrow morning. Time for one last big networking exercise, to alert all branches of the phone tree. Activists from around the country are asked to come, and final preparations made. The last tree house is haphazardly lashed and nailed together, and a steady stream of supporters begin to arrive. Most of us get fitful sleep knowing this could well be our final night here. The alarm is set for 5am.

On waking it is clear today is the day. A team of bailiffs and police is waiting near the front fence. We've heard Andrew Wilson, the Under Sheriff of Lancashire, will be leading the eviction. Apparently an Under Sheriff is a jumped-up solicitor whose main job is to evict families from their homes but is also called up for unusual gigs like this.

The Hulme residents who've said they would turn up have done – refusing that final joint the night before in order to roll out of bed bright and early. Some members of Manchester Wildlife – who have visited the pond a couple of times – appear with cameras more used to snapping voles and badgers. Familiar faces from the EF! gatherings arrive, along with other die-hards from the NVDA circuit. In all approximately seventy people are here. I've been paired up with Bender Del. I put the D-lock round my neck and lock on to the curved ladder, which is, in turn, locked on to a telegraph pole. We're each locked to a concrete barrel. Suffice to say that movement is difficult.

A self-important bloke with a fedora and trenchcoat arrives and is believed to be Wilson. This is confirmed when he tells us through a megaphone. 'You are illegally trespassing on private property. You are required under Section 10 of the Criminal Law Act to vacate the land or you will be removed by bailiffs of the county of Lancashire.'

A couple of excavators are sat in the road, alongside two cherry-picker cranes to remove people from the trees. A tanker is here to 'translocate' or suck the contents of the pond up and spit it out somewhere else. This is what passes as conservation according to Manchester City Council.

Most people are in place when Jane bashes the gong at 6am. This is the Aruga! call or 'Oh shit, we're being evicted' in old money.

'If you want a nip of sherry just tell me. I've got a bottle in my pocket,' says Del.

'Don't mind if I do, old chap. Rationed like in the Blitz eh?' The little mouthful is cheap but reassuringly warming. A feeling of well-being grows in my solar plexus.

One by one we are removed from the site. The process of grabbing people with the hydraulic platform is a blurred struggle of arms, legs and bowsaws. Eventually the tree dwellers are all brought to earth. This keeps the bailiffs busy for a good couple of hours. We try to manoeuvre ourselves to be able to watch the action and be on our guard. There's much shouting – and the supporters around the edge of the site are shocked at the brutality.

Darren, one of the Hulmites I vaguely know, is the last to be brought down. He's been arrested for assault to a bailiff. As he's led away he shouts to us. 'I didn't kick the fucker in the face, but seeing as I'm being done for it I wish I had now.'

Some imperfections in our plan start to become apparent. There are not quite enough people for all the lock–ons. A sorry-looking barrel stands unmanned on the mini-jetty of the pond next to Isaac the newt. The bailiffs use it as a training device and start to whack at it with a sledgehammer. Having been hastily constructed with cheap materials it doesn't last the punishment very long.

Dom and Helen are the first barrel dwellers to take some punishment. As Wilson shouts instructions he looks like the kind of guy who has a butler at home, or a gimp chamber – or both.

'It's a disgrace these dip-shits should be earning good money for this,' says Del.

With every strike of the hammer, there's a cry of anguish, a scream of pain, or loud expletive directed at the Sheriff's men. Unfortunately, Robin Hood has long since hung up his tights.

I'm feeling exceedingly strange. I've not slept well – neither last night nor the fortnight before – and am witnessing friends prone on the ground suffering unacceptable levels of brutality from men with sledgehammers. It's a bit like the scene in Marathon Man with Lawrence Olivier's dentist drill but not as bad for your teeth.

Eventually it's our turn and the hammerers set to work. It is indeed pretty damn painful, and neither Del or I spare the bailiffs exactly what we think of them. As the blows rain down – largely to distract myself – I shout out random comments to the watching crowd such as 'Hulme Regeneration is an anagram of Inhumane Destruction', or 'Dr Henry is a child molester'.

A sympathiser calls to me. 'Why don't you tell these people why you're doing this.' This is sensible enough, and do so for a while. However, this grows boring and soon I'm back to shouting things like 'Graham Lee fists donkeys' to anyone who'll listen.

The barrel takes about twenty minutes of sustained pounding before it succumbs. Del is still locked onto me through the arm tube and I'm still attached to the climbing frame by my neck.

I can see they are trying to get the tanker in position. Fortunately we have spare bodies around. Rachel has locked herself to the front axle. Good on her. She may irritate the fuck out of me but her heart's in the right place. Tango and a couple of his weird mates are on top of the tank itself, doubtless discussing pygmy crop rotation or something like that.

After a couple of minutes the bailiffs try to remove my lock. Wilson comes to have a closer look. His smug grin deserves my spit across it, but I decide that's just going to get my arms broken. 'We'll have you out of there in no time,' Wilson says as a particularly fat and stupid-looking bailiff comes over with a pair of bolt cutters.

This is the same lock I wore at the Texas mahogany action, and I'm experienced enough to know I'm not going to be decapitated, so am not about to lose my head. This time there'll be no wussing out and reaching for the key. This would be a fitting place for my first direct action D-lock to die.

'Do your worst, fuck brain.' I brace myself for the sound and sensation of steel snapping around my neck. The fat bailiff tenses and applies as much pressure as he can muster. There is a sound of metal shearing. After a second or so I realise I'm still tethered to the climbing frame. The bolt cutters have broken, provoking much hilarity.

While another set of bolt cutters are found, the bailiffs take to smashing the foundations of the ladder. I try to put my feet in the way of the hammer and very quickly have my legs held down.

'We're treading on my fucking kneecaps! Cameras quick, they're breaking my legs!' I shout to the crowd.

'Whoever mixed this concrete did a good job, lads,' says the friendliest of the bailiffs.

After several expletives from both sides the ladder is broken free from its base. The ladder, however is still fastened to the D-lock around my neck, and me and Del are still tethered together through the arm tube.

They then manage to cut through the metal bracket of the telegraph pole and we are left on the ground while they have another rest. Wilson wanders off to bark more orders through his megaphone.

Lorraine and Phil, who've been videoing the eviction, come to see if we are ok. 'I saw all that, mate, it looked pretty severe. Good on you.' Lorraine is just about to add to this when I have an idea.

'Hold on, I've got something ... urr ... let's get this right.' It's hard to know if this is sensible or drug-fuelled madness.

After five seconds of weighing up the options I decide on the former and whisper. 'Right, when I say a code word, I don't know, say "banana", I want you to help us up, get hold of this ladder and then walk as quickly as you can towards the pond. Ok? Are you in for this, Del?'

'We've gone this far, we might as well go for it. Besides, I've still got half a bottle of sherry left.'

I look at the three of them in turn, grin and then say the magic word. Within moments we're off at quite impressive speed. A couple of the bailiffs, who by this time are back onto the access road, try to run back to catch us, but it's too late.

An inch-thick layer of ice needs to be broached as we tread ungainly into the pond. We know it's not all that deep, and will probably come up to thigh level in the middle. A cacophany of yips and cheers accompany the breaking of the crystalline barrier between our feet and what we're trying to defend. Bailiffs are either laughing heartily or making 'wanker' signals at us as we acclimatise to the sub-zero waters.

'You ok?' I shout at Del.

'Silly question really mate, but yeah, s'pose so.' He draws in a mighty breath as his genitals submerge. He's a few inches shorter than me.

'Can I have a swig of that sherry?'

As he retrieves the bottle from his donkey jacket, Del shouts to the crowds, 'We're going to get as pissed as newts in here!'

'How long are you going to stay in there? We're very concerned about your health.' The amplification of Wilson's voice highlights his displeasure at our antics.

'We're in for the day, you might as well go off for a pint or two ...' Del replies. 'You know where you can shove your concern ... and your megaphone.'

'Fucking hell it's cold, eh mate?' My feet are going numb.

'Tell me something I don't know.'

After ten minutes trying to think warm thoughts I say, 'Hold on, step up on this ladder, and I'll support you, then we'll see if I can get on, even with this round my neck. We can take it in turns.'

'Ok, if you think you can hold my weight.'

'It'll give us some exercise. More sherry?'

'Yeah, why not, old bean?'

There are cheers from behind the fence as the bottle makes a reappearance. Del raises it to the galleries.

'The latest Citizen Fish album is the bollocks, and I found an old Conflict re-release that's really good too.'

For the next half hour we chat about punk, ska and new wave. Every so often we change position on the ladder. Occasionally Wilson shouts over to enquire about our welfare, and replies such as such as 'fuck off you inbred little shit' are returned.

The water begins to cause genuine loss of feeling from the knees down. Some of the bailiffs come over to chat to us. The friendly one from earlier says. 'I know we haven't exactly seen eye to eye this morning, but I do admire your guts. You must be fucking freezing. Come out now and come for a beer with us. I bet on a normal day we could all have a right good laugh over a few pints?' Some of his pals are nodding.

Del is nonplussed. 'How about when you were swinging hammers at our arms earlier? I didn't hear you saying that then, you twat.'

'Yeah I can see that ...'

'But nothing. Anyway, me and my mate have got other things to discuss, so if you don't mind, piss off. You and your boys can go over there and stand around getting paid for doing nothing.'

Half an hour later and the cold is pretty unbearable. I'm also thinking about what state my Doc Martens are in, and of course my feet. Frostbite and delicate crosses from left midfield aren't really compatible.

'What do you reckon? Shall we get out?'

'If you want to. We've proved our point, and we can't stay in here forever. Besides, my dog needs feeding and I've agreed to look after Kropotkin too.'

'That Tango's a cheeky bastard. Oh well, bet you never thought you could have so much fun getting hypothermia? Let's do one.'

Del and I do our best to share a hug and the final couple of swigs to empty the bottle before emerging. Our exit is greeting by cheers, whoops, the odd obligatory yip – and the sight of Dom being led into the back of a police van. Still locked together, we get to the fence outside the pond and Phil, who's been looking after the key, frees me from the climbing frame.

'Jesus, that feels good. My neck is killing me.'

The ladder is left behind but there's no time for congratulation. Chaos surrounds the tanker on the road. Polly has locked herself to a metal ring on the side. The driver, obviously sympathetic to our cause, says to the bailiffs. 'You cut my wagon and I'll 'it you, got that?' Polly stands merely grinning.

Suddenly there's a whistle – something is afoot; within seconds the cry has gone up that there's a second tanker coming from the opposite direction. All who are able run up the road to obstruct it. Del and I are still locked together as we pass a couple of riot vans. A spotty, sandy-haired constable stops us. 'Where do you think you're going?'

'Just going for a walk officer. That isn't an offence yet, is it?'

'No you're not, you're staying where you are.' By now he has a firm grasp on my coat, as two other officers approach.

'Are we under arrest?' I ask? I can't believe this. Obviously we've been singled out as rabble-rousers. Can't think why.

'Yes,' says the police.

'What for?'

'I don't have to tell you that at the moment. In the van ...' Neither of us move. ' ... Now!' and we're shoved unceremoniously into the vehicle as the door slams shut. As I lay on the floor I remember I'm wearing steel-capped boots. I proceed to repeatedly kick the side of the van. Del covers his ears, but it's the only immediate method of letting off steam during a very stressful day. Before long we can hear blows on the vehicle from the outside, joining in the battering of the van. Result. I hear a megaphone announcement appealing for calm, and some of the banging subsides, but I keep kicking. The van door opens, the same cop looks in, face full of thunder and acne. 'If you don't fucking knock that off, we'll come in there and knock it out of you.'

A couple more symbolic kicks and I stop. Del recommends this because, as a traveller, he's experienced physical policing before. Within a minute the van drives away, heralded by shouts and screams from outside.

Once in the station we're unshackled from each other, and 'processing' begins. I'm ordered to take off my bootlaces and belt. The former are very wet and proving difficult to remove. The piggy-eyed desk sergeant comes over, pushes me to the floor and cuts the laces with scissors.

'Fucking bastard. What right have you got to treat us like this?'

'The law, son. You step outside it, and we step on you. Simple.'

I'm ordered to remove my jeans, then the cord from the shorts I've been wearing to keep out the cold.

'What the hell for?'

'So as you don't hang yourself.'

'You really think I'd kill myself because I've been arrested for walking up a road? You must be stupider than you look.'

'Take the cord out.'

I begin to do so in a lacksidaisical manner. The knot is quite stubborn, as is the cop. He suddenly loses his temper. 'Look sonny. You think you're really fucking clever don't you? Well, I tell you what, you're nothing. This uniform is everything, and you're an arrogant little cunt who stands in ponds wasting police time and public funds. Got that? Now toe the line or I'll bloody well make you, and believe me, you won't like that.' He applies the scissors to the cord and I mutter something about parentage.

'What is that? Did you say something?'

'Not really. Nothing you want to hear. Do you know what despicable means, you fucking prickhole? Beneath contempt.' I can feel tears of anger starting to form.

I refuse to give anything other than my name. After a stern 'If that's the way you want to play it' in response, I'm led roughly to the cells. Going down the stairs I feel a kick in the back, then another. My arm is put up behind my back at the cell door. I stifle a sob.

'Thick, am I?' I hear. My arm is forced further up my spine. 'Filthy pig, am I?' The cell door is unlocked with his other hand, and I'm pushed to the floor.

The cell is barren, and pretty much like the ones portrayed on TV. Various vignettes of graffiti – COLD TURKEY 5/8/91, COP KILLERS RULE OK – adorn the walls. There's a toilet but no paper, and a hard but surprisingly comfortable blue plastic mattress. The only other feature of the cell is a button by the door, marked Ring for Attention. There's a skylight but the glass is so thick virtually no natural light can get through. An infuriating buzz and flicker from one of the stark fluorescent tubes every few minutes adds to my feeling of entrapment.

I ring for attention for what seems like ten minutes, and eventually receive some toilet paper and a small polystyrene cup of tea. A well earned sleep is soon disturbed by the opening of the door panel. I'm very glad to see our lawyer Chris enter the room.

'How goes?' he asks.

'Oh, wonderful. I was done over earlier, and it's not exactly plush in here.'

'You've got it lucky. I've got seventeen of you to see in four stations across the city.'

'Fan-fucking-tastic.'

'Anyway, on the positive side, it looks as though everyone will be released without charge, except Rachel, who's been charged with assault on a bailiff.'

'What? That's a fucking joke. What did she do? Assault the bailiff's boot with her face?'

'I know. We'll just have to see how the case goes.'

Six hours in custody feels a lot longer. However, it's a good chance to rest, get your thoughts together. Nelson Mandela probably got the idea for A Long Walk To Freedom in his cell. A cop I haven't seen before tells me I'll be released without charge if I accept a caution. I agree, and as I'm led out into the reception area I spot the police who assaulted me before.

'I'm going to report you, you sick bastard.' Unlike some captives in the Middle East, I've not learnt to respect my jailers.

'Do what you like, and watch your language, unless you want to go back inside.'

Apparently I've spent the last few hours in Grey Mare Lane Station, in the east of the city, miles from the pond and even further from home.

'Aren't you going to drive me back to where you arrested me? It's only right. Don't you have to do that?'

'Look, you were arrested for behaviour likely to cause a Breach Of The Peace. That's all that concerns us. Now we've found it in our hearts to let you go without charge, so go.'

'I just can't believe this. How do expect me to get home, I've got no money on me.'

'My heart bleeds, son, now sod off.'

I'm leave the foyer goose-stepping with right arm raised aloft.

I continue to think unsavoury thoughts about the police as I walk alone back to Hulme. After a while I begin to recognise where I am and inside the hour I'm back at the pond – or rather a huge pile of mud. A BBC reporter is still at the scene. It's been Northwest Tonight's lead story and Jezzer is being interviewed. I'm just within earshot as he speaks.

'It's our fookin' pond, and look what they've done to it. Where are me and me mates going to hang out now? The ones who were up the trees today were heroes, fookin' heroes I tell ya.'

A small group of us – including Debs – go out for beers that night, but we're mostly too tired to enjoy them. I fall asleep on the floor of the pub, under the table by the cigarette machine. After a long bath at home, I sleep for the next twenty-four hours, getting up only to occasionally put on a CD.

As well as making up for lost time with the woman I love, the next couple of weeks are for rest, recuperation and ending, thankfully, the drug trial. Press cuttings of the eviction are gathered. There's a great photo of me and Del on page five of the Guardian. The headline says 'Protesters make a splash to defend city pond for newts.' The photo has beneath it the caption, 'Troubled waters'. Del looks quite serene, but I look as if I'm delivering a mouthful of abuse to Wilson. According to the piece Dr Henry – the Science Park director I never got to negotiate with – was pelted with snowballs. I hadn't remembered that – but then recall Jez had successfully aimed a couple at Wilson.

I sit back, and look out of the kitchen window at nothing much and reflect on the siege of Abbey Pond – despite the cold, the pain, the arrest and assaults – perhaps the best month of my life thus far.

CHAPTER **4**

SPRING 1994

Ok, I admit it. I've been bitten by the direct action bug – it's one of the greatest forms of self expression I've ever found – and am determined to make up for lost time. The M11 campaign has started something named Operation Roadblock, which is a call for mass site actions every day for a month. Despite Debbie's protestations it's time for a trip to the East End.

At the same time as Abbey Pond a major eviction happened there. The five houses in the self-proclaimed 'Free State of Wanstonia' were taken by over six hundred police and three hundred security in an operation costing £250,000. The opposition was fervent, and the barricading was imaginative if not very effective at times – such as a concrete-filled Citroën 2CV in front of one of the doors with a sign on it saying WANSTONIA WELCOMES CAREFUL DRIVERS. This could paint a quaint picture – rather like scenes from the old film Passport To Pimlico but with more cider – but the reality of the eviction was stark.

It lasted for more than ten hours – and had been both harrowing and empowering. Cherry pickers and sledgehammers again had been used, this time to get people off the roofs. Eleven people were injured. Bailiffs used pneumatic wall pulverisers with no knowledge of who or what was on the other side.

Most of the M11 activists are now living in Leytonstone at Fillebrook Road, next to the tube station. The morning I arrive – day three of Roadblock – approximately forty others also turn up from around the country. We are the hunters – the quarry being diggers, cranes and other plant.

Gary, a wiry bespectacled M11 veteran begins the legal briefing.

'Right, who's been on an action before?' About a quarter raise a hand, and as a virgin to 'digger diving' I am not one of them. Gary used to be an architect – his cut-glass accent and refined demeanour seem somehow out of place in the squat.

We're split into two groups to target different sites. We're not 'told' what to do, but the full-timers lead us through the basics.

'I can't promise you this,' says Ann, who's about my age but half the size, 'but most of the drivers know the score. When you get on a piece of machinery they'll probably stop the engine.'

She adds. 'This doesn't mean it always happens. Without scaring you, we've had people thrown from plant and scooped up in excavator buckets. It's alright – no-one's died yet. Any questions?'

'What happens if we find ourselves out of our depth?' someone sensibly asks.

'No-one should do anything they don't want to do. If it all gets too much, just walk away. It's enough for you to be here in the first place. Any more ... ? Right, let's get going. Has everyone got the legal number on their arm?'

My group go to the site on Dyer's Hall Road. The machinery is big, intimidating, and working at full tilt. Digger diving is a bit like throwing yourself under a slow-moving bus hoping the driver is paying attention. One first-timer looks on in disbelief. 'So we're supposed to climb up those? Madness.'

The security guards (also known as yellow-jackets) see us as we arrive. One with a red hat speaks into a walkie-talkie.

'He's head of site, calling for reinforcements' says Gary.' I think we've got the upper hand here. Let's go.' Gary's approach is part-trainer, part-unit leader, part-tour guide.

We follow as he runs at the cordon of yellow-jackets. Very quickly the gateway is awash with activists, with most struggling into the site. It resembles the British Bulldog rough and tumble games at the gathering, but this time it's for real. When dragged to the ground, some go limp and are carried or hauled back to the gates. The guards have no legal powers of detainment, and are supposed to merely use 'reasonable force' to keep us off the site. However, judging by the extent to which they use violence most guards have a perverse definition of this term. On the other hand, it's fair to say not all the site invaders are entirely passive in their resistance.

Breaking free from a scrimmage I head towards a working digger. On the way I'm rugby tackled from the side. Some have already completed this assault course (with the emphasis on assault) and several diggers are non-operational.

I lay winded with a beer-gutted guard on top of me. 'Fuck off, mate, only my girlfriend is allowed that position. And guess what? She ain't here.'

Machinery is sat, then freed, then sat again. The police are called and before long arrests are made. Two officers come for me as my fingers are prised from the cab door of an excavator.

'Come on, son, you're going in the van.'

I can tell this cop's alright by the lack of aggression in the way I'm being led. Surprisingly, as we reach the van, he says. 'I know you're not really a criminal, and you know I'm only doing my job. But the road'll be built anyway, so you might as well not bother.'

'I appreciate what you're saying,' I reply, 'but if you didn't do everything they told you to, wouldn't you be a better policeman? Acting more on initiative than command?'

The signs of a smile start to emerge but no words.

His follow-up of 'Come on, you've gotta see I'm right here?' is met with a friendly shrug.

'All I'll say is ... ' He holds out a hand. 'Doug. Nice to meet you and good luck.'

As we shake two other officers approach the van and fraternisation reaches a logical conclusion.

'Right, lads, this one's willing accept a caution as long as he doesn't go back on site today. Isn't that right?'

'Hmm.' I take on a pensive guise.

One of the others says, 'You can think about it down Leytonstone nick if you want. This officer's made you a more generous offer than I would've.'

'Yeah, why not?' I don't cross my fingers as I say it. I think lying to the cops is fair game when there's a planet to save.

'Open the doors, lads. Let him out. I'll just take his details and read him the caution.'

I've been arrested, had a chat and de-arrested all in the space of fifteen minutes. I walk around the site and go back to where a lot of the people were gathered before. Some are still stopping the work. Most were looking for a fresh challenge, somewhere away from the cops. A call to Gary's mobile phone gives everyone that opportunity.

'Apparently the yellow-jackets are trying to illegally evict a couple of houses on Claremont Road,' he tells us. 'Who fancies going down there and paying them a visit?'

On the way down there I get chatting to an Irish guy called Roddy. Although we're jogging he's a walking contradiction. He has long hair but a policeman's moustache, and is tall and skinny with a broad accent.

'I tell you man, there's no way they're going to evict any houses in Claremont if I have anything to do with it. I live in that street and they can fook right off as far as I'm concerned.' He says he's saddened at the moment because his favourite comedian, some American called Bill Hicks, has died. Apparently he was only 32. I promise to get some of his material when I get home.

When we arrive at Claremont, the windows of two houses are being boarded up and about twenty guards stand around. Reliance is the main firm supplying the men, who are apparently paid about £2.50 an hour. A good proportion of the yellow-jackets are illegal immigrants from Africa – as are most of the guards outside the pair of semi–boarded houses – the language barrier between evictors and protestors is solid but not impenetrable.

'Are you sure this house has an eviction order on it?' someone asks. There is some confusion as to whether the houses were taken legally or not.

'Look man, the men who pay your wages are descended from people who put your ancestors into slavery,' says Roddy. The only result is a near fist fight.

'Get this fucker away from me before I really say something out of order.'

Roddy isn't best pleased his analysis of colonialism and its legacy has been taken the wrong way.

Ben, a student type in his late teens with round-rimmed glasses tries to intercede. 'I know you're not, ok, but this guy thinks you're being racist, yeah?'

'What ya gonna say next? In my dissertation ... blah blah blah. Ya patronising little cunt. I'm from Derry and know just what racism's all about. I've had to deal with it from pricks like you all me life.'

We have a new plan. For the benefit of the guards I say. 'Well, we can't get in, we'd best go back to the office.' About a dozen of us walk away. We then split up and double back to the rear end of the terrace. Roddy recognises the correct back garden and calls those running ahead to come back. Once over the wall there's an inner fence to negotiate. I see Mark from Leeds shinnying up a drainpipe before climbing in through an already broken window pane. I'm just about to start climbing the fence when Roddy puts his hand on my shoulder.

'Don't climb over it, let's smash the fucker down. Shouldn't be there anyway.'

Within seconds we're all kicking and barging. By the time some guards come round to investigate the commotion, all panels are down. Mark suddenly appears at the back door and lets everyone except the yellow-jackets in. It's high time for a cuppa. Trying to save houses from destruction is thirsty work.

'Bejeez, I thought they were gonna get us then.' Roddy slumps back in the settee.

'The pigs are here,' says Ben. A policeman stands at the doorway demanding entry.

'Bugger off, we don't want Blue Meanies round 'ere. Sling your 'ook.' Old Ron, a long-standing Leytonstone resident and full-time M11er, isn't a huge fan of the Metropolitan Police. Through the letterbox, the officer gives him verbal assurance he isn't going to force anyone out and is allowed in.

'We've had reports the fence round the back has been pulled down. Anyone know about it?'

Old Ron stirred his tea. 'Nuffin' to do wiv us, mate, but whoever did it, good luck to 'em.'

'That's your opinion. Criminal damage is a very serious offence.'

'Wrong on both counts. This 'ouse shouldn't be taken, as the eviction papers haven't gone fru the court yet. And knocking a fence down is 'ardly crime of the century. Not compared to muggings, burglaries, rapes, murders. Ain't that right, son?'

'Mmm.' The cop goes to the door and ushers one of the guards inside. 'Who knocked down the fence?'

A finger points in turn at Roddy, Ben and myself. Within minutes – amid much dissent – we're in the back of a van.

'It's due to scrounging doley layabouts like you that me and my family only get to Spain four times a year instead of five.' The desk sergeant is making the art of being processed the typical joy I'm starting to grow accustomed to.

'That's a shame. You've got less chance of getting skin cancer, you wanker.' I slouch on the desk, elbows at ten to two.

'Stand up straight. Lean against my desk again and I'll give you something to lean for!'

I'm still trying to work out what this actually means when the real questioning begins.

'Name?'

Time for some quick thinking. Has the earlier arrest of the day been logged? Does it really matter? Is it worth giving a false name? Two words – oh sod it – come immediately to mind.

'Roger Mills.'

'Any other names, Mr Mills?'

'Na.'

'Address?'

'101 Fillebrook Road, Leytonstone, E11.'

'Date of birth?'

'Over eighteen. I think I've answered just about all the questions that I want to, so let's cut the crap and could you please get someone to show me to my suite?'

'Look, you piece of shit! I decide when you've answered enough questions. This is my manor and you are givin' me the right 'ump.' Got that? What's your fuckin' date of birth?' Yep, he sounds like some bloke off the Sweeney.

'Thirty–first of February, nineteen seventy-one.'

He's just about to write this down then stops. His face turns the colour of a Leyton Orient home shirt. 'Right! I've 'ad enough. Constable, take this ... this down to the cells.'

Doug, the friendly copper from the morning's antics, appears from the back room and leads me away. When we reach the cell doors, he says: 'You shouldn't wind him up, he's got angina, you know.'

'Good, couldn't have happened to a nicer bloke.'

'Anyway, I thought we had a deal?'

'Well, I didn't go on that site again, did I?'

He smiles wryly and opens the cell door. 'In you go, mate.' At least with police like this around there's some hope. Before long Ben and Roddy join me in the cell. There are only two mattresses.

'This is taking the piss,' Roddy moans as I push the Ring For Attention button until my finger is sore.

'Hey man, stand back. This is an old trick I learnt in Tottenham nick one night'. Sitting about a foot and a half away from the door, Roddy launches both feet at it – the resultant bang is impressive.

'That, my son, is called a two-footed door slam.'

'Yeah – I've done similar myself in the back of a van,' I say.

Thirty seconds later the door flap opens and piggy eyes peer through.

'Oi mate, I don't suppose you could give one of us another cell? This is ridiculous.'

"Fraid not, we're full up today.'

Insult is added to injury within the hour when another prisoner is put in with us who's been arrested for beating his wife.

'That's bloody great,' I whisper to Roddy. 'They're putting us in with all and sundry. Who next? Ian Brady? Dennis Neilsen?'

Mr Wifebeater does have his uses though. His uneaten dinner is duly shared out between me and Roddy. Ben is also not hungry so – like Bolshevik peasants – we hungrily redistribute his food.

We're all questioned in turn. I'm the last to be led into the interview room. A tape recorder is switched on.

Thankfully a campaign lawyer is present and with every question she puts a finger up to her lips. The coaching – though not needed – is reassuring.

After the interview, the tape is put in a sealed evidence bag.

'Would you want a copy of the tape, Mr Mills?'

'Na, but I'll have the CD format if you've got it.'

'Ho bloody ho.' The cop is not impressed. 'I think it's time for you to go back to the cell, don't you?' My lawyer for the day hides a smile behind her hand.

About an hour later the desk sergeant unlocks the cell door and addresses Ben. 'Get your things, lad, you can leave.' Roddy and I look at each other as Ben leaves without a word.

Roddy's 'the little cunt's gone and shopped us, I know it' is accompanied by Ben's departing footsteps.

'You can't be absolutely sure,' I tell him. 'There may be an innocent explanation. He gave his correct address, didn't he? That could be why he's out and we're not.' Our non-eco cellmate sits there, probably very confused.

'Innocent explanation my arse. He's turned us in, and when I see him next I'm gonna have something to say to him, I can tell you. I'm not a violent man but ...' he kicks the cell wall twice – then barely drawing breath 'namby pamby little fucker ... suppose he's going off to Mummy's house right now. Makes me fookin' sick. Those John Lennon glasses, the stupid haircut. He needs a bit of hard living, that'll sort him out.'

'Forget about it, man, get some kip.' By now the cell has been supplied with another mattress and some blankets. We're being held overnight.

Next morning we're taken to Waltham Forest Magistrates' Court after a breakfast about as tasty as Ann Widdecombe, and held for three hours in solitary holding cells. By the time we're called to the dock we've been in custody for twenty-three hours. I give the false name, squat address and correct date of birth and plead not guilty to criminal damage. Roddy does similar apart from giving an unpronounceable Gaelic name, which has to be clarified. The magistrate asks the clerk of the court for a free date in the diary and within five minutes the case is adjourned until the following July.

'We'll see then if we've been grassed up. If that's the case I'm gonna blame the whole thing on him,' fumes Roddy on the bus home.

'Forget about it. These bastards have taken up enough of our time.' I glaze over and look out the window. Although too tired to process it properly, the view of shops, cars and people going about their business is a welcome contrast to four stark walls.

'You're going to love Theresa and Richard. I wished they lived closer.' Debbie's excited at spending her birthday weekend with best friend from childhood and policeman husband.

'I wish we could have gone away – just the two of us,' I say.

'Look – I haven't seen Theresa for ages – please can we not have any nonsense out of you because of Richard's job. It's going to be civilised, cheerful and ...'

'Ok, I'll really try to like them – anything to make you happy. You know how much I love you.'

'You can prove that now we're away from campaigns and your little gang. I've got you all to myself for a couple of days.' There's frisson in the kiss, proof positive that I do love her dearly, but there was no need for that little dig. And since when did EF! become 'my little gang'? Cheeky bitch.

The train rolls into Hemel Hempstead. What a fucking dump – call it misanthropic wiring or merely instinct but something doesn't feel right about the weekend stretching before us like a pair of old man's pants.

I don't want to sound like a misery guts, but we swap expensive train for extravagant taxi – to keep up appearances, no doubt – and arrive at some sub-Brookside close that really puts the sac in cul-de-sac.

A golden retriever jumps up at me as soon as we arrive. I try to push it away without seeming unfriendly but Theresa is straight on the money.

'Don't you like doggies?' She says in baby talk while rubbing the stupid mutt's face. 'How can anyone not like mummy's lickle treasure?' Then she looks at me then Debbie in turn as if to say to her 'You've picked a right one here'.

Here's Richard. He's what? Mid-twenties – balding and developing a paunch already. I almost feel sorry for him.

'Mmm, shall I take our things up?' I say, sensing my attendance isn't required.

'That's a good idea – your room is upstairs on the left. Now Debs – can I get you a glass of Merlot?' They disappear as I struggle up with the bags.

I feel a single bead of sweat run down my temple, but I'm not going to let anything disturb our closeness tonight. Even though it's making my head feel itchy my hands will remain cupped around her breasts, thumbs working away at making her nipples feel loved and cherished.

'That was the best sex we've had in ages,' I say.

'That's cos it's about the first time in ages. What with that bloody pond, then your little excursion down to London ... I feel like some kind of fucked-up eco golf widow.'

'Yes – I know. I'm sorry I've been a bit preoccupied. But let's not talk about it now. I'm here.' I kiss her neck.

'I love you.' I kiss the place between her breasts.

'And I'm very good at this.'

'That tickles,' she giggles with anticipation as I position my stubbled chin for a sustained bout of clitoris licking.

'What's everyone drinking?' I'm doing my best to be primo boyfriend material in their eyes but it's hard fucking work.

'So Lester, what do you do?'

Debbie hasn't told me to lie. 'I'm an environmental activist.'

'What do you mean?' Jesus, this woman is thick.

'I help co-ordinate and participate in direct action, for instance to stop a road from being built.'

Richard says. 'No shit? Really? I've got to ring the lads at the station.' I throw Debbie a 'he's obsessed with work too' glance but she's engrossed with Theresa.

Richard reaches for his mobile and starts gassing to a fellow Nazi. I'm left with no-one to interact with but my pint. No wonder I'm drinking faster than anyone else.

I'm already two pints ahead when Debs turns round from a particularly fascinating chat about hair – something she never usually talks about – and says. 'There's a house party this afternoon at Theresa's brothers'. We're all invited.'

Richard finishes his call and says to the girls. 'Apparently he's known but not wanted in Hertfordshire.' Couldn't have agreed with him more.

Another taxi later and the party is a hoot. There's a huge bowl of punch, cheese and pineapple on cocktail sticks and to top it all a bouncy castle. Not sure how cool the people are cos by the time we arrive I'm pretty wankered. However, it means I can disappear from the disapproving eye of motherfucker Theresa.

'A refill, my dear?' As I take Debbie's plastic cup I tenderly kiss her hand over the punchbowl.

'How many have you had? Daft bugger.'

As I refill our glasses a cry goes out. 'Broomstick game on the lawn in two minutes.' Now they're talking. I finish pouring and rush out to join a team. Neither Debbie nor Mr & Mrs Plod are interested in playing. Boring twats. Like I care – the giddy flow of booze lifts and separates my troubles like a good fitting bra.

My team are winning! The person before me runs back up the garden and we have a good five metre lead. I sprint down as fast my addled organs allow and pick up the broomstick. I place it squarely on the ground and begin the ten spins. One to four are done with consummate ease. I am the master. Five spins and the world starts to lose its edges. Six and my feet are starting to lose the battle. Seven – not really sure what's going on. On the eighth spin I can feel myself picking up speed, but downwards. My face is in freefall accelerating towards earth at ten metres per second per second. I can feel my ear then cheek then nose operating as some crude organic brake block. Good job they didn't see me knock that little kid over on the bouncy castle earlier on.

I'm gagging for a piss. The stupid fucking cow can't turn the key soon e-fucking-nough. I'm trying not to jiggle as I'm carrying both bags containing the curries but can feel the first trickle down my leg. Oh dear. Again, I seem to have forgotten about The 45 Minute Rule – the rule that states it takes time for the last drink to hit you. So, you may feel pissed but fundamentally fine when you take your last sup – but best part of an hour later you're feeling ... like I am now. 'Jusst going to the bog,' I say and as I get up spill some prawn curry over their pristine white sofa.

Part of my brain is aware that I'm half-past sensible. During my wee I realise I'm swaying wildly and compute it's safer to sit down. Not sure how much sprays out as I change position. Then possibly the worst feeling most people suffer in any year – the irreversible, cast-iron certainty of being sick in the very near future. A hot-yet-cold sensation surges through me and the first contraction of my diaphragm catches me by surprise. I try to keep my mouth shut and put my up hand to block, but at least a pint's worth of lumps and liquid shoots onto the floor to the left of the toilet as I try to swing round from a seated position.

'Fucking idiot,' I say to myself.

'Lester, are you alright?' Debbie shouts up the stairs.

'Fine. Fine.' The two words are punctuated with a bile-tainted cough. I hang over the toilet bowl, sweating and shivering waiting for the next wave of nausea.

I momentarily lose consciousness. When it hits I'm lying to the right of the toilet. There's no time for reorientation and I just let it all go.

The next thing I'm aware of is a panicked, 'Oh my God!' Debbie looks like she's going to be sick herself as she tries to comprehend the scene in all its pants-and-jeans-round-the-ankles glory.

'I'm so sorry, Debs. I had a little too much to drink ... Happy Birthday by the way.' She's gone – but shortly returns with a couple of towels. Her activity, however, alerts our glorious hosts.

'You fucking animal,' Theresa says, and I know it's going to be me and not the retriever that's in the dog house tonight. However, this proves to be truer than I imagine when an airbed and duvet are produced and it's made plain I'm to sleep in the back garden. There are two saving graces – one – it's good weather for the time of year, and two, there's a footpump.

A translucent pinky hue on my eyelids heralds the new morning. A quarter-open eye is enough to remind me of yesterday's disasters. I rub my face. There's extensive broomstick game-related scabbing. Despite this, the overpowering sensation is to have another wee. Barely aware of my surroundings I need to lean against the house in order to stand, and, not wanting to disturb everyone make the snap decision to empty myself in the garden. I unfasten, close my eyes and experience a protracted feeling of release. Mid-piss, I look down and see the dog lapping away happily at the golden arc of urine. I'm horrified but don't have the energy to do anything other than finish and go back to the airbed.

'They' come and find me about an hour later.

'That was disgraceful behaviour last night.'

'You should be ashamed of yourself.'

'Someone really needs to grow up.'

Don't know who said what but I sense it's time for us to get going. I make sheepish apologies as we pack and another fucking taxi is ordered.

'I'll send them a little gift, eh?'

'I don't think a present really cuts it, do you?' She can't bring herself to look at me. Can't blame her, and I'm not exactly Mr Handsome right now. The long silence that follows isn't good, but is better than any feasible alternative. I try to make amends by humping all the bags through the station and onto the train, but my old magic charm has yet to work.

'You did what!?' Somewhere around Stoke I decide to break the ice by telling her my little anecdote.

'Calm down. We don't have to tell them.'

'You pissed in Brandy's mouth!' So that was the dog's name. 'How fucking dare you!'

She starts to sob into her hand. I know it's not a good idea to do anything right now so sit very still and hope it'll all blow over.

'That's it! I've had enough. We're so over.'

'Oh Debs, come on ...'

'Fuck off, you fucking loser.' She grizzles as she grabs her bag. Trying to compose herself she takes a deep breath and wipes her eyes. 'I'm moving carriages. I don't want you to follow me. When the train reaches Manchester I want you to leave the train straight away. I don't want to see you.'

'But Deb ... please.'

'I don't want to see you.'

'I'll call you tomorrow then.'

'You don't get it. I don't want to fucking see you. Again.' And with that she slams the carriage door – which comes off its hinges because it has been badly maintained. Rather like our relationship.

'Hi Mum, what's going on down there?' It's only right and proper to phone home every couple of weeks.

'I'm ok, but I've got some bad news.'

A hormonal surge passes through my gut. 'What is it?'

'We had to put Jimmy down. The vet said he had cancer.'

'That's terrible news.' I try to maintain a sympathetic voice whilst performing a celebratory jig on the stairs.

The anti–McDonalds campaign in Manchester is almost entirely Tim's baby. His chemistry degree may be going rapidly down the tubes, but his campaigning's coming along very nicely. He may look like a goth with his long black undercut hair but he's sending out regular email updates for those of us who have grasped the technology and has even built a website for this new internet thingy. Right now though, he addresses the meeting in person.

'I've heard that down in London two people could well be sued for libel for distributing this.' He holds up a leaflet called What's Wrong With McDonalds, and passes copies around the circle.

'I propose we stage an action at one of the stores.'

'What shall we do?' asks Lorraine.

'Firebomb the cunts,' says Tango helpfully.

'Not going to go down well on Market Street on a Saturday,' she replies. 'How about a vegetarian eat-in?'

'There could be some street theatre,' says Rachel. I bite my lip. 'How about some character to rival Ronald McDonald?'

'Yeah, like Reggie the Veggie,' I say dismissively.

'That's it!' she says, without acknowledging me directly. This is a moral quandary – do I want credit for a crap idea? Not sure what Aristotle would've made of that.

It's the only Manchester EF! action currently in the pipeline so I grin and bear it. Phil's experiencing woman troubles and showing clear signs of burnout – I could say the same of myself. Dom's following his love of forests by training to become a tree surgeon. Helen, Lorraine and several other EF!ers are involved in setting up a housing co–op, which is taking up a lot of their time. Basically, the main shakers and movers in the group are becoming less able to come up with the goods. Tim and the other relatively new members of the group are thankfully taking up the slack.

Within a couple of days everything is ready for the action. Leaflets reproduced; rolls, sandwiches and drinks prepared. We've painted a banner which says AT McDONALDS THEY'VE GOT CRIME FOR YOU. Tim's cobbled together a Ronald McDonald costume, complete with red wig, skull mask and chainsaw. Dom is to don the garb of Reggie The Veggie made by Lorraine who is studying textiles. Padded and cartoonish – it wouldn't look out of place on the old BBC show It's A Knockout.

Lorraine's also made a rather fetching brown and green foam tree. I was asked to be the back of a pantomime cow costume borrowed from the local animal rights group but politely declined. Paulo, who as many of you may have guessed is Italian, seems a good lad – he's also a lucky boy as he gets to be in the cow behind Jane. Paulo looks kinda 'normal' too, though his hair is straighter than mine and he can therefore wear it a tad longer without looking like a freak.

I'm one of the first into the Market Street store, clutching a hand-ful of leaflets and a dark secret. As a 6th former I'd been a McDonalds crew member, a five-star one no less. Though a while ago it still gives me milkshake migraine to remember getting my hair and face caked in lard for 12-hour stretches. It had taught me transferable skills such as looking as if I was working really hard but was in fact wiping down a work surface I'd already cleaned a minute or so before.

As I look more like the general public than most, my role for today is mainly. 'Excuse me sir, would you like a leaflet?' Most people at least take one, whether they read it or not is another matter. And, without being prejudicial about some McDonalds customers, whether they can read is another factor.

Outside the store the street theatre is going through its first run. Helen and Phil are about to approach the queues with offers of sandwiches. Not sure how it's gonna go down.

I gaze at those in the kitchens. Frantically shaking this, turning that – most definitely displaying what is called 'hustle', another word for slogging your guts out for less than three quid an hour. When I left in 1988 I was on the magnificent rate of two pounds thirty-eight. I can see scalds and burn marks on people's arms looking as though they'd partially dipped in boiling oil. The management cared far more for the product and profit than the staff.

'Excuse me, madam, would you like a leaflet?' God this is repetitive. I don't want to be right in people's faces, so ironically there's a dreary, mechanistic edge to my work for the day. If you haven't noticed of course I'm still getting over Debs – and no, she's not returning my calls.

By now the staff are aware of our presence and are giving Helen some grief, but as it's the lunchtime rush the stark choice is cash or crowd control. Their compromise strategy isn't working.

I spot Phil going upstairs – must be needing a poo. Well, actually I know he's got a small bag of quick-dry cement in his jacket to put in the cistern.

Rachel is my fellow leafleter for the day. We haven't really seen eye to eye since the Texas action. Uptight bitch.

'Hi Rach, how it going?' I must be bored.

I receive a half smile for my trouble. I say. 'Do you know I used to work for these clowns, or is that possibly "used to work for this clown?".'

'Lester, I'm busy. Why not save it for the people in the store?'

Ok. Will do. Up yours Ms Muesli Muncher. I never can work out if she bats for the other side.

'Excuse me, would you like a leaflet? You know, I used to work for them. You'd never believe some of the things I saw. People spitting in the quarter-pounders. Writing their name in cheese on the grills. Weeing in the sink.' Not sure if I'm putting people off their food, but I'm having a much better time.

Tango arrives late (must have been feeding Kropotkin) and hides some of our literature in amongst the 'McFact' cards.

'Excuse me mate, would you like a leaflet? Do you know a mate of mine used to work for McDonalds and seemed like a really dedicated worker? But his burning ambition was to save up to go to America to visit the grave of the founder Ray Crock and piss all over it.'

As I finish the anecdote I find two of Greater Manchester Constabulary's finest standing next to me. 'Are you the organiser of this disturbance?'

'We haven't got any leaders, we don't just blindly obey orders, unlike some I could mention,' says Rachel. Must be her time of the month.

Tango starts to discuss trespass law with the policewoman. Bet she hadn't bargained on this.

'So let's get this straight. We're in a shop, and for all you know just about to purchase, and you're asking us to leave.'

'If the shop owner wants you to vacate – yes.'

'Come to think of it I am rather peckish. I think I'll queue up for a burger and a shake if it's all right with you.' He tries to get past the cop.

'Don't be ridiculous. Do you really think I'm that stupid?'

'I'd rather not answer that question,' Tango says haughtily.

Another man I don't recognise – but who looks a bit scruffy – is also trying to get through. She asks him to move away.

'Like fuck will I,' he replies.

The officer comes to the end of her fuse and utters those three immortal words.

'Right, you're nicked.' The scruffy man is led out of the store in an armlock by two cops and placed into the van, which – if you ask me – is illegally parked outside on the precinct.

'Oh dear – miscarriage of justice there.' I experience the rare joy of finding Tango amusing.

However, he's on top form today. When the WPC returns he says with a raised thumb. 'You're doing a great job. I thought you'd like to know you arrested our leader just then – not.' Predictably Tango is led away in an armlock. I decide it's time to mingle – I would have done the legal support thing – but he's a knob.

On my PR walkabout upstairs, I seem to have a crew member with me wherever I go. If I give a leaflet to someone, the worker gives them some pro-McDonalds propaganda.

'Hi, how's you?' I try to connect with her on a human level. I sense there's not much going on under the cap the colour of a large haemorrhoid other than the latest Home And Away storylines. Holding up one of her leaflets I say. 'Do you really believe what that says?'

'You'd better talk to the manager about that.' I choose to ignore her and get on with what I'm doing.

'Would you like a leaflet, sir? Have a read, see what you think.' This is a dad out with his two children.

'What's so wrong with them then?' As the father asks this, the younger of the kids is unpacking his Happy Meal with wide-open eyes. The elder kid has ketchup all round her mouth.

'Where do you want me to start?' I say, 'There are six main areas of their business we have difficulty with. Personally, I think the way that they target kids with all their advertising is the worst.'

'Too right.'

'Did you know that the actor who played Ronald McDonald for much of the 80s resigned in a fit of remorse?'

The father nods his head in between chews on his Big Mac. 'These two are terrible for it. Every year on their birthdays they pester me like crazy for a party here.' The younger sits munching mindlessly on some fries.

Parenting advice is beyond my remit – and besides, I don't have any. 'Have a nice day, mate,' I say, 'and unlike this lot, I mean it.' I hand out the few remaining leaflets and go outside. By now the police are intent on ending our fun. One ushers me and several of the others to the doors then stands by the bins making sure we don't re-enter.

Outside I find the assistant manager waving a clenched fist at Phil. 'You wait till I've finished my shift, I'll batter you. Just wait across the street till ten. You're dead.' There's probably half a dozen of us and the same number of them looking on. The lunchtime rush is over and there are two lots of street theatre to watch.

'You're working until ten? In this dump? You're a sad man.' Phil's grin is as broad as the generalisation he's just made.

'Right you wanker.' Phil has to dodge to avoid an acne-covered headbutt which provokes pushing and shoving rather like Premier League handbags after someone's been taken out at the knees by a two-footed tackle.

The guy's co-workers try to cool things down and lead him away. 'Keith, leave it. They're not worth it. Go to the Crew Room and have a break.'

'Yeah, and remember to clock off, or they might sack you.' Phil shouts behind our protective cordon.

During all this the saga of Reggie the Veggie carries on. You've got to hand it to their professionalism. I still haven't seen it all the way through, but have to admit an earlier glimpse of Tim chasing the cow with the cardboard chainsaw was most amusing.

As we start to discuss what to do about Tango a photographer for the Manchester Evening News shows up. 'Sorry I'm late – diamond wedding.' He says it's a slow news day and could well get a photo–led story. 'The picture editor told me this could be the splash but we put the paper to bed at eight.'

'What?' I say.

'Sorry – it could be front page but we've gotta be quick.'

Another police van is making its way down Market Street. Whatever we do – it's got to be quick for various reasons. Tim breaks off from his performance. 'Right guys, let's stage a photo and fuck off. You good with that?'

Within seconds they get in position. Ronald McDonald is wielding a chainsaw over a dead cow and a felled tree with Reggie the Veggie wiping tears from his prosthetic eyes. The sound of the camera clicking away is every bit as sweet for us as the ring of the cash tills is for them.

As the police pile out of the van Dom puts down the chainsaw and tries to pacify the situation. Raising his skull mask he says. 'Officers, we're just going – I promise.' Then he turns to the rest of us. 'I've got a feeling if we don't go now we're all gonna be nicked. Are we done?'

Our offer to leave immediately does the trick. As it's a Friday they don't want us blocking up all the cells as well as all the paperwork. As we leave we give a couple of quotes to the photographer. He's called Lee and could be a decent contact. Jane and Tim go off to the police station to find Tango and we all head to a pub called Tommy Ducks, which has underwear stuck all over the ceiling.

After four pints it's time to cycle up to Abdul's for a veggie kebab. I wobble up Oxford Road way over the limit. I spot an Evening News van and decide to investigate. Like Charlie Bucket opening a Wonka Bar I push copies of Loot aside and bingo! Running along all three bottom columns there they are – like the media whores they are. I decide to hold the front page on the kebab as five copies are purchased and taken back to a jubilant pub.

CHAPTER **5**

SUMMER 1994

Manchester basks in hot summer sunshine – a phenomenon which occurs more often than popularly believed – but not much more. Sunlight diffracts and glares off windscreens, and shimmering waves of low-level ozone rise off Oxford Road's bitumen. A cyclist dressed in only shorts and sandals powers past an ice cream van parked outside the Academy – opposite the University Medical School where mice and monkeys sweat in a secret vivisection department on the fourth floor. Time out from life's cares can be taken on the quad near the library to see broadleaf trees in full flourish, limbs gently swaying. Beneath these can sometimes be found broad–breasted freshers in full flourish, the breeze goose-pimpling tender flesh.

The latest NVDA place to be is the Cuerden Valley Nature Park near Blackburn. Twelve miles long and budgeted at £142 million the M65 extension is the country's largest road scheme currently under construction. That also makes it this year's biggest protester playground. An old police house has been squatted and turned into the Eco-police station – painted green with a black-and-white checkered band around its middle. Tree houses are being constructed and another battle has begun. Unlike the M11, there's much woodland to save; climbing harnesses have replaced yellow jackets stolen from security as the season's hot fashion item.

Phil receives a fair amount of ribbing about his car, but it does come in handy. His old purple Morris 1100 does a daily shuttle run between Manchester and Cuerden. The site is difficult to access by bus and impossible by train. With Lorraine up front and me, Jane and Tango in the back, a Beatles-esque track by World Party fills the car with sound.

One thing which bugs me when travelling by car is the number of car stickers professing concern for things furry, hill-like and tree-like. It's probably the method through which most Britons wear their hearts on their sleeves – perhaps the most inappropriate place to wear them.

Yet again defending his driver status Phil says. 'It's like in this song. Put the message in a box/ Put the box into a car/ Drive the car around the world/ 'Til you get heard.'

'The car's not inherently evil, it's what you do with it that counts,' he adds haughtily.

'Woo-oo! No need to get your knickers twisted,' says Tango, not moving his eyes from the rolling countryside. Phil knows it's best to ignore him.

He's right though. There are a few people who live at the Eco-police station and the camps, but without those who come in, stay for a few days, run around doing actions and then go home, there wouldn't be much energy about. I've found it takes the 'blow-ins' to come in and rouse those living on site out of their domestic routine.

I've seen footage of the Eco-police station on TV, but in the 'flesh' it's even more impressive. The paintwork is quite authentic and it's a great gimmick. NVDA is effective, full-on and honest, but we definitely need publicity stunts to function sometimes.

'Well I'll be buggered, Richard!' I spot a familiar though hairier face coming out the side door.

'Lester! No-one's called me Richard for weeks. They call me Beech here.' We played for different teams in the uni football league but had lots of mutual mates. Turns out he's become a lentil too and is so called cos he lives up an 80-foot beech tree.

'Mate, we'll catch up later. I've got to see my supervisor in Lancaster. I'm doing a PhD on integrated transport.'

There are some veterans of the scene who've made this their temporary home. 'Veteran' somehow seems a silly phrase to use as it's still barely two years since the first Twyford actions. In this peaceful war, a lot of experience has been clocked up in a short space of time. Mark, Nick and Claire – three of our best – are here to provide the welcoming party.

Hugs exchanged, we go inside and catch up on the latest gossip. Mark has a tale for me. 'I was down at a camp in Norfolk and they'd heard that at Abbey Pond two people were up to their necks in ice.'

'What did you tell them?'

'I didn't want to spoil the myth but said the pond wasn't quite that deep.'

The scale and number of camps across the country is beginning to mushroom and we seem to be blatting around covering silly hundreds of miles to make up the numbers. This curse and blessing has been greatly helped by the setting up of Road Alert, which tries to pump information out to the activists on the ground. Shelley and Michael and a few other volunteers do a fine job and the whole operation runs on next to nothing other than hard work.

Nick and Claire have just come back from a few days in Germany trying to stop trains carrying nuclear waste.

'Would you say we've got the most active movement in Europe?' I ask.

Nick says. 'Maybe. The Germans are pretty hardcore, but they don't have the same number of roads to fight.'

Mark chips in with 'So we're like the Juventus or Inter Milan of European activism?'

'This conversation's getting a bit 'boys',' says Claire. 'I'm off to the office.'

On a site this big communication needs to be good. However, the campaign only has two shortwave radios and one of these has been 'lunched out' and one is completely useless without the other. There are very limited CB radio connections between different parts of the site, but usually communication is done in the time-honoured way, by foot. The lucky ones have bikes. Two thousand years of progress and we still have to walk from one place to another to get a message through. This can make a refreshing change or is a fantastic arse pain, depending on the circumstances.

I wander off with Mark and Nick to one of the camps to lend a hand. A lot of upkeep must be done before a single digger can be sat. Firewood is needed in abundance. The kitchen of the station is invariably always in need of a tidy, and has to be kept free of germs and dirt. This is one lesson the movement has learned painfully.

At Twyford plates were not washed very often because there was no running water on site. Normally this wouldn't be a problem. With vegan food there's usually few of the 'stubborn stains' seen in Fairy Liquid adverts. However, one thing there was at Twyford were dogs. Big dogs, little dogs. Dogs. Dogs that left their own organic traces. Dogs that sniffed and licked the organic traces of other dogs. Dogs that would then lick the seldom-washed plates. That – given time for bacteria to fester in the muck – would result in Donga Belly. This condition hasn't as yet appeared in the Lancet, but can be basically described as excruciating stomach pains and chronic diarrhoea. Come to think of it, does any language in the world have a pleasant sounding word for diarrhoea?

One such dog is Strongbow, who belongs to Sparko – obviously both nicknames are alcohol-related. Sparko is 'Brew Crew' – a sub-tribe of 'activists' intent on drinking as much super-strength lager as possible each day.

'Arriteyabassrd,' Sparko tries to stop the barking as we approach.

'What's happening?' asks Mark. 'Any actions today?'

'Err ... mm,' he points to the west.

'Towards Cinder Path Woods? What do you reckon, guys?'

'I think we should help with the action,' I say, as building a bond with Sparko isn't top of my things-to-do list.

The sound of distant shouting mixed with mechanical noise is second nature to me now. I see a young lad halfway up the arm of a digger with three guards trying to prise him off.

As we near the site I see he's taller and stronger than any of us – holding on for all he's worth.

We push a section of felled tree trunk up against the fence and help each other climb over. As I land on the other side I see they're bending back the lad's fingers, pulling his hair and grabbing at his legs and nearby parts.

A few yards away from the digger there's woman with a clipboard. 'Go easy on him, lads, please.'

'Come on, over here,' says Nick. He negotiates the caterpillar track of a nearby earthmover.

'Who's the woman?'

'That's Gill – legal support. We've an agreement with the contractors our monitors can come onto site – so long as they don't get on the machinery.'

'Oo – trouble coming,' I say as three guards are coming to throw us off. 'Who is that kid? He's good.'

'Teddy – he's a local. Only sixteen and wants to join the marines.'

'You've got your lock with you, I trust?'

'Just getting some handcuffs out of my pocket,' says Nick.

'Hurry up then mate, I'll try and hold them off.' The guards start to climb up. I stand between them and Nick as he locks on.

'I see Mark's ok,' he says casually. Mark's shimmied up a pile-driver and has attached himself to the apex with a piece of climbing rope and a karabiner.

'Get a move on,' I hold onto the door handle as they grab at my legs.

'Ok, I'm done.' He's attached to the frame of the wing mirror.

Within seconds they get a proper hold on me and I'm dragged to the floor. I make sure I'm a sufficiently dead weight that it takes all three of them to carry me to the site gates where I'm dumped.

'I'm going to report you bastards for assault,' I say just to keep them on their toes – but as guards go these guys aren't too bad. As I regain my bearings all six-foot-three of Teddy is dropped beside me.

'And stay out, you little twat,' says a white helmet wiping his brow.

'Hi. Lester,' I offer my hand.

'Teddy. Pleased t' meet you.'

'You did well to hold them off back there.'

'Thanks, man – most of them are pussies,' he says rubbing spit into a cut on his arm. 'Besides, kills some time before I join army.'

'I s'pose so, but there's gonna be some wanker telling you what to do. After all this won't you tell them where to shove their orders?'

'Mebbe, but I've set me heart on it since I were five. Anyway, having orders is easier.'

'Not for me. No way.'

Just as we're about to get up Mark's also thrown out the gate.

'Wankers cut my rope. Wonder I didn't twist my ankle.'

Gill comes over to us. 'Are you ok? That was pretty nasty. I'm going to fill out a report.'

'Yeah – I'm fine, fill in the details and I'll sign it later.'

'Ok lads. How about some more?' says Teddy.

I was thinking more of some lunch but male pride intervenes. I nod hungrily.

'Let's go towards Leyland,' he says pointing to the brow of the hill. 'There's usually work going on up there.'

Lo and behold, up the slope there's an action in full flow. A few of the local youngsters and Claire are running toward some cranes with a dozen Group 4 ready and waiting to head them off round the perimeter of the site.

The usual site invasion characteristics then come into play. People going over the fences, some picked off by the guards, rugby tackled, or sat on, or both. One of the local girls suffers what can only be described as a sexual assault. Granted she's not wearing a bra but there was no need for the guard to do that to her T-shirt. And quite why his hands have to be there I don't know. It's suddenly very clear as to why in NVDA briefings in the past women were advised to wear clothing in which they could 'retain their dignity'.

The girl is in tears and Claire is incensed – looking like the N is just about to be taken out of NVDA.

'No wonder you lot are known as Grope 4! How fucking dare you!'

Mark and I decide to use the distraction to our advantage – make a run for it and try to complete the original objective. Teddy follows our lead. Amid cries of 'Oi!' and 'Stop 'em!' we're off toward the cranes and our youth and superior speed mean we get to the cab first. The driver knows the score and turns the engine off. The other two lads start to climb the one to our right.

'How you doing, Teddy?' Mark shouts over to them.

'I've got no water.'

'Oh dear.' Thankfully Mark has this base covered for us. One bottle for drinking and one to hold the inevitable by-product. He holds the former aloft.

'Chuck us some, will ya?'

'What with? A medieval catapult?'

Two hours elapse as Mark and I put the world to rights.

'No, you have to choose one. Them's the rules,' I tell him

'Ok, if I had to shag one of Zippy, George, Bungle or Geoffrey it'd be ... Bungle.'

'And why?'

'Because ...' he's struggling for a reason but I have faith in his bullshitting capacity ' ... I've no idea what species Zippy is and he'd never shut up. George looks like he'd enjoy it too much, being a camp pink hippo. If I chose Geoffrey it would be too near normality, making it seem like I want to fuck a man. Therefore, the logical choice is to shag a six-foot bear with a posh accent.'

'That's funny, I kinda came to the same conclusion.'

We see Teddy waving at us. 'What's the matter?'

'I really need a piss!' he shouts.

'What do you want us to do about it?'

'Dunno.'

'Hard luck. You'll just have to cross your legs for a while, unless you just piss.'

'What, just get it out and go off the crane?'

'Yeah.'

'Nah, I'll hang on. It's ok.'

Another half an hour goes by, but we've found new sport to occupy us. Occasionally we call over 'just piss!' or hold our bottle aloft. Teddy put two fingers up at us and grins, whilst stemming the flow with his other hand. We're pissing ourselves – but only figuratively – as are the guards at the foot of each crane.

We see Claire coming over to where we are. Looks like she's taken the girl from earlier back to base to be looked after. Mark waves and as she nears he shouts and points. 'He needs some water and a piss bottle!'

Squinting up at us Claire raises a thumb and runs back over the hill. I shout over 'It's ok mate, the cavalry's coming'. Ten minutes later Claire has rustled up the Manchester crew to face down the guards. A whole new site invasion takes place – thankfully this time without sexual assault. People are felled, dragged along in the dust, superficially injured amid screams and cries of pain. Teddy is gingerly climbing down the ladder as best he can without wetting himself. Claire, who presumably has the bottles inside her combat trousers, is dodging and weaving, using the others as cannon fodder by allowing the guards to get bogged down in a skirmish then running past. She's making good progress towards the cab but is suddenly taken out with a shoulder barge and falls face down.

'Oi, that's my girlfriend you twat, I'll fucking do you!' Nick's at the gates looking on with half a handcuff round his wrist.

Claire struggles free and is just able to get to the cab and put the bottles on top before she is bundled off. All eyes are now on the mini plastic portaloos. Teddy is only a few feet away, but his desire to urinate is restricting his movements. In what seems like an eternity he grabs the prized vessels and starts to climb a few rungs to safety. Once at a fair distance up, he undoes his flies and pisses. Though he seems to be aiming correctly, a stream of urine flows from the base of the bottle and hit's the ground thirty feet below.

'It must have got cracked when Claire got bundled.' Mark just gets the words out through his laughter.

As Teddy finishes and climbs further up we see a steady trickle coming from the other bottle. Our fit of giggles lasts for twenty-odd minutes. All three of us climb down when the drivers finish their shifts. It's early in the contract and they're not working 24/7 yet.

That night Phil and I offer to do the off-licence run. Among the requests of 'Oh, get us anything cold' there are picky buggers who insist on vegan beer.

'Which ones are they?' I ask him.

'Generally the chemically brewed ones that bring on the bad hangovers. Stella and Kronenbourg. And virtually any cider. Most brewers' brands use fish scales as a filter.'

'Let's see ...' I peer down the list. 'Six three-litre bottles of White Lightning. Fucking hell, how can they drink that stuff? It may be vegan but I don't think it's ever seen an apple.'

'Keeps the Brew Crew quiet and is therefore good for campaign morale,' said Phil. 'They work hard enough, and can survive life up in the treehouses, so long as you keep them good and pissed.'

Our return to the campfire is heralded by the thirsty masses. I catch up with Richard – I still can't get used to calling him Beech. By all accounts he's one of the main players on the campaign and a very able activist.

Entertainment for the evening comes from Tez, an activist-busker who's over from one of the camps near Bath specialises in bastardised cover versions.

'This one's called Sheep,' he says. 'For the Italians in the audience it starts with an arpeggio in G.' He fingerpicks the intro to Creep by Radiohead and begins to sing.

> When I'm on a farm
> And sheep are roaming by
> I like to befriend them
> But don't ask me why
> Their wool is so cuddly
> Their bleat is just right
> They need a good shepherd
> By day and by night

He then strums powerfully into the chorus.

> Cos I shag sheep
> I'm a weirdo

Love to ram them in the rear
When sheep they are near

He takes a deep breath and milks the laughter before continuing
with verse two.

I don't fancy pigs
Couldn't do it to a horse
But my favourite lubes are
Sheep dip or mint sauce
I know it's peculiar
It's just how I am
Idea of a good time
Me, ewe and a lamb
Sheeeeeeeeep, baaa, baaa, baaa, baa-baa-baa-baa, baa

Once he's won the crowd over Tez sings some genuine songs of
eco-resistance. He's good mates with some of the activist-type
bands that have formed, such as the Tofu Love Frogs and the Space
Goats. He sings a collection of sad laments of lost woods, folky
tales of big bad cops and ballads dedicated to the love of the earth.
   Nick says. 'Guys, Claire and I have an announcement to make.'
   'Don't tell me, you're both MI5,' I reply with some rapidity.
   'Not quite. We've decided to get handfasted in August.'
   I deduce it's good news by everyone's reaction and can guess it's
some form of ritual, so ask Jane for guidance.
   'It's a pagan wedding ceremony. It's like getting married but it's
only for a year and a day.'
   The happy couple, as if cast in the glow of their friends' love,
burst into smiles then look to each other and kiss, not in any need
of affirmation but merely to share the moment.
   'Of course you're all invited,' says Claire, 'it's going to be at my
friend's permaculture farm in Gloucestershire on the first of the
month.'
   'On Lammas? That's beautiful,' says Helen. More investigation
reveals to me it's a pagan festival day, a quarter of the year on from
Beltane, whatever that is.
   There's much hugging and congratulation. A few panda-like eyes
can be seen where tears and woodsmoke have combined.
   'Hey,' says Mark, 'sorry to spoil the moment, but who's annoyed
by that light coming from the compound?'
   Competing with the firelight is the fluorescent glow of floodlights
a quarter of a mile away.
   'Shall we sort it out?' says this guy Ian I've been warned about. He's

known for having a big mouth and bragging about the monkey-wrenching he's done. He's either foolish, foolhardy or ... an infiltrator.

'What do you reckon, guys?' Quite a few of us are drunk enough to go for it despite Ian being here.

'Ok,' says Nick going into the mess area, 'we need this.' He picks up a bag of sugar. He then goes to his tent for a pair of gloves.

'Here's the plan. I want two of you keeping watch on the caravan. If they come out one is to run and tell the next group, who are there to be a decoy – if the guards come, run anywhere but towards the lights. That should be enough cover for me to pour the sugar into the generator. Once it's done, make yourselves scarce. I'll make my own way back.'

'It should be ok, there's a skeleton crew out at nights. They're in that caravan.' Claire points to where there is drunken laughter. 'They're playing cards,' she adds.

Nick goes first, using a site fence as cover. There's no movement from the caravan. Group 4 should pay them more and they might do a better job. On the other hand, I just wish we got paid at all.

Mark and Claire get the short straw of being with Ian in group two. They creep into the bushes equidistant between Nick and us.

I'm fifty yards from the caravan keeping watch with Phil.

We hear more laughter. 'Gives us those cards, ya big twat. I'm gonna shuffle them properly this time.' I'm slightly distracted by trying to shoo away the midges.

We wait in silence for a couple of minutes. The floodlights fade to nothing, marked by a cheer from the campfire.

On our return Ian starts bragging.

'That's three lots of wrenching this week. I'm a warrior, first class. Must be my Nordic blood.'

'But you're from Hartlepool. What are you on?' comes back a response from the other side of the fire. Ian falls silent. If you ask me, he's not a spy – just really insecure.

Nick returns from the darkness to loud cheers. 'Thank you, but keep it down a bit,' he whispers jabbing his finger towards the caravan.

I'm sat next to Phil, who – don't get me wrong – is a great guy. However, he's talking strategy with Claire. I've had enough of shop for one day so turn my attention to the woman on my right.

Sure, she's got dreads, but she's wearing tights and they seem to be covering a cracking pair of legs.

'It's better without the generator, eh?'

'Oh, yes. Very good,' she says with a gentle but distinct German accent. 'Hallo, I am Brigitte.'

Turns out she's here for a year at Lancaster University, is from Magdeburg, a little town on the river Elbe and is easy to talk to despite being foreign.

'... the stereotype we see in the media is Germany's much cleaner and more sorted environmentally than we are. You also seem more European than us,' I say taking another swig of beer. This is my second three-litre bottle and it's two-thirds empty.

'I think the English and Germans are very similar. From what I have seen you are not so, how do you say? Insular?' The final word has a Teutonic twang I find quite endearing.

'We're a funny bunch. Especially the half that are a bloody waste of space. They live little lives, consume crappy culture, if you can call it that, and just, just ... bloody annoy me!'

Brigitte smiles, her blonde dreads framing big blue eyes. 'You are being a snob, but I do know what you mean. These people who don't take any chances. Do what they're told. There are too many of them. They are ... dummkopf? What's that in English. It is a test for you.'

'Um, that's stupid or something isn't it? I'm afraid my German never was very good. I can remember now is wie komme ich am besten zum Bahnhof, bitte. It's not gonna get me very far, is it?'

'To the next station perhaps.' As she smiles her head swings back to reveal a very kissable neck in the firelight. There is something very seductive about the way campfires paint us. Perhaps it's the primal romance of outdoor life but it seems to make features more distinct, and mostly more attractive. This is perhaps one reason for the recent rise in on-site pregnancies

It's time to go for it. Do or die – bite the bullet. In the next available silence, I look into her eyes, lean forward and, brushing her hair back with my leading hand, go to kiss her. She responds favourably.

In a break for air, I ask if she has a tent here.

'A treehouse I have borrowed over in the next field. It is quite cold.'

'Shouldn't be a problem. I'm sure we could find ways to keep warm.' It's the oldest line in the book, but gets a positive response.

'But let us stay with the fire some more.' We sit, arm in arm, on the trunk of a trashed tree.

From behind me I hear someone call my name. It's Phil. 'I'm going back to Manchester in an hour or so, are you coming?'

'I'm good, mate. Thanks.' I shout this into the semi-darkness over my right shoulder. I must fancy her. I'm exhausted and could really use a bath. Turning my attention back to Brigitte we snog merrily as sparks rise into the air.

'Ok, we will go now,' she takes my hand and tries to pull me up.

I follow her lead, though trying to stand with a stalk on isn't the easiest or most pain–free activity.

We kiss, hug and generally fondle our way into the next field. Brigitte falls to the ground, and brings me down on top of her and another bout of tonsil tennis ensues. I've got my hands inside her stripy hooded top. Though she's not wearing a bra – she doesn't seem the type to believe in them – there's no sign of sagging. Her nipples are firm and, by her reaction, highly responsive.

We reach the bottom of the tree. There's a couple of ropes and what appears to be a pair of stirrups.

'You can prusik, yes?'

'Hmm ... not for a while.' Truth be told cranes aren't too bad but trees aren't really my medium.

'I will re-teach you.' I sense she knows I don't know how. 'Ok, put your foot in here, push up on this rope, then bring the other hand up to join it.'

After a brief demonstration I grab her and pull her to the ground. 'Very well explained and thank you for teaching me. When we are up there I will give you a present.' I pull her into my groin. Despite the amount I've had to drink it's enough to make her smile.

I have to adjust her harness to the biggest setting and it just about fits. My first attempt to scale the tree is hopeless, but she shows me again, and after a quick trip to the bushes I feel better and start to get the hang of it. It takes about twenty minutes to travel thirty feet, but there's a certain grace to hanging in the air slowly defying gravity. I then have to throw it all down to her and she's with me in five.

The treehouse is cosy. There's a small woodburning stove but we can't be bothered with that. I'm not the biggest fan of ethnic throws but they seem in situ up here. She lights a big scented candle and we start to undress each other.

Oh shit! I've no johnnies with me. I'm one-eighth German. I really don't want a little just over half-German kid playing on the banks of the Elbe in a couple of years' time. 'What's German for contraceptive? You know?'

'It's ok, really.' This turns out to definitely be an understatement. There's something very sensual and exciting about sex in a tree-house – the sustainable version of the Mile High Club.

Next morning it's back to work. As I enter the campaign office Beech is drafting a press release.

'How goes it, old boy?' I ask.

'Burnt out as fuck. Stressed to buggery, 'bout average really.'

'Any good actions lately?'

'Well, we tried to do an office occupation of the contractors in Bramhall, but when we got there all we found wasn't much more than a secretary and a filing cabinet. Cost us all a fortune to get over there and all for nothing. Still, some actions just fuck up like that.'

'Too right.'

'Anyway, tomorrow's vital. In order to get equipment across the river they need to build a Bailey bridge. Word is they're going for it at first light. There's a meeting in half an hour.'

'Originally used for military purposes, these temporary bridges can be carried on a couple of lorries and assembled in a day,' says Helen who's co-ordinating the briefing.

One of the major actions at Twyford had been to try and prevent a Bailey being constructed and valuable lessons had been learned.

'They really need this bridge as soon as possible. Just make sure you get on those trucks, the rest of the plant can wait. If they can't get the bridge built it makes accessing the full site really tricky.'

Ian sees me over the other side of the meeting and approaches.

'Alright mate, been up to anything naughty lately?'

'Might have. How about you?' It's more like we're talking about skiving double geography than major criminal damage.

'Well, did you hear about that crane that spontaneously combusted the other week?'

'No.'

He digs an index finger twice into his chest.

'What makes you think I'm interested? How do you know I'm not a copper? Haven't you ever heard of telling people things on a need-to-know basis?'

'You're alright mate, well sound. If you're a copper then so am I.' This potential double bluff switches my attention back to the briefing.

It's 5.30am – there's about seventy of us lined up for this action; a skeleton crew is left at the camps but every available body is needed. It'll be interesting to see how Brigitte operates on an action. Positions are taken up on the access road and we wait for the lorries. There's only one feasible way in, it's just a question of when.

Twenty minutes later we hear yips from the advance party further up the road.

We run as best we can – the movement needs all sorts of people but more athletes wouldn't go amiss. I resolve to go running more often. There's a few suffering from spliff–related wheezing by the time we reach the trucks.

'Yip, yehah, awoo, yip yip yiiiip!' is the approximate zoological soundscape as we close on the three lorries. Percussion is added by scores of booted feet thudding against the road. I look over to Brigitte and her smile gives me a lift – I've not been on an action with someone I'm involved with before.

There are four full riot vans, two up front, two at the rear, as well as half a dozen Group 4 vehicles.

'We've got our work cut out today,' says Claire, D-lock swinging from her harness as she runs.

We're upon them and the first tactic for the first twenty or so is to sit in the road. When all vehicles are stationary we run past the vans and head for the lorries. Cops and guards are piling out; time is of the essence.

Mark gets jumped by two guards. He'll be ok but we could have done with him on the trucks.

Brigitte is next to be taken out – I feel a certain chivalric urge to help, but it's not in the game plan.

Beech and me are among the first to reach the front lorry. They've made a tactical error, they should have had guards riding on the trucks – an eight-year-old could have spotted that.

Using a wheel nut as a foot-rest I grip the passenger door handle, haul myself up then jump onto the flatbed. There's not much to lock onto other than the sections of bridge.

A guard is just about to climb aboard. I take the lock out of my combats and reach for the key.

'Richard, you ok?' I shout.

'Yeah, I'm underneath.'

I see Sparko's anarcho-mullet as he lifts himself up. I'm surprised he got here this fast.

As I turn the key Dom's climb is aborted as he's grabbed round the neck. His cry of anguish is mostly drowned out by engine noise as he's dragged downwards.

'Geezer – Beech is on the back axle,' Sparko says.

Dom's carried away by four white hats, accompanied by a cop who recites to him. 'You do not have to say anything, but anything you do say will be taken down and used in evidence against you.'

Helen's next to join us.

'Anyone got a book with them?' Helen has a low boredom threshold on actions these days. Even with the most high-adrenaline lifestyles familiarity can breed a contempt of sorts. She now only goes on actions because they need to be done.

We're sitting ducks for the guards now. I have the pleasure of having Mickey being assigned to me. He's got a bit of a reputation for rough stuff. He's getting on a bit, and you could tell by the road map of the British Isles on his nose he likes a drink or two.

'Come on then, my son.' The Irish twang in his voice is accentuated as he digs a thumb into my neck.'

'Camera! He's pressure-pointing me,' I cry, hoping legal support is in hearing distance.

'Cheers,' he says as an angle-grinder is passed to him.

I hadn't bargained on this.

I have one guard holding each of my limbs. Under the circumstances it's not a great idea to struggle anyway. A towel is placed under the lock next to my neck and covering my head. I hear the saw-blade begin to spin. There's nothing I can do other than try and block out the cacophonous noise, which is putting my teeth on edge.

A stray spark lands on my hand and I flinch. I'm at a disadvantage as I can't see when I'll be cut loose.

'Don't worry lad, we'll have you soon.' Mickey's breathing hard and clearly relishing the power trip. The shearing noise is changing pitch – there's less to cut through. Perhaps I can use this as a guide.

'Legal!' I call out for an observer as a plan forms.

'What's wrong?' I hear a voice I believe to be Gill's just above the horrid squeal of metal on metal.

'I'm getting really claustrophobic with all these people around. I feel a panic attack coming on.'

'Oh poor baby,' says Mickey.

'Come on, guys, play fair,' she asks.

'Sorry, love, we do as our gaffer says.'

'I'll go and speak to the Head of Security,' Gill says to me before running off in search of the guy in the blue hat.

She needs to be quick, I can hear the lock is nearly done for. In two minutes I'll be very glad of health and safety legislation when I hear 'Ok lads, give him some air'. I feel the pressure lift off my left leg and right arm.

As soon as I hear blade rotation with no shearing, I throw off the towel, arch my back and struggle for all I'm worth. I'm just able to shove Mickey and the other guard aside and manage to throw arms and legs round the same section I was locked onto.

'You little shitbag.' Mickey's mad now. He's pulling away at my leg. It moves, but only millimetres. He takes another grip, further up the leg, and hauls again. 'Fuck off, granddad!' I'm not feeling at my most tolerant.

His head is now right up against my groin. As loud as I can I cry out. 'You disgusting old fucker! You're trying to give me a blow job! I'm surprised, you don't look like the type!'

Mickey's face recoils from my between my thighs in horror. He's reddening and maddening by the nanosecond.

'You ... you ... fuckin' little ...' He's shocked by my outburst, lost for words for once. Relinquishing his grip, he gathers his thoughts for a moment, snorting with rage.

'You cuntin' little faggot! How dare you! You're the one who's the queer round here not me!' He's lost it and I'm ashamed to say I like it.

'You tell 'im geezer!' shouts Sparko who's got troubles of his own, as has Helen.

'You reckon? I'm not the one who just nuzzled up to my crotch, am I? From where I'm sitting, you're the one who's the queer, ducky?' I would make a limp-wristed gesture but daren't move my arms. It's out of order to use homosexuality like this to score petty points, but from what I've heard Mickey's had it coming for a long time.

'Why you!' Mickey lunges at me, but two more level-headed guards, who see the situation brewing, restrain him.

'Leave him Mick, he's nothing. He's trying to get you the sack. Then where will you and the Missus be?' Mickey is still snarling and scowling trying to push his mates away. I turn to the police and shout. 'Officers, I want that man arrested for attempted sexual assault.'

'Lester, for Christ's sake. This is getting tedious.' Helen's not impressed, and by the looks of it, neither are many of the others.

Mickey is led off in the direction of a Portakabin. I shout after him. 'I suppose you're off to have a wank about it now, eh? Well, don't use me as your inspiration, I'll be terribly offended!' Phil is taking pictures of the action, and, as he passes, Mickey punches him square in the face.

Dom, still straining on my arm says, 'I can't believe that guy, where does he draw the line?'

'Lester, that was your fault though. You shouldn't have wound him up,' says Helen sternly.

'He was bloody well asking for it. I can't help it if he's repressed and has got a problem about certain things.'

'If you say so. I think it is rather childish actually,' Helen's being sancti-fucking-monious.

'What's rattled your cage? It was only a laugh. He deserved it.'

I spot the blue-hatted Head of Security going over and consulting with a couple of cops.

'How about Phil? It's down to you that he got clobbered.' She's not letting it drop.

'If you're going to give a speech on the joys of being PC, you can stick it ... well, you know where you can stick it.'

The guards point at me and the officers nod.

'I can't control what Mickey does. The man's an animal. Now, if you haven't got anything sensible to say, can you please shut the fuck up, or I'm going to leave this action right now.'

'Do that then.'

Five police officers come over, make short work of hauling me off the lorry and 'cuff me for breach of the peace.

I give the eco-police station as a bail address and within the hour I'm inside a cell for the rest of the day.

Lying back on my blue mattress I think about the M65 campaign. It's great but becoming a bit too much of a hippy heaven for my liking, and being rebuked by Helen is symptomatic of this. Also, the trees on the route of the road haven't been 'spiked' with nails. It's a very effective tactic, as it makes a chainsaw operator think twice. But the campaign 'view' is that spiking is not sufficiently 'fluffy'. For fuck's sake, if someone tries to cut the tree down and gets hurt that's their fault. Some on the camps even think that spiking the trees causes them pain. Like being cut down isn't going to hurt at all. Wankers.

Though my bail conditions bar me from the camps I decide that's a huge crock of shit, and return to Brigitte's treehouse. She tells me the action was a mixed success. It lasted eighteen hours, and more guards had to be drafted in. There were 35 arrests, but they managed to secure the area by the river and construct the bridge.

We spend an idyllic day together, gathering wood, hewing water, lighting the stove, picking wild mushrooms. To be more prosaic the water was hewn from the tap at base, but you get the picture. We cook up the mushrooms into a soup and return to our treetop bed. She's delightful but we're very different. Under her crustie mop of curls lies a bookish, rational side. Yet under that is a layer of full-on belief in astrology, tarot, paganism, ley lines and all sorts of hoopla I have no truck with. I've deduced this much after a day and a half spent in her company. Fuck knows what layer is beneath all that but the message I hear is MENTALIST – STAY CLEAR, pumped out through a metaphorical 30k rave rig.

'Brigitte, I have to go back to the city. My life is there.' This is true. Though I fervently wish to defend the countryside I'm not entirely cut out to live here all the time.

'When are you going?'

'I'll get a lift back tonight. I'll be back here, but I'm not sure when.'

'Fine, you go – how do you say it? Whatever.'

'Look, you're great – but ... I can't stay.'

She looks me over then seems to give me the benefit of the doubt. Another away win for Commitment Phobia F.C.

'I know this sounds cheeky but shall we ... you know? It'd be a shame to waste the moment.' We have one more roll around for old time's sake – all thirty-six hours of them. We then swap email addresses – though quite what good it is to her up a treehouse is another matter.

It's time to abseil down before it gets too dark and see if Phil has forgiven me enough to let me in his car.

As she joins me on the ground there's a moment's hesitation. I look in her eyes for clues to her thoughts. Whether I'm going to see her again. We then kiss and hold each other for the length of a television commercial. 'Bye now, take care. See you soon?' she says. There's barely the trace of a half-smile.

'Sure I'll be around. You come and visit me in Manchester?'

She answers with the slightest of nods. She takes a step back, our fingertips the last bodily parts to relinquish touch. I turn with my head full of ifs, whys and might-have-beens as I go in search of Phil and 'civilisation'.

I decide it's time for a trip to Claremont, so hitch down as far as Amersham, then walk to the tube station and travel the twenty-seven stops to Leytonstone without a ticket. Even though Claremont is completely insane, somehow it's reasonably free of yoghurt-weaving hippy bullshit. I notice that the M11 campaign has reverted to being a siege of sorts. Occupation of the street has become the major priority and site actions have virtually stopped, apart from on special occasions. But then again, who can blame them? Hurling yourself at cranes and bulldozers day in, day out is hard, dirty, dangerous, thankless work and there are times when I question why I should want to do it, let alone anyone else.

For 93 years Dolly Watson has lived at number 32 in the house she was born in. Her fiancé died fighting the Germans in '42 and in half a century no suitable replacement came along. Though she lives alone she has everyone on the campaign around as an extended family, and in turn she is always on hand with a cup of coffee and a story. She fears the social services will put her in a home if the street is destroyed. Like the rest of us, she is fighting for a particular kind of freedom.

Claremont Road is becoming world-famous, and gaining a reputation as the place to come to for anarchic types from all around the planet. In its small way it's becoming an alternative tourist trap. Maybe it should qualify for a marketing budget from the borough.

Virtually all the houses have been heavily barricaded in the preceding months. Several can now only be accessed via ladders stretching up to first-floor windows. At one end of the road is the husk of a car, minus wheels, engine and windows. It does still have a use though. Flowers grow out of the bonnet and boot, and the legend RUST IN PEACE is painted on the side. A mock gravestone stands on the grass verge nearby. It's dedicated to John MacGregor, who is still very much alive, but whose lifespan as Transport Secretary has recently ceased. One of the reasons behind his sacking is the treatment he's been subjected to by the anti-roads movement, notably the morning when a posse from Road Alert climbed up onto his roof and obscured the entire front of his house with a three lane banner-cum-motorway.

Towards one end of the street is a zebra crossing with a difference. Half a black and white striped Escort van lies on either kerb. A giant chess board has also been painted, with flower pots masquerading as pawns. A mini model of Stonehenge made of bricks rests on a white spiral squiggle. A couple of armchairs are here in which to sit, chat, drink, skin-up, contemplate or recover. In between them is a coffee table complete with lava lamp. Tailor's dummies sit around the place – some without limbs – others adorned with fluorescent face paint. They sport a range of styles from crustie through to smart. By day, they are comical, if strange. By night, they take on a more sinister quality, especially if you've smoked too much in the Amsterdam-style jazz café a few doors down. It's an open secret that roof tiles and chimney pots are removed and sold to help keep the street supplied with cannabis. It should, however, be known that weed is not for sale in the cafés. That would be wrong – at least plain stupid in campaign terms.

Weird and whacked-out though it is, there's a homely feel. And that feeling is community. Without doubt the most surreal street in Britain, it's also a monument to our resilience and ingenuity as a nation. Somehow though I don't think the Prime Minister or Home Secretary see it that way.

By day it's almost impossible to be bored. New people, new faces, new possibilities and challenges await each morning. At night the place rises to a whole new level. It's become a major hub of counter-cultural life in London. Jam sessions start and musical collaborations form. People randomly fall in love with one another, and some actually manage to maintain the feeling for more than a week. Despite the constant exhaustion, most of the time there's that little bit of energy left over to have it. And this is despite having to fight the guards, police, government and contractors and still run a campaign to make the M11 Link cost as much as possible.

Street parties are held every Sunday night. Sound systems from around London come in from around the capital, Though no stranger to Class A drugs, the appeal of techno still eludes me. For some, repetitive beats are strangely hypnotic. I find them un-strangely repetitive. Without wanting to sound like a young fogey, will anyone be playing techno on Desert Island Discs in fifty years' time? That is, of course, if we're all still here by then.

For those who aren't huge dance music fans, a stage made from the back of a redundant lorry has 'bands' entertaining the crowds. A big effort is made to get locals to attend these. In the world of party and protest, the initial way in for many is the former.

It's Sunday morning after a long drive down. Mark, Jane, Dom, Helen and I are crashed out in the loft of number 34. The sight of

Jane in a sports bra is certainly something to kindle the morning wood.

'Morning,' She stretches. Something of mine does too.

'Likewise. What are you up to today?' Hoping for a response like 'Oh, shagging you senseless', back in the real world my ears pick up sound waves which I decipher as 'There's a meeting in Kentish Town about the Criminal Justice Act'.

'Oi Mark, wake up, you lazy twat. Do you fancy going to that?' A groan comes from the camouflage sleeping bag. A head is nowhere to be seen.

We arrive fashionably late at the Rainbow Centre, Kentish Town. A woman with a bobbed undercut and big blue-framed glasses is addressing the meeting.

'If this is a bunch of shit I'm so going to the pub,' says Mark. The World Cup quarter-finals are in full swing and to miss a single match without good excuse would be sacrilegious.

'Right with you there, bro. It's Bulgaria-Germany unless I'm very much mistaken.'

' ... so as you've seen the Criminal Justice Bill is a real threat to hunt sabs, protesters, ravers, travellers and squatters. Add to that the loss of the right to silence, the ability of the police to take body samples without consent and increased stop-and-search powers. Put them all together and to put it bluntly we've got trouble.'

We've completely missed the briefing so hoover up the literature and get asking questions. Gary comes to our rescue. 'It's mad – they're going to bring in aggravated trespass – which basically is being on land when you have no permission – and you could get three months in jail and a fine of two and a half grand.'

'Fuck a duck,' says Mark.

'That's ridiculous. Will it pass through parliament?'

'Looks like most of it will. Including music being defined as ... where is it ... oh yes ... sounds wholly or predominantly characterised by the emission of a succession of repetitive beats. How about that?'

We go and watch the match – not through boredom but to stave off serious depression.

'I suppose it's a form of flattery in a way,' I say midway through my fifth pint, 'that we've become that much of a pain to Major and his minions that they're bringing it in'.

'That's not going to give me a warm glow inside when I'm doing the prison laundry,' says Mark trying to smile.

'This needs serious attention – next week.' As I say this, the ball is swung into the German box. Letchkov drifts away from his marker and his diving header finds the net. Bulgaria going on to win is the only bright spot in the day – aside from Jane's sports bra.

It's the weekend of Nick and Claire's handfasting and a recent conversion to hitchhiking has saved me a hefty fare or a run-in with British Transport Police.

If you've got the time – and don't mind waiting at junctions – hitching's one of the most interesting ways of getting around. I've made A4-sized signs on the computer – printed on both sides of course. There's North, South, East, West, Manchester, London, Brighton and Next Junction, all concluding with 'Please' of course.

Ok, horror movies may exploit fear of the unknown and portray hitchers as psychopaths, and there may well be the odd nutter who's out looking for someone to lock in a gimp cellar and subject to satanic rituals. However, it's possible – though I admit not probable – that the demon drivers pick up the violent hitchers, and over time cancel each other out.

Back in the real world three lifts from Manchester to my required destination, the village of Owlpen, Gloucestershire is a distinct result. I follow the directions Nick's sent me and Jasmine Lane Farm is a ten-minute walk from where I was dropped off.

Hauling tat across the country on a balmy late July afternoon is sweaty work and I'm thankful my shirt, suit and smart shoes are safe and dry in the rucksack. In the left shoe is a piece of ribbon – we've all been asked to bring one for some reason. Below the sign for the farm is another saying 'Welcome to Possible' in a circus-type font.

Though no expert on agriculture, I can see this is a long way from most people's conceptions of what a farm looks like. There are open fields, but they are some way off. Most of the land is tightly packed and undulating. There are ponds, banks, worm bins, hedges, fruit trees and vegetable beds all crammed into every available space. The place is teeming with life to a ridiculous degree.

It looks chaotic in the extreme, but it's all the more beautiful for the variation. Suddenly the monoculture of the South Downs doesn't seem quite so picturesque. The entire site is on a slight incline, which is great for taking in the wonder of the place but is hard work on the calves after a long day. The farmhouse has a lush turf roof, solar panels and wind turbine. I can't help but be impressed by the positivity of the place. A day early for the ceremony I've been given the privilege of a perspective of the countryside other than getting burnt out and beaten up trying to save it.

Claire runs up the path to greet me. 'Yay, let's get you introduced.'

In the kitchen there's a woman with dyed red hair and a baby at her breast. 'This is Maia – our ... is it host or hostess?'

'Whatever darlin', so long as you all have a great time.' In her early thirties, she bears clear traces of hard living in her sun-accentuated laughter lines. But her and the baby look ten times happier and more content than the average mum pushing a pram round a Manchester suburb. The baby – old enough to control his neck muscles – pauses, lets out an impressive belch – then returns to his dinner. 'Thank you, Oscar,' Maia sniggers as she squeezes him against her. 'Tell you what, do you want a tour of the farm once you're unpacked and his Lordship's had his fill?'

'That'd be wonderful,' I say as Claire leads me to the barn to ditch my stuff.

With Oscar having milky dreams in his cot, Maia literally leads me up the garden path.

'Permaculture is about designing everything so the energy flows most efficiently. The areas closest to the farmhouse are where we do the most work. It's a 60-acre site – designed so that nature does the work for us.'

'Sure doesn't look like it,' I say amazed at the complexity of it all.

I catch the smell of lavender, and look down on a pebble-edged raised bed in the shape of a snail shell.

'That's a herb spiral. The watercress needs to be in the wettest place at the end there.'

Nearby, a multi-decked greenhouse is full of aubergines, marrows and courgettes with a mustard-coloured chicken scratching around the floor.

'That's Charlie, don't worry, she loves the heat. Eats all the weeds, slugs and snails – and fertilises the ground.'

'Let's get this right – you get eggs as a by-product of your pest control?'

'We sure do. And in the winter her body temperature keeps the frost at bay.'

'That's fucking amazing,' I reply.

'Glad you like it. Everything here has at least three uses. See over there,' she points over at some trees. 'That's a chinampas – a floating garden. We grow willows there. Strip them down for fencing and handicrafts or use it to shore up the soil banks. Or it's good for making charcoal and we can even make a tincture out of the bark as an anti-inflammatory. And don't they look beautiful?'

She adds that Oscar gets to munch on a white willow twig when his new teeth are playing him up, as the bark contains salicin, a natural pain reliever.

'It's fascinating,' I say agog. There's so much information to absorb but permaculture also seems to be common sense. Though she's several years older than me – and 'soiled goods' by virtue of motherhood – I can feel a burgeoning Earth Mother crush coming on.

'And there's the geese. Cute though they are in their waddling ways they're also a lawnmower, alarm system, provide great shit for the composters and lay massive eggs all spring.'

'Wow.' This is all so new and there's so much to know.

She says. 'It takes a thousand years for an inch of soil to form from rock. It's the most precious resource we have and everything we do is to make sure it retains its goodness and moisture.'

I bend down and rub a handful of simple dirt between my fingers. 'So this has been coming together since the Battle of Hastings?'

'Yep, pretty much, Charlie might have helped a bit too. Oh yeah – that reminds me,' she turns and points to a little orchard. 'You see those fruit trees – beneath each of those is an old compost toilet.'

'You mean?'

'Yes.'

'Forgive me for asking but do they taste like shit?'

'Come see' We wander over and she twists an apple from a strong yet sagging branch. The fruit even feels unusually heavy and tastes divine. Half a dozen buzzing beehives are shaded by their canopies.

Next is a little patch of woodland. 'These are all oaks. We harvest logs from live trees, then drill holes to impregnate them with shiitake mushroom spores. Give it a few months and they sell for a tenner each.' Interspersed around the oaks is the odd gooseberry bush. I needn't ask if these are also part of the harvest.

'Nature doesn't make any waste. The trees give up their leaves to the soil, and the worms turn it over free of charge. We just design it properly and it all falls into our laps.'

I blow out my cheeks. 'Blimey.' Seldom have I been so impressed, and certainly not by a feat of digger-diving or guard-baiting.

'Ok, there's loads of backbreaking work involved, but it's so worth it. Hungry?'

As we head back for supper the tour continues. 'The farmhouse walls are made of straw bales, and all the hot water runs off solar power. The rest of the electricity for the house comes from here.' She opens the door of a large outhouse and what looks like a sausage machine with a fan in the middle stands before us.

'This is a biomass generator. All the by-products we have no other use for goes through this; it ferments creating heat and pressure and we run the turbine through it. Any excess heat goes through this vent into the blacksmith's forge next door.'

Though not wanting to give up the activist life, I can feel genuine pangs of jealousy at the idyll I've just witnessed. It may be a façade, but if so it's far more seductive than rural life was depicted in The Darling Buds of May – with or without Catherine Zeta Jones.

Claire and Nick have cooked up a wonderful spread in the meantime – honey-roasted squash with cauliflower cheese and garlic mash.

'I think the only thing that isn't from the farm is the nutmeg in the cheese sauce,' says Claire.

'What about the cheese?' I point out.

'You didn't meet Judith the goat,' Maia says with a mix of pride and modesty.

Considering the purpose of the weekend it's not long before the conversation turns to the subject of the handfasting.

'We've had all mentions of God removed from the service,' says Claire.

'Good on ya. God's a twat,' I reply.

'So are you gonna go for the year-and-a-day option?'

'We thought about it and decided to go for eternity.'

'Aah, that's so cute,' I say in the voice of a teenage girl, pinching Nick's cheek.

'Besides, if it doesn't work, we can have a handparting ceremony,' she says, sharing a sarcastic moment with the 'groom'-to-be.

The farmhouse is filling up with hippies now, and there's a good thirty more plus a sound system to arrive for the reception.

'All set for tomorrow then?' I ask.

'Hmm,' says Nick. 'I've got to give my secret mistress one last seeing to tonight, but apart from that.' Nick gets a raspberry blown his way for insolence.

Maia and her staff have worked wonders with the site. The field where the ceremony is to take place is next to a stream, and under a big sprawling oak they've built a willow arch weaved with wisteria. Their marquee is decorated with particular finesse, but I don't feel my feminine side kick in sufficiently to reel it all off for you.

Dusk starts to fall and the fire staffs in the ground are lit.

It's strange to see everyone in their smartest clothes. Even Tango looks vaguely presentable, though he's still a ginger tosser. Jane looks lovelier than ever with flowers in her hair wearing an archetypal Laura Ashley number. Note to self – must be good. Nick's brother Steve's been away in Guatemala but has timed his travelling to return and be best man.

The couple are under the arch with the rest of us holding hands in a huge circle, all clutching our pieces of ribbon. Turns out Maia is also a Wiccan or pagan priestess and will be conducting the ceremony. She's a dark horse that one – though not in a satanic way, I trust.

On that note there's a pentacle fashioned from flowers on the ground before the couple and right in the centre of the circle burns a small fire. Part of me feels like I'm on the set of a Hammer horror film and Christopher Lee is going to turn up and start biting people any minute.

Claire and Nick are decked out his-and-hers white gowns under long white hooded cloaks. He's said he was going to wear it for a laugh and it's definitely an interesting look.

Maia begins proceedings. 'The circle in which you all stand is symbolic of the cycles of life, the womb of the Great Mother, a sacred place created for mortal and divine interaction, in which any negativity from the mundane world can be left outside and all the love and joy we feel for Claire and Nick contained within.'

'Marriage is very much a sacred union, for it is a union of souls in which the bride and groom pledge unto one another their higher selves and all that is divine within themselves.

Claire then bows her head, as Maia continues.

'Lady Claire, I ask you to call upon all that is divine within you, Let it come forth and shine.'

> In you dwells the essence of the Great Mother and the divine
> feminine principle of the Universe
> You are She who has been worshipped and adored for centuries
> and throughout the ages
> You are wife, mother, lover, friend, prophet, and confidante
> In you is everything that any one could ever aspire to be and more
> In you is strength and wisdom, perfection and peace
> Shine dear one and show your true nature.

As she says the same to Nick, apart from the mother part, I check out the circle for potential. There's a couple of lovelies here but it's difficult to work out if they're single. My mind clicks back to the ceremony for a Cherokee prayer.

'Father Sky please protect the ones we love. We honour all you have created as we pledge our hearts and lives together. We honour Mother Earth – and ask for our marriage to be abundant and grow stronger through the seasons. We honour fire – and ask that our union be warm and glowing with love in our hearts. We honour wind – and ask we sail though life safe and calm as in our father's arms. We honour water – to clean and soothe our relationship – that it may never thirst for love.'

Steve steps forward with the rings in a chalice. 'The ring finger of the left hand, the side of the body that holds the heart, next to veins which flow to the heart. The words that were spoken during the placing of the ring will resonate like the circumference of the band itself, through to the heart and soul of both giver and receiver of the most monumental promise of all, the promise of a lifetime as husband and wife.'

Nick takes a ring and says. 'I accept the pledge of your chalice and the eternal promise of this wedding band.'

Now Claire does the same. 'With this ring I thee wed. I take you as my friend, my lover, my husband from this day forth and into the fullness of time where we will meet and remember and love again.'

Maia then asks. 'Is it also your wish today that your hands be fasted in the ways of old?' The couple – on the verge of a mutual giggle – answer with a yes.

'Remember then as your hands are fasted, these are not the ties that bind ...'

We are called in turn to tie our ribbons round their hands. It takes a while, but it means I can check out if the fit ones are as impressive as they move.

By the time I step forward with an offcut from an old tie, their hands are barely visible, enveloped in silk, taffeta, lace, hemp, the odd piece of climbing rope, part of a security guard's fluoro bib and Mark's fragment of an old Leeds United scarf. Claire's been halfway between tears and joyful hysteria for the last ten minutes. I can't recall ever seeing someone so happy.

Maia continues. 'The song your hearts share shall be now be strengthened by the vows you have taken. All things of the material world eventually return to the Earth unlike the bond and the connection your spirits share which is destined to ascend to the heavens. May you be forever as one in the passion and fire of you.'

Maia takes their bound hands.

'You are now as your hearts have always known you to be, Husband and Wife. You may kiss the bride!'

They hold each other like nothing else on the planet exists.

'Now putting the past behind you – alive the combined power to create your destiny – jump together into your common future!'

They kiss again and step forward. Steve is on hand to receive their cloaks.

'Ready?' Nick asks.

'Oh yes,' and with that they leap over the fire.

With the formalities over it's onto the serious business of the reception. The Innerfield sound system has come up from Brighton to provide the tunes.

Cosmo turns up late but laden with goodies. 'Get those down you.' He hands me a couple of orange pills embossed with winged horses. 'They're called Pegasus. You'll be flying in no time.'

I thank him with a big hug. What the hell – I haven't got a date with me and it'll add an edge to the evening. Conscious not to dilute the effect with alcohol I grab a glass of ginger beer, swallow both and go to mingle.

Everyone's at play. The roads programme, current campaigns and the woes of the planet all put aside for the day. I feel this is especially true after about twenty-five minutes when Dom offers me a spliff. One toke sets off the first rushes of the afternoon.

It's nce-nce-nce as the high hat gives way to the bass. I go right up to the sub-woofers and can feel the frequency interact with my diaphragm.

'Pump up the noise, this is a rave,' says the midrange. Whilst personally preferring a bit more narrative in my songs it gets me jumping around in a moonstomp manner.

Jane, Helen and Lorraine are dancing in a little gang, minus handbags of course but the overall effect isn't dissimilar.

During each track new rushes will come and hijack my senses. I look round and most others seem to be gurning away like me. I'm handed a jar of Vic by someone wearing a dust mask and rub some round my nostrils. The effect is cooling yet slightly burns and intensifies the high.

Nick comes over, still in his gown but now with a laurel wreath on his sweaty head. His arms are waving wildly, glowstick in one hand and the thumb of the other tightly over the neck of a bottle of poppers. 'Lester, have a fucking bang on that bastard.'

A piano break kicks in as I breathe deeply through one nostril and it's as though I can feel the brain cells individually short.

'Woooaaaaahh! Do that too often and it's next stop funny farm,' I rock back on my heels involuntarily and can feel a cartoon-like gurn is the default setting for my face.

'Stay still,' Mark comes over to me with some orange dayglo facepaint. 'What shall I draw?'

'Just slap it on, I'll be a fucking satsuma for the night,' I reply.

They're playing one I know – Everybody In The Place by Prodigy. The crowd reaches a new energy apex – like we're all sharing each other's endorphins. Most, but by no means all the guests are fellow activists – so there's an added level of togetherness as we mook about on the grass.

The next track is a techno version of Somewhere Over The Rainbow which becomes – rightly or not – a cheesy hands-in-the-air singalong.

Then, feeling dehydrated I decide I've strutted enough funky stuff for now.

It's full-on dark as I walk away in the direction of the farmhouse to collect whatever's left of my thoughts away from the doof-doof-doof-doodoodoodoodoo-doof.

Passing a section of raised bank and there's just enough light to look, or at least think I'm looking at the life teeming below. I put my face right down to the soil and attempt to comprehend just how the forces which keep us alive come together. I try to look for worms and think I can see a translucent rippling. Then thoughts turn to the microorganisms, the nutrients the bugs absorb and how they interact with each other, the teeming mass of movement I believe I can now understand with the help of MDMA. From there I consider the molecular formations and the quantum vibrations and bonding between the atoms. Rubbing my eyes and returning to life on a human scale I look at the dirt on my hands; the brown stuff I had hitherto given little thought other than washing it off my knees after a match and am truly in awe. Not only do I know next to nothing about it but I'm guessing that scientists haven't got to grips with what earth really is. In this moment of addled clarity it feels more right than ever to stand up for what we stand upon.

CHAPTER **6**

AUTUMN 1994

I can't believe what Gary's just written on the back of an envelope. Normally, he would have just told me, but there are very justifiable fears that the office is bugged. The topic of discussion is where the next major action is going to be. I beam at the words Home Secretary's Home and adrenaline shoots down my spine. Underneath, I write Do WE KNOW THE ADDRESS? Gary takes the envelope, draws a rough map of England and Wales then puts a cross where Kent is.

'Wahaay! That's gonna be great. Any other details yet?' I whisper.

'We're having a planning meeting at Ann's house in half an hour or so. Come along.'

There are six M11 regulars and me present for the brainstorm.

'So, what's going to be the hook, the theme of this little outing? We want to get good press for this baby,' says Old Ron. A full two minutes of silence ensues.

'I've got it,' I say, 'You know Michael Howard has got a dodgy past, you know, they say his family were Nazi collaborators. How about we recreate the Nuremburg trials in his front garden and compare the acts of his ancestors with him bringing in the Criminal Justice Bill?' A dozen eyes look blankly back at me. It isn't quite what's required.

'Nice try, but perhaps something a little less controversial might be better.' Gary is being charitable.

Melanie, who I would say is more of a video activist than a digger-diver, comes up with the next suggestion. 'How about a good old English tea party? John Major's always on about good old English values, tea on the lawn and all that. Well, let's show 'em we can do that as well.'

Most heads are nodding. 'You can't get a lot more fluffy than that. Perfect. It'll still embarrass the hell out of Howard, having loads of crusties picnicking on his lawn,' says Jerry, stroking his wild beard. A carpenter who gave up a life in Birmingham to come and live at Claremont, his main role has been to co-ordinate the barricading.

'Well, we can also combine Lester's idea of a human rights trial, the press'll love that.' Gary is one of our best master tacticians and such an asset to the movement.

Ann concludes. 'Now all we have to do is get as many people as possible there. Lester, do you think you could get a coachload together from Manchester?'

'I can have a go.'

As the weeks pass the Criminal Justice Bill is rising up the news agenda. Some of the measures just seem damn spiteful. Five-mile exclusion zones from raves, ordering squatters to vacate within twenty-four hours, the confiscation of people's vehicles. Ok, I can't really give a toss about the last one but it is pretty heavy. Under Section 154 you can even get six months in prison for displaying 'any writing, sign or visible representation which is threatening, abusive or insulting' to cause someone 'harassment, alarm or distress'. Private prisons, police bail – there's so much to choose from that's scary.

The September issue of the Action Update includes a form.

> Dear Mr. Copper,
> I _____ intend to commit an aggravated trespass / attend an illegal gathering / rave / be a traveller. Please arrest me. You may, under the new laws, take crude body samples, but I would rather if you didn't.
> Thank you very much.
> Signed _____

A variety of Freedom Network groups have been set up around the country to oppose the legislation. A crew in Brighton has launched this new paper called SchNEWS. It's only two sheets of A4 each week, not unlike the Sun for lentils. It's a good read – we'll have to see how long it lasts. The Manchester alliance against the bill has been interesting, bringing together disparate groups. By and large free party people don't have the same interests as hunt sabs but now they share common cause. The one group it's really hard to deal with is the hard Left. They really don't operate in the same way as us and can be slightly scary. Don't get me wrong, some of them are fine if you talk one to one, but together they can be rather like the Borg in Star Trek. Despite this, a new alliance is forming. Slowly, tentatively, imperfectly, but it's happening. Talk about the Bill in the office and in the pub increases until the night of the 2nd November – the week before the Bill is due to become law.

Uncharacteristically Dom has already had five pints of lager. 'Look,' he says. 'We've got to do something on Friday. We can't just let it come in and just sit there like saps. We're better than that. This is a shitty law and we've got to ...' The pause is accompanied with a bang on the table. Seven beers swill within their glasses. A crisp packet I'd twisted into a cone shape falls out of the ashtray.

Phil says. 'Has anyone got any ideas then? We've got tomorrow to get something together.'

Five perfectly blank faces sit round the table, but Helen has an idea. 'Well, there is that crane near the Metropolitan University. We've had our eye on that site all summer wondering what we could do with it. Laing's are building something there. They're one of the companies bidding for the next contract for the M65.'

'Now, you know, that's not such a bad idea,' I slur. I've drunk one pint more than everyone else. I arrived on time. 'Now if you must excuse me, I need a waz.'

I've forgotten to mention that Jane and Tango have split. That's the good news. Shame is she's hooked up with this equally hairy guy called Des. It would seem the Criminal Justice Bill isn't the only recent development that is less than fair.

A plan for the crane-sit forms. Jane's up for ringing round the phone tree to round up some bodies, I've agreed to write a press release and Phil says he'll program his fax to transmit it as the action is happening. Dom and Helen are right up for it.

There is much celebration outside the pub as we all go our separate ways. We rejoice as though we've actually defeated the legislation. 'Ok.' As I speak I trip over the kerb. 'Sorry ... does everyone know what they're up to tomorrow? We may not have sales targets and the like in this game, but I think we know a deadline when we see one.'

'You're pissed Lester, we get the message.' Jane gives me a big sloppy kiss. This becomes the main stimulus for a little self-congratulation when I get home, before sleeping like a koala pissed on fermented eucalyptus juice.

Next morning there's a pretty good response to the ring-round including Polly, who's been on the odd action since Abbey Pond and become an honorary EF!er. The uni campaigns office has become the centre of operations for the day and we get to work. Manchester Freedom Network offers to provide ground support and press liaison on the day. A forty-foot piece of white cloth is procured from somewhere and Dom and Helen set to work on painting NO MORE ROADS vertically down its length. Paulo constructs a CJB WON'T STOP ME' banner. Both of these need to have holes made in the corners, the holes reinforced then rope fed through to attach them to the crane.

Time for an early night as we need to be on site first thing. I've lined up two layers of clothing next to my bed, as well as making enough food for a day up a crane.

Neil's got well used to my antics by now. 'Do you think you'll be the first ones to be nicked under the Act?'

'Could be.'

'You're gagging for it aren't you? Five minutes of fame?'

'Yeah, like a crane sit is sooo glamorous. I forgot to extend the invite to all those premieres I get invited to.'

'You know I'm only pulling your pisser, mate. Good luck.'

'Cheers, dude.'

The 5am alarm sounds and with it the usual 'why the fuck am I doing this' feeling. Pushing my Brighton & Hove Albion ski hat onto my head I grab my bike and quietly shut the front door.

We've arranged to meet outside the Royal Northern College of Music but as ever, some are late and there's a bit quite a bit of 'faffing about' – Helen's most overused words. It's a good job we have the element of surprise a lot of the time. A slick military unit we are not. Then again, considering history can be more cock-up than contrivance, I'm sure the SAS have days when things just aren't going their way.

Drizzle is the order of the day and though a couple of hours 'til sunrise it's not going to be the warmest of days. It'll make the crane slippery and us irritable. All the food and drink is piled into one rucksack along with bog roll and carrier bags – our portaloos for the day. We do our best to reassure the two newbies – Des and Millie, who are from the free party scene. Paulo does a recce – there is a security guard in the hut but from a distance he appears to be napping.

'Come on, I'll stay in this position if we don't move soon,' I say having a little shiver on the college step. To those driving down Oxford Road on their way to work we must look like some penniless Hungarian a cappella band.

Nine of us have braved the weather and early hour.

'Polly, I wouldn't wear those mittens when you're climbing.' Dom's doing his usual routine of channelling his pre-action adrenaline into nannying us.

A number 48 bus passes and who should on it but Bender Del. Momentarily forgetting we're in action mode a few of us yip and wave, but then remember why we're here and get professional.

'Make sure that mobile doesn't get lunched out.' Phil's treated the group to some new technology and this is the first crane action I've been where contact with the ground hasn't meant shouting. However, the per-minute tariffs are such that it's really only for receiving press calls.

Dom and Helen are the best climbers so are to go first and last. The rucksack is passed over after Dom. A metal strut about halfway down the other site of the gate acts as a handy footrest. The obstacle itself is easy – the challenge is getting over without disturbing the guard.

Phil stays on the other side to act as press and legal liaison.

Between us and the crane are girders, rubble, the odd random hole and three-quarter darkness, so we can't exactly sprint over. The guard sees us just as most of us are climbing the first section of the superstructure. He runs out and has a good swear but it's too late. We're on.

The first police car arrives about fifteen minutes later, just in time for the unfurling of the banners.

The width of the crane is such we can all fit within about fifteen feet of each other. Dom has gone to the top – two hundred feet up – to set up the impromptu toilet.

'This is just what we need.' Polly's being mum pouring tea from a huge flask into plastic cups. There's no sugar but it's most welcome nonetheless. It's still not sunrise – headlights are still on full beam and few have seen us yet.

'Here's to a good sit,' says Helen. 'Do you think other groups have done the same as us this morning?'

'They've probably got more sense,' says Jane, offering round some ricecakes. It's amazing what you'll eat at 6am one hundred feet in the air with no breakfast inside you.

The crane driver arrives for work, takes a disbelieving look at us then goes into the site compound. As the other workers show they are directed to continue as best they can. We're treated to the occasional wanker sign and shout of 'weirdos' from the floor.

'Does anyone have to go early?' asks Dom. 'If we're going to be strategic we should offer up a couple of people to be arrested early to see if they take the bait.'

'I'm supposed to sign on later,' says Des, who's clearly not a fan of heights.

'Is this our attempt to get the first arrests in the country then? Should we get Phil to contact Norris McWhirter?' I ask. Talking of records the longest crane sit was set earlier in the summer at the M65 at six days, six hours and 38 minutes.

It's resolved there's little to be gained by this being a long crane sit. Two of us are to come down roughly every three hours.

'If we time each one for about ten to the hour it'll tie in with the radio and TV news,' says Paulo. We agree this is an effective if slightly cynical tactic but today is all about media visibility and standing up to the law so we go with it.

At 8.45 we see a radio reporter at the site entrance interviewing police, builders and Phil.

'What do you reckon then, Jane?' says Des. I can sense she wants to hang around but within minutes they're on their way down. We watch as police officers meet them at the bottom and escort them off-site.

'They haven't been nicked. Does that make them lucky or not? I can't work it out,' says Helen.

Dom waves down to catch Phil's attention then sticks out thumb and little finger into a phone shape and holds it up to his head. The mobile rings.

'Hi mate, what's happening? ... Right ... You're joking ... Ok, I'll tell them. Bye.'

'The police are waiting for the full procedures under the Act to be faxed through from the Home Office. 'Til that happens no-one's gonna get arrested.'

We pass an hour with a game of I-Spy, there's quite a lot of variation with the whole Manchester skyline to pick from. Quite a few people beep their car horns in support and there's a small crowd at the fence who've come along for moral support. I can clearly see Tim, who was supposed to be up here. Must have got pissed and/or stoned instead.

A policeman with a flat hat and loudhailer comes to the bottom of the crane and shouts something inaudible at us. We speculate as to what he's saying.

'Perhaps he's ordered us a pizza,' says Millie, who's clearly enjoying herself.

'How many times have I told him we're not getting married,' Paulo says to some amusement.

The mobile rings again. Apparently the announcement was our formal warning to quit the site.

'But we didn't hear it. Does that count as a defence?' says Dom flippantly.

'Not from today it doesn't. They're just really playing it by the book – now it's arrived,' I say.

'Ok, looks like the cop shop's open for business. Does anyone want to get down?' asks Dom.

Polly says: 'If it's alright with you I'd like to get it out of the way. The kids'll be wondering where I am,'

Helen offers to go with her and they descend to much cheering from above and below. They are 'cuffed at the bottom and led to a van. Although unable to wave they turn just as the back doors are opened. My eyesight isn't all that great but I swear I can make out two huge smiles.

'There you go – the youth of Britain have risen up against this law and who's the first person to get nicked? A fifty-year-old mother of two,' says Millie.

I've borrowed Middlemarch from Jane but it's virtually impossible to immerse myself in polite eighteenth century English society whilst surrounded by the sound of welding, riveting and concrete mixers. Wrapped up snug in an army-surplus khaki coat/sleeping bag, Paulo has no such trouble with his book, The Monkeywrench Gang by Edward Abbey. The subject matter is beyond appropriate.

I put my book down and attend to a more pressing matter. Climbing two hundred feet for a dump is a surreal experience. The carrier bag is reasonably full – and thankfully has no holes in it. I decide to treat myself to a fresh one. Baring your backside to the whole of Manchester is both embarrassing and liberating all at once, but the necessity of it all overcomes any passing emotion. It's also quite a tricky manoeuvre to position yourself over the bag then remain sufficiently balanced to wipe. If in a standing position one hand should always be on crane itself, which can make things interesting. Thankfully in this instance there's a little platform next to the driver's cab providing relative safety.

'The BBC studio is only three hundred yards down the road and still there's no sign of them. Bastards,' I say. They can whistle for the TV licence money this year. Neil will really appreciate another futile stance from me.

It's decided that me and Millie should be next to come down. Dom and Paulo are the best climbers and can take down the banners and collect all the tat. There's enough food for them to have a handsome supper too.

'How about just before the nine o'clock news mate?' Dom says to a nodding Paulo.

The four of us share a hug before we head down to more cheers. After all the fuss made about aggravated trespass in the last few months it's almost a relief to hear it being used in the caution.

We're all released from Platt Lane station the next morning. There's a small crowd to welcome us but Nelson Mandela's release from Robben Island it ain't. There's a distinct lack of journalists, it's like you have to write the fucking story for them to cover it.

On the way back to Phil's for a debrief we pick up a copy of the Guardian. On page three the headline is 'Cambridge hunt sabs first to be arrested under Criminal Justice Act'.

'Bloody liars. We were first.' I'm rather put out that our achievement has not been recognised.

Phil is more stoical about it. 'The press office of the Hunt Saboteurs Association is probably a bit more on the ball than we were last night.'

'Absolutely storming picture. Look at this.' Dom points at the next page. There's some of the M11 gang on the House of Commons roof with a banner.

'Yeah, that's great but where's our coverage?'

'Oooo, looks like someone's jealous,' says Phil.

'While you're being so fucking righteous will someone put the kettle on, I feel like shit.'

What with everything going on, organising a coach for the Michael Howard action has proved a bridge too far, but we have got a minibus of fifteen sorted. On a frosty November morning, our bleary-eyed but happy band set out for a Saturday on the south coast. Advertised as a Magical Mystery Tour, only those present at the planning meeting know the nature of the action, along with Dom and Phil, whom I tell down the pub after a semi-heavy session.

The arranged meeting point is the Burger King store at Thurrock Services at noon. Along the 221 miles of motorway we see the odd traveller van, bus and ambulance we assume is headed to the same destination. We join possibly the least typical group of vehicles in a Burger King car park in history. There is a police presence but it's minimal enough to suggest they don't know what's going on. A hunt sab van containing the Leeds crew comes rolling in without a windscreen. It's been a very crisp, clear morning and the gang are more than cold.

'A stone shattered the glass around Sheffield. We've been huddling together for warmth ever since,' says Lindsey.

Clive shivers vigorously in the driver's seat, unable to share in such sociable heat exchange on the way down. We examine the damage, trying to disguise our mirth with sympathy.

The London posse have arranged three coachloads, complete with paid drivers. I go to Gary, who is looking, as always, burnt out but buzzing with it.

'Where did you tell the coach companies you were going?'

'There's a small animal sanctuary next to Howard's house, so I said we were off to the zoo.' Yet again Gary's logistical skills are A1.

On the way down the M2 virtually every vehicle in the convoy is stopped, but the trespassory assembly part of the CJA isn't used.

Our bus is pulled over around Egerton, halfway between Thurrock and Lympne. Dom slows down and pulls onto the hard shoulder.

Thankfully David, one of the new EF! freshers has stopped making pig faces and squealing by the time the police reach us.

A cop with a large mole above his right eye knocks on the driver's window. 'Good afternoon, and may I ask you where you're going?'

'A wedding in Kent. Is there anything wrong?'

He peers into the back of the bus. 'Not as yet. Just make sure there isn't. Have you got the legal number of passengers in this vehicle? It looks rather full.'

'No, officer. This is licensed to carry fifteen, and that's how many we've got.'

Defeated, the cop fishes for information once more. 'Where did you say you were going again? It slipped my mind.'

'Kent.'

'Oh.'

Five seconds of silence is beginning to be broken by laughter from the back. Dom sits poker-faced, waiting for a response.

Without uttering another word, the policeman makes an 'off you go' hand gesture and our quest is back on.

Only known and trusted drivers have been given a map of how to get to the zoo and the operation has been watertight thus far. Before long the winding Kentish country lanes are full of vans and buses which have mostly seen better days. There is a solitary constabulary squad car at the corner of the lane by the zoo.

'They really haven't got a clue. This is gonna be fun,' I say as we pile out and are handed directions for Howard's house.

The excitement starts to build. Whether he's there or not there's going to be a bit of payback for the cunt who's caused us a lot of grief. A heightened level of pre-action adrenaline plays my spine like a silent xylophone. Dom starts running in the direction of a big hill in the mid-distance. 'Follow me, it's just up ahead.'

The old feeling of adrenaline freefalls down me once again.

'This is great, this is fucking great,' I say, gasping for air. Not playing as much football as he should have done in recent times has taken its toll.

As we reach the crest of the hill, yips, cheers, whistles, and general revelry is clearly audible. A few more steps and the scene reveals itself to us. A hundred or so are already in the garden, a quarter of a mile away.

The house isn't as grand as I expected but has a lovely big roof to sit on, and indeed a couple of people were already up there. I let out a long yip and press on, feeling more alive than I have for a good while.

Once in the garden, it's time to meet new people, laugh with old friends and take the piss out of Michael Howard. I also pause to think how half a dozen people, who were already busy with other things, can plan and execute something as ornate as this action. The icing on the cake is that next to the patio doors at the side of the house stands a lone policeman – yes, that's one, one less than two cops – his only back-up a German Shepherd.

Reinforcements arrive, but not before hundreds more pile over the hill, including a good few photographers and journalists from the Sunday papers.

Clive, who knows his DIY after running a housing co-op for a few years, says Howard's roof has got dodgy pointing.

It would seem that the host isn't here – or he's hiding in the cellar. Despite this the transformation of his garden into a party zone is in full swing.

Some of the London posse are hanging garlands and messages from schoolchildren from the trees.

I ask Gary about them and he replies: 'We've got a woman on the campaign who's a teacher. She asked her class to write them during pastoral one morning.

'Now if you'd excuse me,' he says pulling the aerial up on his mobile phone, affecting an upper-class accent, 'I must ring the Times, old boy.'

I read one of the messages.

> Dear Mr. Howard, I know you have a country to run, and that is very important, but please think again about the Criminal Justice Act. The people that it will punish are gentle people. They don't mean anyone any harm. If you want a gentle country with less crime and more happiness, you should work with these people, not against them. Jenny Potter (Aged 14).

I hear the sound of running water coming from behind a rhododendron. There's Sparko, bottle of cider in one hand, cock in the other. 'Hey man, I'd love to piss on him, but his garden'll have to do,' he says unsteadily though with more lucidity than usual.

'Too right, mate, go for it, but be careful you don't get nicked.'

By now there's about four hundred or more partygoers and about half that many police, virtually all in riot gear. It would seem getting reinforcements out on a Saturday isn't easy.

A banner is unfurled across the front of the house.

INJUSTICE IS NOT ANONYMOUS. IT HAS A NAME AND ADDRESS
Bertolt Brecht

A small sound system appears. If the collective noun for ravers is a 'having it' then this would apply to what is unfolding this afternoon.

In one corner there's a jam session with guitars, digeridoos, penny whistles and bongos. As it's a special occasion I'm willing to forgive the dreadful sound the latter three usually produce.

There are picnic blankets and from the odd basket teacups and cucumber sandwiches are produced.

I join Claire and Nick chilling in deck chairs, looking away from the house towards the Weald. 'It's a nice view, wasted on you-know-who,' she says.

A middle-aged man overhears her and approaches, tracing at the horizon. 'A bypass is due to go right through that lot.'

'Not if we can fucking help it,' I say.

As the partying reaches its loudest, the yips and whistles – though loud and high register – are drowned out as a police helicopter rises from behind the house, flying very low, only fifty feet or so above the balaclava'ed folks on the roof.

'Woah! It's like something from a Vietnam film or the storming of an embassy, not deepest Kent on a Sunday afternoon,' says Nick.

Such militaristic manoeuvres are a clear signal that it's time to go. A verbal message goes round to this effect and the litter-picking teams start their job. People collect their tat and the legal observers attempt to smooth things over with the clearly agitated police.

Gary says to the commanding officer that so long as those on the roof can get down without arrest everyone will start to leave. He reluctantly agrees and it's time to walk back up the slope that four hours earlier I'd sprinted down with such zeal.

Dom asks Corinne, a woman who's been to a couple of EF! meetings but never been on an action before, what she thought of it all.

'Blinding, the best thing I've ever done. I never thought I'd get such a buzz.' It's heartening to hear it's not just me that loves it – else I'd think I was quite mad.

We all dwell on similar thoughts and retell our favourite parts of the day on the journey back north, a trip quite a few of us have made rather a lot recently.

'Are you sure this is the real thing this time? There's been so many false alarms,' I ask. Helen says no. She's received intelligence that finally, after eighteen months of waiting and experiencing some very mad things in the process, Claremont Road is finally to be evicted. There'd been mutterings to this effect at the Michael Howard action, but these were unsubstantiated reports as ever. Until now this has been the eviction that cried wolf.

'Apparently all Metropolitan Police rugby and football matches are cancelled this week.' Helen's been told this by a vaguely reliable source.

'That's as good an indicator as any. Let's stoke some interest up then.' We split the phone tree in two and try and raise as many bodies as possible.

Through the national grapevine Phil has already heard.

'What do you reckon then, are you going?'

'Too bloody right, I haven't been to Claremont at all yet, this is my last chance I suppose.'

The network swings into action. Mini-buses are hired, lifts, pick-ups and hitches arranged. As always, the biggest pain with direct action is actually getting everyone to where the action is.

It is ironic to travel up and down Britain's motorways in order to prevent the building of another one but it's just a matter of course for us now. Four and a half hours later, door to door, we arrive at a Claremont Road on full battle alert. The vibe is so, so different to the laid-back party/protest atmosphere of the summer before. There is, however, still some dossing and lunching out to be done. A woman lies in a huge cargo net strung across the street.

'Exhausting work up there, eh?' Jane calls up to her.

'Too right – getting myself acclimatised for later. Just having a rest, I've just arrived.'

'Where from?'

'Have you heard of Christiania? In Copenhagen?'

'No way?'

'I'm Sandy. Pleased to meet you all. Have a great time.'

We go to the office and find Gary putting the finishing touches to the master plan in deep discussion with Ann who has, a few weeks before, been featured in a Sunday newspaper as an '... eco–warrior, or rather eco–waif, with long blond hair and delicate paper–like skin'. I've read the piece and have been dying to take the piss out of her.

'So, how goes? I'd have thought you'd be too busy on photo shoots being delicate to stay for this?'

'Shove it up your arse,' she replies.

We decide it's best to leave them to it so take some of the M11 virgins on a little tour, taking in delights such as the rubbled remains of Leytonstone High Road. So far 350 houses have been destroyed.

SCHOOL. WORK. DEATH. WHY? is scrawled across a fence. Quite.

At Whipps Cross roundabout the graffiti says CARS POULOUT YOU + YOUR CHILDREN'.

'This lot can sit cranes with the best of them, but their spelling leaves much to be desired,' says Helen. There is some laughter from the newly initiated like Corinne and David, but their reaction is mostly wonderment. Claremont, for all its faults, is without exaggeration the most bizarre and phenomenal thing any of them has ever seen.

On some of the site fences are posted injunction notices.

Tim attempts to read the first paragraph. 'The defendants do forthwith be restrained whether acting by himself slash herself, his slash her servants or agents otherwise however from taking control of, using and slash or occupying or attaching themselves to other items onto goods and slash or chattels in the plaintiff's respective ownership and slash or possession which are used (whether actively or otherwise) for the purposes of construction of the Link Road (as defined in the Statement of Claim therein) and which are situated on the land.'

'What the fuck does that mean?' Paulo expresses what everyone else is thinking as we stand in the chilly early afternoon air.

'I think,' Helen says in matter-of-fact terms, 'that playing with the machinery is naughty, and if these named people are seen doing so, they'll get sent to bed for a while without any tea.'

Corinne – who's a fresher reading English – is baffled. 'Why can't they just say that? This takes half an hour to digest and even then you still don't know what it says. We should send it to the Campaign for Plain English.'

Abba's What's The Name Of The Game? rings out from Old Ron's house as we return to Claremont, and the game at hand is definitely feverish preparation. At times the music is drowned out by banging, swearing, sawing, shouting and the loudest sound on the entire street – Ann's angle grinder cutting scaffold poles for the tower, which is approaching a height of fifty feet above the roof of the house it's perched on. She isn't looking quite so delicate now, although, climbing such a precarious structure a hundred feet in the air takes a fair amount of natural grace.

Carpenter Jerry, looking pale and drawn with purple rings around his eyes, is running around looking for labourers. I volunteer along with most of the Manchester contingent and we're led into a basement.

'Forgive me, Jerry,' says Corinne, 'but you don't look well.' His reddish beard gives the rest of his face even less colour.

'This is what two nights without sleep does to you. I wouldn't recommend it,' he says releasing a huge yawn. 'What I want you lot to do is to start stacking these up in this room.' He points out of the window and one storey above there are three or four hundred dirty, mostly water-filled tyres.

'I'd like to see them bulldoze their way through that lot,' he adds.

We form a human conveyor belt and spend three hours shifting them down a flight of stairs, across the room and arranging them from skirting board to ceiling.

There's so much to do, but once in a while you have to stop for a few seconds and take it all in. Up on the roof sparks are still flying around Ann's welding mask. A huge LET LONDON BREATHE banner has been tied to the tower.

Gary is also showing the strain, as are most. He puts down his own welding torch, takes a bite of a sandwich and stops to chat.

'I bet you'll be pleased when it's all over won't you?' I ask, partially empathising with how he's feeling, but I've not been tied to one campaign for eighteen months. I can't possibly understand what he's going through.

'I'd be a liar if I said it won't be a relief when the street goes, but of course, we've all had some unforgettable times. Somehow, the bad stuff tends to get lost up here.' He points to his short mop of blonde hair.

'You're starting to sound really cheesy. I suppose you'll be saying it's like the Blitz next.'

'It's funny you should say that. Dolly said something like that a few times. I'm glad she's not going to be here for the eviction, but I wish she'd be able to see the last stand. They put her in a home last month. Bastards.'

'That's rough.'

'Do you know what she said on the day they took her out? If she was the Queen she'd give us all knighthoods. I'm not usually one for weepy moments, but that was something special.'

Climbing around the tower isn't too bad, rather like scaling a home-made crane. However, whilst swinging round one of the poles, it slips quite considerably, and it's all I can do to stop myself falling to the street below. Counting my blessings and I quickly inform Ann that it needs tightening.

I go to find Jerry and ask him if there are any action roles other than the tower.

'It's funny you should say that. There is something I think will appeal to you.'

'Oh yeah what's that?'

Even though we're pretty much alone, Jerry reaches over and whispers the word 'bunkers' into my ear.

'Oh right. I take it you need volunteers for them, eh?'

'One or two. The people who made them are also keen to go in.'

I stand for a moment contemplating what to say. I think about what Claremont means to me, and what I'm prepared to give in defence of the place. 'Yeah, sure I will. Is it built for one?'

'No. That wouldn't be too hot an idea. They'll be enough food for two. Find someone who you get on with and make sure neither of you suffers from claustrophobia.'

I go to find a cohabitee – there isn't exactly a shortage of people on the ground. The light is by now fading, and there is upwards of six hundred people on the street. At the far end of the street Clive is working on his lock-on built into the road. The tarmac has been pickaxed out and adapted metal arm tubes sunk into the holes. The design of the lock–on has moved on quite considerably since the days of Abbey Pond.

'That looks comfy.'

'Actually Lester, it's not that bad. Give it a try if you like.'

'No ta, I've already put myself right in it saying I'll do something else.'

Helen and Paulo are chatting next to the ladder that leads up to the office. Having Helen in the bunker will drive me mad in ten minutes, but I think Paulo will be an ok cellmate.

'How do either of you two want a really challenging part in the eviction? Something to get the old blood rushing.'

'What are you up to this time?' Helen says with a three-quarter smile. Paulo is listening intently.

'It's nothing I've done. It's already set up. All they need are people to ... sit there.'

'Where? Excuse my cynicism here, but with your track record ...' Helen's fluffy side is peeking through again.

'That's charming. Alright, here's the story. There's two or three bunkers built below the street. Looks as though they're surrounded by rooms of tyres, so even if the houses got bulldozed, I think we'll be ok.' The lack of evidence I have to support such a claim is minimal, verging on negligible, even negligent.

Helen says: 'What do you mean, we? Count me out, I'm claustrophobic. Give me the tower any day.'

'Paulo, how about it, me old mucker?' I know he loves the buzz of mad actions just as much as me and has the balls to pull it off.

'I want to see the bunker before I say yes or no,' he says.

'Fair enough, mate. I haven't seen it myself yet. It might be under three feet of water for all I know.' Paulo gives me a funny look. 'I'm joking!'

We go to find Jerry putting finishing touches to the tyre room.

'What the fuck do you want?' He's clearly growing more stressed and freaked out by the minute. He needs some sleep. A week's worth.

'We're interested in bunker duty. D'you want to give us a guided tour?'

Jerry gives us a good look to see if we're worthy to inhabit his pride and joy, then beckons with a bloodstained finger, cut by steel mesh jutting out of the perished tyres.

He leads us down to the basement. Then with a crowbar he removes three innocuous-looking floorboards. Below this lies a trap door. It's no more than a foot by a foot and a half. Jerry opens this and just about squeezes his hips through the hole and climbs down the ladder and we follow.

Five foot by six, it is the boxroom from hell. I'm struck by how tall it is, but this is an optical illusion caused by being so tiny. The only way all three of us can be in there at once is for me to hang on the ladder. 'So this place has to hold the two of us for God knows how long?'

'I know it's not exactly Five Star but it's taken me five weeks to build this little beauty. There's a shelf for your food and water and a hook for the toilet bag. Oh yeah, and you'll be linked via intercom with a central communication point away from the street. You're Brown One when you speak into it. Got that? What are you?'

'Brown One. I think we've got that under control.'

'Nice one.' I look around the room then at Paulo. He seems as undecided as I am.

'What do you reckon then?' I ask.

'How many days food will we get?'

'We've prepared bunker packs. Should last you seven days. And enough bog roll for a week too,' Jerry adds with an afterthought and a smile.

Paulo nods and claps his hands together. 'Sure Jerry, leave this to us. You won't be sorry.'

There's still quite a bit of preparation to do, but it feels better now I know what my role is to be. The food pack is lowered down and we kit it out with tat from around the street to make it more comfortable, nay bearable. We line the floor with some polyurethane cushions taken from an old settee. They're thick and warm but also highly flammable.

'Right, well if we're gonna spend the week down here, we'd better leave now and come back when we've got to.' Paulo's right.

Back up on the roof spirits are high. Tez is banging out tunes on his guitar. He's just finished It Must Be Love by Madness. All the old faces are there from around the country. Claire, Nick and Steve are huddled up one end. Mark's trying out his roof lock-on. Des and Jane are being interviewed by a woman with a video camera – one of a dozen or so journalists on the roof. Phil and Corinne huddle together at the foot of the tower. There's been a fair bit of speculation about the relationship status of the two. Beech and Helen are also similarly cuddled together. Ann and her bloke are sharing a double sleeping bag and a spliff. Although in many ways it is a poor decision for one activist to go out with another, it is quite a common occurrence.

Time is a thief and the final days of the street are being stolen away. Built just before the turn of the century, the houses won't survive to see the turn of the next. At 10pm an announcement is made to the crowds – the hundred or two on the tower and roofs, and the many, many more that are on the ground, in the trees and hidden away. Two huge fires blaze away, keeping the masses warm.

From the tower Gary says through a megaphone. 'Good evening everyone, and thank you very much for making the effort to come out tonight. This is it, the eviction – the end of Claremont Road. However, this is not the end of the struggle against the M11 Link Road, or indeed the whole roads programme. It is only the end of the beginning. In the next few days many of us will face danger and adversity, but that prospect isn't as scary as our communities being paved and driven on. With every small defeat we are closer to an overall victory. Last week Brian Mawhinney, the transport secretary said, and I quote, "There should be a ceasefire in the shouting and insults and more discussion with environmental groups." Seems to me like we've got them running scared. Let's give 'em hell. There have been several, as yet unconfirmed tip-offs saying the eviction is due to begin in sixteen hours time – at 2pm. There is no guarantee that this information is correct. They may come in at any time. I wish you all the best and would like to dedicate this eviction to Dolly Watson, who alas cannot be here tonight. There'll be people on watch, so I suggest you get a few hours' rest.'

As the speech and the resulting questions draw to a close, one tune is played. A 10K rig pumps out The Prodigy's Outer Space from the tower, and most upon it attempt to dance without falling off.

And then it all falls quiet. Three hours before the biggest battle the movement has yet faced. There's some muffled conversation, some laughter, some late night drinking. On the whole, however, people sleep and dream weird dreams of the days to come, or failing sleep, they sit quietly with their own thoughts – of what the night will bring as the state comes to take back its territory.

'They're coming!' someone shouts.

'No they're not, you fucking dickhead. Go to sleep,' comes from the street.

Paulo and I do a dry run of getting into the bunker to see how long it'll take to put the floorboards back, shut the trap door and secure it with a steel bar and chains.

'Three minutes give or take. That should be ok. They're not going to get right through all the rest of them by then,' Paulo says. I nod in agreement.

We try out the intercom. It's linked by a wire right out of the street – a stupendous feat of engineering. I squeeze the trigger on the handheld mic. 'Brown One to Base, do you read me?'

'Reading you loud and clear. Are you ok?'

'Yeah we're just testing and will sign off now. Don't want to hog the channels.'

'There's only one channel, but you'll be able to talk to other points on the street. For security reasons I can't tell you what, but listen out for Dolly, Brown Two, Brown Three and Green One.'

'That's a big ten-four.'

'You what?'

'Sorry, yeah, I get it, I'm getting a bit carried away with the old CB radio jargon.'

Paulo grabs the mike. 'Hello, I'm one of the other people in Brown One.' Paulo's sharp. He knows base will know there's only two of us but anyone listening in wouldn't.

'What's your name?'

'Paulo.' Maybe he's not as sharp as I thought. 'And yours?'

'As far as this transmission is concerned, I'm Mother Goose.' It's beginning to sound like something from a spy novel, but here we are living it in real time.

'Ok Mother Goose, signing off now, speak to you later.'

We go to get some fresh air up on the roof and the rave is back in full swing. It's 1.30am, time to say our goodbyes before we go to ground for good.

'Good luck, me old mucker, I know we haven't always seen eye to eye,' I say to Tango.

'Don't get all maudlin on us now, this is going to be fun.' Although cold, tired and – if he's human missing Jane like crazy – he's buzzing. I've not seen him like this before. We embrace. There may have been times when I've thought and said all sorts and indeed meant it – and I have it on good authority he thought I was a laddish twat. But at the end of the day we did respect, even love each other in a strange way.

Corinne's looking scared. 'Don't worry, Phil's right, it's so going to be fun. Actions don't get much bigger or better.' Reassured slightly she kisses me on the cheek.

I go to wish Gary all the best too. Everyone's rushing around to give some love. It's a bit like the minute after midnight on New Year's Eve.

'Have a good'un. I want you to know you're been the worst activist I've ever seen,' he says giving me a huge hug.

'Same applies to you, bum lord.'

'Anyway, you'd best take position, it's ten to two. See you whenever.'

Just as Paulo and I climb back into our house, there's a huge cry: 'They're here!' At the end of the street row upon row of riot police can be dimly seen, marching down the road fifty abreast. Wearing similarly militaristic yet different uniforms, legions of bailiffs follow. Opposition forces far too many to count.

'Oh shit.' I freeze for a moment.

'Quick, let's get down below.' Three minutes later we're sealed into just over two hundred cubic feet of space.

'Brown One, are you in position?'

'Yeah. Everything's fine.'

'Mother Goose to Dolly, come in.'

'This is Dolly.'

'How are you?'

'This is totally wicked. What a sight.' Gary's voice is unmistakable.

'Brown Two?'

'Present'

'Brown Three?'

'We're fine.'

'Green One?'

'Fine.' It's Ann. There have been rumours of underground tunnels from the street to the outside. I've a sneaky feeling this is Green One.

'Hello, Green One, this is Brown One. If your hideout is what I think it is you're fucking insane.'

'You might be right, you never know. It is a bit mad in here.' For an eco-waif with paper-white skin, she really does have a lot of guts.

Life in the bunker is more pleasant for Paulo and I than it may have been for Hitler, although it's a pretty close call. Both of us are quite tall, and there's not enough room to fully stretch our legs. Good mates though we are, conversation runs a bit thin after about three hours. Paulo has in his possession a handheld medium-wave radio, and each hour we tune in for the news. It's Budget Day, and the focus is on the impact of the Chancellor's speech.

'Fucking bastard. Ten pee on fags. How dare he?' I laugh at my cellmate's forthcoming economic misfortune.

'Serve you right, you should try and give up.'

'Who are you, my mother? Anyway, stop talking about smoking, I'm desperate for a puff.'

'You're not bloody smoking, there's little enough air in here as it is.'

'You just farted. That's using up the air. Why can't I?'

'As time goes on we'll have less and less food and so we'll fart less ... Anyway, that's no argument. You're not smoking in here and that's fucking final. Ok?'

We fell silent. Outside tunes bang on. Occasionally there are screams, and cries of 'scum!' 'you bastard!', 'Nazis!', and even the odd 'what right have you got to do that!?'

Suddenly there's a huge commotion. So much so the music is drowned out. Something is definitely wrong.

'What the hell is that?'

'Brown One to base. What's happening.'

'Not too sure. Dolly ... Dolly? Base to Dolly.'

The radio falls silent. Finally after a second or two a signal comes back.

'Hello base, this is Dolly. All I can say is I'm sickened. There was a woman up in the netting. They put a digger underneath her and tried to cut her loose – to the point where she's hanging on by one hand. Then she fell and her head hit the road. She's not moving.'

'Is she ok?'

'To be honest – and I don't want to freak you out – but she looks dead from up here. They aren't even going to see if she's alive. This is fucking unbelievable.'

My thoughts turn to our arrival yesterday, and the happy picture of Sandy lying in the nets.

'Brown One to Dolly, do you read me?'

'Yes, mate, make it quick though.'

'Alright, who fell? Any details?'

'No. All I know is she's got dark hair, and she's not moving.'

'If you get to know any more, let us know.'

'Sure thing.'

The shouts and screams don't subside. Even in our muffled bunker it sounds like a full-scale riot out on the street. Then the electric light which has sustained us goes dead. We scrabble around for the candles in the food bag but find no matches. Suddenly it's a very good thing that Paulo is a smoker.

Another couple of hours pass and things seem to quieten down. Dolly has radioed to say that the woman's been taken away in an ambulance. Apparently she's alive, but serious injury can't be ruled out. Paulo and I have our first meal, a jam sandwich and half and apple each, washed down with a couple of mouthfuls of orange squash.

'Cheers, mate,' says Paulo holding up his plastic beaker

'Up your bum. Not literally of course.'

'No offence, but it'd be really nice to be in this bunker with a beautiful girl, you know.'

'None taken,' I reply. 'But what kind of woman would want to be down here?'

'A really cool one.'

'Where is she? Wheel her in.'

'She's not turned up, I'm afraid. But she'll be out there somewhere. One for both of us.'

'She's probably out there doing something perfectly ordinary at the moment, but she's anything but, and she will be mine.'

'Mine's probably out there doing something other than hanging off a fucking roof. I'm not saying they're all like it – far from it, but I'm not a big one for hairy armpits, piercings, tats and dreadlocks. We certainly aren't born with the last three and if a woman asked me to cut the hair under my arms I'd certainly oblige. If it got me some.'

With such fanciful exchanges we pass the time. It's 6.15am.

'Hello, Brown One?'

'Yes'

'This is base. We've lost contact with Brown Three – not sure why. We've news of the woman in the nets.'

'Go on.'

'It was a Danish woman called Sandy. She's not very badly hurt, but is being kept in overnight for observation.'

The radio news at midnight is pretty much unchanged from the news at eleven, but is still a link with the outside world. It's then my turn to get some sleep, but not before having my first poo in the carrier bag.

'Oh, do you have to? That'll bloody stink the place out,' says Paulo.

'Look, it's better in the bag than in my pants, eh?'

'Just about.'

'Anyway, quit moaning. You'll have to shit before we get out of here.'

'Maybe. I'm trying to avoid it.'

I fall into deep sleep and dream of floating high above the street – sitting on a cloud locked onto a purple buddha. Not only is it surreal but it makes no sense whatsoever. I could be wrong but am pretty sure Denise Van Outen is just about to join me in a naked protest as I wake up with a start.

Paulo's sitting next to me staring at the opposite wall, eyes just about open.

'I'm glad you're awake – it stops your fucking snoring for one thing. I'm going to try and get some shuteye. Do you fancy keeping watch for a couple of hours?'

'Ok, but I'm sure I don't snore.'

Paulo turns over and there's no audible response from him, save for a quiet snore of his own.

In the next three hours I quietly play with the radio frequencies, chat to base and Ann, and Gary in the Tower and to top it all have a piss in the carrier bag on the hook. Mainly though just trying to keep positive. Focusing on why I'm here.

At 3am there's no radio contact, and not just with base. no-one is there. The wires have obviously been cut. They must be close.

Four more hours. I think we've passed the 24-hour period now. I'm just about to fall asleep again myself when I hear voices directly above my head. Several hours ago a couple of people from the tower came to check if we were ok but these voices aren't familiar, not even in type. I hear the sound of wood straining against itself and floorboards being removed.

'Oh shit, Paulo, wake up, mate.' He already is.

Both of us grab onto the bar held by the chains in anticipation of everything coming down on us. Bangs from a sledgehammer rain down but it remains solid.

'How many bailiffs does it take to smash a piece of wood!?' I shout.

'I don't know. How many bailiffs does it take to smash a piece of wood?' replies my comic foil.

'Not enough at the moment. Keep trying, suckers!' We laugh maniacally, probably more though fear than amusement.

It doesn't take long for us to realise the trapdoor is no ordinary piece of wood.

'It must be some sort of wood and metal sandwich,' says Paulo.

'Yeah. Jerry did an amazing job.'

We can hear crowbarring and the unmistakable sound of a circular saw in place of the hammers which haven't been very effective up 'til now.

'Soon have you out of there, boys,' we hear from above. 'By the way, how many of you are there down there?'

'This tunnel goes right down, there must be fifty of us in here.'

'We'll believe you, son, thousands wouldn't,' comes the reply, before the sawing and hacking starts up again.

For another hour and a half the bailiffs struggle with the trap door.

Paulo shouts: 'My arm, you're cutting my fucking arm! Stop it! Stop it!' The second 'it' becoming a bloodcurdling and highly convincing scream of pain.

'Get your arm away from the fucking trap door then and it won't hurt.'

'Never, you motherfuckers. Your father is a motherfucker and so are you. You all deserve to die.' More demented laughter. Paulo loves this and I mostly have faith that he's not losing the plot.

Earlier on I explained the rules of Desert Island Discs and we selected our tunes. Among Paulo's was I Never Gave Up by Chumbawamba. He starts to sing the chorus from it repeatedly in a high-pitched voice. 'I never gave up! I never gave up! I crawled in the mud but I never gave up!' Again and again. Louder and louder, higher and higher. After a quarter of an hour or so it's starting to do my brains in but it is loud enough to drive those above to distraction. I happen to quite like Chumbawamba. The same probably can't be said whoever is above us.

Light starts to filter through the trap door for the first time in thirty hours or so. The gap is sufficient to potentially get quite a lot of leverage with a crowbar. I put my fingers in the way. The bar is pulled out. A pair of eyes replace it in the gap.

'Look, if you do that again you're going to lose them, you stupid prat.' The voice is offering practical if not friendly advice. Losing a couple of fingers might be very worthy, but the experience would lose its sheen very quickly. As I withdraw my hand, the crowbarring restarts immediately. It's not going to take long to get through it now.

With our enemy directly above us now, all planning has to be done with whispers. 'What the fuck are we going to do?' says Paulo.

'I think we've had it, to be honest. What have we got – twenty minutes?'

'Come on, think. We've got creativity on our side. Makes us ten times better than them. I've got it.' Paulo's convinced he has the answer. 'They haven't seen us yet so they don't know how big we are. Quick, grab the cushions and shove them up your coat.' There are indeed four cushions and we do have baggy coats. It is a struggle to get the foam in and fasten the coats. I haul at Paulo's zip and vice versa. All the time the trapdoor is giving its last few moments of valiant struggle. A quick check to see that none of the foam is showing through and we're ready. I'm not convinced they're going to fall for it but it might buy us some time.

We step back to the sides of the bunker when it is obvious that the door is going to smash. It falls down between us, with Paulo narrowly avoiding concussion. Harsh fluorescent light floods in and a range of police, bailiff and security heads peer into the hole, only to see two sumo-like figures looking back them. I'm hoping they can't see us too clearly.

One of the riot police speaks: 'Evening, lads. My name's Dave and I'm responsible for getting you out safely.' He has MP5 in yellow lettering on his helmet.

'Well you're going to have your work cut out. We've been down here for three days eating nothing but lard. There's no way you're going to get us out,' says Paulo keeping a straightish face.

'I'm going to give you a little time to think over your options.' Whether through exasperation or puzzlement Dave leaves us to it. Save for a solitary security guard, the two of us are left alone. I pick up a fragment of the ex-trapdoor and pocket it as a memento.

'Give me five,' says Paulo. 'I'm gonna get some shuteye.'

Five are given and yips hollered before Paulo gets his head down.

I look up at the guard. 'What's the score?'

'Dunno really, I know the police aren't too impressed to see you and your mate being as big as you are. We were hoping to get you out and then go for another of the bunkers. I'm covering while they most of them change shift.'

'How long have you got left?'

'Eight hours. I hate it in here. Really I sympathise with you lot, but hey.'

'Why are you doing it then?'

'I'm trying to get some cash together to get my little girl something for Christmas. She's got really bad asthma, and I've been on the dole all year.'

'Surely there's something else you can do?'

'Come on, you know what it's like. Are you on the dole?'

'Yeah.' Not that I've really looked, but I appreciate it can seem like decent jobs don't grow on trees.'

'Do you smoke, mate?'

'No. Nice to meet you though. Lester,' I tell him. I climb onto the first rung of the ladder and stretch my hand out to the guard.

'Colin.'

'And you. Do you want an orange?'

'Are you sure? Have you got much food?'

'Yeah, go on. We've been light eaters, despite how we look right now. I promise it's not poisoned.' Colin laughs and gratefully takes the fruit.

We talk of the relative fortunes of West Ham and Brighton until Paulo wakes up dying for a cigarette. Colin obliges. With the trapdoor open it's more acceptable to smoke, but it still irks me somewhat.

'How long have you been in there now?'

'I don't know, what's the time now?'

'Eight in the morning, more or less.'

After a quick bit of mental arithmetic I declare with some amazement, 'Jesus, that's forty-two hours.'

'Fucking 'ell, I don't envy you. Twelve-hour shifts are bad enough, and I'm getting paid.'

'Yeah I know, tell me about it.' Paulo's financial state is seldom less than parlous.

Within the hour the police and bailiffs reappear. Dave reacquaints himself. 'Good evening, gentlemen. May I come down and join you?'

'No, fuck off.' Paulo is intent on defending our advantage. I'm very committed to this action, but for Paulo it's deeper and intensely personal. Him against the Met. I just hope it doesn't end up like a sticker in the M11 office which says 'I've met the Met, and I've got the bruises to prove it'.

'Very clever, son, but that doesn't really answer my question. I promise you here and now, if I come down, I won't try and remove you. Ok?'

'What do you reckon?' I ask Paulo.

'No. We've got to hang on. Every minute is more cash we're costing them. Thousands.'

Dave interjects, 'Come on, lads. You've made a good show of yourselves. What you've done is really brave and there are people up here, including myself, who respect that, but it's time to call this quits and have a bath, a decent kip and some food.'

'We need some time to talk it over, ok?'

'Alright, you got two minutes, but I'll leave you with two choices. When I come back, you can either leave with your heads held high, with dignity. Or you can do things the hard way, which will involve no dignity and a fair degree of pain.' He leaves us to confer.

'Come on, mate,' I plead, 'we've been in here forty-four hours now. He's right, we've done well and there's not a lot more we can prove down here.'

'You're submitting to them, that's what they want.'

'We haven't any choice. I'm going out when he asks. Please come out with me. It's a choice between pain or dignity, and I know which I deserve, and which I'd rather avoid.'

'I'd rather die.'

'Paulo, listen to me. They're going to hurt you. I don't want that to happen, but I'm not going to let them do it to me as well, not for you, not for anyone.'

'See you later then, I'm staying.'

'For fuck's sake, will you listen to me?' Paulo sticks his fingers in his ears and mouths a silent sentence, as if to say 'I can't hear you.'

Dave reappears. 'Well then, gents, what's it to be?'

I take the cushions out from my coat as I speak: 'I'm coming, but only because it's clear that if I don't you and your men will assault me. I haven't the slightest respect for you or your tactics.' Paulo, sitting on the floor, shakes his head, awaiting his fate.

'I can't agree with you, but I understand. Give us your hand.' I climb the ladder rungs unaided and refuse any contact.

'Well done. If only your mate had more sense.'

'He won't listen. Don't hurt him, eh?'

'We'll see whether he responds to reason. If not we might have to try something else.' I notice the side-handled baton and wish more than anything he'd change his mind. I call down to him, 'Mate, are you sure about this?' He nods.

'Ok,' Dave says, 'my men have to escort you off the site now.' One of the officers goes to grab hold of my coat.

'Fuck off, you animal.' The policeman tenses, and looks to Dave for direction.

'Let him walk of his own accord, he's a good lad.' As I climb the basement stairs into the main body of the house, I can hear faint singing. 'I never gave up, I never gave up, I crawled in the mud but I never gave up.'

With an officer at each flank I walk in silence along Claremont Road for what I know is to be the final time. At the end of the street stand Jerry, Dom, Helen, a few locals and a couple of Brew Crew.

I'm inundated with hugs on the other side of the crush barriers and feel quite overwhelmed.

'Are you ok?

'What happened?'

'Where's Paulo?'

The latter is most in need of an answer. 'He's still in there. We were given the choice of dignity or pain.'

'Oh. Oh shit! Shit!' Helen immediately bursts into tears. She's seen enough in the past to fear the worst.

'There's nothing we can do for him right now. What happened to you two?' I say trying to change the subject.

Dom wearily scratches his dreads. 'Well, I got down here late in my girlfriend's car and tried time and again to get food into the people on the tower. We tried throwing stuff up to them and all sorts. Then I tried to smuggle some through the graveyard next to the street.'

'What happened?'

'It was crawling with cops. I got nicked under eighteenth-century ecclesiastical law. Trespass in a graveyard. I got released after five hours and got out about nine o'clock.'

'What the fuck is ecclesiastical law? Helen, how about you?'

'I sat on the roof until I couldn't sit there anymore. You wouldn't believe how cold it was out there last night. In the end we were out of food, out of water. I was actually quite glad when the cherry picker came to get me off.'

'Oh shit, here comes Paulo,' says Dom. He's being dragged along the street by his underarms by three officers. He's clearly in a lot of pain. At the edge of the cordon the kwik-cuffs are released and he's dumped carelessly before us.

'What happened, mate? What did they do?'

Fighting the tears and holding his wrists, he blubbers, 'They 'cuffed me and then pulled me out of the hole by my wrists ... They went tight, I think they've broken my thumbs ... I can't feel a thing in either.'

Helen tends to Paulo's wounds as her reddened face streams with tears. 'Kwik-cuffs are only supposed to be used on violent offenders.' She straightens to shout at the retreating cops. 'Under no circumstances should they be used in such a way!'

Incensed they should treat Paulo so abominably, I grab the cordon fence and shriek at the pigs. 'Some people think that anyone who murders a policeman should receive a death sentence! Personally I think they should get a fucking knighthood!'

'Too fuckin' right.' One of the Brew Crew is in full accord.

Unsurprisingly the police aren't in agreement. One comes over and says to me: 'This is a formal warning. Any more of that and you will be arrested for Threatening Behaviour.'

'You would as well, wouldn't you? Nazi fucker. I suppose all this is a bit relaxed for you, eh? I do apologise! I'm deeply sorry that the law doesn't allow you to beat me to death right here! You fucking disgust me!' By the time I'm halfway through that little lot Jerry and Dom have pulled me away from the street. It takes thirty full seconds for the diatribe to stop.

'Come on, lad, you've done all you can. Let's go and have a cuppa. The others'll make sure your mate gets to hospital.' In truth, Jerry looks more in need of some tea and a sit-down than I do, but he's still on the go giving his all.

The next morning, back in Manchester, it's great to listen to the eight o'clock news on Radio 4. ' ... an estimated eight hundred police and as many bailiffs and security guards are still removing the protesters from the street. The eviction has currently cost three million pounds, making it the most expensive since World War Two.'

The next day the story is fifth in the running order. Amazingly Claremont still hasn't been taken. There are apparently two people left in the welded cage at the top of the tower. I go to the phone and ring the M11 campaign office.

'Give my love to Ann and Gary from me when you see them – fucking storming.'

'They're running short of food and water now. Word is that Gary is coming down soon, but Ann isn't. She's been whacking the cutting tools with an iron bar when they come anywhere near the cage.'

'Good on her. Fucking keep it up, everyone.'

The eviction ends midway through the afternoon of day five. It's cost £1million per day. Gary was right – we may have lost the battle but – hey, you know what I mean.

END OF PART ONE

PART TWO:
PUNISHMENT

CHAPTER 7

WINTER 1994/5

It's January 3rd and I'm at my parents' slumped in front of South Today, the BBC's saccharine-heaped regional magazine programme. Obviously there was no New Year's resolution to replace the cheesy wanker news presenters. They must go out of their way to search for the smarmiest twats they can find. For once, however, there is an issue of substance to report.

'Protests against live animal exports at the port of Shoreham escalated last night. There were more than twenty arrests as demonstrators clashed with police.'

'Oh, that's dreadful. There are some wicked people around.' My mum's getting quite into the coverage of the crowd trying to stop the lorries. I'm still recovering from New Year excess. I don't remember throwing up, nor having a nasty scatological experience but I did wake up fully clothed with four different hues of brown stain on my shirt. If anyone has any ideas as to why – answers on a postcard, please.

It's not exactly my issue but it's nice to see protest hit the true-blue south coast and refreshing to see older people getting done over by the cops instead of us youngsters all the time.

The TV news continues: 'Philip Lacey, managing director of Shoreham Port Authority, said today the port was bound under contractual obligation to take the lorries. The protests are expected to continue with increased numbers tomorrow ... Tragedy today struck a Hampshire village after a vicar's wife and three children died when the car they were travelling in collided with a ...'

'Looks like it's all kicking off down here. Who'd have thought it?' I say to Mum.

'People just aren't going to stand for it. The way they treat those calves, it's just not right.' This is about as close to a soapbox moment as my mum ever gets.

'Don't you think we should go down there? You could actually see some protest first-hand. See what it's like for me, week in, week out.'

'There's no point in turning out, you'll never stop them. Besides, do you know how cold it is out there?'

'Oh come on, what would you be doing otherwise? Watching the box, that's what.'

'No, I just don't fancy it, that's all.'

Later that evening I meet up with my old mate Dave for a couple of festive pints. 'I can see this live export thing is cruel,' I say, 'but people are going mad about it. Just because the countryside – the planet whatever – doesn't have a face we can't pull in the same level of coverage.'

'Are you jealous? Or is it your anti-animal stance kicking in?'

Rightly or wrongly I associate two types of people with animal rights – the old woman with ninety cats who runs a donkey sanctuary, or some shadowy gimp in a balaclava who sends incendiary devices in the post and rescue monkeys from research establishments.

'I'm not anti-animal,' I reply through a thirsty slurp. 'I have full respect for a gazelle roaming the plains or whatever it does, but domesticated animals are just ... unnecessary. And cruel.'

'Why?'

'Take cats for example. What's cat food made of? All sorts. You show me the face of a cat and reflected in its eyes are the souls of a thousand dead horses.'

'That's just weird.'

'Weird but true. And don't get me started on fucking dogs. Besides, I do my bit for animals. I've been veggie for years now.'

'I've seen you eat meat. Take that barbeque last summer. You were tucking into that quarter-pounder like there was no tomorrow,' says Dave, no doubt thinking he's stolen the moral high ground.

'Yeah – but it would have gone to waste. As would all the land, water and labour used to produce that burger. I was doing the decent thing by making sure it wasn't going to die in vain ... and damn tasty it was too.'

'So you're not a veggie at all then?'

After a couple of moments I respond hopefully, 'Could I be described as a pragmatarian?'

'More like a bullshitarian.'

I get off my chair to visit the bogs. 'The logic stands up – you just can't deal with it. The sound of my piss hitting the urinal will make far more sense than you ever will.'

On returning to my parents' house, Mum and Dad are watching the blanket coverage of Shoreham on the evening news.

'Oh come on,' I say, 'let's go down there. It'll be a laugh.'

My dad, sitting in his usual place on the settee, joins the debate for the first time. 'We've already told you, we're not going.'

'Look, you've had all these pets these years, the cats, the birds, the rabbits, those bloody dogs. Now there are some animals that genuinely need help, and you're not going to get off your butts. That's rich that is. There's a word for that – hypocrisy.'

'You'll never beat them,' says Mum.

'You don't know 'til you try. And those calves are what, six months old. They're tiny, defenceless creatures.' Though it goes against the grain, playing the animal lover's card is the best way to get my way.

A moment's pause. Her eyes go skyward and after taking a deep breath she says: 'Alright. Just this once.' I go upstairs to put some warm clothes on. It's well below freezing outside.

From our house to the port is a three-mile drive along the coast. As we near Shoreham the streets are filled with hundreds of people of all ages and classes all on tenterhooks waiting for the trucks to arrive. The holiday season could well be a reason such a turnout. It'll be interesting to see if numbers keep up once most people return to work. Also, due to the tide patterns, the lorries come in midway through the evening – which is very convenient for those working in the day who wish to express their discontent.

One of the three possible access routes is a small road next to the King's Head pub. As we walk along to check it out my dad says: 'It's too narrow, you'd never get an artic down there.' He knows what he's talking about, having been a lorry driver for years.

Five figures, largely obscured by darkness, are turning over an old car – blocking the road completely.

'Ooh, I hope that's theirs,' says Dad, probably visualising his Vauxhall Cavalier suffering the same fate. Shoreham isn't used to such scenes, nor are its residents.

I reply: 'Who gives a shit? Best thing to do with all of them.'

One of the houses on the front has rigged up a PA system and what sounds like a sentimental dirge pours forth. I approach a woman in the crowd.

'What's that music?' I ask.

'It's called God Gave Life To The Animals. Isn't it great?'

'Hmm, enjoy the evening.'

We head back west along the coast road and can see ahead of the beginnings of a commotion.

'Looks like it's kicking off, I'm going to run ahead,' I say to my folks.

There's about as many protestors as police as the lorries crawl up the main road. Many people are trying – and largely succeeding in sitting, standing and lying in their path. There's a line of 200 or so cops between me and the lead truck, which has a couple of people in balaclavas climbing on top. One of them is shaping to smash its windscreen with a brick. Oh yes.

Suddenly there's some movement in the police line, and seeing a gap I think to myself, 'What's the worst they can possibly do?'

I sprint and make it about ten metres without much hassle apart from shouts of 'Oi' and 'Stop him'. Although this isn't my issue it feels like the skills are definitely transferable.

However, just as I feel I'm going to get a clear run towards the truck an officer kicks out and takes me down just below the knee.

The bad news is I'm lying on the floor with three officers on top of me. The good news is I can see the guy on the truck is making pretty short work of the windscreen.

I feel a kick in the small of my back. 'You won't be trying that again will you?' says one of the cops.

There are cries of 'Leave him alone, you fascists!' and 'He hasn't done anything wrong!'

Quite unfazed, one of the officers asks me: 'Are you going to walk or be dragged?'

My lack of response is rewarded with me being dragged, facing forwards and downwards.

In mid–drag a woman with a LEGAL OBSERVER bib goes over to the officer who kicked me and says: 'I saw what you did to that young man. What's your name and number?'

She receives no response. Trying to identify individual officers is a tough gig because virtually every epaulette is covered up with fluorescent yellow jackets.

I can see my dad behind a crush barrier – I don't think I've ever seen him so irate. He's arguing with one cop pointing his index finger at him vigorously. It looks as though he's being given the old '... if you persist in using that tone of language, sir, you will be arrested' routine.

I'm dumped behind a crash barrier near to where my parents are.

Mum says: 'Are you ok? That looked nasty. The one who kicked you, he was a right evil bastard.'

'I kept telling you what the police are like, and you never believed me. Now you've seen it for yourself.'

Many of the police holding the line are required to remove the people sat in front of the trucks. The cops remaining try to hold people back, but once a bold few make it through, and show how easy it is, the cordon is no more – force of numbers seems to be winning the day.

The crowd treats itself to a hearty recital of 'We shall not be moved' to help boost spirits as the police really start to wade in.

Although there are many being assaulted, pulled, punched and shoved one couple catches my eye a few yards away. A middle-aged man and someone I assume to be his wife. He's greying around the ears, with slacks and sports jacket – looking to all the world like a magistrate, who, after dealing with one too many protest cases, had gone native. She has signs of a demi-wave under a bobble hat, Barbour jacket and a long smart skirt.

Steam rises from the officer's mouth with every syllable. 'I'll give you one more chance to come peacefully, sir.'

The couple exchange a look – presumably formed through years of happy marriage – and stay just where they are, a shared concern for dewy-eyed calves outweighing their obedience to the forces of law and order.

'But I am being peaceful. I'm being totally passive,' the man says meekly, but clearly. Then an officer goes to hold him down, whilst another puts his shin across the man's windpipe while a third grabs his legs.

'Are we coming now?' This question is nearly drowned out by the wife's screams. She's seized by the hair, pulled upright by it and thrown several feet across the carriageway in almost one movement.

Our section of the crowd – having seen what's happened to the woman – surges forward. The barriers are felled and the police are surrounded by incensed citizens. The funny thing that occurs to me is the range of headgear – flat caps, balaclavas, headscarves, Arafat scarves. Whatever folks are wearing to keep out the cold or their identity hidden, they are all united in their fury.

One woman goes up to the officer who had pulled the woman's hair, six inches from his face, and eyeballs him. 'I could call you an animal, but that would be to say that these poor creatures are in some way like you. That would be an insult to them. You disgust me.'

The cop is grinning. 'I'm only doing my job, madam, no-one's perfect,' he says smugly.

'I'm not asking you to be perfect, I'm asking you to be human,' as he walks away from her to cries of 'Scum!', 'Cowards!', 'Murderers!' and 'Come and do that to me, see what you get!'

As the couple receives some first aid and tempers cool, attention returns to the stationary lorries. I walk past the first lorry with the broken windscreen. As I do so a man says to me, 'It's alright, this ain't going nowhere, my mate's just done the brakepipes.' The outburst reminds me of Ian at the M65.

There are dozens of people round the side of the trucks consoling the animals. A woman in her thirties in a cute yellow mac sobs, holding her hand between the bars of the truck out to a calf whose snout is in close proximity.

'There, there,' she snivels, 'good boy. It's alright, you're not going anywhere today.' She tries to collect herself with a deep breath, 'not if all these good people can help it'.

She looks like an estate agent's secretary or something similar, doubtless another one of the car sticker brigade.

I earwig silently as she says. 'Don't worry, we'll be here as long as it takes, all bloody year if we have to. I haven't got anything better to do.'

I'm tempted to go suggest something better for me and her to do than freeze our arses off down here, but I suppose it wouldn't be appropriate. My thoughts return to the calves as I see one which seemed to have a trapped hoof – cooped up so tightly it could not turn around. There's a pair of mournful eyes looking out between the slats.

'Are you ok? What do you reckon about all this? Confused? No, I s'pose not, I wouldn't of thought this was an issue you'd really sit on the fence about.' I feel like a bit of a prat talking to a cow, even in this matter-of-fact way.

'I tell you what,' I continue, 'if they play that bloody song again I might kill you and me – put us out of our misery.'

The calf sniffs my hand with dry nostrils. Word is they haven't been fed or watered for at least six hours.

Suddenly a huge cheer goes up from in front of the truck. I say goodbye to the calf and go to investigate. People are jumping up and down, hugging each other. Compared to twenty minutes ago the mood has completely changed.

'What's happened?' I ask a middle-aged woman who was gleefully waving a Union Jack. Around her neck is a placard which reads

ACTIVIST
ANARCHIST
EXTREMIST
FANATIC
If this is what I am to be called because I care
I shall wear each name with pride

'There was an announcement. They're sending the lorries away. Isn't it wonderful?' she says.

I shake hands with the woman. 'Good on you.'

After finding my parents in the crowd, it's decided it's time to head home. Driving back through, we see a woman holding up a BEEP IF YOU SUPPORT US placard. My dad honks the Cavalier's horn, which is reciprocated by cheers.

'Well, what did you think?' I ask.

'I've never seen anything like it,' said Mum. 'The police just kept charging the crowd. Children were getting separated from their parents, and the language! And I'm not talking about the demonstrators. I've certainly learnt some words I never knew before.'

The next day virtually one story dominates local coverage. BBC Southern Counties Radio receives a record number of calls about the animal exports and the story has broken onto the national news, which mainly focuses on the guy smashing the windscreen and describing the protests as violent.

On the TV there's footage of many coachloads of police being drafted in from London and Kent to bolster the numbers. Apparently there are to be 1,500 police on duty tonight – twice as many than there had been at Claremont Road. The fluorescent yellow force of the state army versus a chaotic ragtag army of compassion.

'Christ almighty, look at them all,' Dad says as coach follows coach follows coach on the screen.

'Shit yeah. Let's hope they're on best behaviour tonight.' I don't expect this will be the case.

'Shall we go again tonight?' I'm thinking they at least understand what I do now, even if they don't get the same kick out of it.

Mum replies: 'I don't know, it was awfully rough and very cold, wasn't it?'

Socialist Worker Wanker 1: 'What you don't understand is that while Habermas addresses critical theory ...'

Socialist Worker Wanker 2: 'Oh but ...'

Why? Why did I agree to do this talk? I'm on a coach en route to a Criminal Justice Act rally in Glasgow and am surrounded by Socialist Worker types. I seem to be the only green on the bus and I'd rather bite my ears off than listen to this. I've only ever been to Scotland once before – just over the border in Dumfries. Drank eighteen pints and I think I met someone who said they held the world record for riding backwards on a horse.

I've never spoken at a rally before – there's going to be one of the Birmingham Six and Tommy Sheridan, the first person to be jailed for the Poll Tax. I should be jailed right now – for the crime of forgetting my CD player and having to listen to this Marxist twaddle all the way there.

The saving grace is that most on the coach have been informed – maybe through their central committee – that I am one of the first arrestees and am not one of them – and consequently leave me alone. At least I can visit the M77 camps while I'm here – and yes it means I'm not coming back with the Trots unless Donga Belly strikes.

Rain is no stranger to the more northerly parts of our fair isles and lo – it is verily pissing it down as we arrive in Prince's Street. The weather doesn't seem to have affected numbers or indeed the spirit of the crowd. There's a rather good samba band complete with brass section currently having a creditable stab at White Riot by the Clash and I decide this is the best part of the march.

A couple of women in fairy costumes are brandishing powerful water pistols, going into local pubs and burger joints to fill up when they run out of ammunition. I can't see any of the Manchester socialist crowd around and for once the occasional smell of patchouli is reassuring.

Though not one for chants my favourite is some bloke in a mullet wig shouting 'Major!' as loud as he can. 'Pain in the arse!' is the crowd response.

Walking next to me is a woman of no more than twenty, looking like an identikit student – red and black short stripy dress combined with the classic tights and red DM look – although the red woollen beret is a strange addition.

'It's great isn't it?' I say.

'Absolutely. It's terrific to get everyone together to show how they feel, don't you think?' This isn't a Scots accent.

'Certainly. I'm Lester by the way, pleased to meet you.'

'Charlotte.' As we shake hands as I move some scrappy bits of paper from one to the other.

'What are they?'

'Them? Oh, I'm just trying to memorise what I'm going to say at the rally.' Atta boy, there are definitely sharking tokens available here. I knew there was fringe benefits to this game after all.

'You're speaking today? Get away! You're having me on.' Told you.

'No honest, look.' I produce a copy of the running order. 'There you are, four down the list – Lester Stype – one of the first CJA arrestees.'

She's giving me a promising look, but as most men know, the looks that blondes with blue eyes give you can be wildly misinterpreted.

'So Charlotte, less about me, let's talk about you. What do you think of me?'

She laughs – bingo. 'I'm studying here – classics. I was with friends but they seem to have disappeared.'

'That's terrible. We'll have to stick together as protection from all these police.'

'Indeed.' She links my arm and we enjoy the parade. After a while I even start to find the silly hat rather fetching.

The first announcement from the PA on the stage blunts the blade of my spadework. 'Will all speakers please report to the stage.'

'That's my call. I'd better go.'

'Feeling nervous?'

'Um ... na. I'm going to play it for laughs. I can't go wrong hopefully.'

'Good luck.' She turns, takes both my hands and kisses me squarely on the lips, adding: 'Knock 'em dead.' I can feel all is present and correct in the pants barracks.

'Well cheers. I'll try. Mmm, I know this sounds forward, but I may be rather parched after I finish speaking.'

'Ok, I'd love to go for a pint,' she replies. 'I'll get up the front so you can find me.' I walk to the stage trying to think my erection out of existence.

Paddy and Tommy are great speakers, and even the bloke from the Scottish TUC holds his own. Now it's my turn, armed with one sheet with bullet points of what I'm going to say.

Ok, it's only a stage. And two thousand people. No-one's gonna die, it's a sympathetic crowd, I'll be fine. Gulp.

I've decided to go for a populist style à la Keith Chegwin out swapping things on the Multi-Coloured Swap Shop or Radio One Roadshows.

'HELLO GLASGOW!' I shout into the microphone, the four syllables taking up the best part of ten seconds to say. The crowd loves it. I look in the front row and can see a red beret and a smile.

Crowd Reaction Key

I would start by telling you about a funny thing that happened to me on the way here, but this isn't the London Palladium, so I'll just get on with it. Instead, I'd like to start with an apology. You can probably tell from my accent that I'm not exactly from round these parts. As a Southerner [😠], I'd like to say sorry that we have given you Tory government for the last fifteen years, and to say we're not all like them down there. Honest. [😀] On November the fourth, the day after the Criminal Justice Act was given Royal Assent, myself and some friends climbed up a crane in Manchester. Did we do this to get a panoramic view of the Manchester skyline? [✗] Or because we'd had one too many beers? [😊] [✗] No. It was because the government is taking away rights from us that no decent administration would even consider taking away. We also went up there to protest about the M65 extension, a motorway that's currently being built near Preston. I understand that you've got a few motorway problems of your own up here. [✓] So I'd strongly recommend finding a

crane or bulldozer building the M77 and do the same as I have
done. Try it, you might just like it.

The Criminal Justice Act is a very strange piece of legislation in
many ways, but it is very peculiar in one particular respect. It
gives the police the power to arrest people if they imagine that
you are going to go to a rave, or a protest or something like that.
[😫] I don't know about you, but I think the only thing that
sparks the imagination of the average policeman today is the
thought of bringing down repetitive beats on the head of someone they don't like the look of. [😵] Now, I'm sure all the police
in Glasgow are very nice, and I'm sure none of them ever forget
their mother's birthday, but it's just an impression about cops in
general. Everyone, are Glasgow cops nice people or not? [✘]

There are several things that the government's tried out in
Scotland before the rest of the country, such as the Poll Tax [🙁]
and Brian McClair [😃], but this time they're implementing the
CJA all over the country at the same time, so we can fight it
together. [😃]

We may have been the first people to be charged under the CJA,
but we certainly won't be the last. Lots of subsequent arrests
since ours have shown that. I would heartily recommend that
everyone here today breaks the act. Why should I have all the
fun? Get a CJA case of your very own. [😃]

The act will only be defeated through sheer weight of numbers,
made unworkable by filling up the courts with cases. [✔] The
Poll Tax was defeated with mass civil disobedience, thanks in the
main to good people like yourselves, now it's time to rise to the
challenge again. The Act is an inherently evil piece of legislation:
small-minded cultural cleansing to criminalise anyone whose
lifestyle differs from that of John Major and Michael Howard.
Think on. I'll bid you good day. Thank you for listening.' [😃]

Applause and cheers ring out around round the park and I'm
loving every moment. As I walk off, Tommy comes up to me and
pats me on the back.

'Aye, that was a cracking bit of rabble-rousing there. Good on ya.'
I'm not getting all bigheaded now, but could definitely get used to
doing stuff like this on a regular basis.

As I go to find Charlotte I spot a few of the Manchester commies.
One looks over and directs a wanker sign in my direction. Fine. I'm
just off to go meet up with a very cute woman and have a distinct
chance of some action. They'll go back to Gorton tonight and jerk
off into a sock about Cuba. What are these people like? Maybe
they're jealous cos we're off actually doing something while they're

just full of very dull talk and shite theories.

Charlotte greets me with a huge hug and a big sloppy kiss. This is what it must be like if you're in a band on tour, only multiplied by a million. I feel very lucky and extremely jealous all at once.

'You were fantastic,' she says. 'Let's go to the 13th Note for that pint.'

Halfway there she slips her arm down and puts her hand inside the back pocket of my jeans.

'My wallet's in the other one,' I say as I push her against a garden wall and we lose the next ten minutes in each other.

One pint turns to two then four. Having barely eaten all day two bags of crisps doesn't do much to stem the tide of alcohol. Taking one of the empty packets I fold it several times longways then wrap it over to form the shape of an AIDS ribbon and place it against my chest. 'This is to commemorate all the crisps that die every year.'

'I'll join the cause.' She takes my hand and the ribbon and places it to her breast. 'Let's go back to mine.'

In bed there's a real connection between us – retaining eye contact all the way to mutual climax. Apart from being fit there's a lot to be said for Charlotte – she's bright, positive and knows what she wants. The best thing about her is a randomness of mind to create her own humour from scratch.

I disappear under the duvet and start to run my tongue over her pelvis. Ensuring I whisper loud enough to be heard under the bedding I begin to commentate in a David Attenbrough voice. 'Here, on the rolling plains of the Netherlands, the great licker stalks his prey, the lesser spotted G-Spot.' There's a dirty giggle and sounds of anticipation and I suck and rub away until she's begging for me to stop yet hopefully aching for more

The mood is brought down by news on the radio just as I'm about to broach the serious issue of blow jobs.

'A woman has died during a live animal export protest at Coventry Airport. Jill Phipps, who was 31, fell beneath the wheels of a lorry carrying veal calves.'

We recoil from each other in shock. 'That's terrible,' she says curling into a ball.

'I've never heard of anyone dying on an action before. Not in this country. Despite all the mad shit that's happened you never think anything like this will happen.' I go to be alone with my thoughts and the kettle.

For some reason I ask Charlotte if I can ring my mum. The latest news from Shoreham is that the Port Authority has decided not to renew the contract with the company shipping the calves. Also, the Chief Executive of the port, Philip Lacey, has resigned. All this and a £2.1million policing bill caused by heavy numbers of protesters turning up each night. Perhaps Jill, who according to Radio 5 had been to Twyford and the M11, hasn't died in vain.

It's funny, I feel really energised and motivated, but can also tell that the relentless nature of the lifestyle is starting to have an effect. Just like with Debs, some areas of my life wither through neglect. I haven't been out on the beers with the lads in a good while, and Neil probably feels he's living in a house by himself most of the time. Then there's the financial pressure – my overdraft is pretty huge, and I haven't wanted to go on about having to sign on but it is a pain in the prostate. I'd like to see an advert like the ones in magazines to adopt African kids.

The ad would read: 'Would anyone like to sponsor an activist? Just 51p a day can keep Lester supplied with D-locks, veggie kebabs and the odd pint, please give generously.' Anyway, rant over – for now.

We wrap up warm and Charlotte leads me through the frosty streets to catch the bus near the Bridge Street Metro Station.

Licking a roll–up she says, 'I always like to have a fag here. This part of town is called the Golden Z, and the streets are all named after tobacco and slave traders.'

'I'm sure you could have your post-cancer ashes scattered here if you like it so much,' I reply. It really feels like I can be myself with Charlotte – I can be sick and dark if I want to and not have to skirt around her sensibilities.

At Buchanan Street bus station there's a statue of a man and woman in a passionate clench. Funnily enough she's wearing a beret. I suggest we copy the pose and use it as an excuse for a protracted snog.

'Haven't you got lectures today?' I ask coming up for air.

'Come on – classics – I only have six hours a week. They let us get on with it.'

One the bus she tells me that Pollok Park is over a thousand acres – Europe's largest urban green space. 'It was left to the people of the city by the Maxwell family who'd owned it for 700 years,' she adds.

'Blimey that's,' – I look upward up to do some calculation '28 generations if I'm not mistaken.'

'Depends how often you fuck,' she says, running her hand inside my thigh.

'Come on, play fair. Sitting next to you and the vibration of the bus is enough to set me off.'

At the side of the existing road is a sign welcoming all to the Pollok Free State.

I've forgotten just how muddy camps can be. Within seconds my virtually indestructible size 11 para boots are already heavily caked in thick brown biological soup.

'Urgh. Do you fancy giving us a piggyback over this?' I ask Charlotte.

'Oh yeah sure. You weigh double what I do.' As ever, she has a smart answer for a dumb question. Like a gentleman it is I who carries her over the worst of the mud, and of course threaten to drop her in it a couple of times.

'Wow, this is so impressive,' I say. The main camp is like no other I have seen.

To keep the central part clean and dryish, tonnes of gravel have been blagged from somewhere, and have been spread around the site in neat paths. In the middle stands a huge octagonal treehouse in an imposing beech. At each corner of the camp are four huge wood carvings, Tartan totems.

'A lot of this is Colin's work,' she adds. 'He'll be around some-where.'

Sure enough he was in the next clearing chopping firewood with a huge axe. At six foot five, with long black hair and beard to match, he looks as though he's just used the implement to slay a few English at the Battle of Culloden. I definitely don't want to ask if he's wearing anything under his kilt.

'Well Charlotte, where'd ye get this new laddie from?' he says, leaning on the axe.

'I'm Lester. I'm up from Manchester for a few days to help you out.'

'I dare say you are. Well you can start by loadin' up the barra.'

I look confused. Thankfully Charlotte darts her head to a wheel-barrow a few yards away.

In no time last night's fire is reignited and a Dixie pot for tea hangs above it.

With a hot mug in one hand and Charlotte's hip in the other, I ask Colin about the North American Indian-style totems.

'These ravens symbolise enlightenment, and the eagles, well they represent many things. Power, healing – but most of all the inner strength that freedom gives ye.'

'The best thing about the Free State,' says Charlotte, 'is virtually everyone involved is from the housing schemes.'

'Aye – too true, but it's good to see the likes of you coming to visit – ye supportive Sassenachs,' Colin says with the trace of a smile.

More folk start to appear and we're given a tour of part of the route by Colin's girlfriend Gehan.

Posted on some of the trees are pictures of security guards.

Gehan says: 'These are the ones who've used rough stuff, but once their face gets known round Pollokshields the lads know what they'll get if they don't calm down.'

'We haven't got anyone quite like Colin down in England. I wish we had,' I reply.

'He's terrific but drives me to distraction sometimes. Last month he sat up a tree for two weeks, with only a copy of Burns and a hammock,' she says with an air of exasperated pride. 'And there was the 20-day crane sit over in Malletsheugh.'

'Twenty days! fuck me, that's a new British record.' I'm aghast.

'Aye, it probably is,' she says without fuss. 'There's a lot to the Free State that doesn't happen elsewhere.'

'Go on,' I'm like a kid in an NVDA sweet shop.

'About 300 of the local kids have staged a school strike. They come over and give the guards hell. The headmasters of Bellarmine and Crookston Castle keep slagging us to the press, but it doesn't seem to make much odds.'

'And,' she adds, 'on a different tack there's a couple of Wimpey sites round the city which have been ... er ... a wee bit unfortunate.' Charlotte aids the explanation by miming the striking of a match and going 'boom'.

Heading back to the main camp I see a notice on one of the trees:

Pollok Free University

Aims:
> respect and service to ourselves, others and nature
> learning with hand, heart and head
> taking responsibility for the education of one another
> and ourselves
> listening deeply to others with sympathy and tolerance
> gender, ethnic and social justice
> standing up, speaking out and being true

Courses in:
> Social empowerment – how we can be bigger than
> ourselves through others
> Social history – why the rich are rich and the poor are poor
> Spirituality – how to grow strong in love from the soul,
> Living skills – literacy, childcare, cooking, wood and
> stonecraft
> Creativity – self–expression through music, art, poetry,
> drama, dance and writing

For more details see Colin by the fire.

'Jeez, have you got time to run this as well as everything else? This is mental,' I say, not knowing if this was incredible or the biggest load of bollocks I've ever seen. With this in mind I go to find Colin by the fire.

'You see, son, this is where I grew up as a kid. This is my soil, you know what I mean?' says Colin. I certainly do, though there's still been no word from the Worthing public enquiry so far as I know.

Through the trees I see a shock of red hair and think nothing of it. If the stereotypical view of Russ Abbott, etc. is to be believed all Scots have ginger hair. However, as I look closer the beard and small face and plaid shirt seem familiar. It's Tango! And Dom, Helen, Phil, Jane, Paulo and Lorraine.

'Fucking hell, look who it isn't,' I cry running to greet them.

'Colin, here's some more supportive Sassenachs,' and introduce them all to him and Charlotte.

Phil says to me: 'We couldn't let you have all the fun up here by yourself.'

'I've been having immense fun,' I say, hugging Charlotte round the waist from behind.

'Wooooo!' they all cry in a really fucking mature way.

'Lester and Charlotte / Trying to save the trees / K I S S I N G,' says the ginger tosser.

'Well, guys,' says Colin, 'this is great but there's conservation work to do if anyone fancies it after you've put up your tents.'

There's all this emphasis here on being local. I suppose that's fair enough, but pollution moves about, as does CO_2. We may not be local, we may even be foreigners but alien troublemakers we definitely are not. Well, unless there's a good reason to wind some fucker up.

The conservation Colin has in mind is tree spiking, and making sure there are bodies back at the camp we go with him, Gehan, a couple of others and a huge bag containing nails of various lengths and widths.

Unlike the M65, Pollok has a very healthy view on the subject of spiking. In the surrounding hills and troughs around the Free State, as well as many other parts of the route, there were trees with a large white 'S' painted on them.

'Are all of the spiked trees marked?' Charlotte asks Colin.

'Now that would be telling. As far as I want the chainsaw gangs to know there isn't a spiked tree without an 'S' on – but I could be wrong.'

'Are you getting loads of press?' asks Phil.

'Aye. There's an arsehole or two pushing microphones in my face here every day.' Colin's smile suggests a tinge of sarcasm in virtually everything he says.

Gehan says: 'There's been a couple of good actions lately. We visited the council planning meeting with a pipe and drum band. They really liked that.'

'Who? The councillors or reporters?' I ask.

'Then there was the day we went down to see the jackasses at the Town Hall where the model of the route was. We had made a mock-up of the Free State, including benders, trees and hippies, and ... redesigned their design.'

The trees aren't very difficult to hammer into, but it's the sheer volume of trees and the number of nails needed for each one that makes the task backbreaking. I'm getting blisters on my thumbs that look as though they'll swell to the size of golf balls.

After two hours of hammering, Gehan's mobile phone rings. 'Bloody thing. I hate the fucker, but we need them.' She presses the answer button and her expression changes for the worse.

'Right laddies ... oh yeah, sorry, and lassies. There's a spot of botherc. It's nae too far from here. I'm going over there now. You're all welcome to join me.' Just about everyone's glad of the break from hammering.

'We've got the mini-bus if that's any help?' says Dom. It is and we run off to find it.

On the way, Gehan briefs everyone. 'We've got a bit of an unwanted visitor at one of the other camps. The local MP, Allan Stewart. He's a right nasty piece of work, but he's also an endangered species.'

'You what?' says Jane.

'A Scottish Tory,' says Gehan as she rings the local press to alert them of Stewart's presence.

It's a couple of miles to where the action is, but the landscape is quite different. Colin points at some windswept housing blocks. 'This is Corkerhill, one of the biggest housing schemes in Europe. You've probably heard quite a lot about places like this. Well two-thirds of that is crap, but the rest is as true as it could be.'

'So what do the locals think about the road?'

'It's mainly being built for the rich folks over in Eastwood,' says Gehan. 'Unless the contract's putting food on the table everyone's pretty solid against, but you know what it's like, or maybe you don't. These folks have a tough enough time keeping their lives together as it is.'

'You could say that. Between you, me and the gatepost, that's what we're hoping. There's already been quite a lot of plant smashed up that we can't account for,' Colin says with a wink.

In the time it takes to get a round of drinks in, we're at the camp. A couple score of people are already there. It seems like word had spread fast.

'That's Stewart, the fat cunt with the lambchops,' Colin points to three figures walking past a couple of tents. 'That one with the air-gun is his son. And oh yes, that's the head honcho for the project on the end.'

Colin leads our deputation towards them. I wish he was with us on all actions, I'd have a lot more bottle.

'Afternoon, Mr Stewart. Pleased to see you're out taking your kids out to see the local beauty spots before they disappear. Did you really need Mr Dyson to accompany you?'

'It's no business of yours,' says the MP.

'If you say so. If you say so.'

Stewart's son takes the airgun from his shoulder and waves it in our direction. 'Yeah, fuck off, you freaks.'

'And what are you gonna do? Shoot us?' asks Jane.

'I don't know what the people of Eastwood did to deserve an MP like you,' says a steely Gehan.

'You people and your way of life are a disgrace. You're wasting everyone's time.'

'At least I'm not a waste of space, Mr Stewart,' says Colin. The distance between us and them is narrowing but I sense from the Manchester crew that we should all stay out of this. I merely hold Charlotte's hand and spectate.

Like a schoolboy with a temper Stewart goes over to a nearby campaign banner and starts to rip it down.

'You leave that be,' says Colin calmly.

'Get out of my face, McLeod,' says Stewart as he bends over to grab a pickaxe handle lying nearby.

I see Gehan look behind the men and smile at a woman running up the path with a notepad and camera. No prizes for guessing who she is.

'Useful weapon a pickaxe,' Stewart says, brandishing the handle in Colin's face, 'there's a lot you can do with a pickaxe.'

'Get off our camp. This is a place of peace,' says Colin.

He prods Colin a couple times in the chest with the handle. 'I've had enough of you, McLeod.' And Allan Stewart, junior minister for the Scottish Office, takes a swing at the big man.

Although the blow doesn't land there's a reassuring click of a camera shutter rapidly opening and closing before a scuffle ensues. Dyson instinctively puts his walkie-talkie to his ear. Gehan moves quickest to try and protect her man.

The journalist is on the edge of the fracas. 'Mr Stewart. Is attacking peaceful protestors becoming of a Member of Parliament?' There's no response.

'You don't see this every day, eh?' I say to Charlotte. We start to laugh more through surprise than anything else.

Two squad cars pull up and escort Stewart and the boys off site. As the officer with a greying beard approaches, Gehan asks him, 'Are you going to arrest them?' Again, there's no answer.

We huddle round the journo giving her some choice quotes.

'I've definitely seen our side charged with assault for less than that,' says Jane. 'In fact, I've been arrested for a lot less.'

As the MP climbs into the car with his son, Phil shouts: 'Well done, you've just fucked your career, mate!'

Dyson has his mobile clamped to his ear and the worries of the world on his shoulders. Back at the Free State word has spread of the incident. One camera crew is setting up and another is panning around the camp. A reporter comes over to us by the fire with the cameraman.

'I've just heard from my office. Stewart's been charged with breach of the peace. He's resigned from the government,' he says. I can see the cameraman's smile as he captures our screams, shouts and yips.

'And his son's been arrested for possession of an airgun without a licence.' We all go schizo. Dom's jubilant dance nearly results in him landing in the fire.

It's time for serious celebration. Gehan climbs down from the octagonal treehouse with a huge rucksack. She opens it and within are three half-gallon demi-johns. 'Birch sap wine anyone?'

It tastes like alcoholic maple syrup though not quite as sweet.

'I'm not quite sure what flavours are in this,' I say to Charlotte. 'Can I borrow your palate?' I can taste hint of menthol on her tongue but am not sure if that's the wine or the roll-ups. Still, it's a good ruse to snog her, as if I needed one.

'Shall we go back to yours? I want you to grasp my pickaxe handle,' I say cheekily.

We ask if we can decant a bottle's worth of the wine and stop at the off-licence for three more.

Within thirty minutes we're naked – two hours later we're soft-focus – swigging, sucking, shagging, secreting, sweating and serotonin-soaked.

Next morning I'm awoken to breakfast in bed and a large bottle of Irn-Bru.

'This is the king of hangover cures,' she says as I try to drag her back into bed.

I'm feeling pretty wrecked and my mood isn't helped by reality crashing back into my world. 'You know Dom's driving back later today,' I say rubbing a hand over my face.

'And?' She pushes the breakfast aside and lies on my lap demanding eye contact.

'Not sure. I wish I could clone you and take one of you back with me.'

'The original or the copy?' She pins me to the bed.

'Oh, the copy would do, I suppose,' I say with fake nonchalance.

She flops onto the other side of the bed, facing away from me.

'These few days have been amazing, you're the best thing to have happened to me in ages.'

'But.'

'But I live in Manchester. I have a fully formed life there. Granted, it'll have a you-shaped hole in it. I can come and visit ...'

'When? Every six months? In between the last arrest, latest action and next court case?'

'I promise. Next month?'

'You'd better. Or I'll come down to Manchester and squat your house.'

'If it wasn't for your degree I'd suggest it right now. I suppose we'll just have to see how it goes, eh?' She's receptive to a hug but I can feel our closeness ebbing away by the second. What can we do? As Billy Bragg once sang – here I am a victim of geography.

I get dressed, pack my tat and she walks me back to the camp to meet the others. As we arrive Colin's sweeping the paths and Gehan's cooking – yes – porridge.

'You've been a lucky charm to us this week,' says Colin.

'You guys have got more going for you than luck from what I've seen this week,' I say vainly squeezing Charlotte's hand.

Phil's running up the path. 'Lester, there you are. We've been waiting for half an hour for you to show. Dom's getting jumpy about the traffic.'

'Ok ok, don't spit your dummy, I'm coming.' Perhaps a quick get-away will be less painful.

I turn to Charlotte. 'Feels like we've crammed a year into less than a week.' I see a tear form on her lower lash and I start to well up.

We share each others' mouths once more – who knows – perhaps for the final time. I don't know what regret tastes like but I'm sure think I'm getting some right now – and break away while I still have the chance.

Dom isn't impressed as I climb in. 'Just because you've had a little shag palace in town doesn't make it right to make us all late getting back.'

'Fuck off, I'm having a bit of a moment here.' As the van turns a hard right out of the camp all that is Charlotte starts to slip away. She runs on behind the van – I wave and we share final diminishing eye contact before we're lost in the lunchtime traffic.

'We should do something to support those guys,' says Jane. 'Let's see if Wimpey have any projects in Manchester when we get back.'

Four days in February. What would sane people do with 96 hours during the coldest month of the year? Visit a solarium? Fly to the Canary Islands? Watch the Simpsons on video with a big pot of soup on the stove? Wrong – the Manchester EF! answer to this conundrum is to sit up this fucking Wimpey crane that a quick examination of the city skyline has provided.

Yes to shitting in a carrier bag 200 feet in the air (again). Deffo to sub-zero sleep on a metal platform – it's a good job I don't sleep-walk. A big 10-4 to slowly running out of food and sensation in my legs, which isn't exactly the best way to get down.

Don't get me wrong – it isn't all suffering – Helen has a copy of the complete works of Winnie the Pooh and each night she reads to those of us who haven't got down and been arrested. We fall about reciting:

> The more it snows
> Tiddley Pom
> The more it goes
> Tiddley Pom
> The more it goes on snowing
> And no-one knows
> Tiddley Pom
> How cold my toes are growing

Highlight of the first evening is some of the workers setting a fire to smoke us out. We use the mobile to call the Fire Brigade who come and tell them to put it out. Ok, Wimpey are building an office block and not a road here but it'll learn 'em anyway.

Day two sees us getting acquainted with our new surroundings. We have four tarpaulins to hang around one section in order to provide a bit of shelter, and Tango treats us to a prolonged explanation of the world of the pygmies of West Papua. Hoo-fucking-ray.

Day three ... seems to just be there. I think we're all spending a little too much time living up cranes and it's starting to show. Still, we're getting some decent TV coverage. Before our mobile ran out of power Phil was keeping us informed of where we ranked in the news bulletins. Oh – and my lips are more cracked and broken than a leper's loins.

On day four, when I rise to have a piss, the calories-for-movement exchange has broken down and all I'm getting from my calves is severe cramp. At this point a sensible person would decide it was time to come down. Indeed, that I do is a clear indication I haven't quite yet lost the plot in all this madness just yet. Tim agrees to go down with me. Helen massages my legs to get the blood circulating again. I don't want to let on to the others but as well as feeling weak, hungry and cold – I'm not enjoying this action one iota. Perhaps it's just the extreme conditions up there which are sending me slightly delirious. Maybe I should join Neil and get a proper job.

I try not to think about my demotivation as we climb very slowly down to the ground where we are arrested for Aggravated

Trespass by a couple of cops not much older than ourselves. One looks strangely familiar but I can't quite place him.

'Where do I know you from?' I say.

'Nowhere I can think of,' he replies. I look at him intently.

'Something tells me I don't know you from here, so you must be from Sussex, yes?'

'Yeah, what of it?' Then the penny drops. This wanker was a couple of years above us at school and used to pick on me and Dave for being smarter than the average comprehensive kid.

'You're Paul Reed, aren't you? From Boundstone?'

'Yeah.' He looks somewhat taken aback, and I can tell from his expression he hasn't an earthly who I am.

'How's your brother Mike? Pretty decent midfielder as I remember. Did he trial for Pompey in the end?'

'Nah, dodgy cartilage in both knees.'

'Yeah, I always remember he was a decent guy, whereas you were a total cunt through the whole of school.'

'Who are you?'

'That's for me to know, twat brain.'

'Leave it L ... ' says Tim, before I give him a stern look stop him saying more. Ok, I can see this is childish, but I think I've earned the right to some fun after all I've been through. There's an over-riding sense of injustice about all this. The whole point of doing all this in the beginning was freedom, now I'm going to get it taken away yet again. I'm just trying to do the right thing. Ok, we might get up people's noses every now and again – a bit like now, but they're either planet trashers or people getting in the way of our objectives. And why am I always skint? Where's my pension fund? Why isn't the rest of society backing us? I've spent the best part of two-and-a-half years running around fighting everyone else's battles and what have I got to show for it? An ever-expanding criminal record. Let's just say I'm not in a good mood. Rant over.

'Still trying to work out who I am there, Paul? Brain not quite up to it? Perhaps that's why you joined the force,' Even though it was years ago there's a bit of payback for all those times he hacked me down in the playground, held us down and administered dead legs for no reason.

'Shut the fuck up, whoever you are. We'll be at the station soon and I think a night in CDC is just what you need,' he says with a grin, reaching for his notebook.

We soon find that CDC is the Central Detention Centre – what others would call the drunk tank. During processing I decide to play ball and give my real name through sheer exhaustion.

I'm in a cell with some guy who's clearly coming off of something. Shaking, retching, muttering, crying and screaming his way through the night. Needless to say the quality sleep I had virtually hallucinated about for most of this week is not forthcoming.

In the morning I'm transferred to the main holding cell at 7am and see Tim there.

'How was it for you?' I ask Tim.

'I was in with him,' he points to tiny bloke – not more than five-four, wearing a paper boiler suit. 'Apparently he stabbed his wife to death last night.'

'Shit. So we can assume from that getup his clothes have failed the boil wash.' I look at the little guy. I've never been in the presence of someone who's taken a life before, and didn't expect it to be a near-midget.

Court doesn't start til 10am so we've got three hours in here. I can smell the sickly sweet odour of my smackhead cellmate. Like I said, last night he was sleeping like a baby – crying, with his pants full of shit, wishing he had a bottle in his hands.

'Where are the others?' I ask.

'Don't know how, but they must still be up there. I'm glad you had cramp when you did.'

I dare say there's a cross-section of Manchester's low-lifes in with us this morning. A wife beater here, a petty theft there. Joyriders, burglars, drink drivers, drug dealers, mostly alone with their thoughts or pacing around. I overhear a couple of crims in the corner sharing a story. I only make out the final line of '... he keeps going to the doc to get it cleared up, but she don't know he's given it to her, so every time he fucks her he gets it again,' and the resultant gale of laughter.

Our solicitor Chris arrives, a hefty stack of folders under his arm. 'Morning, lads, we haven't got long before the hearing. Word is the police aren't too happy about your little publicity stunt over the last few days.'

'Well tough tits,' I reply. 'It's a free country. Still. Isn't it?'

'Well, let's put it this way, I don't think they're going to go easy on the bail conditions this time. Good news is at least they are open to bail.'

'Christ, you'd think we've raped and murdered some granny the way they carry on,' says Tim.

'I think they definitely want to take this to trial to teach you a lesson. If you plead guilty you can avoid that.'

'I'm not pleading guilty to aggravated trespass. It shouldn't be a fucking law in the first place. Sorry, Chris,' I say.

'That's ok, you know I agree with you. Tim?'

'I'm with Lester on this one.'

We're led up from below into the dock around 10.30, the hand-cuffs removed and we're flanked by a couple of Group 4 guards.

Tim takes off his jumper and beneath it is his 'Too Drunk to Fuck' Dead Kennedys' T-shirt. I stifle a giggle.

'All rise,' says the clerk of the court and we reluctantly stand.

The three magistrates come in – two women and a man in that order. After a minute of paper and pen arrangement and water pouring, the woman in the middle, who has a pair of those glasses which hang from a chain around the neck, looks at us. Her eyes narrow and it's obvious she's looking at Tim's chest and taps the other two on the elbows.

'Young man,' she says after some conferring. 'I must ask you to cover up the message on your shirt or you will be held in contempt of court.' Tim and I share a look as he reaches for his jumper. A snort of mirth is the only sound in the entire court. And it's coming from me.

'This is no laughing matter. If you have no respect for this court, perhaps you should be led down to the cells to contemplate your attitude. Is that what you want?'

'No, ma'am,' I say with roundest middle-class vowels I can muster. Tim puts on the jumper. It's plea hearing take two.

'Lester Stype. It is put to you that from Monday, February the sixth, until Thursday the ninth you occupied a crane on Clarkson Street, Manchester ... How do you plead?'

'Not guilty,' I say. Tim does the same when the charges are put to him. We are allowed to sit down.

The magistrate looks to the clerk below her, and he is already on the phone to check for available dates for the trial.

Great. Another court case. More days spent listening to all this legal crap.

The clerk announces: 'June the twelfth, thirteen and fourteen are available ma'am.'

'That only leaves the matter of bail conditions,' she says. 'Given the nature of the incident I believe there is a strong possibility that similar offences may be committed between now and the trial. Mr Binns, do you have anything to say on behalf of your clients?'

'These are community-minded young men of good character. I think a residency bail would be sufficient on this occasion.'

The ruddy-faced prosecutor pushes himself to his feet. If I had to guess it looks like a lifetime of knocking back post-court port has given him gout. 'Ma'am, it is view of the CPS that a residency bail would not prevent similar incidents from occurring.'

Again more conferring, looking like a dimwitted veteran version of University Challenge. Tim has his arms crossed with his middle finger raised on his cheek. Nice touch.

'Would the defendants please stand,' says the main magistrate. 'We are inclined to agree with the prosecution stance with regards to this matter. Both defendants are ordered to reappear at 10am on June the fifteenth. If – in the intervening time either of you enter any building site with a mind to carry out a similar stunt – a warrant will be issued for your arrest. Is that understood?'

This is unreal, it's even taken the wind out of Chris's sails. 'Just to clarify, ma'am,' he says, 'is that any site in Manchester or in the country as a whole?'

'It is a nationwide restriction.'

'But ma'am I must object strongly to these bail conditions.'

'And why is that, Mr Binns?'

'In my experience no peaceful protestors have been given such stringent terms.'

'You are free to take this up with the CPS but unless you or the clerk can make any point in law and everyone understands the nature of the conditions I think I can speak on behalf of my colleagues in saying the matter is closed. You are free to go – for now.' She nods at the clerk who stands and says: 'All rise.'

Chris treats us to a coffee and sticky bun in the café.

'I'm sorry, guys. I had an idea they were going to try something but this is way off the scale,' he says dejectedly.

'Not to worry,' I reply. 'You did your best. Anyway, I don't know about you, mate, but I'm kind of proud of these conditions. Makes me feel we've had an impact.'

''Spose so, says Tim, 'it's a good job we're not out-of-work builders or else we'd be pretty fucked.' He continues, 'Of course I didn't say this, Chris, but I couldn't give a toss about this bail. Fuck 'em all.'

'Too right,' I say. But right now, all things considered, I could do with some sleep and a steady income more than all this hassle. And while I'm at it, a decent girlfriend who lives in the same city as me rather than sharing the night with a shit-covered junkie. Still, as John Major once said – when your back's against the wall you have to turn around and fight.

CHAPTER **8**

SPRING 1995

Having not been to Oxford before, I always imagined it was full of rosy-cheeked girls from Walton-on-the-Naze called Rosalind – the kind you could romp with in a haystack if you ply her with enough Pimms. And ex-public schoolboys sticking their heads up each other's arses on the rugby field every Wednesday and Saturday afternoon – the adolescent replacement for slamming each other's dicks in the desks at prep school.

Basically, I always thought Oxford was posh. Don't get me wrong – some of it is – but sat here in Cowley Road Community Centre it's all a bit council, as my mate Dave would call it.

Helen and myself have travelled down on the coach to talk tactics with this Third World campaigning group. Highlight of the trip was some little kid in the seat in front. He was trying to say 'sugar' to his mum but it was coming out as 'shagger' and the more she tried to stop him the louder and more frequently he said it. I suppose direct action's like that in a funny kind of way.

Jeremy is the co-ordinator of the Lloyds and Midland Boycott campaign, otherwise known as LAMB. His threadbare jumper on top of a crisply ironed check shirt makes me think he's a trustafarian – someone who's playing the activism game 'til he gets bored and then gets a job at Daddy's insurance company in the City. Someone who'll inherit the family estate one day. The only estate I'll ever inherit is a poxy Vauxhall Cavalier and I don't even want to pass my driving test.

My eyesight isn't all that good but Jeremy is wearing those bottle-end glasses. Someone told me that being that shortsighted was a sign of stress. If that's the case Jeremy needs the world's biggest spliff and a year-long blow job to chill him out. Still, he's got the stupid wispy facial hair to go with it once he is. I suppose it's reasonable to say he hasn't made a good impression thus far, and lecturing to the two of us from the front of the room isn't helping.

'The banks currently have a total global exposure of £1.3 trillion in HIPCs,' he says with a squint. I look blankly at Helen only for him to continue. 'With the impending risk of mass defaults multilateral agencies have devised structural adjustment programmes and debt-for-equity swaps to reschedule the repayments.'

'Woah, dude, in English, please,' and to think I'm missing my friend Tessa's birthday drinks tonight. Still, considering Debbie will be there I suppose this is my punishment for past deeds.

Helen seems to be more in tune with this inbreed. 'Jeremy, what Lester is trying so diplomatically to say is that we're not familiar with the terminology of this sector.'

'I see,' he says, wiping his glasses on his jumper. Yeah, like fuck he does.

Slowly we go through and Helen translates the financial bullshit. This is the Noddy version we arrived at after a couple of hours:

> Once upon a time there were some countries a long way away. We invaded them and made them poor.
>
> The banks lent lots of money to these poor countries in the 1970s.
>
> Many of these countries were, and are, run by nasty men who spent it on guns, torture equipment and palaces.
>
> The money wasn't spent on schools and hospitals for the starving types.
>
> There was lots of interest to pay on the loans. The countries could not pay. The banks were angry.
>
> The banks talked to the nasty men. The nasty men agreed to cut spending on schools and hospitals for the starving types to help pay the loans.
>
> The only way to pay off the loans was to chop down the forests, dam the rivers and sell off the crops the starving types depended on. The nasty men also had to sell the gas and electricity companies to the banks.
>
> Some pop stars sang a song and held a concert to raise some money for the starving types, but they said nothing about the real reasons they were hungry, and bought them some sacks of grain.
>
> The starving types make up a quarter of the world's population, most living on less than $1 a day.
>
> Many, arguably too many of these starving types had children, and a lot of them died before their first birthday.
>
> For every £1 the UK gives in aid, the banks take £11 back in debt repayments.
>
> And the moral of the story is ... the banks are destroying the planet even more than the Department of Transport. And the starving types don't get to live happily ever after.

'Ok, Jeremy,' I say, feeling more co-operative now it's all been explained. 'What can we do?'

'Well, the Annual General Meeting of Lloyds Bank is coming up soon and some of our committee have suggested you might like to attend.' I sense from his tone he's not so sure.

'Ok, not a problem. Helen, do you think we can raise some numbers for this?' She nods.

Jeremy asks, 'I've not been involved in this kind of thing before. This may sound like a stupid thing, but what tactics would you employ?'

'Well,' I say with emphasis to freak him out. 'We've never done such a meeting so I couldn't possibly say. I suppose we'll leave the incendiaries behind on this occasion.'

Almost as a reflex reaction Jeremy manages a startled, 'What?'

'Lester, stop it.' Helen shoves my arm. 'He's only playing.'

We can't just turn up to this meeting – we have to be shareholders. Seems a bit weird to have to give the bank some money, but the campaigners have a bought a load of shares and can transfer them into our names. We only need one to be able to attend.

I stay in Oxford overnight and I go drinking with Andy, an old uni mate studying for a PhD here. He takes me to the Turf Tavern for a few pints. Apparently it's where the drinking scenes in Inspector Morse are filmed.

'There's been another don murdered at St Egbert's college, Inspector,' Andy slurs. We've been acting out alternative episodes of Morse in between catching up on each other's lives.

'You're fucking joking, Lewis, that's five this month.'

'Yes, she was professor of Lesbian Sex studies and had worked night and day inventing the vibrating double-ended dildo.'

'What? A case of 'build it and they will come' you mean?'

'Quite, sir – and like the batteries we found in the murder weapon – she's quite dead.'

With such fun Andy and I pass the evening and ten pints later stumble over the cobbles to the night bus to the ring road. There's virtually no light pollution and it may be the booze but it's one of the clearest skies I've ever seen.

'I suppose this is like the skies they get in Africa,' I say. 'This bank action'll feel weird. If it does any good chances are I'll never meet any of the people it benefits.'

'But that's not why you do it, is it? For the feedback?' asks Andy, picking up a traffic cone and putting it on his head in classic student style.

'I s'pose not, or else we'd all have packed it in a long time ago.'

Back in Manchester Helen and I do a ring-round and get a list of forty names and addresses to send to Jeremy. Within a fortnight a Lloyds share certificate arrives in my name. We're also sent some literature about the LAMB campaign. Apparently each new student account is worth £18,000 in profits over a lifetime and according to some survey they did there seems to be lots of students who haven't banked with Lloyds or Midland – the two UK banks who are owed the most by developing countries. One thing the debt crisis is linked to is the drugs trade as it forces poor countries to grow crops which can generate the most money. Not sure if this is a good thing or not. Will have to give it some thought next time someone offers me a line of something.

Thankfully a lot of the old guard from Manchester and Leeds are here to make up the numbers. Yet again we drive down in a minibus from north to south, filling up with petrol on the way, swelling the profits of the oil companies and consequently the banks. However, short of walking, there isn't much of an alternative.

The AGM is to be at the Barbican so we've arranged to put everyone up in the Rainbow Centre the night before the action. A squatted ex-church in Kentish Town, it's warmish, dry and costs nothing – perfect for our purposes. Jeremy and a few others from Oxford have turned up. I hope he speaks something approaching English in the briefing later on. Also, there is Melanie from the guerrilla video group Undercurrents, who is making a short film about LAMB. While everyone is settling in, staking out sleeping bag space and being media tarts, Helen and I are off to Soho for a special mission.

'Six pairs of thumbcuffs and six pairs of handcuffs, please.' Call me naïve but I've never bought anything from a sex shop before. We won't be able to get D-locks through security.

'Don't worry,' Helen says to the bloke behind the counter. 'It's not for sex.' I'm not sure this has clarified our purpose but am glad Jeremy gave us the dosh to cover the bill.

On our way out the shop I have a quick look through the videos.

'Look Helen, The Cock-Mess Monster. That's a genius title.'

'If you say so. Let's go.'

I should have known nearly fifty people sleeping in one room would make setting the alarm for 7.30am unnecessary. Still, better to be safe than sorry – just like the precautionary principle states. I read about it in an article recently and it means that if we aren't sure if global warming and the like is taking place, we should definitely act against it just in case.

We cook up a huge pot of the best precaution against mid-morning hunger – porridge – and everyone starts getting ready for the action. Dreadlocks and suits make for a strange combination, but Mark, Dom and most of the others seem to pull it off. There's some pretty dodgy Oxfam shop efforts knocking about but on the whole people look pretty presentable. Tango looks stranger than ever – I suppose it's difficult to find a suit colour to match if you're a raving ginger. Of the ladies, Jane is predictably the pick of the crop in a turquoise off-the-shoulder number. Still, it isn't a fashion parade – we have serious shareholder shenanigans to perform.

Again, Jeremy has fronted the money for the tube tickets – he isn't all bad and seemed to have had a really good time when we arrived back last night. I could get used to these subsidised actions – it'd take the heat off my overdraft. However, there is a bit of a feeling that our hands are tied. There was talk of doing the fire alarms but we don't want to go too far this time round. Having said that, there are no leaders in EF! and if someone wanted to do so I wouldn't condemn them.

There's isn't loads of security but Grope 4 have been hired and there are enough for us to be on our toes. Like with the Texas action all those months ago, due to our age no amount of dressing up is going to conceal why we're here.

We'd guessed there'd be metal detectors on the door, so we've advised everyone to hide their thumb and handcuffs in their shoes. It's a good job most of the women are wearing suitable footwear. I go to the toilets to remove the cuffs and on leaving see Melanie outside the ladies armed with a camcorder.

'How did you get that in here?' I ask astounded.

'It's a spare. I hid it in the sanitary towel bin yesterday and hoped it wouldn't get emptied overnight.'

There's about 300 chairs arranged in rows and we're by no means the only people interested in this event. Seems for people with nothing better to do than follow their share portfolio it's an excuse to dress up and come to London for the day. Three big floral arrangements grace the front of the stage, and the bank's logo is projected onto the back of the hall like in a cinema. I'm buddied up with Jeremy of all people and we sit a couple of rows from the front. If it's not going to be fun, it'll certainly be different.

While Sir Robin Ibbs, the bank's chairman, makes his opening remarks I look around the room and share a smirk with some of my fellow 'shareholders'.

Claire and Nick grin back at me. I assume now they're married they must need the handcuffs every now and again to spice things up again. Some of the M11 bunch were up for coming along, and it's good to be on an action with the likes of Gary and Ann again.

To my left about three rows back I see something which causes me to momentarily forget about Sir Robin, the meeting, the troubles of the world and my role in trying to sort them out.

Female of course, five-foot-eight, maybe nine. Black hair cut into a longish bob, framing a face I immediately fall for. What is it about love at first sight? It must be something to do with what your DNA wants your kids to look like. And I didn't think I ever wanted any. Green or blue eyes? Too far away to tell exactly. And is that a nose stud or a freckle? She's my age, or perhaps a smidgen younger, and although she's about fifty feet away I can see she's got it all going on bodywise – athletic but with pronounced breasts – just the way it should be in most lads' utopia.

I can't explain why adrenaline is shooting up and down my spine. It's certainly nothing to do with Sir Robin's speech. Considering I haven't spoken to her yet that's quite an impressive effect. I've no idea who she is, where she's from or if I'm going to meet her again, and yet in five seconds I've fallen in love. Is that sad or what? I suppose I do know something about her. Making a snap judgment from her appearance and age I guess she's not here to check on the performance of her portfolio.

'What are you looking at?' Helen leans over and whispers from the row behind.

'Nothing, just trying to psych out some of the shareholders, that's all.'

My attention reverts back to the meeting when Jeremy asks a jittery question. 'Er, Sir Robin, my name is Jeremy Tugwell, ordinary shareholder.' I feign a sneeze to cover my amusement at his surname. 'In the last twenty years banks across the globe have received £2.5trillion in debt repayments and Lloyds holds twice as much debt as the Midland Bank. My question is, does the bank have any plans to write off any of this sum in debt forgiveness?'

Sir Robin looks down over his half-moon spectacles. 'Our position is currently under review but in the main we take our lead from international institutions such as the International Monetary Fund. Next question?'

I can clearly make out Jane's voice calling out, 'Answer the question, Sir Robin!' and this provokes the first flashpoint of the morning. After a few months' travelling, Rachel, she of the politically correct police, is back – complete with a long African print skirt and righteous indignation to match. She steps out into the aisle and speaks without a microphone. 'I've travelled extensively within Africa over the last year and I have seen with my own eyes the hardship the banks are causing.' A slow handclap starts among the non-activist shareholders.

'Young lady, there are certain rules which dictate how this meeting is conducted, and speaking out of turn is not allowed.'

'Well you should learn to answer the questions put to you,' she says, the red rushing into her cheeks, looking not unlike how I'd imagine Rosalind from Walton-on-the-Naze to be.

'If you do not stop this, I will have to instruct the guards to remove you from the meeting.'

'Whatever, you don't have the right to silence me,' and at this he signals four guards to take her from the room. At this she wraps herself around the legs of her chair. From where I'm sat it's impossible to see what's happening, but the pitch of her voice has raised to a scream and – to give Rachel her due – she's stronger than I'd imagined. Before all four guards are in position Paulo has dived in to join her – good on him but it's not part of the plan.

'He's just kicked me in the head, the bastard!' Paulo shouts at the top of his lungs. You've got to hand it to him in terms of bottle after what happened to him at Claremont.

Four more guards approach and both of them are carried kicking and screaming from the hall. I look for a reaction from Jeremy, and though he's clearly outside his comfort zone there's the trace of a smile.

'What do you think of the show so far?' I ask him.

'Fascinating. I trust this is just the entrée?'

'You could say that, mate.' I've been working on my party piece for later.

With order restored a middle-aged woman I assume is a 'real' shareholder is given the microphone. 'Sir Robin, may I congratulate the board about the record profits this year. I would also like to praise the staff of my local branch in Kidderminster. There's always a ready smile whenever ...' Sorry, I've lost the rest of what she's saying. It's like those bits of Prime Minister's Question Time when MPs have a minute to jam their nose firmly up the PM's backside.

Now the next person to be given the mike has my full undivided attention. It is she – the new organic apple of my eye – the mysterious target of countless sideways glances so far. I've yet to catch her glance.

'Ladies and gentlemen, my name is Sarah Jenkins, ordinary shareholder.' There's a Northerly lilt in her voice, hidden in part by higher education somewhere more southerly. 'I would like to address this meeting on the subject of Lloyd's involvement in the finance of arms to Indonesia. For those not familiar with the background to this, I will explain ...'

'Excuse me young lady, are you trying to ask a question or deliver a lecture?' Sir Robin interrupts with a smug, fat grin.

'I have a very pertinent question to ask if you would only let me speak.' She certainly puts the pert in pertinent. 'The military dictatorship of Indonesia invaded the island of East Timor twenty years ago.'

'Where's East Timor?' I whisper to Jeremy.

'Indonesia.' I look blankly. 'North of Australia.' Like I said, he has his uses. I don't want to seem ignorant if I get to speak to her later.

Meanwhile I keep one ear on the rest of her question. 'Since then, a third of the East Timorese people have been murdered. Two hundred thousand people wiped out by this highly undemocratic regime. The question I would like to ask is, how can you possibly justify this bank helping to finance the sale of Hawk aircraft to Indonesia, especially considering the planes have been used to attack East Timor?'

'Well Miss ... Jenkins,' replies Sir Robin, 'the sale of armaments to foreign governments is of course a sensitive subject, and we take every care to maintain the most stringent standards in deciding who we do and do not do business with. The Indonesian government is an ally of this country. The deal to which you refer has been granted full government export credits and, to my knowledge, the Hawk Trainer aircraft are indeed, as the name suggests, for the training of pilots, and have not been used in the governance of East Timor.'

'I do believe you are mistaken there, Sir Robin.' Authoritative. Intelligent. Gorgeous. With every word she speaks, I can feel myself completely lost in her intoxicating presence. If you could bottle how I'm feeling right now, it would outsell anything the Body Shop has to offer by a factor of a hundred.

She holds a document aloft and prods a finger at the front page. 'This is a transcript of a first-hand account of the Dili massacre, which clearly shows that Hawk fighters did indeed bomb the village.'

'This isn't a matter I can deal with right now. Perhaps you would like to send your findings in writing to Corporate Affairs. Right, are there any more questions, perhaps about other aspects of bank business?'

Over the next half an hour there is the odd question about conventional bank business, but in the main it's a torrent of queries about the bank's ethics – lending to projects that cause environmental damage, the effect of the boycott upon the number of student accounts and so on.

There's a disturbance towards the back of the room. Melanie's video camera has been seen and a couple of the shareholders are taking it upon themselves to try and take it off of her. I get up out of my seat to get a closer look. Dom dives under Helen's chair and locks his leg to hers. Top move.

Sir Robin has clearly had enough. He shouts above the din. 'All those in favour of ending the question session and moving onto the resolutions of the meeting, please raise their pink voting cards!'

Despite howls of protest, the shambolic vote takes place and we lose. It's clearly time for the real fun to start. Helen feels it too, as she pokes me in the back and winks as I turn to acknowledge her.

She's standing on her chair and shouts: 'Sir Robin, please could you try and maintain some order in the meeting? I'm sure everyone would appreciate it if you actually did your job!'

I cup my hands and shout 'Wave one go!' The plan is for all activists without locking devices to get up and storm the stage. There is insufficient security to deal with us all but police are starting to pile in through the back doors. We haven't got much time. I secure my thumb inside one end of the cuffs inside my jacket pocket.

'Wave two go!' Everyone with locking devices is to attach themselves to anything which comes to hand. I run towards the stage, the chrome-coloured cuffs now visible to all.

'Christ, he's got a facking blade!' I hear a guard shout as I climb onto the stage.

There's no time to correct him as I jump over Lindsey wrestling with a guard.

Another guard is directly at my back but I have youth on my side and my objective right in front of me.

I lunge at Sir Robin's microphone lead and secure the cuffs around it with my free hand. Come on.

Within seconds I'm bundled to the ground surrounded by police.

A WPC with a tense, pinched face bends down and asks me to unlock. I shake my head and sit tight.

'Where's the keys?' she asks. I shrug.

Displaying a genuine lack of common sense she tries to pull on my arm, presumably to prise my thumb from confinement. 'That's not gonna work now, is it?' I say.

'I wouldn't give the Sarge any shit if I were you,' said another of the officers.

Throwing me a foul look she signals for one of the venue technicians to come over. I look over to Sarah's chair. She's standing on her chair, looking towards the stage and clearly loving every minute of it. Result.

My view of her is obscured as the rotund technician unplugs the microphone lead then kneels over me trying to thread the lead through the end of the cuff. It won't go.

'Again. Where's the key?' says Sarge in a hard-faced bitch kind of way.

I can hear the unmistakable sound of Tango being carried out. 'The logging roads of Kalimantan are bringing dysentery and death to the Iryan Jayans!'

'What's he on about?' asks one of the officers.

Fascinated by the inch-long hairs growing out of the techie's nose, I say: 'Sorry about him. Bit of a prick.'

'It's no good. The only way we're going to shift him is to cut the lead.'

'You might as well. I think the meeting's adjourned,' I say.

'This'll do it.' Mr Nosehair says producing a Stanley knife.

The blade gnaws through the copper and the last of the plastic casing succumbs. Four guards are summoned to lift me and I'm carried out through all the pandemonium, suspended by the feet, one shoulder and my tie. Sarge follows in close quarters. I sense another notch on the arrest bedpost is imminent.

'I can't believe this is how the bank treats its customers!' I shout as I'm unceremoniously dumped on the front step heralded by the click of camera shutters. Jeremy has done a decent job alerting the financial press to the action.

'Are you ok?' asks one of the LAMB leafleters. Next to him is an effigy of the Lloyds Bank horse lying dead on the floor as another guy flogs it with a home-made whip.

Sarge says: 'It's lucky for you the bank didn't want to take things further, or you'd be in Bishopsgate nick by now.' It's best I don't give her any lip – that's what she wants. 'It just shows how neutral you really are.' I reply.

Sarah appears through as I regain my breath. She leans over me and I stare right into her vivid eyes the colour of leaves in a vibrant jungle canopy.

'You ok? That looked pretty rough,'

'I've been worse. Lester.' I offer my hand. As our fingers meet the tingly, fizzy feeling of infatuation surges through me. I haven't felt this good for months. Debs, Brigitte, Charlotte and all the others seem like they memories from someone else's life. She's hotter than Joan of Arc's arse when she was burnt at the stake.

'Sarah,' she says. 'I work for CAAT.' Despite rolling my eyes knowingly she adds, 'Campaign Against the Arms Trade,' and points to some other activist types, for some reason mainly dressed in green and purple.

As I push myself up from the pavement she offers her hand again. In my book that's a sign of flirtation if ever I saw one. 'So did you enjoy that?' I say, 'By the way, I thought you were good in there. Very persistent.'

'Compared to you lot we were a bit tame. I didn't even get thrown out, although they were threatening to at the end when I wouldn't shut up. I would have been more raucous but I am officially at work today.'

'No worries, you've scored loads of cred points already if you ask me.' I want to add a wink but feel that'd feel like I was playing the Sid James role in Carry on Protesting. 'Did I miss anything exciting?'

'By the end it was a complete shambles. They had to take the final votes above a load of shouting and screaming. By the way, this is

Francis, and this is Erin.'

It was only then I notice she has two people with her. My field of vision back to normal, I shake their hands.

'Francis is a leader of the Timorese resistance, and Erin works with me.'

'Nice to meet you,' I say, immediately turning my glance back to Sarah.

Dom comes over to the four of us. 'I think everyone's moving off to the pub now, how about yourselves?'

I try to play it cool in the boozer – if that can be defined as sitting next to Sarah and offering to buy her a drink inside two minutes.

'So,' she said, sipping her pint of cider, 'What do you do when you're not getting thrown out of AGMs?'

'You know, this and that. Help keep things ticking along in Manchester, and travel around doing actions. I was at the Claremont eviction, and a couple of the other biggies.'

'You were at Claremont! I missed it, I was abroad after my finals. What was it like?'

'I'm not really the person to ask as I was in one of the bunkers. I couldn't see much,'

'I heard about those bunkers. They sounded amazing! I think that's where I'd like to have been if I'd been there.' I want to tell Paulo I've found 'the one' but that would mean leaving her side. Oh shit I've got it bad this time.

Jeremy comes over clutching a lime and soda.

I stand and salute him. 'All hail the chief. Come on, man, live a little. Toast the trashing of your foes with a fucking pint.' I think all the excitement of the day has made me a mega lightweight booze-wise.

'Thanks, but alcohol doesn't agree with me,' says Jeremy, 'but I'm sure the campaign could just about stand buying a round.'

'Steady, mate, I'll feel like a semi-pro at this rate. Mine's a lager.'

There's time for two more pints before the minibus has to leave. As the last quarter of the second one drains away, I feel my mood change for the worse.

'What's the matter?' Sarah asks.

'Can I be honest?'

'Fire away.'

'I didn't think you peaceniks agreed with that kind of thing. Ok – joking apart – I want to get to know you better and would give up my space on the minibus to know what's going on in your head right now.'

'If it's any consolation I think you're great too. Look, here's my card. Give me a ring anytime. We'll hook up next time you're in London.'

'Sounds like a deal.' I scribble down my number on a beer mat. As I place it in her palm I leave my hand resting in hers.

We draw each other close, the pint glasses reflecting in her eyes.

'Do I deserve a kiss for trashing the mike lead?'

'You sure do,' and my lips receive a gentle cider-tinged caress.

It's been a week since the AGM and I've been in a foul mood ever since. No prizes for guessing why. The phone rings, and as I reach over to grab it, I spill a cup of tea over myself.

'What!'

'Hello, can I speak to Lester Stype, please?'

'Yeah, this is me, what do you want?'

'It's Sarah, Sarah Jenkins. Shall I phone back? You sound a bit stressed out.' My maladjusted state of mind undergoes instant reform.

'Sarah, why hello. Sorry about that, it's just been one of those days ... in fact it hasn't been one of those days, actually I don't know why I was out of order just now.' Stop babbling, you muppet, and get on the case. 'Anyway, why do I have the pleasure of this call?'

'You know you said I should call if I needed help? Well, there is something.'

Despite the quasi-porn running through my mind the words, 'what's that then?' go down the receiver.

'It's the British Aerospace AGM in two weeks. I'm helping to plan the protest there and thought that the event could do with some more, how should I put it ... impetuous shareholders.'

'So, stop me if I'm wrong here. What you're trying to say is that your bunch are too fluffy to kick up a stink at the meeting, and so it's time to wheel out Rent-a-Mob.'

'Of course not. You must be joking!'

'I am. Of course I'll come, and I'll see who else is into it from here. Ok?'

She laughs. 'Thanks. You had me worried there for a minute. Can you get back to me with the details of who's coming so we can get share transfers in time.'

'Sure.' I make a note of it in my diary. This is a top priority job.

That evening, I meet with Helen, Dom and Phil in the pub. The conversation very soon turns to getting priorities right. 'I've been asked if anyone fancies doing the British Aerospace AGM?'

Helen ruffles my hair. 'Oh – and who asked you that, may I ask?'

'Yeah, alright. So Sarah did ask me to sort it out. It's perfectly innocent.'

'Oh yeah. I suppose next you'll be saying you're not angling to stay at hers after the action.' Now why didn't I think of that?

'Count me in anyway, lover boy.' She tweaks my right cheek between thumb and forefinger.

'Get off me, you old cow, and get us a beer.'

'With charm like that, she's bound to fall at your feet.'

Three days later I ring Sarah at work. 'Hi, I've been doing some spadework and I've got some people for the action. Do you want their names and addresses?'

After each name she replies with a 'mmm'. Images of other circumstances whereby she might make similar sounds flood my mind.

'Listen, I was thinking. I've got to meet up with my solicitor about a case down there the day after the AGM. Is there any chance of staying over at yours that night?' There's no way she can know it's a lie, but I cross my fingers nonetheless.

'Yeah, that wouldn't be a problem, although I am flying out to a conference in Brussels the next day.' It's very difficult to read anything into a statement such as this. 'Lester,' she says. 'It's all a bit hectic around here at the moment, I'll have to go. I'll get the share certificates sent off this week.'

'Well Sarah, I'd love to sit and talk, but things are a bit pushed here as well,' I say printing off guitar tablature from the internet. Yes – I've decided to live on bread and jam for the next fortnight after spending my entire Giro and more on a Tanglewood acoustic. Maybe it's a sign of burnout but activism is starting to lose its charm, and most nights I'm making my fingers bleed trying to learn some easy Beatles songs. Call me a hippy, but learning how to form a C# minor seems far productive than freezing my arse off somewhere with a load of hippies.

'Please can someone stop.' Helen's got another fifteen minutes holding up the hitching sign. We've been on the road since 5am and are at Coleshill just outside Birmingham and trying to change from the M6 to the M42. We need to get to the Marriott Hotel on Park Lane. Traffic, traffic everywhere, and not a ride to hitch.

'All these fucking cars with one person in them. Makes you want to shoot them all,' I say.

'That attitude's not going to get us a lift is it. Smile,' she says as another two cars shoot by.

'The government should bring in designated hitching posts at each junction. Maybe we should negotiate for that next time there's a big campaign.'

'Oh yeah – I can so see John Major going for that.'

'It's no worse an idea than the Cones Hotline.'

'That's not the point. Smile, here comes a lorry,' she says.

Too many hours later we arrive at the eastern end of Hyde Park via a pint in the Bricklayer's Arms. I see Sarah and a dozen other women lying on the pavement at the intersection with Park Lane. A couple are covered in shrouds, the rest are all covered with liberal splatterings of red paint.

'This is no time to be lying down on the job. There's an action to plan,' I say as I stand over her.

'I'll have you know the women's vigil is a very serious and symbolic act.' She's trying to suppress a grin.

'I suppose I can't join in then? In solidarity and that?'

'No.'

'Why not?'

'I don't have to spell it out to you, do I? This is the woman's vigil.'

'That's discrimination. That's disgraceful.'

'Report me to the Commission for Sexual Equality. Or set up a men's vigil if you like.'

'I might just do that,' I beat my chest repeatedly like a gibbon on heat, 'After I've been to the shareholder briefing.'

'Run along then, I'll see you later. I'm supposed to be dead at the moment.'

'And that paint had better be eco-friendly.'

'Be off with you. I'll see you outside the action.'

Inside the hotel, I ask one of the waiters for a cup of coffee and help myself to a couple of biscuits. Helen gives me a holier-than-thou look. 'Aren't you worried about where the money came from to pay for those?'

'Urhgh,' I say through a mouthful of crunch cream. 'If you look at it that way, you're right, but no one else will drink this coffee now it's poured, and I've had most of this biccy.'

Grand Prix drivers, particle physicists and the extremely terminally ill all deal in milliseconds. So do thumb lockers. I was about three inches away from pulling the same trick on BAE's Chairman Bob Bauman as I had on Sir Robin. The action went tolerably well, though you had to hand it to Bauman – he was good – had the avuncular folksy American thing off to a tee. You could imagine him being the devoted grandfather of any Yank under the age of ten.

So convincing was he I almost felt guilty performing my special move – the microphone lunge – but I had a woman to impress so perform it I did. The guards were better prepared than at Lloyds. Maybe they'd been watching a video of our previous match like Manchester United preparing for a big Champion's League game. I was caught by a guard in mid-lunge and all at once my world turned upside down – my body moved violently downward, my torso rotating clockwise, eyes pointing toward the ceiling. Helen fared no better. Within sixty seconds we were both dumped out on the front steps of the Marriot. Sarah's still lying on the other side of the road caked in fake gore.

'Having a good die-in?' I ask, wiping the dust from my suit trousers. Her silken hair is matted red, and the face I would do anything for looking like Carrie from the old horror film.

'Not bad. The fake blood mixture is really doing its job. I made up three bucketfuls.' The only other corpse I recognise is that Welsh lezzer Erin, who looks completely shafted too.

'Looks like I missed out on a lot of fun – if you happen to be a sicko like you.'

'You can talk? You're the kind of person who hangs from things by his thumbs. How did you get on?'

Before I can answer the question, a woman organiser brandishing a megaphone comes over. 'Why don't you make an announcement to everyone what went on in there?'

'Mmm ...'

'Oh go on,' Sarah goads me.

'Alright then, give us that thing ... Hello everyone. As you may have seen, a few of us have been turfed out of the meeting. We got to within a hair's breadth of sharing the mike with the chairman, quite literally.' I hold my thumbcuffs aloft to cheers.

'Though the last I saw of the meeting was through a headlock, it seemed as though we had the upper hand.' I look down at Sarah, who's beaming back.

Just as I finish, the cheers begin again, but this time the heads of the crowd are raised aloft. Hanging from the roof of the hotel is a huge banner BAE, MURDER BY PROXY.

'Nice trick. How the fuck did they get up there?' I ask Sarah.

'Just a little something a couple of us have been working on.' Like Rose West and Myra Hindley before me, I've completely fallen under someone's spell – without the sadistic murders of course.

It's mid-afternoon and I've had enough but try not to show it. All this peace shit is fair enough, but everyone's really serious. It's all death this and genocide that. At least on anti-road camps we have a laugh and muck about. You daren't say anything out of place with this lot. Especially with Sarah's colleague Erin – her mood is as spiky as her hair. I don't know if it's me or blokes in general, but I get the distinct impression she's a labia lapper.

I help Sarah collect up banners, placards and leaflets as she hails a cab.

'Taxis in London, that's a bit swish isn't it?' I say to her.

'We could never have managed this lot back on the Tube. I get the fare back in expenses. It's part of being a paid employee.'

'It's alright for some. I'm fucking good at what I do. I should get paid ... not sure who by.'

'God, you make it sound as if I'm earning a fortune, by the time the bills are paid I'm probably worse off than you.'

She continues, 'I've just got to bung these into the office and then we can go back home.'

In the cab the exertions of the day hit us both. I rest my weary bonce on her shoulder, and she rests hers on mine. We're both off in micro-nap land, gently rocked by the suspension negotiating the potholes of the capital.

She gives me a nudge – the engine gently turning over. I'm relieved to see I haven't dribbled on her.

'Only be a couple of minutes,' she says to the cabbie. I want to object, but I've had enough of being right-on for one day and she's paying.

As we reach the top of the office stairs she says proudly: 'So this is where it all happens. This one's my desk. We're working on trying to free Lucinda and Felicity at the moment.'

'Oh right,' I try to muster maximum enthusiasm, but even I can see I'm not into arms trade stuff, it's just not my bag.

'You know, the ones who smashed the Hawk nose cones with hammers. They've been on remand for a few months now.'

'Oh them. Course I do. It's terrible.' Forgive me for jumping to conclusions, but part of me reckons Lucinda and Felicity smashed up the planes to get some action in prison after lights out.

Though I'm not the World Pulling Champion, based on previous experience I reckon we have sufficient mutual chemistry to make a move later on, but I've sufficient doubt to point and pant like a dog as we pass an off-licence near her flat.

'It's ok you daft bugger, I've got plenty of wine in,' she says patting my thigh. There's physical contact, but it's a pat not a caress. It's a tight call – she's harder to read than A Brief History of Time in Arabic.

Her flat resembles a T-shirt I picked up at Wimbledon one year – mainly purple and green. 'I like it, but what's with the colour scheme?'

'They symbolise the international women's movement,' she says pulling the cork out of a bottle of Sauvignon.

'Cheers.' We chink glasses large enough for me to hope she'll be good and drunk within the hour.

'Thanks for coming down for this. I'm exhausted. A few more days like that and I'll be a prime candidate for the funny farm.' She lays her head on my accommodating shoulder next to her.

'It was a bit mad today, I have to admit.' I stroke her head, my fingers coming to rest on her cheek and move my face to within inches of hers.

'I think you know what I'm going to ask you now.' I stroke the back of her neck.

'I think so.'

'Well?'

She smiles, and I detect the slightest movement of her head toward mine. Our lips meet, then again ... and there's the clincher. The feel of her mouth is every bit as sensuous as it looks. It seems as though everything that ever mattered is slipping away – replaced by unconditional devotion.

I break to say, 'I've wanted to do that ever since I laid eyes on you. I've thought of little else since.' Soppy yet sincere. She reacts with a smile and further petting.

My hand traverses her right shoulder blade, across her back, down to the top of her leggings. Temptation to forage is extreme, analogous to a pig in a truffle field, but I resist. I'm guessing there'll be other times when I can explore freely and get my snout right in there.

Breaking from the latest clinch she says: 'I've just remembered, I've got a flight to catch in the morning. It's not that ... What I'm trying to say is ...' Our hands are entwined, fingers laying and moving within fingers.

I'm going to trust whoever it was who said the best things come to those who wait. 'It's ok. I'll sleep on the sofa bed tonight. It's not a problem. You're exhausted – I'm exhausted. I don't think either of us are fit for much tonight.'

I stroke a stray eyelash from her cheek with gentle precision. 'Sarah, I want you to know I care for you very deeply, and I think you feel something similar for me.' She casts her eyes upwards and shrugs but the accompanying grin is reassuring. 'Look, I'm not about to go all pathetic and pronounce my undying love from the rooftops or anything.'

'It sounds like that to me.'

'Ok, I admit it. I'm falling in love with you.'

'Look – you're great but I don't want to rush things. I've just come out of a relationship and I don't think I'm ready. And there's the distance thing. Let's take it one step at a time. Ok?' She kisses my hand.

'Fine by me. Now, you need to be asleep or you'll miss your plane. I'll come and tuck you in.' Upstairs we went – and though it's all very innocent and I get no further than first base, it's fully forty-five minutes before I finally close the her door and creep down to the sofa bed, punching the air in jubilation as I go.

Signing on – a necessary evil at present – means I can get the odd round in on a Friday night and keeps a roof over my head – on the relatively few occasions I'm in Manchester.

I think they make the place where you sign on deliberately soul-destroying as an extra incentive to get you to fuck off into the work-force.

Whenever I take the numbered ticket from the little machine it makes me feel like asking for meats and cheese like at Tesco's deli counter. My number – 42 – eventually appears on the electronic display – and I stroll over to the nearest available paper pusher. Plonking myself in the seat I hand over my signing card to her and on her return I notice alien material in my file. I don't mean glowing green slime or secret papers from Area 54, but some kind of directive from above.

She's about fifty and nervy – I get the distinct impression she prefers cats to people for some reason. But if I worked in Withington dole office I probably would too.

'Your file shows it's time for your periodic review. Mr Stype, you've been signing with us for the best part of two years.'

'Yep.'

'As far as I can tell here, you left university in the summer of 1993 with one of the best arts degrees this country can provide and you've had not a day's work since.'

'Uh-huh.'

'Well– what have you been up to?'

'This and that. Not much really.' I don't want to tell her about the activism, or they'll probably force me to end it. I'll be made to take voluntary work with old people – or worse.

'The Jobseeker's Agreement you've signed means you must actively apply for at least two jobs a week. If there's evidence that you aren't – as seems to be the case here – your benefits may be withdrawn.'

'But.' I didn't expect this when I rolled out of bed this morning.

'But nothing. You're just not trying. If you'd been travelling or something I could understand. And your signing record has been most erratic.'

'I've been trying so hard. You don't understand.'

'As far as your records show you haven't applied for a single job since graduation. I want you to sign a new Jobseeker's Agreement now promising to apply for two jobs a week. If you don't do that your money will be stopped. Do you understand?'

'Doesn't look like I have a choice.' She enters the new details on the computer then goes over to collect the printout.

'Sign here.' She prods a bony finger towards the bottom. I take the biro and hurriedly squiggle across the dotted line with a loud sigh.

'Excellent.' she says, chalking up another victory against sloth. 'If you bother to check the boards I'm sure there'll be something there for you.'

'Good morning to you too.' I add 'cunt' under my breath as I turn to go.

I meet up with Neil for a pint after work in the beer garden of the Red Lion, Withington.

'Cheer up, you miserable motherfucker. I've had my boss twisting my bollocks about end-of-year figures all day. Count yourself lucky,' he says as he puts the pints on the table.

'Look at those bubbles,' I say pointing at the tiny air pockets rising from halfway up the glass. 'They travel up, and they keep going 'til they reach the surface. Then that's it – release.'

'What's your point, Plato?'

'I don't know – things are all a bit complicated at the moment. The dole nazis are gonna start shoving a red hot poker up my arse soon if I don't get a job.'

'Maybe you should. I'm sure the lentils could manage without you.'

'Thanks – it's just really unfair. I think activism's been one of the best graduate training programmes there is. Responsibility, starting projects from scratch, teamwork, using your initiative under pressure, dealing with tight budgets ...'

'Oh yeah – talking of tight budgets – have you got that tenner you borrowed on Friday?'

'Hmm,' I look in my wallet and hand over the only cash I'll have for five days.

'Thanks. So what's all this philosophising about the bubbles in your pint? Bet you this tenner it's about that bird in London you've been on about.'

A small nod of the head reveals my true source of angst. 'I really miss her, mate. She's everything I ever wanted.'

'Sounds like a fucking lezzer from what you've told me.'

'Some of them are deffo grade one carpet lickers, but not this one. She's amazing.'

'Mate – a bird is a bird is a bird. Look around.' Granted, there are some sorts around us, but they've got white jeans, dangly earrings and seemingly not much attitude.

'You don't understand.'

'No, mate – you don't get it. Have you fucked her?'

'That's the kind of question that proves my point.'

We're near the end of our pints – the only trace of the bubbles ever existing are random smeared trails on the glass, and a gentle giddy sensation stirring in our brains.

'Your round, mate.' Neil lifts a thumb towards the bar.

'But that was my last tenner 'til next week. Sorry.' What is this? National Make Me Feel Guilty Day?

Neil reluctantly pushes himself up and grabs the glasses. 'I'll get 'em in, but maybe you should think about that fucking job, eh?'

Another week, another court case. The planet may be in a bad way but it's a good job the end isn't imminent as I – like so many other activists – am increasingly tied up in too much red tape and bullshit to do anything about it. I don't remember superheroes having to repeatedly appear in court or sign on or get bailed off of every construction site in the country. It would make for very dull Marvel Comics, wouldn't it?

I really can't be arsed with all this trial. Ok, this is the first Criminal Justice Act case and I suppose it has some legal significance, but it's just another day or two of having to sit there while all the procedures roll out. I might as well not be there.

There's only four of us on trial today as everyone else accepted a caution. I meet with my fellow accused – Dom, Helen and Paulo – outside the Cornerhouse Cinema on Oxford Road and as we walk through St Peter's Square it's obvious Dom is much more into this than me. 'Manchester Freedom Network has organised a demo for the opening day of the trial – a Teddy Bear's Picnic – tea, sandwiches, costumes the lot. And people have been asked to bring balls of wool to wrap around Crown Square.'

'Ooh, the cops'll be shitting it I'm sure.'

My sarcasm couldn't have been more misplaced. As we arrive at the court there's cops everywhere. Cops on horses, cops on bikes waiting in the side streets, cops on people's cases tearing down wool hung from trees and lamp posts. There's a good hundred or so people here supporting us – not bad for 9am on a Monday morning – but nearly as many boys in blue.

'Christ, anyone would think it was a murder trial,' says Helen, completely amazed at it all.

As we pass a cluster of three officers Paulo says to them, 'I bet all the burglars in the city are having a field day,' but they barely acknowledge he's there.

'At least we won't get mugged,' I add 'unless it's by them.'

Phil has been on the case and had some T-shirts made. They're black with THE CJB WON'T STOP ME on the front. To maintain accuracy the B is crossed out in red and an A added to show the dreaded legislation is now law.

There's a couple of photographers and a few journalists. We pose for some photos and I try my best to look defiant, but my heart's really not in it. Helen says to Lee from the Evening News: 'Of course we'll fight this stupid law. It's our basic rights at stake and we're willing to go to prison to defend them.' I'm trying to work out why Sarah didn't ring to wish me luck this morning.

While we're hanging around waiting for the magistrates we're all sat in the café. Most of Manchester EF! has turned up to support us and we spill over three whole tables. The talk is of the impending eviction of Stanworth Valley at the M65 – dubbed the 'village in the sky' in SchNEWS – the national direct action newsletter – as a network of walkways connects all the treehouses.

'If it kicks off next week,' says Tim, 'I'm sacking off all lectures to go.'

Helen asks me: 'Are you up for it?'

'Hmm ... well there's my bail conditions to think of, and we're probably going to get more shit today.'

'Come on, we need you there.'

'But Helen, today's a classic example. It's cool that loads of people have turned up to support us, but unless there's a massive outcry they have the power to send us to prison. And I'm not in the mood to get banged up in the showers just yet.'

'I bet as soon as the aruga goes up you'll be gagging to get in the van.'

Chris Binns comes to call us into court before I get chance to answer. 'Ok, we're in in five. We've got a stipe today.'

'Yeah, Lester's the Stype,' says Paulo.

'No – a stipenduary magistrate. Like a district judge.'

As we enter most of the seats in the public gallery are taken up by police, and there's only room for a dozen or so of our supporters.

Chris turns to us and says: 'This is unbelievable for a case of this level of seriousness, but if I raise it as a point the magistrate will think I'm trying to score political points.'

Tim thinks this is so most of our supporters will get bored and go home – and he's not far from the truth I reckon.

The stipe takes his place. He looks younger and more with it than most magistrates. The woman from the Crown Prosecution Service calls the first witness, a building worker, to give evidence against us.

There isn't much of a case for us to fight. Aggravated Trespass is now a criminal offence and all they need to prove is that we were disrupting their work.

I glaze over during the first witness who really hasn't got a lot to say apart from he was prevented from working. Apparently it's contempt of court to draw images of the court, but I amuse myself by doodling, sketching and caricaturing. The two I'm particularly pleased with are the usher bumming the stipe, and the prosecutor being licked out by an Alsatian. I'm no artist, but hey, it amuses me. My boredom is broken by the showing of video footage when Inspector Bishop gives his evidence. It's jerky, the detail is poor and it was taken from the police helicopter. I can just about make out Dom at the top of the crane.

I write WERE YOU ON THE WAY BACK FROM A DUMP, DOM? on a scrap of paper and pass it along the bench and am glad we've something to giggle about.

Helen leans over and whispers: 'Fucking hell, how much did that cost to put together? It's at least four grand to put that thing in the air.'

The most annoying thing about police giving evidence is the way they kiss the magistrate's ring at every turn. They all swear solemnly on the bible to tell the truth, atheist or not. I'm sure atheist cops must exist. Maybe no cop has ever given it any thought – some university should research it.

Correspondents from a few, but not many newspapers sit in the press box, scribbling the odd bit of shorthand every so often.

There's a young woman reporter who I've made a quick doodle of whilst imagining what she's really like – at work, at rest, at play, or even what she'd do with a Mars bar. She's not in the same league as Sarah, but certainly a contender for the end-of-season playoffs.

Chris does his best with the defence case, and we dutifully answer the questions he puts to us, and argue the toss with the prosecutor, but the law we're charged under is so wide-ranging a difficult sheep could probably be charged with interfering with the work of a shepherd.

The usher orders us to stand as the stipe leaves to consider his verdict. I half-heartedly lift my bum off my seat whilst still heavily leaning on the bench. Enthusiasm, respect, anticipation – you name it – I've an absence of it. To be honest none of us think we'll be acquitted, but it's just a question of what the punishment will be.

Well, for those who wish to check their pools coupons, the result was this. 'Section 68 of the Act states that in order for an offence to have been committed, intimidation, obstruction or disruption must have taken place, and that you must have had the intention of doing so.

'There is no doubt that you did not intend to, nor did you, intimidate the workers on the site. We have heard that no attempt was made to obstruct the crane driver when he tried to gain access to the crane.

'The lion's share of the case of the defence has been that you did not intend to disrupt work on the site, that the demonstration was an awareness-raising exercise, both against the building of the M65 motorway, and the Criminal Justice Act. We have heard from arresting officers that you were polite and civil throughout, and that you conducted yourselves very well.

'However, it is my opinion that there were many other, and far more appropriate, and indeed effective methods of displaying your discontent for these issues than the course of action you took – actions and methods that would have kept you the right side of the law. Being intelligent individuals, it is very difficult to believe you did not know that the consequence of your act would cause disruption of the work on the day in question.'

I let out a tut, Dom breathes deeply and looks skywards. Paulo's grinning – I'm not sure what at.

'It is also equally the case that, as intelligent fellows, you would be able to deduce that Inspector Bishop was asking you to come down from the crane, even if you could not hear his order. Bearing both of these points in mind, this court has found all of you guilty of both of the charges put before you.' It feels like we're getting a telling off from the headmaster, and we can't help but smirk. There's a cry of 'shame', and another of 'disgrace' from the public gallery. One of the policemen turns around looking disapprovingly but doesn't escalate the situation. They've got their guilty verdict, and that's enough for them.

'Mr Binns, do you have anything to say for your clients in mitigation before I pass sentence?'

'Yes, your worship, I do indeed. I realise this point verges on the political, but these fine young people are symbolic of more widespread opposition to the Criminal Justice Act. I would urge leniency in this matter. This case is just as much about our basic human rights as much as preventing work on a building site.' At this all the supporters in the gallery cheer and even I find myself clapping my hands together.

Chris continues: 'On a more mundane level, I would point out that all my clients are in receipt of state benefits and would not be in a position to pay heavy fines.'

The stipe replies: 'Court is adjourned while I decide sentence. In this interval, could I also ask that the four of you fill out Statement of Means forms so that your financial position can be assessed? Thank you.'

We rise and fill in the sorry tale of our personal finances on the forms during the break.

Half an hour later our fate is decided. Sections 68 and 69 both carry maximum sentences of three months in prison and £5,000 fines. All four of us are ordered to pay £50 in costs and receive a year's conditional discharge, which means we need to be good in future or we're supposed to be locked up, but it never happens.

'What a bunch of crap,' Helen says in the pub after.

Paulo shakes his head and says: 'That whole case must have cost tens of thousands, maybe more. And all we got was a little slap on the wrist. Pathetic.'

Chris raises his pint in salute. 'Well guys, you might think that but I really enjoyed today and I want to thank you. I know it's not about notoriety, but I've had the news editor from The Lawyer on the phone for quotes. And it was a bloody interesting case.'

'Are you sure? I beg to differ,' I say, holding up the various sketches in my notebook.

Tango's been on good form lately – maybe his new girlfriend has something to do with it. She's called Eloise and is as ginger as he is. I've come up with a little nickname for them – the Orangs – but I haven't used it to their faces yet. He's more chilled, less obsessed with pygmies and has actually been organising his own actions.

A couple of weeks ago I passed a newsagents and the Evening News A-board read 'Car Park Hoax Closure Chaos'. I heard he'd got a copy of the council logo from the internet, designed a poster saying 'Car Park Shut for Essential Repairs' and got up at 4am to fly-post every multi-storey and pay-and-display in the city centre. Genius. He still looks like a pomeranian with dreads – but hey – he can't help it.

Now he's one of the main movers and shakers behind Manchester Critical Mass – a coming together of as many cyclists as possible riding on the last Friday of the month. I couldn't make the first one as I was visiting Sarah but am intent on being there this evening to celebrate the humble bicycle – along with the radio, perhaps the most elegant invention ever devised – apart from fucking punctures of course. Critical Mass has no leaders – it's an 'organised coincidence', but it needs foot soldiers to spread the word, so yesterday I spent a couple of hours photocopying fliers and putting them under the brake cables of bikes around the Arndale Centre.

The meeting point is St Peter's Square at 6pm and as it's June next week there's no need for lights. It's a good job as mine got nicked earlier in the year and I haven't had the cash to replace them. If I was Home Secretary car thieves would be able to get time off their sentences by torturing those who nicked bikes. Reactionary? Surely not – just sensible policies for a happier Britain.

My trusty – some would say rusty – old bike has done me good service. Ok, maybe I'm not the best at giving it love or even oil in return, but I think we have a good understanding overall.

Some EF!ers like Dom and Helen are away preparing for the Stanworth eviction but that's not a problem. It would seem the great thing about Critical Mass is it's on the respectable side of direct action and easier to get people to come along. There's young professionals in suits, young mums with kids on the back seat, city straights and beardy weirdos. Also present are a dozen police, including three on motorbikes. And there was me thinking cycling was a right not a privilege. Silly me.

Jane, Des and Corinne are chatting to some skinny bloke with all the lycra gear and wraparound shades. As I near my suspicions are confirmed – he's American. I thought Yanks were only called Chuck in films, but no, unfortunately he's right here.

Sucking on a Gatorade bottle he says: 'Man, I was at the first Critical Mass in San Fran in '92. It was like, so stoked.'

I'm a) trying to work out what he's saying and b) wondering if he's bullshitting when our Keanu Reeves soundalike pipes up again.

'You should get some strategy going – like junction corking. And do you do Chicago Hold-ups?'

'Do what?' I say. Trust the Americans to take something as simple as riding a bike with your mates and turn it into a pseudo-science.

'Dude, corking is blocking an intersection so the mass doesn't get broken up, and a Chicago Hold-up is this.' He takes his black Cannondale and raises it high above his head with a loud 'Yaaaaaaaa!' Corinne mouths the word 'wanker' whilst rhythmically shaking her fist up and down.

Jane shouts. 'Dom! Hi! Sorry, Chuck, we have to meet our mate over there.' Hooking up with an imaginary friend is the best excuse we have to disengage from this twat.

Des says: 'Apparently we're to start dead on six and head towards Chinatown.'

'Where's the route going from there?' I reply.

'Umm ... I don't think there is one.'

Jane puts us all right. 'Basically, there isn't a route. If you fancy taking everyone in a certain direction you can. The more spontaneous it is the harder it is to control.'

'Fantastic, let's do it.' As we set off the air is filled with horns, bells and whistles of all manner of pitches and tones, accompanied by yips and several examples of its recent successor – the whoop – which sounds rather like the mating call of a howler monkey.

We're also honored to have the Rinky Dink bicycle powered sound system along for the ride, which is pumping out Movin' On Up by Primal Scream.

Sarah goes on the Critical Mass rides in London when she's not breaking into British Aerospace sites around the country. I rang her the other day and I'm still none the wiser as to what's going on in her head. Though I still think we'd make an amazing couple, and I want to shag her into the middle of the next century – I find it hypocritical that she's always going on about defence industry secrecy yet can't give me a straight answer as to how she feels about me. Anyway, sod it, I'm not going to let those thoughts spoil my evening.

There's a guy with a cool T-shirt with ONE LESS CAR stencilled on the front and a woman who's easily keeping up with everyone on her skateboard. Riding aabout ten abreast, we hang a right onto Market Street. We thin out to let a bus through, but there's a taxi trying to sneak in behind it.

'Looks like we've got trouble,' says Eloise, whose purple helmet is another source of amusement for me.

'Let's see about that,' I say and double back towards the rogue vehicle.

The cabbie's about forty-five, looks Greek or Turkish with curly hair and a big porn moustache. There's a couple pedalling as slowly as they can in front of him. A police motorcyclist pulls them over.

'What happening, officer?' I hear the woman ask.

'I'm arresting you both for obstruction of the highway.'

'Jesus Christ, we were moving.'

'Not fast enough. Now stay there.' He reaches for his radio and calls for backup.

Freed from this obstruction, the taxi accelerates up to the next cluster then over-revs behind them. I pedal as fast as I can to get right in front of him. As I cut in front of the cab it lurches forward, catching my back wheel and I'm thrown through the air and land on my kneecap, fortunately to the side of the cab. There are screams and a shout of 'Get his fucking licence number' as I hit the ground. The next sound I hear is the smash of someone sticking a boot through both headlights. I look up to see them quickly ride off into the pack.

The sound system's playing Fish's Eyes by New Fast Automatic Daffodils and I'm trying to block out the pain surging through my leg by trying to work out what the opening lyric – Take your time with the Devil's fish law – actually means.

Of the faces crowding over me to check on my condition, Des and Jane's are the first I recognise as the cab steams off, the driver's mouth forming unheard expletives.

'Should we call an ambulance?' Des asks.

I shake my head. 'No, I think I'll live. Fucking hurts though.'

A policeman comes over and Jane says: 'Aren't you going to arrest that taxi driver? He knocked over our friend and has mashed up his bike. That's dangerous driving surely?'

He screws up his face dismissively. 'The guy's got the right to earn a living. I don't blame him for letting off some steam with you lot playing silly buggers in the road.'

'That's outrageous. He could have been killed. Look at the state of the back wheel.' My favourite eco-babe arguing my corner slightly stems the pain in my rapidly swelling knee.

'I'll be ok, you guys finish the ride.' As Des helps me up, I find I can't put any weight on my left leg.

'You might have to get a cab home,' he jokes.

He checks the condition of my bike and informs me the back forks have been bent out of shape as well as the wheel.

'To be honest, I'm sorry to say it's fucked. You might as well leave it for people to scavenge for parts.'

I prop it up outside the amusement arcade, run my hand over the crossbar as a final goodbye and hobble off with barely the bus fare to catch the number 48.

CHAPTER **9**

SUMMER 1995

'I've got tar on my DMs – motherfucker!' Paulo's less than chuffed at the latest sign of global warming, picking at the black mess in the tread with a stick. The summer's so hot all the roads between Manchester and Glastonbury seem to be melting.

'Shut up moaning. You're about to experience your first Glasters.' I've been several times before as a student and before – but haven't had time since 1993 ... can't think why.

'Are you sure we're gonna get over this ok?' he asks, as we face the fence.

'Don't talk wet. Compared to some we've had to get over this is a piece of piss.' Eight feet high and made of corrugated iron. Paulo puts his foot on my back and he clambers on top of the fence.

'Bollocks!' he cries, but it's a cut finger – not what could get hurt if sat astride a structure such as this.

I throw the rucksacks over and Paulo leans down and pulls me up to his level. There aren't any guards on the other side and reinforced rivets even serve as footholds on the other side.

My knee's fully mended now – took three weeks before it stopped hurting, and as far as I know that bastard taxi driver got away scot-free.

'I feel bad about not paying,' Paulo says as we get our bearings. We've been walking round looking for a Scouser-and-snarling-dog-free section of fence for an hour or two and the lights of the small temporary city below us makes me think we're not too far from the Stone Circle.

'Bollocks, it wouldn't be the same without people blagging their way in,' I say. 'It used to be a free festival for travellers in the first place anyway – we're just keeping the legacy alive.'

We make a beeline for the Green Futures field, both to pitch up, and because Sarah'll be 'personning' the CAAT stall over the weekend.

I find Erin behind cellotaping posters of dead people to an awning.

'Hi, is Sarah around?'

'Not right now. She's popped down to the vehicle to pick up some leaflets and stuff. Can I give her a message?'

'Not really, I'm just anxious to see her.'

'I haven't seen as much of her myself of her myself in the last few weeks, less than I should have done anyway. I'll say you called.' In all this time she doesn't look at me once – as if blokes aren't worth scratching the retinas on.

This festival is to be a special time of celebration as Mark is off to Brazil to do the research for his PhD in rainforest ecology. Lucky bastard. Still, we'll do our level best to give him a decent send off.

This year Leeds EF! is running a café to raise much needed funds. I find it tucked away in a corner, with Clive putting the finishing touches to the ambience – ethnic throws on the walls and floors, beanbags and a coffee table strewn with the odd Action Update.

'Salutations my friend. Long time no see,' says Clive. 'Did you hear about Sparko?'

I immediately fear the worst. 'Oh no, he didn't, did he?'

'Yes, I'm afraid he did,' Clive says with a laugh.

'I think we're at cross-purposes here. What's he done?'

'Well, he jumped over the fence yesterday, loaded up with gear, pills, speed and a few other bits, and where do you think he landed?'

'In some cow shit? On the moon? Between a pair of thighs? How the fuck do I know?'

'Right into the police enclosure,' he says as I double up laughing. 'One full intimate body search later he spent last night in the cells and appeared in court this morning.'

'Hey Clive, you go and enjoy yourself, I'll put a few hours in on the stall this afternoon.' Just because I got in for free doesn't mean I'm not gonna do my bit.

He shows me how to work the video projector. We've got some footage of actions to show as well as some stoner movies such as Microcosmos and off he goes.

The café starts to fill up and I'm rushed off my feet. The main attraction is a herbalism workshop by some beardy Scottish bloke. About all I got from it was that various plants like dandelion are diuretics and make you piss a lot. I'm sure there's more of a scientific basis to it than that, but it was kind of 'Hungover? Eat some dandelions. Got cancer? Eat some dandelions'. He'll say that having a good piss cures AIDS next. One thing I did learn was that celery is a herb. I just thought it was disgusting.

Mark arrives and I get the feeling my shift is nearing its end. 'Are we gonna party or what?' he says.

'Hey Mark, I've got a leaving present for you,' says Paulo, who's been lending me a hand. He places half a dozen pills into Mark's hand. 'These are snowballs, all the rage at the moment – they're from Russia I think.'

'Come on then, boys,' he says, giving us two each. 'We've got some hours to lose out there.'

Lindsey takes over the café and we're off ... just as soon as Paulo skins up a fat one to get us on our way.

'Hold on, I've gotta get some water to take these with.' says Mark, going behind the counter.

'Pah – what a poof. I'm gonna go without,' I say necking both.

When we emerge it's getting dark. By the Tiny Tea Tent there's a woman selling hash truffles for a pound each so I get a round in.

'These'll get us there in no time.'

'No alcohol tonight chaps, it'll only muddle the effects,' says Paulo as he swallows the chocolate treat.

There's a bunch of people dressed in white tunics coming towards us looking like a cult. A woman hands me a piece of cardboard and says: 'For your protection. They will soon make themselves known to us.' It seems to be some sort of device to prevent you from being abducted by aliens.

Turning to Mark I show the 'device' and ask: 'Do you think the average Joes in the street think we're as mad as them?'

'Some do, some don't I s'pose. Most probably think we're a bit over the top,' he replies, 'but hey – fuck 'em, we know we're right, eh?'

Mark bumps into a friend from Leeds on his way to the toilets.

'Hey Spence! How are ya?' he says with a hug.

'Off for a shit,' says the friend, holding a new roll of toilet paper aloft.

'Wow, may I?' I say, wanting to examine the roll.

'Mark, looks like your friend is über-fucked.' Spencer turns to me and speaks very slowly. 'Do ... you ... need ... a ... shit?'

I nod enthusiastically.

'Come to think of it, I do too,' says Paulo, the irises of his eyes barely visible. And yes, the power of suggestion on drugs is such that Mark feels the need as well.

'This way, fellas,' as Spencer leads us, holding the toilet roll aloft, to the nearest bogs.

I still really need to go but my mind wanders onto the subject of Sarah. I grab our new-found shitter-bound saviour by the arm and ask. 'Have you seen Sarah? She's missing ... and I love her.'

'Don't mind him, he's bollocksed,' says Mark as he prises me off. 'It's ok, mate, we'll find her, once you've had a dump I'm sure she'll turn up.'

'Really? That's brilliant. I'm so gonna miss you, mate,' and I give Mark a huge bear hug.

'Ok, how many sheets do you need?' I'm asked as Spencer winds bog roll round his hand. I just gurn and nod.

'Here you go. There's a cubicle, yes, there,' he gives me a wodge of paper and I'm gently prodded in the right direction as another rush surges through me.

I just manage to put cheeks on the wooden seat before the deluge begins and the feeling of release is exquisite.

'Mark!' I shout, 'I thought Sarah would turn up once I'd had a shit. Where is she?' I put my head in my hands and feel like I'm going to cry.

There's a response – but not from Mark. 'Woman trouble, eh?' comes a voice from the next cubicle.

'Yeah – I love her and she's never around. It's like Paul Weller refusing to reform The Jam.'

'I'm with you, pal. And if this woman wanted to be with you, she'd be right here.'

'What, in the toilet?'

'No, you doughnut – you know what I mean.' He continues: 'Look, man, you're at one of the best places on earth to have a good time. So have one. I bet she's not fretting about you right now, is she?'

'But I'm crazy about her – I really am!' I complain.

'Course you are, man, but if you're meant to be together, you will be. And right now you're not, so quit fretting.'

'Yeah you're right.'

'Course I am, man. Go and have a great big toke and have a wicked time.' And with that, the Sage of the Bog was silent. After I wipe the clag and pull up my jeans I open go to say thanks but there's no-one there.

'You took your time, you twat,' says Mark, grabbing me round the neck and rubbing my hair with his knuckles. 'Now you're gonna forget about that woman and we're off to dance our tiny tits off. Ok?'

As we go in search of a party down the disused railway track and much to the lads' amusement I lose my footing and fall into the bushes. Landing among huge rhubarb-type leaves, I take one and put the stalk inside the back of my T-shirt, and emerge, seeming to have a metre-wide frond growing out of my head and saying 'Take me to your leader'.

The rest of the night is pretty sketchy, suffice to say I think I lost everyone and didn't dance to anything much. Around 5am I wake up in the stone circle and watch the peachy sunrise. On my way back to the tent I'm just about lucid enough to notice people are staring at me as I walk past. I borrow a mirror back at the campsite and find NONCE written on my forehead in green marker pen.

Punctured bicycle, on a hillside desolate. Well not quite, it's 2am and we're in Phil's car somewhere in the arse-end of nowhere and Morrissey's giving it large on the stereo.

There's always that feeling of nerves and excitement before an action but it's especially keen tonight. Fear and anticipation merging into a heady mix that fights off any thoughts of sleep. Given the nature of what we're about to do we've never been better prepared than this. I – like the others, I hope – have shifted my body clock over the last few days and tried to get as much rest as possible in the last 24 hours.

I wind down the car window. Cold country air fills the car. I stick my head out into the slipstream to savour the feeling of mild asphyxia as the rushing air leaves my face feeling icy cold. I can't hear anything over the whooshing turbulence. It's a feeling I link to childhood – going on day trips with my parents; sticking my head out of a train window – withdrawing it just before another rattles past in the opposite direction. The best part is it's merely a matter of moving my head back inside the car to make the feeling go away. It's all about control – and with any luck our level of preparedness will give us that this morning.

There's only five of us who know anything about this – Phil, Jane, Dom, Helen and myself. Phil's playing his usual co-ordinating role but there'll be no press release faxed out to the media this time. His job is to get us from A to B and back to A without a heavy prison sentence. For extra security he's even wrapped the mobile phone in tin foil. Paranoid? Perhaps – but as a wise person once said – just because you're paranoid, it doesn't mean they're not out to get you.

We had a briefing meeting last night – going through an eight-page dossier containing the layout of the site and proposed actions. There had been only one copy of this document and once we'd memorised the details and familiarised ourselves with the map the plan was burnt, and from that point onwards – even though there is explicit trust between us – no-one's been allowed out of the others' company to ensure secrecy.

We're all dressed in black – long sleeves, gloves, I've even had to buy a balaclava for this one. This isn't some glib anarchist statement – I can't say where but we're off to sabotage machinery at an opencast mine.

Everyone's been completely silent apart from Jane's request for me to close the window – alone with our thoughts and the possible consequences the next few hours may bring. In SchNEWS each week people have been asked to write to one of the M11 crew who's on remand for several months for sabotaging plant – allegedly.

I was asked a week ago if I was into doing something major. There were several reasons for saying yes – I think we're really quite good at what we do and have every belief we can pull off more hard-hitting actions. It's also keeping things fresh – if you use the same tactics time after time you're going to get stale.

My role in preparation for the action was simple. Phil gave me some money to buy the following from any DIY store which didn't have CCTV cameras:

Bolt cutters – 3
Molegrip pliers – 3
Cordless nailgun – 1
Torches – 4
Large car jacks – 2
Large adjustable
    spanners – 3
4 kg Builder's sand
Plastic funnels – 4
Bottles of etching
    fluid – 4
Bags of sugar – 10

Obviously the last item had to come from the supermarket instead – I don't look like the average person who makes jam, but an unusually sweet tooth doesn't usually arouse suspicion of nocturnal sabotage plans.

Opencast mining is what happens when you need coal but no longer send men underground to retrieve it. Diggers grab at the ground, obliterating the earth beneath it until giant pits the size of a small city and 200 metres deep are formed. The briefing said the site we are targeting used to contain ancient woodland, badger setts and was the breeding ground for protected butterflies before the mining company got its hands on it.

Phil says: 'Ok, folks, I'm going to park here. Dom, you've got the compass to find your way to site?'

He nods: 'Having done the recce I don't think anyone's going to miss it once we get over the hill. Is everyone ready?'

Helen's eyes are shut and she's taking deep breaths. Jane says as she massages Helen's shoulders: 'Well, it'd be a bit silly to come all this way for nothing. Let's do it.'

Phil looks at his watch. 'Right, it's five past three. I'm going to stay here 'til half four. After that I'll be at the post office in the village. If you're not back by six I'll assume you're not coming. Does everyone remember how to get there?' We do – allegedly. On go the balaclavas and we look like we're going to an IRA funeral.

Four rucksacks containing the tools are taken out of the boot. They aren't exactly light and I secure the waist strap around me to give increased back support. 'Health and safety, boys and girls,' I whisper as it clicks into place. There are also eight double-bagged half kilos of sand to shove in our pockets.

We each of us pick up a torch and four beams cut through the darkness. I want to shine mine into the air like the Bat Signal, but this isn't the right time to muck about.

It's only a five-minute walk to our destination – the pit is vast – far bigger than the photos in the dossier had me believe.

Dom points to a track running down a few hundred yards away. 'We can get to the bottom down there.' He moves the torch beam down into abyss. 'And can you see some of the plant there?' I can just make out tiny bulldozer-type shapes an eighth of a mile below us.

'Ok, speed walking go! Try to keep together,' says Helen. In order to give ourselves maximum time on site we're adopting a ridiculous accentuated waddle as we're carrying too much to be able to run.

As we pass the site office Helen notices it's supported by scaffold poles. 'I've a feeling they'll come in handy. Never know when you need more leverage.' We all reach for our spanners and within five minutes we've added a new bit of kit to our inventory. Getting them down the slope is cumbersome and we set down next to each other first chance we get.

It's like wandering around the surface of some new barren planet – there's nothing to see but ridges, undulations and contours slowly narrowing down into a huge bowl at the bottom.

A large Komatsu excavator is first the digger we encounter. Helen takes off her rucksack and whispers: 'I've got this one, carry on.'

Nearby is a dump truck. I take the mole grips and cut all the hydraulic cables just behind the cab. We've been warned to replace each tool after we've finished with them as scrabbling round for them in the dark isn't the best idea – especially if something's left behind by mistake. Next I unscrew the fuel tank cap and struggle to open a bag of sugar with gloved hands. There's a satisfying shushing sound as granules flow like a mini-avalanche into the hole.

Dom's got the nailgun and it's his job to do every tyre on the site. Each one costs hundreds of pounds. I signal for him to 'service' my vehicle.

'Will do,' he says, 'hopefully won't be too noisy,' as he places the gun against the tyre wall. Fortunately it's more of a thud and a hiss than a bang. Three more identical sounds follow within a minute. The sides of the mine will muffle some of the noise we make, but the safest strategy is to carry out the quieter operations first.

This is so great – it's us just doing our thing. No police or security getting in our way. It's the kind of action that builds strong and deep bonds. I can tell by everyone's body language how much they're enjoying it. Watching Jane climbing up to the oil inlet on that earth scraper really is a joy to behold, but unfortunately she's still with Des.

There are no sounds of nature to freak us out. We're not doing this to save this site – it's buggered – but it will put quite a dent in end-of-year profits – one the company would rather not put on their shareholder report.

Though I've not done it before, I know there's a subtle art to monkey wrenching. According to the briefing, smashing things up leaves only superficial damage. The best method to permanently put these machines out of action is by adding abrasives to the lubrication system – and that's what the sand is for. I crawl underneath a large tractor-type thing, torch in mouth, wrench in hand, and look for a screw to release the oil. Granted, it's going to spill into the ground, but we can't bring everything we need. Omelettes and eggs as they say.

The nut comes off and I just manage to roll out of the way before the viscous liquid starts to empty away. Then it's up and round to the side to unscrew the oil filler cap, in goes the funnel and out comes the sand. A couple of handfuls should do the job.

It only takes a couple of minutes to find the radiator and pour some of the etching fluid in. I'd like to be here when they try to turn the ignition key on this baby tomorrow.

Helen's waving her arms – our signal for a group chat. As we reassemble there's smiling eyes beneath the balaclavas.

'Come on!' cries Dom as quietly as his excitement will allow. We share a big group hug and an exuberantly muffled yip.

Helen whispers: 'Ok, it's ten past four now. I think we've done most of the quiet stuff. Time to plan the big exit. What have we got?' We look around. There's a few lighting rigs and a dumptruck, which has been carelessly parked rather near a steep bank.

Jane heads towards in that direction. 'What's keeping you? Plan B awaits.' We help each other scramble up the bank and put down the rucksacks. Dom and Helen take the jacks and start racheting up the truck. Me and Jane are sent to go and grab the scaff poles from below. There's a lot of fetching and carrying in this business. We could really do with some machinery to help us trash these machines.

We have to take the long way round to get back to Helen and Dom as we've got a pole in each hand. By the time we return they've done well. The truck is up on it's two right-hand wheels at angle of thirty-odd degrees. The ground feels like it's already been compacted by being constantly driven over so I don't think it's about it give way.

'Brace yourselves,' says Helen. The jack's given us about all the help it can and we have to provide the rest. 'And be careful. We don't want this fucker falling on us.'

Dom says with a laugh, 'Did I ever tell you how insightful you were?'

We place the poles into the gap under the chassis and on the count of three take the strain amid puffing, grunting and various other sounds, which shouldn't normally come out of a human.

'If anyone feels like dropping it, say so pronto,' says Jane. I wish I could see her in this heroic pose, but I've got other things on my plate right now.

My shaking arms are the outward sign of the aches running through most of my body. During a workout lactic acid usually takes at least an hour to build up but this is instant muscle exhaustion.

'Come on, find it from somewhere,' I shout as we gain another couple of degrees, getting it right to the tipping point.

'Yeaurrrrghhhhh!' is the mutual zoological noise as gravity suddenly frees us of our burden. There's the subtle sound of the tyre treads shifting on the last couple of centimetres of earth but after that there's a couple of seconds of silence – watching as the truck gracefully starts to rotate like a platform diver – before it hits the bottom with a delicious smash. With ricochets, echoes and the displacement of the ground below it's a while before there's total silence once more.

Our bloodlust for killing inanimate objects is so heightened we don't pause for congratulation, it's straight onto the first lighting rig, which is child's play compared to the truck. Only on turfing the third metal monster into the pit do we feel sated.

Another group hug. 'Wow, that was amazing,' I say in the huddle.

'I know,' Helen replies, 'but we've gotta make tracks now, or Phil'll leave without us.'

It's rucksacks back on and off we go without further celebration. God, it's like being in the fucking paras. Helen and Jane are far tougher than they look. Well, Helen is a bit on the chunky side, but you know what I mean.

We reach the original path we came down and waddle down the hill. Out comes the compass. We follow the bearing towards the village. Like I said – we've never been so organised. Once away from the site it's just walking – no noise, no jubilation until we reach the village, when it's even more important to be silent. Rural folk are notoriously nosey, or so we're led to believe in TV programmes. Maybe they have fuck all else to do and it's true – we're not taking any chances. It's four minutes to five when we reach the Post Office and I've never been so glad to see a car in all my life.

Dom knocks on the driver's window and a dozing Phil nearly jumps out of his skin. A smile nearly as wide as the mine appears as soon as his brain works out where he is. Leaping out of the car he bearhugs us each in turn and unlocks the boot.

'Boy, was I starting to shit it!' says Phil once where all back in the car. 'I think it's worse for me – at least you know what's going on.'

'Bollocks, you were so asleep,' says Helen lighting up a well-earned rollup. 'Get us out of here.'

It's Billy Bragg's turn to kick out the stereo on the way home, a car-full of party. Howling out the lyrics like a band of strays – there's a shared feeling of achievement no-one can take away from us. There's beers to be had at Phil's on our return, but the buzz is more than enough for now.

When World Turned Upside Down – a jolly song about the land and political rebellion in the English Civil War comes on the stereo – we listen to the original words:

> In 1649, to St George's Hill
> A ragged band they called the Diggers
> came to show the people's will
> They defied the landlords,
> they defied the law
> They were the dispossessed,
> reclaiming what was theirs.

We try to rework them. After a few attempts the 'finished' version comes out like this:

> In 1995, on some secret hill
> A team of five came tooled up
> with a plan to make the 'dozers still.
> First we trashed the engines,
> then we smashed the trucks
> We'll get away with it
> with any fucking luck.

'So, done any good actions lately?' asks Sarah as I dump my rucksack on her kitchen floor.

'No – my knee's taken longer than I thought to heal – but it's better now.' It's not fair – I should at least get some reward for fucking up those diggers but I can't tell her.

She got out of the bath to answer the door. Her green towelling dressing gown is doing a poor job of containing her contours and I'm horny as a sex-starved goat cloned with a triceratops.

Embracing her from behind, penis straining against my boxer shorts I ask, 'I know you've just had a bath, but do you fancy getting dirty again?' Slipping my hands inside her gown I lock them onto their lovely targets like heat-seeking missiles.

'Hold on,' she says. 'I meant what I said on the phone. I don't know where we stand at the moment and about the only thing I'm not confused about is the fact we need to talk.' That said she's not removed my hands and if she can't feel that up against her buttocks then there's something wrong with them. Which there isn't – they're perfect – like the rest of her.

We gently sway for a couple of minutes, her arms around mine and she pulls me in closer to her neck, which smells how I think Spanish lemon groves would.

She takes my right hand and kisses it then each finger tenderly before placing it on her breast and doing the same with the left. It's all I can do to stop myself hoisting her up and beasting her on the kitchen table.

'Ok, I'll get the sofa bed ready for you.' She pulls away and goes to the airing cupboard to get some blankets as I'm left priapic and confused.

She's into hyperactivity mode. On goes the kettle and a cup of tea with soya milk is the only thing I'm going to get my hands on tonight that's hot, sweet and wet.

I don't want to push the issue so look in the side pocket of my bag for toothbrush and paste – I'm sure it's only a matter of time. It takes me the best part of three hours to fall asleep without the distraction of radio or masturbation to put out the fires in my mind and groin.

It's Friday and Sarah's taken the day off work to spend time with me. Tomorrow's work and leisure – I'm to experience my first Reclaim the Streets Party. The M11 campaign has risen from the rubble of Claremont and become even better than before. They've done banner-hangs at the Motor Show and shut down the British School of Motoring for the morning – good on them. I'm sure we'll be running around most of the day like headless soya-substitute chickens helping with the party.

Catching the Tube, we're just on the overland part of the Piccadilly line and Sarah's got the A-Z on her lap. 'Where do you fancy going?'

'How about a picnic in Regent's Park,' I reply, lost in the possibilities of the day.

You don't have to have loads of dosh to be romantic – wine can certainly help – but we lie next to the bandstand feeding each other in the sunshine. She spills hummus on my nose, so I rub salsa-dipped pitta on her cheek and lick it off to delicious squeals of protest.

There's that golden pause when a couple read each other's mind and go in for the kiss. I've still no idea what she thinks in general but the Lesterometer has at least swung as far as snogging in the park. There have been few moments today when I've not had that wonderful fizzy feeling in the pit of the gut. It's a given that each time you fall in love feels more intense than the last time, but I can certainly vouch I've never felt like this before. I'd murder a dictator and face the death penalty in a filthy Third World jail if she asked me to. We wander round the park, our fingers entwined, stopping every few hundred yards for kissing, tickling, or merely to look in each other's eyes. It's fantastic not only to be 'normal' – doing regular things like fool about with the woman you love – just like everyone else does – and put the cares of the world to one side for the day. Caught in such an embrace she says: 'We've got a busy day on tomorrow. Do you fancy the pictures?'

Grudgingly I stop nibbling on her neck to reply: 'I can do that any-time. I want some you time.'

We wander past the dog walkers, hackysackers, pram pushers and sunbathers, oblivious to virtually everything except for Sarah and the desire to share glances with couples walking in the other direction – as if to say – yeah, I'm feeling it too, isn't it wonderful.

'Where are we?' she pauses to consult the A-Z.

'Dunno, you're the local round here – with all the directional sense of Mark Thatcher in the desert. How about we find a secluded spot and get lost in each other?' I pull her close to my cock – hard and at full action stations.

She pulls away. 'I think it's time we had that talk.' Fucking hell.

'Ok, let's head back to yours.' The spontaneity and magic of the day seems to be vanishing with setting sun and we're off to find the Piccadilly, still hand-in-hand, but I'm losing trust in her touch.

'So,' I ask flopping back on her sofa next to her before taking a large swig at my wine. 'How do you feel about me right now?'

'It's very difficult as you know. I am attracted to you, though I really don't know how much. I'm still not entirely over my last relationship, and I think that sometimes you're trying to rush me.'

'That's because I love you.'

'You think you're in love with me.'

'You don't know 'til you've tried.' I put her hand on my ever-active groin.

'See what I mean about rushing me?'

'So – I find you vastly attractive and want to have sex with you. Is that such a crime? Does that make me some patriarchal bully?

What's your problem.'

'When you speak like that, yes you do sound like a bully. Erin ...'

'Oh don't bring that fucker into it. She's no expert on how men think.'

She turns away from me. As I gently rotate her back tears well in the corner of each eye.

I cup her face and kiss the wetness away. 'Look I'm sorry. I just want you so much and this is more frustrating than I can ever say.'

She takes my hand and says: 'Ok, you don't have to sleep on the sofa tonight,' and leads me to her bedchamber.

As we climb the stairs I'm trying to convince myself to let her make the first move. She hasn't said, 'I want it now, and I want it from you', but I've had less obvious come-ons than this and got lucky before.

I'm first into the bathroom and make sure face, teeth, torso, armpits and old fella are all clean. There's a spot of pre-cum on my boxers but as things stand going out there naked is not going to help my cause. As I re-enter the bedroom there she is – dressed in a 'Stop The Hawk Deal' T-shirt, skimpy white knickers and nose stud. Nothing more. No make up, perfume, earrings or bra. Perfection.

We're upon each other and fall onto the bed and in no time she's lying astride me on top.

'You don't know what I wouldn't do for you,' I say, 'does that make sense?' I check with a snigger.

With my hands supporting her bum I lean forward and run my tongue along the elasticated top of her knickers, stopping at a little embroidered flower in the middle. My hands ride up to her hips and very slowly start to roll the material upon itself, lowering my tongue in unison with the progress I have made. She lets out a pant, which turns into a sigh midway and throws her head back and I respond by running a hand up and down her arched spine.

'I want you so, so much,' I say, continuing to peel her underwear southwards. Her pubic hair – of which there is more than I anticipated – is now visible and I lick each side of the border between thigh and pelvis before moving in for a full site inspection. She pulls her thighs together to get knickers further down then shifts her weight to allow them to pass each knee.

I reach for the G-spot round the back whilst lustily licking at her like a yoghurt pot which still has fruity goodness to deliver. Her breathing becomes shallow and she reaches under the T-shirt for her breasts. Moans go deeper before morphing into gasps, and the build–up to orgasm begins. Her erect nipples are showing through the 'S' and the 'P' of 'STOP' on her T-shirt.

Strangely though, there's no reciprocation. Though I can feel myself harder than a constable's side-handled baton, she's making no attempt to undress either me or her. Maybe she's caught up in the moment – can't blame her, even though I say it myself, as it's currently the convulsions and whimpers of climax.

As soon as she's finished she casts herself aside. No kiss, no caress, no wandering hands. Just silence. Then sobbing.

'What's the matter?' I cradle her – still beautiful despite the snot and snivels.

'You,' she fights for breath, 'you know I told you I hadn't got over my last relationship?'

'Yeah?' not knowing what to say but I can sense the play isn't about to turn my way.

'Well, I've started to see them again. Last week.'

'Well, I can see that might be a tad difficult, but you said you're attracted to me, right?'

'Look, I know this is the last thing you want to hear but I don't want to talk about it now. We've got to be up in the morning. 'Night,' and she pulls away from me to the edge of the bed.

I roll over as the seeds of tears are starting to come but I fight the feeling. Just as I feel myself drop off to sleep after an emotionally exhausting day I hear, 'Thanks for the orgasms by the way,' and feel a solitary stroke on the small of my back.

Awake at 9am and out the door in twenty minutes. I've showered, but after last night's lack of getting sweaty there's barely a need. No names or explanation from Ms Mystery – she's seems perfectly happy to leave me in the dark – the bitch. Sad truth is I'd forgive her in an instant.

Not a dozen words are uttered between us until the bus drops us near to the Battlebridge Centre, just off King's Cross – the temporary HQ of Reclaim the Streets. The police surveillance teams seem to be doing their job 'cos as we arrive there are vans a-plenty.

We casually walk past as a cop points a video camera at us. It's a good job the Nazis didn't have them or else there wouldn't be any Jews alive today. In my present mood feel like grabbing it and changing the aperture of his arse but yes, I know, I'd get in trouble – again.

I see Ann loading up a van as we approach. We share a hug and my curious nature gets the better of me. 'Come on, you can trust me. Where is it, p-leeeease?' I cup my hand in hers. Why couldn't I have fallen for a sensible woman like this?

'It's going to be somewhere in Islington,' she says, 'but we still need to keep hush of course. The cops are crawling all round King's Cross. How's you and ...' Ann crooks her head in Sarah's direction – who's off chatting to someone else.

'Don't ask. My guts feel like I've done ten rounds with that lot,' pointing to the riot vans parked up the road.

'Well, hopefully you'll have a wicked day. I've gotta get on – you know what it's like when you've got a party to organise. There's never time to enjoy it yourself.'

I offer to help but all the strategic lifting and shifting was done over the last couple of days. She hands me a bundle of A6 leaflets, whispers 'Angel' in my ear, makes her apologies and runs off to ensure another part of the masterplan is in place.

The leaflets have a picture of King Kong lifting a car high in the air and contain the following words.

Rave Against the Machine

Streets are where urban life is lived, from chance encounters to the building of strong, solid communities over decades.

Roads are for traffic to get from one place to another in a hurry.

Today is not a protest – it's a celebration of life as it should be.

There are no such things as roads – merely streets that haven't been reclaimed!

I'm not trying to be a control freak here, and don't want to jump rank – if indeed there were any – but I think someone of my experience can be better used. I cram the leaflets in my bag and go off in search of someone else to play with. I spot Jerry looking tired and stressed as ever in the foyer. 'Hey mate, is there anything I can do?'

'Not right now,' he says, barely stopping to talk, 'everything's pretty sorted. The crews are in position and it's just a question of hit and hope now. Best thing you can do is grab a cup of tea and relax 'til we take the street. Gotta go, ok?' and trots past me in what would have been a run if he did regular exercise.

In the hall I spot Gary. Surely he's got a pivotal task for me.

'Sure, you can help me fold this up if you like,' he says as he drags the front corners of a huge multi-coloured CARS CAN'T DANCE banner on itself. We manage to just cram it into his rucksack. It barely fits – in the same way there's never enough room for a damp tent in the bag when it's time to pack up camp.

'Ok, is there anything else to do? I could join one of the teams taking the street, or lock-on to something.'

'Lester, just chill. We've been planning this for ages. There's loads of people on board and they all have a specific role in getting this together. There's not going to be any locking on and the crews know exactly what they're doing. Go for walk and I'll see you nearer the time.'

He's right. I am being a control freak – gotta accept I'm not saving the planet single-handed and learn to have some acceptance and trust in the deeds of others.

'Ok, ok. I give in. I'll see you there,' I say as Gary pats me on the shoulder and disappears out the door, doubtless on an important mission.

On the wall there's a display of photos from the first street party they held in Camden a couple of months ago. I'd heard sketchy details about it, but this tells the story rather well. Looks like two second-hand cars 'crashed' at a junction and this blocked off one end of the High Street and allowed a party to unfold. There's some shots of loads of people, including kids, taking great delight in whacking the cars with sledgehammers. It says 1,500 people were there – and by the look of the level of preparation and the glorious weather there's going to be more than that today.

Time is ticking on and Sarah's done one of her usual vanishing acts (at least last night's little revelation explains why some of them occurred) so I walk round to Angel, thinking I'd have to look non-chalant so as to not give the game away. I arrive at 12.45pm having bought a six–pack of Red Stripe en route. I find a huge crowd on the pavement outside the Tube station. There's also hundreds of police, but they're heavily outnumbered and by the looks of it don't quite know what's going to happen. Same here.

There's a load of beardy drummers, knocking out some kind of bongo rubbish, and a rather attractive woman – though too crustie-cum-Tank Girl for my taste – in purple dress-and-leggings comb-ination expertly spinning a diablo, throwing and catching the plastic eggcup-shaped thingy without really looking at it. I've never really been a fan of noodling about, especially with bongo players, but I suppose today is when I start to learn to relax and enjoy myself. Let my hair down – if only it were long enough. After ten minutes of rocking back and fore on my heels and passing the time of day with the hippies I'm actually having quite a nice time.

Though it's clear this is no ordinary Saturday on Upper Street, the traffic is still moving – a mother and karate-suited son drive by in a blue Skoda; a post office lorry, among white van men and cherry-red cabs off in pursuit of a fare. At the lights I spot a white flatbed truck with Jerry at the wheel and know it's time.

Dead on half-past one a foghorn sounds and around a dozen folk – some of them I recognise from Claremont – run towards the stationary vehicle.

Looks like scaffold poles are this season's must-have NVDA item. Each of the two tripods is made of three poles connected to each other at one end with jubilee clips. They are lifted out, stood upright and the legs pulled apart, so each looks a bit bit like a headless giraffe with a missing limb.

One of the crew shouts: 'Everyone come onto the street please! Come protect the tripods!' and within seconds there's a couple of hundred people surrounding the now fully opened pyramids.

Some guy with what seems to be a blanket on his shoulder climbs hand-over-hand up one of the legs as a rope is secured half-way up the poles to add stability. The climber hooks the fabric – which is a sling made of a sheet and some rope – over the apex of the poles then eases himself in, fifteen feet off the ground. On the other carriageway another bloke swings jubilantly in his sling.

Coming up Pentonville Road is the sound of bicycle bells – and hundreds of Critical Massers ride in to provide extra numbers. What an operation! People are swarming onto the road and the street party begins.

We've taken the street! It's been well and truly reclaimed. With sheer force of numbers and the liquid nature of crowds the cops don't stand a chance.

I decide to walk up the other end of the street, give out some leaflets and admire the beauty of the operation. Looks like the police aren't going to try and step in, at least for now.

Near a CAR FREE banner shaped like a pair of red pants I spot Ann, and she's next to a ... it can't be ... a tank! What seems to be an armoured sound system playing Wonderful World by Louis Armstrong. Nearby there's a couple smooching, lost in each other's arms. The woman kisses her partner tenderly then nicks his panama hat and puts it on her head as they dance, lost in each other's eyes and the moment.

'What the fuck!' I say to Ann as we hug.

'Yeah – it's a bit mad eh? Didn't know 'til the last minute they could make it. This has been out in Bosnia for the last couple of weeks,' she says slapping its camo-painted flank.

Rugs and carpets are laid out and people recline with a can of choice. Sure there's whistling, drumming and whooping but also a pleasing silence – an absence of traffic noise.

There's a kids' area complete with sandpit and climbing frame – I wish my parents had taken me to something like this when I was five. There's even buckets and spades laid on – what attention to detail. I pass two twelve-foot women in bikinis. I've always liked them tall but will have to learn to stilt-walk to get with them today.

The street has been transformed. A billboard with a Rover cruising down an exotic stretch of desert road next to the word ENJOY has had the words MORE POLLUTION expertly added in the same font.

Nick and Claire are dancing to the plinkety-plink-plink the sound system's now kicking out. I crack open a can and go to join them through a smiley sea of moving bodies.

Someone's 'played' with a water hydrant and a spectrum of spray cools the dancers raving to the dede-de-dede-wooooaaaahhh or however it goes. Whatever.

'This is the fucking dog's, despite the playlist,' I mouth into Claire's ear.'

'Come on. What are you, some sort of rock dinosaur?' she says, taking my arm and spinning me round.

'Don't get me wrong. I'm having a fab time, but since when did lyrics go out of fashion? And guitars?'

'Bollocks,' she shouts, blowing her whistle.

I wince and waggle a finger inside my poor ear. 'Thanks for that. All I'm saying is I can't see you listening to this in fifteen years' time.'

'Course I will,' she replies dismissively with a yip and a swig.

Despite my minor gripes, this is amazing. So many faces, there must be – what – three thousand people here. All doing their bit – even if it's just showing up, having it large and getting mashed. It's a bit different to being stuck up a crane on your own in the pissing rain. Fundamentally I'm in a good mood. I even smile at a hippy in fluorescent orange trousers juggling some clubs.

I see Sarah waving a donation bucket around near a bus shelter which is shaking under the weight of ravers and wander over.

'Fancy seeing you here,' I say directly after a long slurp of Red Stripe.

'What are you on about?' she says distantly.

'I was, what is known in even the remotest parts of East Timor, joking. Fancy a stroll?' Shit – base to mouth – don't be friendly to enemy. Too late.

'Mmm, I'm supposed to be meeting someone in a bit.'

'Anyone I know?'

'Not really'

'Oh.' Be like that then. I chuck a pound coin into the bucket and start to walk off.

She runs after me. 'What?'

'You know what.'

'Look,' she says, 'shall we go for a pint when this is over and we can talk? Yes?' I'm finding the ground rather fascinating, not wanting to be snared in the driftnets of lust.

I limply nod and move on in search of cheer – and crack open another coldie.

There's two welcome sights – a band stage has been set up and some young punks are doing their thing, and Gary's tapping his foot – finally getting some downtime.

'Respect my old son,' I say with a hug. 'This has taken the mantle as the best action ever. Well fucking done.' Next to us a skinny bloke in a tartan cut-off shirt is dancing with a white-on-blue road sign.

STREET FESTIVAL TEMPORARY ROAD CLOSURE

'Glad you like it. This is only the start with any luck,' says Gary with the hint of a grin.

I point out a row of fat, sweaty cops standing around looking all frustrated. 'They're the only ones here who seem to be having a down sort of day.'

Gary replies: 'They're not getting the chance to play with their truncheons – yet.'

'Do you think they'll be bother then?'

'Very probably, if only so the press can write it up as a big riot tomorrow.'

'It's so wrong. In four hours the only thing I've seen thrown is a four-year old chucking some sand in the air.'

Gary suddenly puts his hand to his face: 'Don't look now, but you see those two on the left with the camera?' I look to see the same cops who videoed me earlier.

'That's Sergeant Sully and his mate Barry Norman of the Forward Intelligence Team.'

'Barry Norman? Making films about us? No shit.'

'Yeah, that's his name. They've been on our backs ever since Claremont. Apparently Sully's got a budget to pay informers.'

'Cunt. Hope he's proud of himself when the planet's totally fucked.' I can't resist raising a middle finger to them. I lower it just as a BBC radio journalist comes over.

'Would you be up for doing a vox-pop piece?' she asks. We agree and she checks for levels.

'What do you think about today?' she asks. The furry microphone looks like is been made out of a Scottie dog.

'It's a great day out,' says Gary. 'Fantastic for families, and it's great for an ordinary person such as myself to send a message about air pollution and car use to the government,' as I try to stifle a snigger.

She turns to me. 'Are you a London resident?'

'Yeah, I've never done anything like this before, just came down for the party.'

'And do you think you'll be coming along to anything like it again?'

'Too right, it's brilliant. I've really caught the protest bug today.'

'Could you describe to us what's going on?'

'Thousands of people. Plenty of music and dancing, and best of all no traffic. It's a carpeted cacophony of car-free carnival.' It was the best sound bite I could come up with at short notice.

I'm out of cans so am off in search of the offy – the intrepid Beerhunter. If there's one on this road they're in for record takings today.

A rather fetching girl-shaped tree comes bouncing along, manoeuvring past a couple of blokes in Major and Blair masks having a snog on the makeshift dancefloor of the A1 arterial.

Bin bags are distributed and the clean-up process begins. I take one and am assigned to be on the look-out for green glass. Sarah's also part of the clean-up crew – chatting to Erin. Hold on – I think to myself ... No – that's ridiculous. As Sarah bends down to pick up another can, she even has a way of picking up rubbish that drives me wild. I fill up the sack as quick as I can and return to my own drinking and am reasonably spannered after an afternoon of alcohol, sunshine and not much to eat, off past some folks bagging up the sand from the temporary beach.

Shouts. Trouble at the other end of the party. The alarm goes up and it's time to revert back to activist mode.

'The police are trying to take the tank!' someone shouts, and the middle section of the party moves toward the commotion.

What's left of the sunshine is reflected off police visors and shields. In the first couple of rows I can see someone with a gun – a fluorescent water pistol – squirting the police lines.

They're trying to push us back, batons swinging and catching anyone too near. I squeeze through, near enough to be in the way but not in face-battering range.

'We're just having fun. Why don't you just fuck off?' shouts one crustie woman getting up close and personal to one officer.

The shield connects with the side of her head and down she goes. 'Now get back! The lot of you,' says the cop and we withdraw a metre or two and make sure the woman is ok. She's pissing blood from her temple.

'And to think he's getting paid out of our council tax for doing that!' comes a shout from behind me.

'And all on double time,' says the cop nearest to me to his grinning colleague.

More sirens, more vans. They've let us have our fun and now it's their turn.

A cop with a megaphone comes through the ranks and shouts,

'This is your direction to leave. If you do not disperse within two minutes you will be arrested.'

It's the old choice between dignity or pain once again. I turn around and see Sarah and Erin several rows behind. I wave to catch their attention, then point a raised arm behind them suggesting we get the hell out of here and make a drink-lifting gesture with the other. She mouths ok and I push through to where they are. As we pass the line of blue I throw the cops a hard stare, rather like Paddington Bear once did to Mr Gruber.

'Right, where's the nearest boozer,' I ask Sarah, trying not to notice she's holding hands with Erin. Game, set and lesbian match.

'Not sure. Anywhere really. Do you fancy coming along?' she asks the shaven-headed minger.

'It's ok, I'll let you sort this yourself,' says Erin as she gives Sarah a big fat smacker on the lips! Millions of men would pay good money to see this. I'd hand over the rest of my overdraft not to.

The vast majority of people have the sense to move when asked, but there's a couple of hundred refusing to budge. We make our way to the King Edward VI, only three hundred yards or so, but the difference between getting a good pasting and not. As we're queuing for the bar we see more riot police are changing into riot gear in a side road. Riot briefs put over the top of ordinary cop trousers, then strapping on shin pads, thigh pads and elbow protection. Then comes the all-in-one suit, which looks more like a babygro than anything else. On go the stormtrooper helmets before grabbing the side-handled batons out of the van. All to the irritating sound of alsatian barks. Then off march these brave boys to go and quell this huge threat to civilisation.

One woman, looking particularly distraught, is clutching a one - year-ish-old baby, and screaming, 'They've shut off all the exits. My partner's in there somewhere.' There's nothing I can do for her but I dwell on losing a partner too – the woman of my dreams stolen away by an ugly Welsh lesbian.

It seems the poor bastards are being funnelled in our direction for a good kicking. Down the street the shouts and screams intensify, with the odd thud of missile on shield and the sound of broken glass.

'So,' I say. I stand on a stool to try and get a better view of events outside, 'no prizes for guessing your mystery lover now, eh?'

'I'm sorry,' she says trying to hold my hand, 'I was going to tell you last night but it didn't feel appropriate.'

Outside there's a smash followed by a car alarm's wail. Nearly as loud is a woman's screech of 'Leave him!' above the rest of the mêlée.

'Was that before or after you came?' I enquire.

'You're not being fair,' she says, starting to turn on the waterworks.

'You know what I think?' I say. She cocks her head to one side. 'I'm less likely to get hurt out there,' I continue as I grab my bag, pause to kiss her on the lips one last time – and leave.

Can't believe I've got to go to court again – should get some kind of fucking loyalty card. This time it's the Wimpey crane climb we did in solidarity for Pollok last winter. Me and Tim are in the dock for this one, and we want to be able to put forward political rather than legal arguments for our defence. Chris Binns has told us the only way we can do this is to represent ourselves in court.

Nice though the jam doughnuts in the café at Crown Square are, I'm growing tired of having the opportunity to buy one. Tim and I haven't had much time to get a case together. In fact, the trial starts in an hour and this is the first I've seen of him for two months. Though his bail conditions say he's not supposed to leave the country he's been in Denmark with his new girlfriend. Even now, when we should be getting our arguments together he's trying to teach me the language.

'No, it's pronounced yi, like eye with a y at the beginning,' he says exasperatedly.

'What's that again?' I ask. Languages never were my strong point.

'Fuck it. Where were we?' Tim says, wiping the curtain of hair from his eyes. It really doesn't go with the suit. Whereas I look the business of course.

'Ok, as usual with aggravated trespass we're pretty guilty. I reckon the best position to argue is that we weren't trying to stop work, just trying to raise awareness of the issue. Do you think they'll buy it? We were up there for nearly four days.'

'Haven't got much else have we?'

'We'll just busk it and see. All this court bollocks looks easy on the telly. It's just professional arguing.'

As we walk into court I'm unsure whether we need to be in the dock or at the benches used by the lawyers; I explain our position to the usher. He shows us to the bench and I take an immediate dislike to the prosecutor. He looks like I'd imagine Ratty from The Wind In The Willows to be, but prematurely balding with an ill-fitting suit complementing an equally ill-fitting moustache. 'Crebbins, CPS,' he sneers, extending a bony, intensely veined hand.

'Lester, human being,' I retort, and Tim and I reluctantly shake.

When out of Crebbin's earshot, I lean over and whisper, 'This geezer looks a right penis.'

Tim giggles and says: 'What was his name again? Crevice?'

'No, but I think it's going to be for the rest of the trial.'

Once more we have a stipendiary magistrate rather than the usual line-up of three amateur buffoons.

The first prosecution witness is Richard Evans, senior project manager for Wimpey. Crevice serves up obvious questions to volley home like, 'Do you recognise the defendants as among those who occupied the crane?' If that's what it takes to be a prosecutor I've obviously missed my calling in life. Then we get a bit of a shock. Exhibit B is a ten-page list of costs incurred during the action to the sum of £11,199.

When we're each presented with a copy of the figures, Tim and I swoop on them intently – more out of simple curiosity than any desire to make a legal case. There's some surprises within the document – including a five-hundred-quid bill for the security. Cheeky bastards. Ratty's had his go and it's my turn to cross-examine.

'Thank you Mr Crevice. Now, Mr Evans, is it true that there was no environmental impact assessment carried out on the M77 motorway in Glasgow?'

Crevice stands up. 'Your honour, this line of questioning has absolutely no relevance to the case in hand and Mr Evans does not work in Glasgow.'

I'm not done yet. 'I realise that, but I'm keen to show from the off this company has little interest in playing by the rules.'

The magistrate seems like a decent guy, but he also has a court to run. 'Stick to the point, Mr Stype.'

'Thank you, Mr Stipe,' I reply, rather pleased with recycling the joke.

'Mr Evans, on each day of the protest, did we hang large banners from the tower of the crane?'

'Yes.'

'And what would you surmise the purpose of this would be?'

Crevice is on his feet again. 'Your honour, the witness is here to report what he saw – not speculate as to the motives of the defendants.'

'Point noted,' said the magistrate. 'Please ask questions that the witness will have direct knowledge of.' This is no fun.

'Right. I'll lay it out in very simple terms everyone can understand. If I was to say the protest was a stunt raising awareness of your company's activities in Scotland, would you agree with that statement?'

'Perhaps. It's hard to say.' I look to the ceiling and then to the magistrate in some silent appeal to his humanity.

'Ok,' I say, 'can we turn to these so-called costings?'

'If you like.'

'To start with there is clearly stated the sum of ninety pounds for a typist, yes?'

'Yes?'

'Is it not alleged that I sat up a crane, not on a keyboard?'

'I'd say it's a rather silly question.'

'And I'd say – Mr Evans, that this is a rather silly list. There is also the matter of five hundred and sixty-eight pounds for 'expenses and cars'. Is the prosecution seriously suggesting that anti-road activists pay for the running cost of motor vehicles?'

Crevice pipes up again, 'Your honour – I would again question the relevance of the line of questioning.'

This time I've had enough. 'Mr Crevice – this is my witness and I would appreciate it if you waited your turn.'

He's really mad now. 'Your honour, I'm sure it's not escaped your attention that for some reason the defendant continually refers to me by the name of Crevice. Could you please remind Mr ... erm ... Stype where he is.'

What a pussy. Getting the magistrate to fight his corner. I could have this twat for breakfast.

The main man in the chair looks me square in the eye. 'Mr Stype, please could you give the representative of the CPS the courtesy of referring to him by his proper name? That is Mr Crebbins.'

'Fair enough. I simply misheard the gentleman's name. May I continue?'

'Please do.'

'Above all, Mr Evans, the five hundred pound bill for the cost of policing the demonstration is the one which sticks in the gullet most of all. Having witnessed first-hand the activities of the police many times in the last few years, there are many things I would like to do to them, but personally pay their wages is not one of them. All of these figures are wildly inaccurate, and it is a damned cheek for Wimpey to even try to extract payment from us.'

I can see the patience of the magistrate is wearing thin, but I'm really starting to enjoy this and continue. 'Your honour, I have no prior accounting experience, but looking at these figures it would seem these were compiled and audited by the Bank of Toytown,' and I throw the costings document across the courtroom – there's even a ripple of applause from the public gallery. Tim's trying not to laugh, something he's been concentrating on for the last half an hour.

Crevice is up on his feet again. 'I must protest. This young man is making a mockery of this court and urge you to take him in hand.'

'Yes,' the magistrate turns to me, clearly impressed with my degree of flippancy. 'Mr Stype, could you please get on with the point you are trying to make and cut out the attempts at comedy, you are not helping the proceedings. I have decided to issue you with a formal warning for contempt of court. Any further nonsense and you will be taken from this court and remanded in custody until such time as you have learned some manners. Is that understood?'

'Yes,' I say, trying to conceal my contempt for the court.

'Right, now Mr Stype, are you trying to say that you would like me to disregard the claim for damages?'

'Yes. I thought that was perfectly obvious.'

'Then pray tell me why you did not simply say so instead of going round the houses?'

'Now we're really communicating. I like that!' This extension of friendly banter is met with a stern glance.

'Tim, your witness, mate,' I feel it's high time I faded into the background for a while. In the run-up to home time Tim has a go at cross-examining Evans, but to be honest it's nowhere as entertaining as my efforts. I pass the time drawing doodles of Crevice, but make sure he doesn't see my artwork, including one depicting him with a huge cock where his tongue should be.

At the start of day two it's the arresting officers in the witness box, and it's the same fatuous bollocks that usually comes out of their mouths. What gets me is that it's just assumed that what the police are saying is the truth when more often than not they're trying to twist the truth to ensure your guilt. The depressing thing is so long as this is the way things are I don't know how we're gonna save this planet of ours.

Tim's first into the witness box – and Crevice is over and done with him in twenty minutes. Now it's my turn and my guess is it's payback time from earlier. Let battle commence ...

Dear reader, to save us all paper and time here's an excerpt of what I had to put up with over two hours in the dock:

CREVICE: *Mr Stype, do you not think that climbing up cranes without the proper safety equipment is dangerous, even life-threatening?*

STYPE: *In my experience, it's not as dangerous as it looks.*

CREVICE: *Can we assume from this that you have done this sort of thing before?*

STYPE: *I do not feel that I can answer that question at this juncture.*

CREVICE: *All right then, would you consider that nine people clambering all over a crane was nine times as dangerous as one person doing it?*

STYPE: *That is a mathematical equation I had neither to date calculated, nor do I think is relevant to this case.* (To the MAGISTRATE) *Excuse me, objection if I may. Can I question the relevance of this line of questioning? It seems to be bordering on the insanely surreal.*

MAGISTRATE: *Mr Stype, you are currently a witness. You will have your chance to make your witness statement soon enough. This is the third time you have uttered the word 'objection'. May I remind you that this is not Perry Mason, and once again that your conduct is not helping matters.*

Stage two of the questioning looked into the motives of the climb.

CREVICE: *You saw what was going on in Glasgow, you have admitted yourself that you had seen the destruction first-hand. You were angry, and wanted to avenge what you felt was clearly wrong.*

STYPE: *Yes, I wanted to draw attention to the building of the road.*

CREVICE: *Oh, but it was much more than that. You and your colleagues wanted to hurt Wimpey – attack them economically – hurt their profits, didn't you?*

STYPE: *The object of the exercise was to get media and public attention, nothing more.*

CREVICE: *And what better way to get coverage than to bring the construction of an inner city building project to a standstill. Is this not true?*

STYPE: *No, it was neither our intention nor our decision to stop the work on the site.*

CREVICE: *If publicity was your sole intention, then why did you not get off the crane after the press had covered the story?*

STYPE: *The longevity of the publicity stunt was a factor in the amount of press we received.*

CREVICE: *But to stay up there for nearly four days, even after much of the press attention for the story had faded?*

STYPE: *The longevity of the publicity stunt was a factor in the amount of press we received.*

CREVICE: *Oh come, come, Mr Stype. That simply wasn't your sole motive, was it? What kind of fool do you take me for?*

STYPE: (to MAGISTRATE) *I'd rather not answer that particular question.*

In the end I must have said the words 'longevity' and 'publicity stunt' fifteen times each, trying to play word games with Crevice until he lost the will to carry on.

The verdict eventually comes. 'I find it difficult to see how those up the crane could not see the consequences of their actions, both before and after they scaled the structure. Therefore I can only surmise that you did indeed intent to disrupt work. I have no option but to find you guilty of Aggravated Trespass. Would the defendants like to say anything in mitigation before I pass sentence?'

I let Tim deal with the closing statement for fear I'll say something that'll land me in the cells. 'Yes, Your Honour, I would like to say a few words on behalf of both of us.

'There's an important distinction in life that courts cannot deal with – the difference between what is legal and what is right. As we all know – but not all of us accept – not everything that is legal is right, and not all which is right is legal.

'We may have contravened the dogmatic letter of a bad law, but in essence we have done no wrong. We were acting in order to prevent a greater evil occurring – the building of the M77 – an act criminal in all but law.

'Acting to prevent a greater crime may not be acknowledged as a proper legal defence, but it is something perfectly justifiable to all except those who have something to hide. If a law is wrong, it is the moral obligation of all to break that law; if those who make that law are unjust, it is our duty to use all peaceful means at our disposal to make them accountable.

'Our lawmakers are drifting from us, riding roughshod over our civil liberties so as to appeal to a narrow band of voters in an undemocratic voting system.

'In this climate of indifference, we are left with no option to defend our lifestyles, our beliefs, perhaps even our lives. It is better to die on your feet than to live on your knees.

'Personally speaking, and I believe that I also speak for my co-defendant, we will not pay any fines or costs set by this court, and as far as the compensation that Wimpey has requested, it'll be a cold day in hell before I give them a penny as recompense for what I have done.

'In a society where a murderer can serve as little as four years, it is the justice of the madhouse that merely walking on private property could make a person liable for three months' imprisonment.

'The judiciary should not used be used to protect the people who destroy our environment, it should be there to protect the planet, to uphold justice. It should actually do what we are told that it does day in, day out. In the case of the M77, Wimpey broke the law, and the law turned its back on the crime. We tried to redress this wrongdoing, or rather bring it to the attention of the people of Manchester, and we are the ones being punished.

'Hounding young people through the courts with vindictive legislation is cowardly in the extreme and I would suggest that the Criminal Justice Act should be in the dock today and not ourselves.

'Concluding, Your Honour, if it is the case that I am to be criminalised for conducting peaceful protest then so be it, but then what option does that leave me, Lester and other people in a similar position?'

Stopping for a mouthful of water he continues: 'By outlawing the right to peacefully protest, its occurrence may be greatly reduced, but the architects of that law may find that other less peaceful forms of direct action may increase. If this happens, it is not something to condone or condemn, but should be looked upon as a course of events which could have been avoided if cases such as this had not concluded in the manner which it has. Thank you.'

Good old Tim, spoken like a true lawyer. We share a hug as cheers ring out from the EF!ers in the public gallery, provoking disapproving looks from the clerk of the court and magistrate.

Crevice opens his mean little mouth again. 'Your worship, if I may be so bold, there is the matter of previous convictions to consider. The defendant Timothy Pilton is of previously unblemished conduct. On the other hand, I have in my possession the printout on Stype from the Police National Computer, and there are a few previous incidents that Your Worship should be aware of.'

Crevice hands me a list of dates and cases, but it doesn't say in plain English the outcome of any of them.

He continues: 'Stype was found guilty of in his absence on a charge of criminal damage at Waltham Forest Magistrates Court ....' I have to interrupt before I lose it completely – the result of listening to the best part of two days of complete crap. 'Excuse me!' I shout. 'Sorry, if he reads out any of that I'm walking out of this court and I'm not coming back. I was acquitted of that charge and that is wrongful information that could well be prejudicial to the punishment I receive.'

'Your Worship, I really must ...'

'Button it, Crevice. I've just about had enough of your incompetence. Now, are you going to do it properly, or am I going to walk out of here? It's your choice.'

The magistrate interjects. 'Gentlemen, please. This is not behaviour worthy of a Court of Law. If Mr Stype's concerns are genuine, and I have no reason to believe that they are not, then that case should not be referred to. Indeed, Mr Crebbins, I will save you the time of reciting Mr Stype's previous convictions. I have decided to give both Mr Pilton and Mr Stype a nine-month conditional discharge and a fine of one hundred pounds. Also, regarding the awarding of compensation to Wimpey, I am of the opinion that the claim for costs has not been sufficiently well-presented before this court, and Wimpey will have to pursue this through the civil courts. Would the defendants care to stand ...'

In the pub afterwards, a toast is raised in our honour, and one in Phil's absence – he's gone down to London to prepare for a new job he's sneakily got – chief researcher for a Labour MP.

'Well done, Lester,' says Helen, 'but that was a bit risky kicking off about that conviction at the end there, wasn't it?'

'Yeah,' I say, 'especially as I didn't actually turn up to that trial.'

I decide to give Chris Binns a call the following afternoon, when the hangover is just about bearable.

'Hi Chris, just thought I'd let you know how we got on yesterday.'

'It's ok. I know. Well done, you.'

'I s'pose we were never going to be found not guilty. We put up a good fight, and we got their bloody eleven-thousand-pound pisstake claim thrown out.'

'So I hear. One of my colleagues was in court this afternoon and he took a look in at your case. He said you were really giving Crebbins some stick.'

'I'd like to think so. If he's got a daughter, we've definitely blown an invite to her wedding. Especially after I called him a wanker on the way out of court.'

'He's one of the best prosecutors around. You two did well to get him rattled.'

'If he's the best they've got, then it's a good job that the magistrates are corrupt, otherwise no-one would be found guilty.'

'Mmm, maybe. The important thing is, did you enjoy it?'

'Oh Christ yeah. Best crack in ages. Nearly as good as the actual action, but without getting freezing cold and cramp.'

'If you loved it that much, judging from the report I received you could carve out a career in the legal profession.'

'How about my record?'

'Some of the best lawyers I know have got records. It's probably why they're so good at what they do.'

'I'll bear it in mind for the distant future. I don't think I'd enjoy defending someone else as much as myself. I don't mind fucking up my own case, but if I got someone else in the shit – well, you know.'

'Mmm, I'm glad you enjoyed it. See you soon for another case, no doubt?'

'We'll see about that, mate. I think after the next one I'll be a prime candidate to go inside for a while.'

'To be honest, you could be right. All the best.'

I've never been to the Houses of Parliament before – don't know, why, just hasn't cropped up on my things-to-do list. However, Phil's invited me for drinks at the Strangers' Bar in the Commons and it would be simply rude to turn down such an offer – that's how I've justified it to myself anyway.

He meets me at St Stephen's Gate – in a suit and tie!

I fish for reaction with an 'Ooh – get you,' but he's not for biting.

He sticks my visitor's pass to my long sleeved T-shirt, and we head off to the metal detectors.

'You've got to watch this one,' he says to the official with a comedy wink as I'm being frisked. Bastard.

He leads me on a quick tour – I never knew there was a fully working Post Office right in the central lobby. There are huge paintings of Nelson and the Duke of Wellington in between the two Houses. I wonder if they'd be on the side of the activists or the authorities if they were around today?

The House itself is a mix of being completely over the top and deliberately shabby. The chair in the Queen's Robing Room is in dire need of new upholstery – cheapskates.

'It's all very decorative,' I say turning to Phil, 'but you get the feeling there's more pomp and tradition than actual work going on.'

'Mate – after four weeks here – I couldn't agree with you more but the holidays and pension are pretty decent. Let's go and get pissed.'

The Strangers' Bar is decked out in a lot of dark wood panelling, perhaps taken from somewhere equally dark and Amazonian.

Apart from the Commons crest above the optics, it resembles a slightly dog-eared hotel bar.

Phil's looking very much at home, waving a tenner and his pass at the barman. 'You're supposed to be an MP to get served here,' he says, 'but Tom's in here quite a bit and most of the staff know who I am.'

We go to a table in the corner with two pints of the guest ale, Horndean Special Brew.

'So, tell me the latest gossip,' says Phil clutching two bags of crisps in his teeth.

'No. You first. What's it like working in this geriatric kindergarten? Are those green leather seats wipe-clean?'

'It's not so bad. You're right, they are a load of egotistical big kids, and you have to have your bullshit detector removed from day one to get on with anyone, but apart from that it's a great place.'

'Sounds divine. Don't you miss going out on the piss like we used to? Isn't it all a bit civilised now?'

'Maybe,' he replies, 'the majority of Commons researchers aren't the most scintillating bunch of people in the world. Besides, you look at the sort of hours we clock up.'

'No excuse, you're just a fucking big girl's blouse these days.'

'Look, I'm nearly thirty. We've all got to grow up at some point.'

'I think you're being a poof, pardon my French.'

'Alright,' Phil says, thumping the table as hard as he can without causing a scene. 'Down-in-one competition now. Let's see who's the Jessie when it comes to drinking these days.'

'What? At these prices?'

'I'll buy.'

'You're on. No spillages allowed though.'

We've barely touched these pints so Phil takes a couple of sups to get level with me and the glasses are then set on the table to be grabbed, like gunslingers going for their Colt 45s.

We brace ourselves, take a deep breath, and on a nod of the head from Phil, I thrust the pint to my mouth and try to disengage my Adam's apple.

'Finished,' Phil says, wiping his mouth clean.

'So have I. Look.' A white foam round the edge is the only trace a pint was ever there.

'I won that.'

'Fuck off, it was a draw at least.'

'No way. If anything, I just about edged it.'

Phil rises to his feet and points jabs a finger at me. 'Now that's the most ridiculous thing I've heard all day, and I was in the gallery for Prime Minister's questions.'

'Alright then, let's have a re-run. I'll get 'em in.'

'No, mate, I insist.'

Two more pints are laid on the table. 'Right – ready – set – go,' and we're off again – willing the fluid downwards with no consideration for taste, dignity or later consequences. In a funny way it's bigger than me versus Phil. It's establishment versus underground; public school versus comprehensive – there's a lot resting on the result of this silly contest. Both our glasses come to rest on the table simultaneously somewhere around the five-second mark.

'Now that was definitely a draw. Decider?' asks Phil, with the same competitive glint I must be exuding.

'Ok, one more and then we'll have to stop or else we'll get chucked out and you'll be fired. And we need a referee this time.'

'I'll get Tom, he'll understand.' I hand him a fiver. 'Ok, I'll get 'em in, then go get the Honourable Member for ... now what's the proper name of his constituency again.' He's showing the vital signs. Victory will be mine.

'Who gives a fuck what his seat's called, get his arse down here,' I say delivering a belch and fart concurrently.

'Aah, I bet your MP bloke can't do that,' I add, very pleased with myself.

'I bet he can't, but to be honest, I haven't asked him.'

'Ooh ...,' he yelps, holding his nose. 'You're not allowed to do things like that in the House.'

'Aren't you? I thought that was why the chamber was really empty sometimes. Picture the scene – the chamber is packed, six hundred bums on seats, then Michael Portillo or Dennis Skinner suddenly lets rip and it's every man for himself.'

'Lester – you amuse yourself with that and I'll go and get Tom.'

It's an unusual situation – I'm in a pub, I'm over eighteen but I can't get served. I go over to the window and there's a terrace overlooking the Thames, a great place to get nutted on a Wednesday afternoon in late summer. Checking that I've got a pen in my pocket, I go to the toilets and scrawl IF VOTING CHANGED ANYTHING THEY'D ABOLISH IT on the cubicle wall. Graffiti isn't really my scene but this is a special occasion.

Phil returns with palms extended. 'Can't find him, sorry. How are we gonna do this? Another?'

'We'll have to get another judge, won't we?' Phil goes over to some guy in the corner who's eighty if he's a day and within a minute I can distinctly see the old fella nodding.

Returning to me clapping his hands Phil says: 'You know we were in need of a judge? Well Gerald there just happens to be a Law Lord.'

'Great. Get 'em in then. Does he want one?'

This is the moment of truth – where we will be pushed to our limits – forced to produce a world-class performance over a short space of time. Not unlike the Olympic 100-metre final.

Our esteemed official takes a sip on his gin-and-tonic, grabs his pocket watch then says: 'Ok chaps. You're under starter's orders as it were. And go!'

I'm trying not to swallow or breathe, just relax and tip the glass at the steepest appropriate angle to let gravity do its work.

Feeling the last mouthful fall from the glass I slam it down as fast as my addled reaction time will allow.

The two thuds are virtually inseparable once more.

'I'd say that was five seconds for both of you, but for the life of me I couldn't say who won. Thanks awfully for the drink though.' and with that Gerald returns to reading the Telegraph.

I hold out my arms and we embrace. 'Dude,' I say, 'thanks for all the help over the last few years. I don't know what we're gonna do without you.'

'Come on, you were the one running round getting nicked left, right and centre. I was more technical support than anything else.'

'Bollocks, man,' I say slapping him hard on the back. 'You've held Manchester EF! together. Not just things like buying the mobile – it was your ideas and confidence that we could do things ... and your ability to ferry us around,' adding the last bit with a cheeky grin.

We order two more beers and go back to our table.

Phil rubs his stomach and winces. 'Urgh – that was tough. Now, tell me about this woman you've been seeing? The grapevine says you're besotted.'

'That subject is off limits today, mate. Let's just say I've not been lucky on this one.'

'Oh dear – has she run off with another bloke?'

'Yes and no.'

'Eh?'

'Another woman. Ok. And that's all I have to say. Right?'

Phil rocks with laughter and can barely get his response of 'Absolutely!' out.

'Oh dear,' he says wiping his eyes. 'As we're here in the belly of the beast, a toast – to direct action and those of us who've been out there. We've had some fine times.'

'I just hope there's a new set out there to replace us when we all hang up our harnesses,' I reply.

'Course there is. The next lot will be even more radical than us. They'll chuck us out, tell us we're old hat.'

'I hope so – I really do,' I say, not knowing whether it's the booze or my lack of faith in human nature that's causing a sudden downturn in my mood. It isn't helped by Phil asking me what I'm going to do after activism.

'Not a clue. But I s'pose I can't do it forever. For loads of reasons.'

'Yep – there's a big world out there and at some point you have to do something for yourself. When's that going to be? Where's the biting point?'

'Phil – can I email you a mind map of the answers when I'm sober? I think it's time we leave before I lose my deposit down the toilet.'

'Ok, mate, you can stay at mine if you like. I'll give you the key and I can stay at Flick's.'

'Yeah that's cool, thanks. But who's Flick?'

'Well – not all Commons researchers are anally retentive – though she can be if you ask really nicely.' That's the dirtiest joke Phil's ever told for as long as I've known him. I like to think he's learned something from me too.

As I walk him to the bus stop he writes down the address. 'It's walkable if you could use the air,' he says.

'Something tells me I'll appreciate it tomorrow if I do.'

After he's gone I walk along the river and take in the hustle and bustle of eight million people all plugged into the London Machine – virtually all of whom aren't going to change their ways just because some know-it-all youngsters stage a few stunts.

I turn back and look up at Big Ben but the only faith I have in it is that it's telling the right time. How is the future of the capital to play itself out? In fifty years time will it be floods or famine? Will Eastenders feature riots over fresh water, or indeed will the BBC even be around to make the programme?

I'm not sure, but as I find Phil's mews house and turn the key to the permanent background hum of the sound of burning hydrocarbons I feel far too small and powerless to change any of it.

CHAPTER **10**

AUTUMN 1995

It's my mum's birthday and I've hitched down to Sussex to do the dutiful son thing for a few days. Caught up with Dave and a few people from school last night. Perhaps it's growing maturity, but I managed to pace myself to have six pints instead of double figures and wake up hangover-free.

Bob Geldof once sang I Don't Like Mondays. Well, I disagree. Granted, I don't have a nine-to-five to drive me mad, but I'd like to think I work hard for little reward.

On Radio 4 at 9am there's Start the Week, which gives the brain a bit of a workout before facing the challenges of the day. There's the residual thought of what you did over the weekend, and the extra energy you get from having a couple of days off, if I haven't been on an action.

Today is indeed a Monday, my parents are out, Start the Week is on and I'm tucking into a bit of breakfast intently listening to some bloke who's written a book about Bonobo chimps. By all accounts the upside of being a Bonobo is they are very happy and peaceful creatures, however, the constant incest and penis fencing with your dad I could do without. As these weighty philosophical musings occupy my mind the doorbell chimes.

As I walk barefoot up the hallway a yawn forces its way to the surface, and I have to consciously keep one eye open to identify the visitors standing in the porch – two men wearing police uniforms.

They flash their Met IDs, and names are mentioned but I'm too shocked to process the words other than 'Nigel' – cos it's such a shite name. I'm brought back into this dimension by the one on the left asking 'Is Lester Stype there?' in an accent that could be from the English/Welsh border. Not Gloucestershire. Hereford maybe? Perhaps Wales itself. I allow everything and anything to flood into my mind other than the distinct possibility that I'm in trouble.

The other cop, whose front teeth are so big he could almost use a broom to clean them, adds: 'He was supposed to appear for trial in Waltham Forest last year and didn't show up.'

Come on brain, say something useful ... 'No, I'm his brother Paul.

Pleased to meet you, come on in.' I lead them into the sitting room with no plan other than to lie and hope. I turn the radio down and sit on the edge of the sofa. There's an armchair either side and each is shortly occupied by a cop's arse. The opening lines of Caught By The Fuzz by Supergrass starts up in the secret gig venue of my head.

'Would you like a cup of tea, lads?' I ask.

'No thanks, not on duty.'

A vague cover story comes into my head. 'Yeah, I'm afraid Lester's gone to live with his girlfriend in Portsmouth for a while. I'm due to see him in a couple of weeks – I'll tell him you called by.'

There's a silence. They're both looking at me – and smiles are not to be found. A horrible chasm has opened up in my Monday morning and the chances of Monday afternoon being one to savour are as likely as Nick Leeson being made Governor of the Bank of England.

The non-Welsh one says: 'You're not Paul, are you? You're Lester. We've got pictures,' and before I can say anything more they're upon me. I try to get off the couch, but they push me back. My legs go up to defend myself but as it's two against one and I'm barefoot it's not going to be much of a fight. The Welsh one pulls me round, pushes my face into the recess of the sofa, where only lost coins and Glacier Mints usually dwell. I feel what I presume is a knee pressed into the small of my back as he says to the other. 'Right Tony, you grab his legs and I'll put the cuffs on.'

Compared to kwik-cuffs these are like a light massage applied to my wrists, but this isn't exactly play fighting.

'Get up. You're coming with us,' says Nigel and I'm pulled backwards by my arms onto my bare feet.

'At least give us a chance to get some socks and shoes on,' I ask.

'You should have thought about that before you started lying to us.'

As we leave the keys to the porch door – which are never used – are in the lock. For some bizarre reason they lock the door behind them and shove the keys in the pocket of my shorts.

'But ...'

'But nothing. Get up that path, you tosser,' says Nigel, not willing to listen to anything more.

'Bundled' is the common verb used for being put in a police vehicle, and it's well observed. With restricted movement in the arms and shoulders, combined with the lack of respect shown by the officers, you might as well be an unwieldy parcel to be crammed into the back seat.

I meet Nigel's eyes in the rearview mirror and say: 'This is kidnap. I don't recognise your authority.'

'Christ, Tone, we're not going to get this between here and London are we? He's giving me earache.'

'Look, I didn't even do anything. This is total bullshit.'

'That's for the magistrate to decide, I'm afraid,' says Tony.

Right now the only freedom I have is dissent. For the next hour, until even I get bored of the sound of my voice, I give it large about the questionable nature of the police force, how duty is a four-letter word and how I was trying to do the right thing.

I try to use my phone call to explain to my parents why I've disappeared but surprisingly no-one's home. Instead I leave a message on my sister's ansaphone. Three hours later Nigel comes down to see me with a cup of tea and some biscuits.

'There you go. Sugar?' he says, somehow anxious to please. I dunk a bourbon cream and say nothing.

'There's been ... a bit of a mix-up. Your parents are locked out of their house.'

I let out a laugh-cum-snort. 'No – I think you locked them out by nicking that porch key.'

'Whatever. The reality is your parents need to be let back in, so I just need you to sign a release form and we can get all this sorted.'

'Look – Nige – I know this sounds harsh but I know my Police and Criminal Evidence Act, and if you so much as touch my bag I'm gonna sue your arses.'

'Come on – be reasonable.'

'Yeah – like you were when I was eating sofa earlier on. Fuck you.'

He picks up the remaining biscuits and storms off. I think that's called one-all. I'm later informed that Nigel opened up the evidence bag without my consent and him and Tony drove the hundred-plus-mile round trip to let my folks in. Greatest police force in the world? Cunts.

I'm led up into the well of the court still in T-shirt and shorts, handcuffed and flanked by security. In the public gallery there's Dom, Helen, Gary, Ann and Paulo, who's wearing a big cow-spot print pimp-style hat. Once I am free of the cuffs, I raise a thumb in their direction and mouth a special 'Thanks for coming down' to the Manchester posse.

As the magistrates come through the door the usher asks Paulo to remove his hat and beneath it his hair is bleached and dyed in Friesian cow black and white. Even the usher is fighting the urge to smile, though the magistrates look less than impressed. I'm torn between basking in the surreal qualities of the moment and the overwhelming feeling that I'm sunk.

'Can you confirm your name?'

'Lester Stype.'

'Not Roger Mills?'

'No.'

'So you gave a false name on arrest?'

'Yes.' Why can't they ask me some easy questions like what's the secret of quantum physics.

'And is it also true that you failed to appear at trial when asked to do so?'

I know I'm the accused, but the whole process feels so removed from me. I might as well not be here, which was one of the reasons I didn't turn up for trial in the first place.

The magistrate looks down his glasses at me. 'Mr Stype, the fact you have given a false name and failed to attend trial gives me little faith in you turning up if you are given bail. I see no choice other than to remand you in custody until the time of your retrial in two weeks.'

Remanded in custody. Prison. Freedom – that lofty concept I had gone in search of nearly three years ago – will be something which happens to other people. Suddenly, as the cuffs are reapplied the full gravity of this hits me and I snap. 'This is total bullshit. Someone should bomb these fucking courts.' As I'm led below I raise both arms aloft towards my supporters shouting, 'Bomb the courts!'

I'm led into a courtyard, then to a Reliance prison van with individual cells. Sat at a right angle to the tiny window, I suppose this is where my sensory deprivation begins. Through it I can only see about four inches of life at a time – slice after slice of the outside world I will shortly relinquish for the time being. 'You've done it now Lester,' I say to myself passing the last object to fall into my eyeline before the austere arched prison gate – a humble lamppost.

'Right. Time for your strip search. Trollies down.' The prison officer – or screw as I suppose I have the right to call him from now on – has appalling teeth and looks like an extra from a bad pirate film. He takes a cursory look up my arse but thankfully isn't taking full pride in his job.

As I have no other clothes I'm left with little option other than to wear prison uniform. I'm issued a couple of sets consisting of a blue and white striped shirt and ill-fitting jeans. To say I don't feel a certain frisson in being a con would be a lie.

I'm informed it's now time to see 'the vet', which seems to be the post-ironic term for the prison doctor. In the 'waiting room' – for want of a better term to call it – there's one other inmate. We get chatting and his name is Les. I can accept he's on remand for multiple arson but find it difficult to get my head round his resemblance to John Cleese.

Shown to my new temporary lodgings, my cellmate-to-be is lying on the top bunk. Though he's not much older than me it's kinda like the scene in Porridge when Godber gets introduced to Fletcher.

When the door slams behind me, I'm addressed in even middle-class tones. 'Roger. Nice to meet you.'

'That's never your name?' I say as I reach up to shake hands.

"Fraid so.' and the inevitable 'What are you in for?' conversation ensues.

He's a really nice bloke – for an ex-public schoolboy – and is here because he fell out with his fiancée, got really drunk and decided to set fire to her car. Unfortunately, the flames got out of control and from a sense of both remorse and twisted decency went and knocked on her front door to warn her of the impending inferno.

Ok, that was a hyper-dumb thing to do, but when sober you could not meet a nicer bloke – at least one looking at a five-to-seven-year stretch in the near future.

The cell is about seven-foot wide and a little longer lengthways. A cockroach scuttles from under the bunk towards the toilet and I step back in alarm.

'Don't worry about them,' says Rog. 'They can be quite entertaining. I sometimes line them up and stage a race.'

In the first few days it's the simple things that irritate me. Not being able to just go for a pint, or even things I would never normally do like spend the afternoon in a betting shop or car boot sale. Everything the state has deemed me not deserving of doing. After all I've done I should be held shoulder-high through the streets – huge crowds with burning torches and battering rams should be storming the gates to break me out of here. However, as it stands I'm left with me, the ceiling and my thoughts.

Within three days I'm firmly into the regime and in a funny way it feels like second nature. It's kind of scary how fast you can be institutionalised.

At 8am our cell is unlocked, we collect our breakfasts in stainless steel trays and go back to eat. Toast and cornflakes with UHT milk is about the most appetising option. Next highlight of the day is exercise from eleven 'til twelve. In the yard it's possible to tell the old lags from the older guys who've recently found themselves in prison. Don't know why – just something about the way they carry themselves. Roger says a major purpose of the exercise hour for most is to swap phone cards for smack.

'How many people on our wing are on class As?' I ask. They all seem a pretty decent chilled-out bunch. Then it dawns on me we've possibly got the drugs to thank for this. He says 7 out of 10 are using and I'm grateful I'm kind of on the 'Just Visiting' section of the Monopoly board.

The main topic of conversation is how everyone's been 'stitched up by their brief'. Rog is about the only person who freely admits to what he's done.

At 1pm we collect lunch to take back to our luxurious quarters. It's a bit like school meals except the dinner ladies have slightly more facial hair and tattoos. I remember a couple of people at the M11 said they were freefall fruitarians – wishing to only eat that which has fallen from a tree of its own accord. Not sure how they got on with that. According to the rules, the food is supposed to be 'wholesome, nutritious, well-prepared and served'. It's the best joke I've heard since I arrived. There's even times when the food runs out before everyone's been served – a mixed blessing for those at the back of the queue.

We're left to our own devices 'til 3pm when we have two hours of recreation – a daily competition of the best pool and table tennis players you're ever likely to see.

There's usually a Scrabble round-robin, and I most enjoy playing Tafari. He's Ethiopian and his name means 'one who inspires awe'. Sentenced for a year for credit card fraud, he's been in an extra nine months awaiting deportation. Though his spoken English isn't great he lives up to his name when it comes to piling up points with little white tiles. He struggles to tell me he's had so much spare time he's memorised the Scrabble dictionary and more often than not beats me by more than 100 points.

There's a crew of three Yardies on life sentences for murder who ironically play killer pool every afternoon. They're decent enough so long as you're polite and don't get in their way. In crime terms I'm plankton compared to some of these sharks. It's not that scary in here – although Roger told me of a sex offender who didn't take the 'Rule 43' option – to be segregated from the other prisoners. Word got out as to why he was inside and he was attacked with razor blades in the showers.

He adds: 'They cut deep into his buttocks as that controls the muscles for getting an erection.'

We go to collect tea at 5pm, and are then expected to entertain ourselves 'til eight when it's lockdown and lights out at ten. Roger has a radio constantly tuned to the crappy local commercial station. If I hear Whigfield or Kiss From A Fucking Rose by Fucking Seal one more time I'm gonna be up on more serious charges.

As a remand prisoner I have certain privileges compared to those who've been convicted. I can shower in my own time, and wear civilian clothes. I'm also allowed three visitors a week, which breaks the monotony but I haven't requested anyone comes to see me unless they really want to. It's only two weeks after all. Have received a fair few cards and a couple of books – at least I know there's people out there thinking of me.

Having said that, it is starting to get to me in here. It's subtle, draining your spirit, taking your get-up-and-go and replacing it with curl-up-and-mope. I'm proud to say I've felt low, but haven't shed a single tear. I know there's nothing wrong with crying but it's still a personal badge of honour, however misplaced.

Due to staff shortages there are few opportunities to visit the prison library. Even when you get there you don't fancy reading anything. There's all this talk of rehabilitation and education of prisoners, but about the only thing I've learned in here is I never want to be this bored ever again.

Pentonville is shaped like a part-finished cartwheel, with spokes leading off from a central hub. Hopefully I'm not talking like a hippy here, but there's a strange energy about the point where the various wings join. The almost constant soundscape of bangs and slams, shouting and crying, alarms and buzzers echoes through this central chamber – like a sinister discordant symphony of wasted lives.

'There's been three suicides this year already,' says Rog. 'Hangings. Always hangings.' Rog is a good laugh but are are times when the prison is the only thing to talk about and things get dark. He says our exercise yard is where the prison's gallows used to be, and that all who were hanged here – including Dr Crippen – are buried in a lawned area near the back wall.

Each day one of us is 'randomly' chosen to be strip-searched and have their cell turned over for drugs and weapons. Of over a hundred in our section, I've been selected in just over a week, and if you include the search I'll get on the way out of here that'll make four times I hear the dubious request of 'trollies down'.

It's the night before my trial and Roger's lying on the top bunk reading his John Grisham novel – can't really see the attraction of reading crime fiction in here. About every half hour he'll lean over on his other side, producing a sleep-breaking creak from the rickety bed.

'Rog,' I say with that just-awake grogginess, 'I've been thinking.'

'What about?'

'Just the nature of what people are in here for.'

'Go on.'

'I suppose it's all about not having what you think you need and acting on it. Theft's the obvious one, but domestic violence is – I don't know – about not feeling secure in your relationship. Do you see what I'm saying?'

'Kind of.'

'How can I rephrase – ok, if you take money, drugs, women and cars out of the picture I think there'd only be me in this place.'

'Yeah, I can see that. What's the solution?'

'Fucked if I know. Good night.' I turn over and the top bunk obscures just enough artificial light to dream of being trapped in a velvet curtain – huge, heavy, constricting. I'm just about able to breathe but it's impossible to escape until I wake with a start in the middle of the night. I spend the hours 'til breakfast lying there with little hope of drifting off again listening to distant crazy shouting from the psych ward.

At 10am I'm whisked off to court where I'm as meek as possible and given another 12-month conditional discharge, a £100 fine for the offence and a £50 fine for jumping bail the first time round. Then it's back to Pentonville and the process of release begins. I reluctantly hand back the uniforms – apparently they can be sold on for a decent price on the outside and am given my property back. I don't thank them – seeing as I shouldn't have been here in the first place.

The Manchester minibus has been blagged to come down and meet me at the prison gates. It's a lovely gesture but they shouldn't have. Even Neil's taken the day off work to come down with the lentils to celebrate my release.

Dom recommends the Hemingford Arms from when he lived down here – a few minutes west of Pent-upVille.

Neil gives me a big hug, fakes a microphone in front of my face and asks: 'What's it like to be free again after all these years, Nelson?' I grin to acknowledge the gag but don't have the energy for a witty response.

Two weeks without alcohol has been ok, it's not like I'm shaking or anything but I'm craving oblivion and self-destruction rather than festivity. I take any drink on offer and slug it back with abandon.

Dom went to prison for Twyford so understands some of what I'm going through, which is probably more than I do. 'Don't worry, mate, you get good and pissed tonight – we'll look after you.'

Despite everyone chipping in to buy me lunch it doesn't take long for the effects of booze to spill over into the day.

By 3pm I go to the bog for a tactical chunder – something I haven't done since the first year of uni. Making yourself sick to make room for more alcohol isn't the exactly the apex of achievements in life.

Two more hours leads to four more pints. No one's going to tell me what to do for a good long while after this.

Tim asks: 'So, did you get it from Mr Big in the showers?'

My witty repost is 'Fuck off, you goth cunt'. He backs away – I must have the look of a pub drunk itching for some handbags.

'We're all doomed, it's fucked,' I say putting my face into the crook of my arm. 'Why do we fucking bother?'

Neil holds a hand up to the barmaid to say he has the situation of me under control. Patronising arsehole.

Helen puts her arm round me. 'Come on, Lester, we've been going great guns, you're just a bit emotional after what's happened over the last couple of weeks.'

'Bollocks,' I say, brushing her aside. 'Fuck it. Fuck the planet, and fuck you all.' I run out of the pub with no idea where I am but with one destination in mind.

As I try to cut across what I think looks like Clissold Park I realise Dom and Neil are in hot pursuit. Relative sobriety is victorious over my desperate drunken lurching and Neil bundles me over.

'Where the fuck were you going?' The whole point of us coming down was to give you a lift back to Manc,' he says, pinning me to the floor.

'Where's Sarah? Why isn't she here?' I slur, struggling to push him aside.

'She doesn't care, mate. Get with the programme.'

I stop thrashing about and lie back at the sky, my mind racing with images of Sarah being tongued by Erin – writhing and begging for more.

I'm taken back to the minibus. Everyone's more subdued than before – and some I'm sure wished they'd never come all this way.

'I'm sorry, guys – 'specially you Tim. You may be a goth but you're not a cunt.' As I give him a hug I swallow down a mini-sick burp. This is a precursor for an emergency chunder stop on a hard shoulder just outside Hemel Hempstead – reminiscent of the weekend Debs dumped me. All hail – the conquering hero returns.

My 25th birthday is looming on the horizon three weeks hence. Of course it's only an arbitrary date, but since getting back I've been having a good hard look at my life and not liking what I see. We can all be our own harshest critics, but coming up to the old quarter century I've got no job, no work experience relevant in the 'real world', no money, no girlfriend, a big fat criminal record and absolutely no idea of what I'd do other than activism.

Ok, over the last couple of years I've had a right laugh – most of the time – while sharing some unique experiences, but that isn't going to take care of me in old age. I suppose there's a flipside thing about prison – it makes you appreciate freedom all the more, but also – perhaps for the first time ever, I realise I'm not indestructible. Perhaps watching lives being destroyed from the inside has brought it home that one day there'll be a little gathering somewhere – hopefully not a church – to commemorate the fact that I am no longer around.

Wish I could get better sleep. Have started waking up around three and not being able to get back off – even knocking one out doesn't seem to help. I just lie there, caught up in inconclusive thoughts. Of course, there's the consequence of being knackered during the day that leads to ... not much to be honest. Haven't had the energy to think about organising actions – furthest thing from

my mind to be honest. It sounds horrible – considering the support
they showed me on my release – but I haven't been in touch with
anyone from EF! since. I'm burnt out and need time to work out the
angles – my balls are on the baulk cushion and I've no idea what
spin I can use to get me out of the snooker I'm facing.

Trouble is, it makes me feel guilty that I'm not out there doing the
business on the activism front which leaves me feeling even worse.
Then I feel guilty about not being in touch with the gang and feeling like I haven't the energy to explain puts them further to the
back of my mind.

All the prison business has messed up my signing on and so I'm
completely broke, and they're on my back even more now they
know what I've been up to. I've had a cursory look at the jobs
section, but have no idea of what I want to do when I grow up. Not
one iota of progress on that score since the day I talked of
working for Viz with Ken Bierce in Worthing Job Club.

Don't know if it's connected but along with the lack of sleep
there's been a loss of appetite. By the time I haul myself out of bed,
get thoughts together, dwell on quite a few of them, stare without
seeing for maybe an hour at a time, snap out of it, then fall into the
same pattern, most of the day has gone by without troubling the
kitchen other than for the odd cup of tea.

Neil senses something's up – that I've gone from being a doley
lentil who's too busy to get a job to just being a layabout. He tries
to chivvy me out of it – takes me to the pub to meet a couple of
women from work, and is there to listen to my ranting and whing-
ing. But the women lack the depth of my sorrows and besides – how
can I show a girl a good time on £12.51 – the current balance in my
graduate account. Things aren't helped by losing my wallet
containing £30. Fell out of my pocket on the bus – should have
spent it on a new second-hand bike.

On a more positive note I've definitely lost weight – probably a
stone and half in the four weeks since I got out. And that's with me
drinking a good few cans a night. It's ok, they were good and cheap
from Aldi and I bought a lot with the last Giro I had. The one EF!
person, come to think of it about the only person, I've seen on a
regular basis is Paulo, who gives me the odd tenth out from what
he knocks out to students. Hash was never really my thing, but
anything to get some sleep. Not that it's really working.

I keep thinking someone out there has the life which had been
mapped out for me in the summer of '93 – an interesting burgeoning career, a supportive, mentoring boss grooming me for even
better things. Someone else's got the girlfriend I should have been
seeing for about eighteen months by now, who I would have met at
a tennis party through a client.

Whoever the fuck it is please give it back to its rightful owner. Boss – I could do the job better, and as I'm cheap to run wouldn't be on at you for constant pay rises. Girl – I have three times the passion, four times the humour and five times the bedroom skills of that loser ... who am I kidding – where's that rolling mat?

Neil has a spare portable TV and I've set it up in my bedroom. Don't really care what's on as long as it's not soaps – but to be honest there's not much quality other than Father Ted, Frasier and the Private Life of Plants. That said – Jennifer Ehle in Pride And Prejudice is about the only thing to get me going at the moment. Surely my libido should be higher than this in my mid-twenties?

Went to the library and got some David Icke books. Always thought he was a bit whacked out – and still do – but some of what he says makes some sense. He used to be in the Green Party after all. I totally agree there are people with too much power in the world but that they are eight-foot lizards from the sixth dimension? Please. All his conspiracy rants are making me a bit jumpy and I decide that, contrary to what we were always told at school, reading is bad for you.

At night I stare at the artex on my bedroom walls and see different shapes – mainly creatures. Some cartoonish, others sinister. Demons, like mini-gargoyles, looking down on my new prison. As the headlights from passing cars traverse the walls their features change, as if laughing at my predicament. I turn over – eyes shut tight wishing for the sleep which never comes for long enough.

On the Open University each night I've learned what it's like to be an occupational therapist, veterinary nurse or electronic engineer – and no, I don't fancy being any of those.

It's been weeks since I checked my emails – I probably have hundreds by now – or do I? Would anyone be bothered to write now I'm not doing actions? Where are my other friends? Why don't they ring? Why can't I get it together?

Happy birthday to me. Celebrated by going to the doctor and being prescribed temazepam. Decided to go for a swim to try and make myself feel better. Did five lengths then found I didn't have the energy to kick my legs and have to leave. Don't fancy drowning on my special day. Get home, force down two Cup-a-Soups and some toast and go to bed for a smoke. It's uncomfortable craning my neck to watch the telly so lay it on its side and it's much better. Even managed to do all the numbers games on Countdown this afternoon.

My present from Neil is a video of Cinema Paradiso – my favourite film. Not sure why – might been cos I was on hash cake first time I saw it and wept buckets. Never fails.

Make a rare appearance in the lounge to watch it but fails to raise the barest emotion. I feel don't feel connected to it, to Neil, to anyone, to me.

I dump teacup and plate in the sink and say to Neil: 'Doctor says I've got depression. That's bollocks, isn't it?' Shows I've been slow on the uptake lately as he reckons I've had all the symptoms for weeks now.

He clamps his hands onto his face, takes a deep breath and says: 'Lester, this probably isn't the best time, but there's something we need to discuss.'

'Don't tell me. You're coming out.'

'Hmm ... my mum and dad have offered to help me out with the deposit on a flat, and I'm going to take them up on it. I'm seeing a mortgage advisor tomorrow.'

'I'm made up for you, mate.' Great. Can we add to the earlier list of life failures imminent homelessness?

There's a theory that happiness depends on four spheres of life – love, home, work and social. If more than two of these aren't going according to plan, the plain and simple truth is you will not be happy. If you include the fact I've shunned virtually all my friends lately that makes four out of four. Bingo. Jackpot. We've got a winner.

Over the last few days the tablets have stabilised my sleep, and as I can't drink or smoke feel a bit more together. The depression still clings to my system like flu, but I'm a bit more like the old me. I feel like there's an emotional blockage and if I can just breach it everything will be ok.

An experiment comes to mind based on theory that music is the language of emotion. It's a long shot but I'm willing to try anything to stop feeling like shit all the time. I shut my bedroom door and flick through my CD collection with a solitary purpose – to try and cry myself better.

Like most males of my age or above, it's difficult for me to shed tears without the aid of alcohol. And besides, booze-induced tears aren't the real deal.

As a warm-up track I select Wonderful Life by Black, and as the synth intro gives way to the verse lie back and consider all the ways my life ain't so wonderful. Next I bring out one of the big guns, I Want You by Elvis Costello. Hugging two pillows, I can feel something start to well up as he sings unaccompanied: 'Oh my baby baby, I love you more than I can tell...'

The following seven minutes of this, perhaps the saddest, most heartfelt song I've ever heard, does have an effect. Especially when I think of Sarah and all the other women I've loved and lost, who are now in the arms of someone else.

Something by the Beatles is good but unsuccessful, but the blue–eyed soul of Paradise by Aztec Camera manages to say more about my situation than anything I've heard thus far. The Only One by Billy Bragg, an old favourite, somehow lacks the magic ingredient. Prefab Sprout's When Love Breaks Down again was a nearly but not quite. U2 try their best with One and REM may know that Everybody Hurts, but it's not everybody I'm interested in – the only thing that matters right now is my own personal pain and pity. For the next hour I line up track after track to storm my emotional barricades. Cavalry charges from the Stones and Richard Thompson, musical mortar attacks from Christy Moore and the Beach Boys. Attempted ambushes from Van Morrison, the Saw Doctors and the Small Faces. All to no avail.

Next I try Bridge Over Troubled Water as it's Sarah's favourite. I've always thought it was a great song, but had never really listened to it before. As the final verse begins I start to feel on the brink; my eyelashes moisten and throat contracts. My nose begins to run, and as the track ends I'm sobbing on the bed. It's the last track on the disc and I lie dribbling snot onto the duvet. Don't know what is released in tears to make you feel better, but a lot of the tension in my head has gone and I can even detect the trace of a smile in between snivels.

I put on one last track for the evening. During the Style Council's You're the Best Thing, a compilation of images over the last two and a half years come flooding into my mind – the little moments of joy experienced on actions, camps, bedrooms, or the pub. My wonderful world of birds, booze and bulldozers.

Part of Neil's house-buying plan is to move in with his girlfriend to save more money for fees. Couldn't blame him if my recent behaviour has been a factor in him moving out. I'm feeling better but the upshot of my recent spin-out is I've got to move out too as I can't afford to keep the house on by myself – besides, the old place wouldn't be the same with anyone else.

Have been looking in the Evening News for jobs, have even re-jigged my CV and have applied for a few things but I can't say your average employer is going to give me an interview – even if I promise to walk over broken glass to get there.

I'm all boxed up and need a new plan by the end of the week. A job would be best but all the letters coming back my way over the last couple of weeks have started 'Thank you for your recent application. Unfortunately ...' you know the rest.

As we're moving out there's nothing to break so have taken to practising my volleys in the lounge with a tennis ball.

PHOCK. One-nil. A wonderful goal by Stype.

PHOCK. Two-nil to Brighton. Man United simply have no reply. Cantona's got his head in his hands.

PHOCK. And there's the hat-trick on his FA Cup debut. Lester Stype. Remember the name – he'll be on a back page near you very soon.

PHOCK.

Hang on ... was that the ball or someone at the door? I go and check. It's Dom, Helen and Jane each holding a bottle of wine.

'Hello, stranger. Fancy hanging out in the park?' Helen asks. 'We've got something to ask you.'

It'd be rude to say no, and I'm allowed the odd glass now my sleep is back to normal. 'Ok, as long as I can go on the big slide.' I get my jacket.

The last gasp of late autumn sunshine is watery but welcome. There's a sign in the playground prohibiting alcohol but we ignore it like the A-grade anarchists we are. We swing and swig, though it's difficult to get any momentum going with a bottle in your hand.

'Lester,' says Dom.

'Dom, says I.

'I know you haven't been involved lately, but have you kept up with the news?'

'Kind of, but I've had shit of my own to deal with lately.'

'Did you see the news about Newbury?'

'Yeah.' They've decided to give the go-ahead for the bypass.

'Well,' says Jane, looking better than ever. We're trying to retain eye contact but our swing rhythms aren't synchronised. 'This is the going to be the biggest battle yet. And ...'

'And what?'

Jane drags her feet to stop the swing. 'And we need all our best people there. You're right up there, Lester. We need you.'

Helen, swinging higher than any of us, says, with each sentence coinciding with a forward motion. 'You don't have to answer now ... But we're off there tomorrow ... I'm staying 'til the job's done ... one way or another.'

I screw up my nose, unsure at the proposal. 'I'm trying to get my act together, get a job. I can't tell you how skint I am. Isn't it some-one else's turn?'

'Mate, this is everything we've been working towards. You never know – I'm not saying we're gonna win, but everyone's so up for it.'

He's right. One last push. Unless we try we'll never know. Besides, there'll be somewhere to stay, even if it's a treehouse. And it's so, so lovely to be wanted. 'Go on then,' I say, 'put me down for a space tomorrow. What time are you leaving?' They all jump off the swings, knocking me to the floor in a swamp of hugs.

CHAPTER **11**

WINTER 1995/6

I'd like to say the minibus is crawling through Newbury but this would grossly overestimate our current speed. Dom headbutts the steering wheel saying: 'Someone should build a bypass round here.'

Leaving Manchester – at least for the time being – will be a wrench but I suppose things haven't been working out. At least me and Neil are still on good terms despite all the shit I've put him through lately. Over Christmas I dumped virtually everything I own in my parent's loft and so I'm down to one rucksack of clothes, toiletries, a couple of books, a sturdy pair of boots, sleeping bag, a climbing harness I bought myself for Christmas and most importantly a cashpoint card for the pub.

It seems that while I've been wallowing in my bedroom there have been new developments. In November over a hundred road schemes were axed, the roads budget was cut by 30% and Newbury is the only major project currently going ahead. Looks like we're on top for a change. Losing battles but winning the war.

'I think this is the office over there,' says Helen, who's said Newbury is her last hurrah. I think she deserves the break – at times she's held her life together on pure bloody-mindedness and if there was any justice on this planet, society would club together to buy her an overland round-the-world ticket as a thank-you.

'Office space? In the centre of town? That's a bit posh for us isn't it?' I ask.

'Friends Of The Earth are picking up the bill. They're actually supporting us this time,' says Tango, sat hand-in-hand with Eloise.

'No way? So they've finally grown a backbone. That's great news,' It's really good being back with the gang. I think a few of us are getting itchy feet but we're still in there fighting. Jane wants to start a family with Des, which naturally is a disappointment for me but it's a free country. Dom says he wants to go and live in the countryside somewhere but, unusually for him, the plan is a bit vague.

We eventually find somewhere to park and haul our stuff up an anonymous-looking alleyway. One door and a staircase later the Manchester EF! battalion is reporting for duty at HQ. In reality, we're cluttering up the office not knowing quite what to do or say.

A big fella in his forties with sandy coloured hair and glasses acknowledges our arrival whilst continuing his conversation on the CB radio. We dutifully wait until he's finished telling someone how many miles of polyprop rope to buy, where to get it and what price to haggle for.

Dom waves an arm in his direction with a flourish, as if he's introducing a Las Vegas headliner. 'Guys, this is Radio Bob. He's a legend.'

'Please, no autographs,' says Bob, 'you have to go through my agent.' He seems like a great laugh. If he's typical of the folks on the campaign this is gonna rock.

Putting an arm round Bob's squidgy shoulders Dom says: 'He's our ... what's your title again?'

'Quartermaster. I deal with all the kit. If you need anything, just ask. And I'll say no.' He turns to the corner of the office, where a pair of hands can be seen putting paper on top of a filing cabinet. 'Matthew?'

A younger, geekier version of Bob sticks his head round. 'This is my nephew everyone. Mate, could you get these folks something to drink, please?'

Matthew nervously threads his way through the computer gear and goes towards the kettle, not making eye contact with any of us.

As Bob shows us a map of the proposed nine-mile route of the road Matthew scrabbles about for a bit before saying, 'We're out of teabags. Sorry.'

Bob looks at his watch. 'Oh well, as Dom and Helen are particular friends of mine I think a quick trip to the pub is in order. It's not like the evictions are going to happen tomorrow. Besides, they've brought all you fresh cannon fodder for me to play with.'

Eloise looks worried. 'Joke,' says Bob with a reassuring smile. 'Come on, let's go to the Clocktower.'

We wend our way through the gridlocked streets to a real spit-and-sawdust dive.

'Traffic's bad here, isn't it?' I say to Matthew trying to engage him.

'Yes, well, that's because there's only 25 yards of road for every car in the UK, you see,' he says with a twitch. Strange. Nice, but strange.

'You're gonna love this place,' says Bob as he pushes open the door. 'Well, let me rephrase that – you're gonna have to love it. Most of the pubs in town won't let us in.'

Behind the bar is a huge woman with huger hair and classic Hell's Angel black leather jacket with quilted lapels.

Bob takes out his wallet. 'I'll get them in as it's your first day. Everyone, this is Barb, if you play nice she's the world's best land-lady. I think you can guess what happens if you're not. Now, what're you having?'

The biggest table in the pub is soon covered with pints and it looks like we're going to christen our arrival with a few.

'Weeeeeeaaaaaaaggggggggghhhhhhhhh!' Helen screechs as if she's seen a nine-foot mouse, running over to hug some muddy woman at the bar who she drags over.

'Everyone. This is Jesuit Jo.'

'That's a funny name,' says Tango.

'Hmm, the nickname kinda stuck cos people say I'm always on a mission. Besides, Joanne's has been awarded the most boring name eight years running.'

'Who by?' asks Eloise.

'Me. Call me JJ to save time eh?'

JJ has set up a camp in the woods nearest to the river Kennet.

'So my lovely,' she says to Helen. 'Where are you lot going to set up home?'

'Would it be ok if we show the guys round Kennet, see what they think? It's so beautiful there,' she replies and turning to us, enthuses, 'there's kingfishers, big fat chub and pike swimming through the reeds. And the sound of the river lulls you off to sleep like you wouldn't believe.'

'Before you need a piss halfway through the night,' cuts in JJ with a wink.

'I know we all know road building is wrong, but it's especially crazy with this route. There's badgers, bats, nightjars, dormice – the works. All of them should be protected, but there's been no ...'

'... Environmental impact assessment,' I finish her sentence with virtual certainty of being right.

'Thank you. Mine's a pint of cider,' JJ says with a trace of Margaret Thatcher about her. I meekly pull out a fiver and head to the bar where I can still hear the conversation.

'The road's going right through the site of two battles from the Civil War,' says Bob holding court.

'That's why the campaign is called the Third Battle of Newbury,' explains Tango to Eloise in quite a patronising manner.

'So are we the Roundheads or Cavaliers?' asks Dom. 'I'm not sure. Politically we're more like Cromwell's lot, but I think the King's men had more similar hair,' he says patting his dreads.

'Going back further in time there's even Mesolithic remains up near Donington Castle. The archaeological people are up in arms. Thanks, darlin',' says JJ as I hand over her pint.

'And old fossils like me,' adds Bob.

'There's some pretty Stone Age thinking behind the building of this road if you ask me,' I say to a chorus of groans.

'Quite,' says Matthew, having hardly touched his half of bitter. 'Traffic surveys have shown 80% of Newbury's traffic is local and only 10% of the journeys are long distance, going against the whole raison d'etre of the road – to reduce traffic volume from the town centre by 25%.'

'Fucking hell,' I say to Matthew, 'you're like Statto from Fantasy Football on the telly, and I begin to chant 'Statto, Statto' as if I was on the terraces on a Saturday afternoon. He blushes and hides behind his half.

'That's a great name for him,' says Bob, patting his nephew on the back. 'Statto. I like it.' Statto is mortified, as am I for suggesting it. But it looks like the nickname may just stick.

We walk along the river to along a canal towpath to the Kennet camp through the cold, dark night, alcohol easing the aches in our shoulders and shortening our perceived journey time.

JJ shines a torch up to a massive treehouse about forty feet off the floor. 'This is the Mothership – it sleeps twelve at a push. Should do for you all tonight,' she says holding a prusik loop for the first person to slowly pull themselves up the rope. 'Leave your rucksacks there and we'll winch them up afterwards. Come sit by the fire with Izzy and Trev while you're waiting. They're from Brighton. They don't bite.' Two identikit hippies in multicoloured woolly ponchos huddle by the fire.

Not wanting to sound like a wuss I sidle up to JJ and quietly murmur, 'I'd say cranes were more my thing than trees.'

'Well, just watch and learn and you'll pick it up. No worries. You've just got to treat the tree like a best friend,' she says going on a firewood mission, leaving me somewhat perplexed as to how to do this.

After having the biggest possible piss I can muster I eventually pluck up the courage to clip onto the rope and scale the tree. Left hand knot up, followed by right, then pull my legs up to take up the slack. I can feel the strain on my abdominal muscles immediately. Given a few weeks of this with any luck I'm gonna have a mean six-pack. Sarah'll be sorry then, or maybe she's more impressed with the size of Erin's clit. About halfway up I lose confidence and call up to Helen who's sorting out the tat.

'My arms hurt. I can't do it,' I cry.

'Stop being a big baby and get on with it. I've some aspirin up here as a special treat.' I resign myself to the thirty or more crunches I need to perform to reach the trapdoor. The gentle sway of the rope complements the woozy boozy feeling and I try to ignore the bicep pain and focus on my pharmaceutical treat at the top.

Upstairs it's blankets a go-go and an old-fashioned oil lamp is the only source of light. About half the size of a tennis court, The Mothership is the most impressive structure I've seen at any camp.

'Right – here you are,' says Helen, handing me two pills, then gets back to unpacking her sleeping bag. 'If you really get caught short in the night the middle of night the container in the corner is for urine,' she says pointing to a plastic gallon-sized tank. 'But to be honest, it's less disturbing for everyone to climb down.'

'Can't I just piss off the top?' I ask.

'I don't think JJ wants her camp covered in wee. You're not a tom-cat now, are you?'

'No, Mum,' I say wanting to brush my teeth but having to wait 'til all the bags are up with us.

'I'm sure once you've got your own treehouse you can make your own arrangements. Personally, I have my trusty blue teapot,' she says proudly.

Within half an hour everyone's settled down, and using my ruck-sack as a pillow I drift off to the steady trickle of England's most biologically diverse river.

I wake the next morning at seven to a varied chorus of snoring, farts, whispers, groans, giggles and a 70% full bladder. Jane's up and about so I get her to give me a refresher course in abseiling.

'Make sure you're clipped on,' she says, positioning a terrified me at the top of the rope. 'Use your bottom hand as a brake and feed the rope through at a rate you're comfortable with. Pull it up towards you to slow down.'

It's stop-start-stop, about ten minutes and much mutual laughter at my expense before my feet gingerly touch the ground. Thanking her for the help I unhook and go for a nose around.

Although everything's in January dieback, there's still much to take in. What sunlight there is flecks the surface of the water giving that silver-and-gold effect. A water vole surfaces breaking the pattern, looking like a hamster with a scuba diving qualification. I thought they hibernated but obviously not. If only it knew that these could be the last few weeks of tranquillity.

I return to see JJ stirring a steaming porridge pot.

'What do you reckon to Kennet?' she asks.

'It's beautiful. How could they?'

'I know. Breaks your heart. But there could be some karma coming their way if they fuck about with the river. Affects the flood plain and years down the line goodness knows what'll happen, especially if they build houses nearby.'

'Good. Fuck 'em. Teach 'em a lesson,' I reply.

'Sounds like we're going to get on. Porridge?' she says, dipping a ladle into the gloop.

'Would it be ok to build a treehouse here?' I ask. 'I think I've fallen for the place.'

'Helen says you're a mouthy shit,' says JJ, 'but a fucking good activist. Welcome aboard,' she says with a hug.

I decide there's no time like the present so get to it straight after breakfast, compiling a list of what I'm going to need to build a new home for myself. Well, actually I bug JJ all morning for tips, but at least I'm trying. She talks me through the basics. I need pallets for a floor which need to be lashed and nailed securely in the right part of the right tree. I don't know if it's a male thing or just basic self-preservation, but the uniform nature of cranes is much easier to trust, and I need to be able to transfer that faith to these random, organic and eminently snappable structures – and quick. Not being the most practically-minded person on the planet I offer to help Eloise and Tango build their treehouse if they help me put mine together. Enlightened self-interest I think you call it. Their assistance – and a hasty refresher course in tying the knots correctly – could well save me from having the worst treehouse on the entire route. How embarrassing – and arguably fatal – would it be if my new abode was to come loose and go ow-ow-ow crashing through the branches like in an episode of the Simpsons. Trees aren't the most symmetrical things, but I eventually spot a mid-sized oak with a decent reach of its branches.

'If we're going to try and save a tree, it might as well be the best one we can find, eh?' I say to Eloise and apologise to the pines surrounding us.

The camp has a CD player powered by a car battery and we're allowed to borrow it to lift our spirits on the build and we strap it to a nearby bough. We're also 'aided' in the construction process by Trevor offering us a line of speed.

'This base is the bollocks,' he says sniffing back a nostril's worth. Now I wouldn't normally advocate the combination of Class A drugs and heights but we've got to get on with it – I don't fancy spending too many nights with everyone in the Mothership.

'Woah!' I get a rush prusiking halfway up the tree with a hammer and nails in the hood of my parka.

Tango is the most experienced of the three of us in living on site. It's irritating but we have to rely on his instructions most of the time. It takes the best part of a day to get four pallets secured in the right position, covered over with board and a bit of carpet nailed on top.

By the time Rocks by Primal Scream pumps out of the stereo we're jumping around in drug-fuelled celebration on the newly built floor, being very careful not to fall to a reasonably certain death.

I try to get as much done on each trip up the tree as possible. The speed is making us work on a supercharged level, though it can make you forget what it was you went down to get.

'I think that's enough for today,' says Eloise, attending to a blister.

'Definitely, I'll go to the offie for us all after dinner,' I say very pleased with the progress we've made. There's a rudimentary field kitchen but I dare say it'll be a struggle to get all the domestic chores done whilst preparing the trees for defence.

That night there's a blazing fire to ward off the freezing temperatures. We're all sat around in fingerless gloves, many layers of mostly muted tones and big facefulls of facial hair. Let's just say if Scott of the Antarctic were still alive he'd assume we were part of his latest expedition.

To be honest, despite the growing media image of 'eco-warriors' living in trees, it's been a while since I've lived outdoors and it's gonna take some getting used to. Still, there's so much to get absorbed in, plans to execute and no doubt fun to be had. The average psychiatrist may disagree, but right now this feels like the ideal place to get over feeling a bit depressed.

Over the next couple of days the treehouse takes shape, with a hazel branch roof covered with tarps, and we even have time to fit a walkway from my tree to the one Tango and Eloise have chosen to occupy. We become part of the larger network of polyprop linking each treehouse with every other. Without touching the ground I can get from my as-yet empty home to the Mothership in about five minutes, gripping the top rope and edging along with my feet to the next set of branches. Every piece of polyprop on site starts and ends with a black wizened melt to prevent them from fraying. This is achieved by dabbing them in the fire.

The tension on the ropes needs to be just right, or else, as I found out to my cost about day four, you can be stranded in midair and have to get someone who really knows what they're doing to come and rescue you.

The rest of the Manchester gang are getting on with creating their new homes at Kennet and it's not unlike moving to a new flat anywhere else. We have little parties to celebrate, and climb over to a neighbour's to borrow something for that little DIY task. There's going to be a need for a shit-hot neighbourhood watch pretty soon.

One afternoon Bob drops by in one of the campaign vans.

'How's it going?' he asks.

'Yeah – pretty damn great. Any news on how long we've got before the forces of darkness arrive?'

'Could be any day now. We've not had any leaks on tactics and the like. Gotta keep on our toes.'

'How long do you think we can hold out?' I ask.

He shrugs but adds: 'If it all seems like it's going on forever, they need to be finished by the end of March so they don't disturb the nesting season. That is, if they're going to obey the Countryside Act.'

'So in a nutshell it'll just go on for as long as we can hold them off and fuck the legal niceties, yeah?'

'You've got it. Now, do you need any stuff for your treehouse? I've got a loads of donations in the back of this.'

I grab two plastic containers for water and wee, a bucket and a couple of bog rolls. Added to this I blag enough blankets to ensure warmth, a roll mat, a bag of tealight candles and a couple of jam jars to act as makeshift lanterns. There's also a copy of Treasure Island, which looks like it needs reading on dark, cold nights to supply some Caribbean sun.

Some people's treehouses have dreamcatchers and hippy-shit hanging from the ceiling. My abode is minimalist, functional and plain – rather like my bedroom in Manchester used to be.

After a while the confidence with the ropework increases, and abseiling is transformed from a cumbersome stuttering task to a rapid exhilarating operation. The rope makes a pleasing whistling sound as it whizzes through the metal descender and within days I've developed enough control to moderate my speed quite well. So long as you have some idea when the ground is coming towards you, slow down a little and bend your knees it's a fantastic way to travel, the closest to being Spiderman I'll probably ever experience.

Next morning I see JJ heading to the river carrying a load of pipes and a bag of cement. 'Fitting some plumbing?' I ask.

''Fraid not, we're gonna build some underwater lock-ons.'

'No shit?'

'Shit.'

'Wow.' I don't fancy JJ in the slightest but she really is some woman.

In seven days amid much swearing, hairy moments and tea drinking, Manchester EF! has managed to get a motley collection of five treehouses together and decides to have a little party to celebrate.

For the first time we meet Spanner, JJ's boyfriend, who lives in on a different part of the route – famous for a 16-day tripod sit blocking the area where security wanted to build their compound. Local vigilantes pushed the tripod down one night and threatened to come back with a pickaxe if he went back up. Spanner's good value but really likes his cider.

'Considering I'm a vegan I'm fucking leathered,' he says jumping over the firepit for the fifth time in as many minutes. Slipping slightly on take-off there's an inevitable loss of momentum and the bottom of his combat trousers catches on the flames.

JJ, who's sat on 'her' chair – which she carved herself from a section of fallen tree, rocks back with laughter and struggles to come out with the joke, 'What's orange and looks good on hippies?'

'I'm guessing the punchline is fire. Am I right?' I say with a snigger as Spanner beats at the flames with his hands and Dom gets up to throw some mud on the fire-affected areas. Spanner may be one of the best climbers on the campaign, but – perhaps as a consequence of this, you get the feeling he's ever so slightly nuts.

On the rare moments there's some free time away from camp, it's nice to see some of the route we're trying to defend. It's good to try and drag Statto away from the office as a guide. Towards the north there's Mary Hare, where badgers have been seen scurrying about, yet English Nature didn't seem to be able to find them when compiling their reports. Cowardly bastards. A little further to the south is the heather-and-heath beauty of Snelsmore Common containing six species of bat in the nearby woods, all of which are supposed to be protected. Also at Snelsmore is a burrowing creature called Swampy, who's been swotting up on Viet Cong-style tunnelling techniques. He's actually called Dan and he and his mates are a really cool bunch. Also, it's one of the many parts of the route where ancient woodland currently reigns supreme – oak, ash, birch and the like. It's easy to focus on the mammals and the trees that need protection, but Statto says a single mature oak can, apparently, be host to over 2,000 species of insect. There's the wetlands of the River Lambourn where there's supposed to be colonies of the Desmoulins Whorl snail, which is about the size of a match head, and no doubt swallowed from time to time by the odd passing swan. This leads down Rack Marsh, a perfect site for otters to twitch their whiskers, be cute in a web–pawed way and teach their young to catch fish. Talking of our scaly friends, trout happily swim down the Kennet looking for a tasty cranefly unless JJ's out in her coracle trying to catch one for supper. Arguably the most beautiful part of the route, the Kennet is the main tributary of the Thames and combines woodland and river in a way even a townie like me finds quite awe–inspiring. Next, the site of the First Battle of Newbury is set to be trashed, where in 1643 thirty thousand men fought – and 7,000 died – in a bloody stalemate witnessed by the king himself, who lost his Secretary of State Lord Falkland when he deliberately rode to his death in despair at the horror of civil war. Somehow, I can't see the Transport Secretary doing the same when this all this kicks off. Towards the south of the route dormice are currently snoring away in Reddings Copse, completely oblivious to the impending destruction of their nests. There's also a 160-foot Corsican pine there, the tallest tree on the route. Finally the road is to plough through the National Trust land of The Chase and Great Pen Wood, where more badgers and bats should be afraid, very afraid.

There's currently about 15 camps along the route where other rare things can be seen, like this bloke who's convinced he's the reincarnation of King Arthur. He's got all the robes, a broadsword and everything. Not sure what the cops are going to make of him. There's Bagnor camp, just below Snelsmore, where the Cambridge

bunch are, and thankfully there's a good few from the M11 here, just up from Kennet at a 'place' called Rickety Bridge. A lot of the Leeds gang are at Tot Hill at the bottom of the route, which is a bit of a pain when it's time to meet up with Nick and Claire for a few pints in the Clocktower, but we manage somehow.

As we walk in our harnesses past the Hatchet, a pub particularly known for its pro-bypass clientele, a couple of balding blokes bang on the window and mouth 'We're gonna fucking kill you'.

'They're probably the ones who threatened Spanner,' says Nick with disgust.

'Wouldn't bet on it,' says Claire, 'There's plenty like that round here.'

'Have you heard what they jam the CB channels with?' I ask. 'Like "We're coming to burn your camps and rape your women". Nice.'

'And it only seems to stop when the local news is on the telly. You'd think they'd have better things to do,' says Claire.

'Obviously not,' I reply. The airwaves can be so full of abuse we arrange in person which channel to go to for ten minutes of uninterrupted chat.

'The old small-town mentality can get to you a bit,' says Nick. 'Apparently one aim of the road is to make Newbury bigger than Basingstoke one day.'

'Wow!' feigns Claire, 'Basingstoke? What lofty ambition.'

'You only have to look at their fucking MP to see this place isn't normal,' I say. David Rendel – supposedly a Lib Dem, is fervently pro-road and says those in favour of the bypass are the 'true environmentalists'.

I suspect Nick is a bit of a closet Lib Dem, and it'll be interesting to see how he deals with this. He says: 'If the party's really as green as they say, they'd tear up his membership card tomorrow.'

'Rendel is a total cunt. I'd rather be bum raped by an ebola-infested gorilla than vote for any party that supports him,' I diplomatically add to the debate.

'Yes, quite,' says Claire. 'I'm not sure I'd vote for you with comments like that.'

'Oh cram it,' I say with a smile and upraised finger.

We pass car after car after belching car, heading to our destination with a rapidity those stuck in the traffic can only dream of. Any one of these could contain the vigilantes and CB 'enthusiasts'. A woman winds down her electric window and throws a lit cigarette out without looking, hitting Claire on the hand.

'Hey, watch it, you stupid bitch,' she says, jutting her tongue against lower lip to 'spaz' her.

'Sorry – and keep up the good work by the way,' says the driver, noticing our harnesses.

Claire accepts the apology but is still riled. 'Electric windows sum it all up. How lazy have we become that we use scarce resources to open and close a fucking car window? And then it's seen as a status symbol to be that lazy. No wonder people are getting fat these days.'

'Steady, dear, you'll blow a gasket. Let's get you a lovely pint,' says Nick stifling a laugh.' Thankfully we've reached the sanctuary of the Clocktower and leave the mean streets of Newbury behind.

Barb's welcoming smile from behind the bar is arguably the first I've seen today. 'What's it to be, my love?'

'Three pints of Dog Bolter please.'

'How are you faring? Keeping warm? Is JJ looking after you?'

'Yes thanks, for a camp commandant she's ace.'

The beers line up in old-style dimpled glasses and I carry them over to the table where Claire is wildly gesticulating. 'Could you believe that fucking woman? She could have burnt my hand.'

Nick puts an arm round her. 'She is on our side, and it was an accident. You're just pissed off with the world. Besides, some of the locals may be bad, but our lot aren't exactly perfect.'

'Too right. Kennet's quite sorted, but there are some right head-cases knocking around,' I reply, suddenly seeing Nick's strategy for domestic peace, which is go on, have a rant, let it all out.

'Don't get me started,' says Claire, wiping the traces of a big gulp from her mouth. 'We seem to have become a branch of the social services down at Tot Hill. People who constantly sit by the fire and never chop any wood, eat daily yet never cook, who can't look after their stupid dogs let alone help out on an action.'

'Oh, those pesky Brew Crew.' Nick shakes his head looking gloomily into his pint and I bite my upper lip to stop myself laughing.

'Don't get me wrong,' she says barely drawing breath. 'There's some of the most organised, sorted and inspiring people you could ever meet in this movement. But trying to stop the road is stressful enough without having to look after people who, let's be honest, have severe mental problems. We're not social workers are we? How can we be expected to look after people on the verge of a nervous breakdown most of the time.'

'Yeah, wasn't Bim sectioned only last week, my dear?' Nick says, stirring the pot.

'Oh don't talk to me about him. Wanker.'

'I dunno. He's a decent bloke when he's not off his head.' I interject. 'And not being sectioned.'

'He's a fucking Dime Bar,' says Claire using the latest slang term for camp casualties, derived from the imbecilic Harry Enfield character in the TV ads. There's other terms though – energy vampires, kettle watchers, lunch-outs, and 'Jakies', a fucked-up fusion of junkie and alkie.

Claire's in full flow now. 'I heard someone at Tot Hill fell forty feet and ended up in a back brace 'cos some pissed-up moron cut short one of the abseil ropes – probably sold most of it for skag and used the rest to keep their trousers up with.'

'Not that we're getting sanctimonious about getting out of your head though, eh?' says Nick, stepping in just at the right moment. 'Who wants another pint?'

'Too right,' says Claire, 'I suddenly feel much better.'

It's January 8th and the campaign's had tip-offs of both good news and bad news. The bad is the clearance of the 10,000 trees on the route is due to start tomorrow. A convoy of coaches rolls into town and thankfully our route-monitoring team, consisting mainly of friendly locals, follows them. The good news is we've heard on the q–t that the campaign has a mole in the security. They'd best keep it very tight or else it'll be another species that'll be in dire trouble. If the Newbury bypass is Star Wars then we are Ewoks and Darth Vader is to be Nicholas Blandy, the Under Sheriff of Berkshire. We'll have to see if we can fuck up his Death Star.

Finally for both sides after decades of frustration and anger, years of mustering troops and finances, and months preparing tactics and 'weapons', the Third Battle of Newbury has begun.

We awake to jubilant news on the radio. Two five-metre tripods have been put up at the gates of the specially built compound at Newbury Racecourse, blocking the dozens of coaches inside. Looks like the guards and bailiffs will be stranded there most of the day. One-nil to us.

We're off to a flier. Over the first three days of clearance less than a hundred trees have been cut down and everyone's on a high though there have been reports of guards beating people up. At this rate the road'll never be built. Most of the time we're at camp fortifying the trees, but we do venture out occasionally.

On day four the police start to intervene. Thirty-four are arrested for aggravated trespass and bailed off the entire route. A new term is heard over the radio – the 'Newbury Sausage' refers to the long, thin area most arrestees are forbidden to enter. Some have to report to the police station several times a week. The threat of jail will deter many, and after my little holiday in Pentonville it puts the willies up me a bit. Neither the guards or bailiffs get bailed off site or arrested when they beat someone up. The police should be fucking ashamed.

One morning I go at 5am to help with the route monitoring with Wendy, a well-heeled mother of two who's voted Tory up until now. Still, everyone's entitled to a change of heart, I suppose. Rumour has it Transport Minister George Young is a lapsed member of Friends Of The Earth. With the help of in-car radios we've managed to get in front of the convoy and Wendy's doing about 15 mph to the accompaniment of police sirens urging her to go faster.

'Can't you go any slower?' I ask.

'They'll arrest us I'm sure. This is about as slow as I dare. Sorry.'

Apparently Edna is the best at this – she's 75 and yesterday managed a speed of 8 mph before she was ordered to put her foot down.

I look out of the window behind us see a huge snake of about twenty coaches, digger after digger, and more riot vans than I thought the cops possessed. There must be some very unpoliced streets in the Home Counties at the moment.

'Can you believe they've got so many vehicles out? God knows how much this is going to cost them,' I say.

'Yes, it's like being up against the fucking army,' says Wendy, glancing worriedly in her rear–view mirror.

It is like a civil war. We're up against the state on 24/7 alert and there's no knowing what they're going to do to us if we don't give in.

'Things are going to get nasty, aren't they?' says Wendy, looking apprehensive.

'I think they wouldn't be as rough if there were more people like you up the trees,' I say. I don't want to guilt-trip her into doing so, but it's the truth. Failing the law, all that's protecting you is your fellow activists and a rapidly perishing faith in the humanity of the opposition.

As it's such a big route, the worst thing is the uncertainty. You don't know where they're heading, not knowing whether a particular site is going to be trashed today until the convoy has gone past it. The camps are still safe – for now. If Blandy follows the law he has to apply through the courts for an eviction order for each one, and that hasn't happened yet. In the meantime every tree which hasn't got a treehouse in it is vulnerable. Today it's Pen Wood which has the dubious honour of a visit from Blandy, and it's my first opportunity to see the bloke close up. To be honest, if the Star Wars analogy is to hold any water he's more like Jabba the Hutt than Vader. A podgy country lawyer, he's got a very smug air about him, and looks certain to be more of a hate figure than your average sheriff.

There's no set pattern to a clearance, but basically it's this – long lines of security try to surround an area and allow chainsaw gangs to start their dubious task. Added to the snow, cold and discomfort, the sound of the chainsaws both near and far is distressing as it means some tree is gonna get it but it's also just plain annoying.

Once a site has been targeted we try to get as many numbers there as possible. The local cops have noted some of the regular campaign vehicles, including an anonymous looking van from Brighton with the Tasmanian Devil from the cartoons painted on the side. As soon as we've got numbers on the ground it's a case of trying to make ourselves as much of a nuisance as possible. Sometimes it's just us running at the security, like a scene from the first civil war. White hats get knocked off amid much swearing and manhandling. Today this African guard totally lost it and took a swing at someone. It just shows how stacked against us it all is when the police don't arrest a black guy who's just tried to assault someone. I suppose it's a case of my enemy's enemy is my friend working against us this time.

At well-defended sites there are some lock-ons at the base of trees, but in the main it's very primitive, trying to get between the blade and the trunk so the operator has to stop. At least that's the theory.

The trees are cut and then burnt, or piled up to be sold to a timberyard. At the end of most days we have people who go out and spike the fallen trees so they won't be fit to go under a bandsaw somewhere else.

'Wendy, look,' I say to her, not believing my eyes. A black-and-white pantomime cow is trying to get through the cordon, and a senior security guard in a red hat is on the radio trying to work out what the fuck to do.

'A pantomime?' says Wendy, 'I thought this was a farce,' as she grabs her camera to capture the moment. Within two minutes the cow is herded by three officers towards a riot van and both ends are read their rights.

'I suppose in court the back end'll argue it didn't know where it was,' I quip.

Day-to-day living back on site is all about keeping up 'normality' with all this madness around us. We've asked the campaign to foot the bill for the milkman delivering to the camp each morning, as it's embarrassing if we've got nothing to offer any guests. It's the little things that keep morale high, even if we have to wipe snow off the kitchen table most mornings. Some days no-one can face cooking and we have to send someone off on a bike to the chip shop.

We had some great news the other day. The Mothership is named after a Julian Cope song, and he came to visit the camps wearing a fluorescent jacket with POLITE on the back. Class. Anyway, he's said he's going to stage a benefit gig for us in Portsmouth in the next couple of weeks. What a geezer.

We had another strange but welcome visitor. There's a new group called Business Against The Bypass and one of their lot came to see us in his Jag and slipped Dom fifty quid for us all to spend down the pub. Marvellous.

Up in the trees it's a fine balance. You need a bit of fat on you to keep out the cold, but the less you weigh the more forgiving the branches are going to be. Keeps you bastard fit though – should send fat people here to do courses – we'd get paid by the social services.

Today is particularly exciting as we're expecting some of the

Manchester posse to come down and visit. The pecking order has changed – it's their turn to sleep in the Mothership. Ha ha.

Tim, Corinne, Paulo and the rest arrive about 6pm. We've tidied up specially and a path lined with tealights leads from the edge of the camp to the bottom of the Mothership. It's like a little post-Christmas grotto. Tango's especially excited as Tim's brought Kropotkin along to visit.

'You're still alive then,' says Tim as he hugs us all in turn.

'Barely,' I say puffing out my cheeks. 'How's the frozen wastes of the north?'

'Fucking warmer than here.' Tango and Eloise fall upon the dog like they're gonna crush the horrible mutt.

'How's the McDonalds stuff coming along?'

'Well, you know it's the longest libel trial in history? Well, it's not gonna finish for a few months yet. Poor old Helen and Dave are knackered.'

'Yeah, I know how they feel. Right,' I say as we approach the prusik rope. 'Who needs some climbing training?'

Just as on that first night here we get eventually get bodies and bags up into the Mothership. Our Helen's been out of action for a few days with some kind of lurgy but she's plucked up the strength to come and sit with everyone tonight, clutching her teapot.

We've stocked up on the wine and hoisted up one of the wood-burning stoves to make things even more homely.

'So what's been the best bit so far? I can't wait to get stuck in,' says Corinne excitedly bouncing up and down on her haunches.

'I particularly liked one morning when a policewoman couldn't control her horse,' says Tango while Eloise fusses over the dog. 'It was like someone had smeared Ralgex on its bollocks.'

'What? The horse or the policewoman,' I ask and get a piece of hummus and pitta bread thrown at me by a slightly tipsy Jane.

'It's just really ... hard,' says Dom. 'But good. It's what we've been gearing up for all these months I suppose.'

'It's nice watching the guards suffer as well,' says an unusually outspoken Eloise. 'Like, deep down we want to be here, but they stand there bored to tears for what? Three-pounds-fifty an hour?'

'Radio Bob told me some of them have been coughing up blood because of inhaling all that smoke,' adds Jane.

'Good – fuck 'em. They deserve it,' I add.

'Sorry – gotta go,' says Helen rushing towards the trapdoor not knowing which end to hold. I wouldn't fancy abseiling down in the dark trying to keep everything in.

'To be honest guys, it's been like Doctor-fucking-Zhivago most days, but with no Julie Christie to brighten up the place,' I say, rather proud of my filmic analogy.

'Don't be such a sexist wanker,' says Corinne.

'What? So finding someone attractive from an old film is suddenly sexist? What a bunch of shit.'

'Ok, I'm sorry. It just wouldn't wash on the women's mini-bus at the Union. I know,' she says grabbing the teapot Helen's left behind. 'Shall I put the kettle on?' she says and is most perplexed as to why we're all falling about on the floor.

As the evening draws to an end I have a bit of a drunken cuddle, with Jane but Des is a decent fellow and they're trying to make a go of things. Besides, there's more important things to be doing right now than fuck up my life by going out with someone who's seeing someone else.

Making extra sure I'm clipped on I wobble across the walkways to my treehouse and am just able to fasten my sleeping bag before dreamless oblivion envelopes me.

Considering the time of year it's a lovely clear day. You can see your breath as you wake but the sun is bright and cheery.

'Looks like scrambled eggs would fix a few scrambled heads. Shall I cycle to town?' I ask looking in on the fumes and fogginess of the Mothership.

I hear something beginning with a 'y' and so go to collect the camp bike only to find that viggies have trashed it in the night. Wheels bent, brakes cut and tyres slashed. Determined not to be perturbed, I jog along the river to town and feel all the better for it despite the burning rage.

On my return Manchester are mingling happily with Brighton. I suppose we've a fair amount in common, being the big activist towns in the north and south. Paulo and Trev have discovered a mutual fascination with varieties of ecstasy, and Izzy and Corinne are getting on like a vigilante's house on fire. Sorry, just wishful thinking there. I don't want to spoil the mood so I get on and cook breakfast and save the bad news for later.

As January draws to a close they've only cleared about half a mile of the route. I think that's some kind of victory, but there's been over 200 arrests and God knows how we're going to keep up the momentum. However, there are buses from London and Brighton every day to ferry people here and back. As usual we rely heavily on people to come along for a couple of days with energy, a fresh perspective and kick-ass attitude. On this front our prayers have been answered in the form of Tim, who's got a mate doing a chemistry degree.

Arranging to meet me, Helen and Dom in my treehouse he shows us a couple of plastic bottles containing an innocuous-looking colourless fluid.

'I think we can have a lot of fun with this stuff,' he says

unscrewing the cap. 'Go on, sniff it.'

Dom puts his nose over the bottle and inhales. Within a couple of seconds he's thrown himself under my duvet. 'Urghhh, that is so grim! What the fuck?'

The odour is spreading round the room and I don't really need to get near it to get an idea of the full horror.

'Cor! Tim, put the fucking top back on. I've got to sleep in here. Please,' I plead.

'It's butyric acid,' he replies as he complies. 'Totally harmless apart from the obvious.'

'I'm trying to put my finger on the smell,' says Helen, 'That's it! It's the exact smell of Lester's treehouse.' I throw a cushion at her head. 'No, seriously, it's ... it's like week-old pus mixed with farts, the taste of earwax and what I imagine dead bodies smell like. Yeah?'

I lean out over the edge to spit onto the ground. 'I think that just about sums it up. Now what are we gonna do with it?'

'Let's take it to Bob. He'll know what to do,' says Helen with a mischievous grin. 'Tim, I think your mate has developed a new secret weapon here. Can he mix up any more?'

We go and tell JJ the details and use the CB in her treehouse to reach base.

'Bob, it's Kennet, can you come over? Over,' I say.

'Umm, bit tricky at the moment. Couple of hospitalisations this morning. One broken arm at Pen Wood and a suspected hypothermia at Granny Ash. Over,' says Bob.

'It's important. Please. Over.'

'Ok, give me an hour. You're all wankers. Over.'

'We know. Over. Thanks and out,' and we get on with camp chores until he turns up.

Tim puts the bottle under Bob's nose. Knowing what's coming I try to stifle a grin but crack up as he recoils in horror.

'Christ alive!' he says, 'have you been draining corpses? What kind of sick shit is this?'

'All perfectly legal. What we need to know is how we can best use it,' says Tim with some pride.

Bob stops for a moment's contemplation, then lets out a kind of contented purr. 'Somewhere in the madness of yesterday I seem to remember one of our secret sources talking of a brand new fleet of bailiffs' vans having been delivered. And I know where they are.'

'Brilliant. Tonight?' asks Dom. There's no need for a reply. All heads within earshot are nodding.

'I'll get onto my little mole,' says Bob with a wink.

Six of us – Tim, Helen, JJ, Spanner, Dom and myself have been selected for this action. 'Selected' overplays it, I suppose – this isn't the England football team we're talking about here. We're the ones stupid enough to volunteer. Bob's told us where to be and when, and wait for the code word 'acid'.

We've decided to go SAS-style on this one – that is we're going to walk to and from the action without using a getaway vehicle. If all goes to plan we can melt into the countryside before anyone knows what's going on.

I've neglected to bring my balaclava with me so I've got a T-shirt to wrap round my face at the vital moment. Considering the stink we're gonna create that's just as well. Dom draws the short straw and has to decant the stuff into half a dozen smaller bottles.

Since the early days of the clearances we haven't really targeted the security compound so it's a reasonable guess they're not on full alert. It's 2am and we're about four hundred yards from the compound, skirting round in the shadow of the woods.

Spanner's local so knows the terrain best. 'Ok, according to Bob's directions we should meet with him just by this tree here.'

We wait. 'He's fucking late. I knew this was a bad idea,' says Helen.

'Bollocks, you were totally wired for this earlier on,' I whisper.

'Well, where the fuck is he?'

'Acid,' says a clear, calm and somehow familiar voice above us. We look up with some amazement to see Clive from the Leeds tent at Glastonbury looking down. He jumps onto the ground and we greet him as quickly and quietly as possible.

'Right,' he says, 'we've gotta be quick. I've not been able to get hold of any keys for them, but I've stacked some crates either side of the fence near the vehicles just past the second lot of floodlights there,' as he points to where he means. 'Is that ok?'

'Fucking storming,' says JJ.

'As usual they're not on the ball. Even the red hats are pretty dumb. There'll be two guys with a dog doing circuits all night but if you time it right you should be ok. I'd best get back to the dorm or they'll smell a rat. Give us a couple of minutes to get in, eh? Good luck.' And with that our 'mole' turns and heads towards the compound in the opposite direction to our entry point.

'Clive, well I'll be buggered. Who'd have thunk it?' I say to Dom. 'I always saw him cleaning up the kitchen with Lindsey, not this kind of thing.'

'It's the quiet ones you have to watch sometimes,' says Spanner anxiously looking at his watch. 'Right, fuck it. Let's go.'

We run as silently as our boots allow up to the right section of fence, and there's eight milk crates stacked in two lots of four.

'They probably have the same milkman as us. We'd better watch what we say to him,' whispers JJ as she climbs over, signals the coast is clear and is followed by the rest of us.

Half a dozen white Land Rovers stand in a row fifty yards away.

We've all got about a litre of 'acid', and in absolute silence pick a vehicle each and start to pour about half into the air vents. My feeling of exhilaration is added to by the overpowering stench. This is definitely another unique experience. Tick in the box.

JJ pulls the hammer out of her jacket and waves it in the air. This is our cue to be ready with the tools we blagged from the camp earlier, be they spanner, wrench or metal bar.

'Now,' she says and we smash the windows in unison, creating a noise loud enough to be heard back in town. As fast as we can we pour the rest of the fluid on the seats and carpets then we scarper back to the crates as fast as our legs will allow to the sound of shouts and the slamming of Portakabin doors. Dropping straight down onto the grass safe-side we sprint into the woods disappearing like rabbits and I try to remember the directions back to the camp JJ had told us. That's about £60,000 worth of kit they won't be using again in a hurry. Add it to our bill.

The nature of the protest is slightly changing. Theoretically, as long as each camp can be identified as a separate entity, every one needs a separate eviction hearing in the courts before that bastard Blandy can move in.

Our latest tactic is to set up as many new camps as possible.

Just north of Bagnor there's Elephant Tree, then Bagnor Lane and Quercus Circus, which is something to do with the Latin name for Oak. In between us and Rickety Bridge is Camelot, where King Arthur lays his broadsword at night. South of Reddings Copse is Sheep Dip, Birthday Party and Babble Brook. Pen Wood has a profusion of half a dozen camps now; Seaside, Manic Sha, Heartbreak Hotel, Horseshoe and an off-route visitors' camp for blow-ins. All in all about thirty little cells of resistance – more than enough to keep the DoT lawyers busy for a few weeks.

People are using their skills in all kinds of ways to do their bit. Tree FM – a pirate radio station has been set up and is pretty decent; news, views, reports and tunes on a six-hour loop. Not as good as Radio 4, but then they should be getting their arses down here to report what's going on a whole lot more than they do. And that goes for the whole mainstream media.

The station is a handy way to get non-sensitive information out to the camps, cutting out the squelch and stress of the CBs. Lately it's been truckers late into the night with firebomb threats and claims that camp water supplies have been contaminated. I think they're just bored – all the snow blocking the roads over the last week has probably made it worse. We report it – Bob even gives the police recordings – and they do nothing.

Like prison and most other things associated with NVDA, being on the front line provokes a mixture of feelings, in turns fascinating or mundane, inspiring or frustrating, hilarious or just plain old depressing as fuck.

It's the relentless nature that gets to you most. Talking day after day with the same guards, knowing they're not going to change their minds. With reasonable certainty they ask, 'Why don't you get a job?' and I reply, 'I've got one. It's here. Why don't you get an education, you ignorant cunts?'

Without doubt this has been the maddest, and felt like the longest, month of my life. Though some days you just can't shake yourself out of bed at 5am to try and get up a tree and stay there in the hail, wind, sleet and snow. It's times like this you find out where your limits are, but it's also good to know they're being pushed. In short, it's an adrenaline junkie's paradise here – if you can handle it.

Three days into the month and all the empty threats over the radio gain substance. Some woman's car has been firebombed over at the visitors' camp. It's lucky she wasn't in it. And Rendel says we're the violent ones. Twat.

We're running round like Ben Johnson on double his drugs ration trying to get Kennet ready for the eviction. Eloise is winding barbed wire round the branches closest to her treehouse, JJ's fitting a cargo net underneath hers for provisions – of which whiskey and cake will feature heavily, so she says. Jane's banging spikes into the base of her tree and Helen's putting up more walkways between the trees – more options in a tight spot, another possible way of avoiding capture by the forces of darkness. As for me, I'm helping Tango build a lock-on at the base of one of the undefended trees. Thankfully, our part of the route hasn't been savaged too badly yet, but there are camps where it's just the defended trees left. Now that must be a kick in the balls each morning.

'It's mad, isn't it?' I say to Tango. 'We're kind of living like Robin Hood and his merry men, fighting for good against the Sheriff and all that.'

'Yep, can't think of any other situation in history that fits as well. Who would you be? Little John?'

'As long as it's not Friar Tuck and his religious mumbo-jumbo I couldn't care less. I suppose we don't have a Robin. I reckon if it's anyone round here it'd be JJ.'

'Yeah, but they got to fight with arrows and all sorts of cool shit. We've got some paint bombs made out of rubber gloves, but we'd get so mashed if we fought them properly, and lose public support.'

Seems like Tango's definitely mellowing with age. I thought he'd be doing the whole pygmy thing with grass skirt and blowpipes by now.

One of the guards has told the press that a demonstrator attacked him with a syringe. I'm sure it's not true – not even Sparko would do that – but the worst thing about it is because we're not a proper 'organisation' we can't sue the arse off the papers. Besides, there isn't the cash to pay the lawyers. Donations have been flooding in and Friends Of The Earth have done good work in meeting the bills but the whole thing's not too far off being run out of what's in the petty cash jar and people's giros.

The court proceedings to evict the camps have begun – a sure sign that the evictions are only a matter of days away.

Still, it's not all about money. I saw Wendy with her mate Lady Genevieve Butler the other day when the chainsaw crews were clearing the Chase and both of them were in bits. I dare say they'd had a quiet word with everyone and anyone before this madness kicked off properly. But there's powerful forces behind this road, like Vodafone, the biggest employer in the town. In fact, it's worse for Wendy and the other vol-au-vent-teers as we call them. I'm not a local – this isn't the Downs around Lancing – and thank fuck for that.

'I'm not coming, and that's final,' I say.

'Come on, it'll be a laugh. I don't believe in it any more than you.' Jane's trying to persuade me to accompany her to a religious service up at Snelsmore.

'Oh go on, there's a lift going in twenty minutes, and I'll get you a couple of pints afterwards,' she says seductively running a fiver under her lower lip. Game, set and match – even though it's pissing with rain today.

We drive north in the mini-bus. I'm amazed I've agreed to be here. Must be something to do with spirituality, man. At least Tango's stuck to his guns and is back minding the camp, good on him.

'Did you hear some of the security guards defected to our side this week?' asks JJ

'Did they give any particular reason? Conscience transplant?'

'Well, you know they've not had it easy? Three of them just went fuck it. I suppose they just got fed up with being treated just as badly as us. And you know what one of them said?'

'Go on.'

'I'm joining the tree people. They've got all the birds and drugs,' JJ delivers the punchline just right and for a moment we forget the increasing devastation we're driving towards.

As we pull into the 'car park' for today – a.k.a an area of very recently ex-ancient woodland – the full extent of recent work hits us all. The two elements dominating the scene are smoke and mud.

'Fuck me, it's like hell,' says Dom, summing up what must be in everyone's thoughts.

There's a broad mix of locals and 'layabouts' as Rendel would no doubt call us. It's a good job him and Blandy aren't here, or there could be a reconstruction of the crucifixion this afternoon.

I ask with an air of innocence, sensing there's a churchy element to her upbringing: 'Eloise? Are we expected to pray today?'

'Why of course, Lester.'

'And what should we pray for?'

'Whatever's truly in your heart. I suppose what you really want for the earth.'

'Would Blandy having a massive heart attack this afternoon count? Or Rendel being ripped apart by a pack of rabid dogs?'

'I don't think that's quite in the spirit,' she says turning from me.

'Shame. I think if the church is to survive into the twenty-first century it needs put the requirements of potential customers first. So, where's the bloke in the dress?' End of conversation.

Once again – this is quite high in the Surreal Life Moments League table. There's a cop and a security guard for every one of us – loads of my mates and colleagues stood in stair-rod rain waiting for a man we don't know to talk about something that shouldn't have happened to big-up somebody that doesn't exist. Confused? You should be.

Jane is wrapped in a long cloak and the rain is dripping off the end of her nose. 'You look like Tess of The d'Urbervilles,' I say. 'just before she got hung,' and stick my tongue out in a playful manner.

Then the vicars arrive – five of them. Yes, five of them. Haven't been to church apart from weddings since the Cubs and I'm suddenly inundated. One of them is the Bishop of Baths and Wells ... surely not the one from Blackadder?

'Oh God,' pipes up the first priest or whatever he's called and I'm already fighting the giggles and feel a gentle kick in the shin.

He continues: 'We are gathered here today in trying circumstances to ask you for the strength to overcome and ask forgiveness for those who would ravage the earth for their own gain.'

I nudge Jane and whisper: 'He's pretty rad for a vicar, eh?'

After the initial shock of hearing pretty much my own thoughts come out of the mouth of a 'Man of God' it all starts to lose its novelty and I start to drift off in the sermons, in my mind's eye trying to resurrect the forest, closing off from the Apocalyse Now reality and imagine red squirrels chasing each other over sturdy boughs; sparrowhawks swooping onto voles sprinting in vain towards their burrows, laying Jane down under a mighty oak, removing her undergarments and giving her a mighty seeing-to ...

'... Oh Lord, you are so big,' shouts the vicar over the downpour and brings me back to the here and now. Can't speak for anyone else, but I suppose that was the highlight of the service for me.

There's more tub-thumping of a secular kind three days later at a mass rally organised by Friends Of The Earth. As ever there's stuff to be done around the camp – but in a funny kind of way it'd be like not turning up to your boss's birthday party ... not that I've ever had one, but I imagine it would be if I had.

'Apparently Johnny Morris is going to be there,' says JJ.

'What? From Animal Magic?' I ask.

'The very same.'

'And Maggie Philbin.'

'Well, I'm so gonna be there. Who said being an activist wasn't exciting?' I say, trying to outdo her sarcasm. But secretly I think we're both really impressed two faded stars of children's TV are on side.

The walk is from Bagnor to Snelsmore and when we arrive there must be the best part of 10,000 people. I've never seen so many at an anti-roads demo before.

'God – if only we could get this many for an average day at Gotan,' I say to Helen.

'Well, it is a Saturday – and there does seem to be this gap between 'activist' and 'supporter' we can't seem to bridge,' she says, giving bunny ears to the two key words.

Feeling a little star-struck I make a special point of going to find Mr Morris. When I eventually track him down I find a frail hero of my youth – he must be eighty if he's a day – but is a true gent, signing autographs and not even getting annoyed when someone asks him to do a silly animal voice. I don't have anything for him to sign – still, the moment is enough, shake him warmly by the hand and leave him to his day.

I gently push through the crowds trying to get back to the Kennet posse and, no ... it can't be ...

'Stewart ... Stewart Johnson? Well I never.' He hasn't changed a bit. We share a warm embrace.

'Lester! How the devil are you?' he says patting me on the back.

'Well you know. Living up a tree in a war zone – cold, wet, muddy. Bloody great actually, mate. What's the latest with the enquiry?'

'They're still sitting on their hands. No announcements one way or another.'

'We've got them running scared. That'll show them.'

Stewart looks at me with what I take to be pride. 'Look at you in your harness and all. Must seem like light years from that meeting in Nikki's lounge, eh?'

'To be honest, mate, it's all been so manic it's gone really quick.'

'Well, for what it's worth, we've been hearing little reports of what you've been up to – we're very proud.'

I suddenly feel a little teary and need to go. 'Well Stewart, it's been great to see you, but I need to find my crew, they're over there.' I point vaguely, trying not to seem rude.

'Ok mate, maybe see you later.' I leave with a hug and turn to take deep breaths and rub my eyes dry.

The walk along the route reaches the rallying point and the speeches begin. Lady Butler is first up speaking on behalf of the Third Battle campaign, and gives the cops a good going over.

However, Nick's up next and I'm thinking his contribution to the event will be edgier.

He approaches the microphone with a confident air, takes a deep breath and begins: 'The decision for all this!' he projects in a strong, clear voice, sweeping an arm around at a panorama of trashed trees, 'was made by Brian Mawhinney, the ex-transport minister, three hours before he quit the post! How dare he. Messing with our lives and the heart of England at the stroke of a pen the afternoon he leaves. If that fact alone doesn't make you scramble up the nearest tree in blood-boiling anger you're not paying attention. This road is not about party politics, it's much bigger than that, but this could be the time we seize the agenda. Building the bypass is a crime, but this is far more important than that. This could be when society starts to see things just can't go on as they have. It's gonna be a long, slow process – especially with a spineless goon like Major at the helm and thousands of fascist cops and attack dogs snapping wildly at any opposition, blindly protecting the old from the new.

'And this is nothing to do with a general election around the corner and the Labour Party galloping to the rescue. If he becomes Prime Minister Tony Blair putting planet before profit is about as likely as me being made Home Secretary.

'The next few weeks are crucial in the fight – not only against car culture, but also for a sane, sustainable future. When the Sheriff and his men arrive, give them a damn good hiding. Not with bottles and stones, but with force of numbers, fresh ideas and fire in our bellies.

'We can become more possible than you can powerfully imagine! Let battle commence!' He ends with a single raised fist and a cheeky smile.

Charles Secrett, the director of Friends Of The Earth is the last to speak, and he does a good job of appealing to his membership base, but isn't a patch on my mate Nick – part-Churchill, part-visionary, part-lunatic.

After the rally some old bloke comes up to Nick clutching a wooden box. He says: 'You lot are bloody heroes. Here are my medals from the war. You deserve them.' Nick's completely choked and doesn't quite know what to say.

Like a late present from a reticent lover there's some surprise news the morning after Valentine's Day. Desmoulins snails have been seen on the route, growing in the sedge near Rickety Bridge and there is to be a legal challenge. We celebrate by cracking open a bottle of sherry.

'Cheers everyone. This could be what we've been waiting for,' says Eloise. 'Maybe they'll have to postpone the evictions.'

'I think there's more chance of Blandy winning the Nobel Peace Prize,' says Tango.

'Too right,' says Dom with an air of certainty. 'It'll be like Abbey Pond. They'll say they've created a new habitat for them, pay some bullshit ecologist to sign off the paperwork and that will be that. And from what I know of these snails – which ain't much – they're picky buggers. They don't just live anywhere.'

Final mad preparations begin; people start to dig tunnels, not knowing if they'll be finished in time. There's a gungho attitude in the air, with no-one knowing if their camp will be evicted first.

I visited Reddings Copse the other day and the Corsican pine is standing proud with a 15-foot ladder fixed to its highest branches. Above this proudly stands a Union Jill, the adopted flag of the movement – like a Union Jack but featuring any other colour than red, white and blue.

It would be easier to handle but Newbury isn't the only eviction happening at the moment. In Wales at a place called Selar there are camps to stop an opencast mine from being built. They must feel really neglected as Newbury's getting all the attention. We would've sent a couple of vanloads of our people over there but it's not as if we have any spare ourselves.

In the office uncle and nephew are not happy chappies. A dartboard has been donated and Bob has stuck a photo from the paper on it and he's throwing the arrows with all his might.

'Who's this?' I ask.

'This twat,' he says not breaking rhythm, 'is John Watts, the roads minister. He's accused us of making hoax calls to the fire brigade. I've just about had enough.'

'I'm feeling it's not been a good day. Shall I get the kettle on?' I say squeezing past about twenty bags of cement.

'Yeah, watch out for them,' says Bob, throwing a dart right between Watt's eyes. 'Some fucking builder dropped them off. Can't he see this is an office?'

'He's not to know, is he? Bob, to be honest I think you need to chill. Shall we go for a quick one at the Clocktower?'

'Can't – no time. Tonight is crucial.'

Statto explains Bob's manic mood. 'All the current appeals

against evictions failed today. They're going in, probably tomorrow.'
'Shit – I'd best get back to Kennet.' I grab my stuff and abandon tea-making duty.

At first light Blandy goes into the Pixie camp near Snelsmore using half a dozen pro rock climbers as bailiffs to get people out, along with the cherry picker crews. We were expecting the latter but these scab climbers? Some people will do anything for money.

When we get there the camp is completely cordoned off. As it's the first eviction they're putting on a good show. There must be seven hundred guards for an area about the size of three football pitches.

There's no way through, I'm stood with Dom and Helen and the best we can do is to watch and shout from the sidelines. JJ was at Spanner's last night and they're both doing their best to elude the hydraulic platform, nimbly shifting from tree to tree, unclipping their harnesses at crucial times to attain a new position.

I can just about make out the look on JJ's face – exhilaration but there's also the definite lines of a scowl. There aren't any rules here, but calling in the climbers really seems to have upset her.

It's similar to Gladiators on the telly, with the likes of Spanner's mate Lee Tree swinging from bough to bough with a confidence I could only dream of.

'How could they?' says Helen close to tears. 'Aren't climbers supposed to have a love of nature?'

'Apparently they're on £700 a day. Fuckers!' Dom replies and shouts the final word as loud as he can.

'Well,' I say, 'I hope if they go out for any posh meals on the proceeds they'll choke on it. Or if it goes towards a house it falls down.'

There are tears forming in Dom's eyes. 'It's a shame the planet doesn't act in retribution, like ancient peoples believed. Maybe it had better start – and soon.'

The scene above us is like a twisted Chinese circus cloned with a horror film. At times it's as if it's been beautifully choreographed – then within minutes of these displays of grace someone will be cornered, assaulted repeatedly, then dragged into the bucket of the cherry picker to the sound of chainsaws. The platforms are slow to manoeuvre and without the climbers it'd be virtually impossible to get people out of the trees.

'This is too upsetting,' says Helen, just as the final branches comprising JJ's escape route are sawn away. 'I've got to go.' With an overwhelming feeling of powerlessness I follow on in silence.

The next morning we're more ready for them – a good couple of hundred people on the ground and a fair few locked on to the bases of trees. Thirteen were arrested yesterday but there are still three treehouses left.

However, Blandy's got another trick up his sleeve. He's divided up the convoy and sent half to The Chase and half to Pixie. It's not rocket science to do so but such tactics are going to make it so – so hard for us to have the right numbers on the ground in the right place at the right time.

It's difficult to know what to do – whether to be up the trees or be ground support. I'm still not the best climber in the world and will probably be a hindrance to those still up in the canopies. Besides, they can't lower any ropes down to us for fear of being ambushed.

Again we're restricted by using peaceful tactics. The best we can do is to lie down between bailiffs, diggers and the trees to stop them. I join Wendy and Genevieve who are sharing a flask of tea.

'Lovely day for it, ladies,' I say squeezing in next to them.

'Lester, how lovely to see you,' says Wendy. 'Care for a cuppa?'

As she hands me the cup the sound of a woodwind instrument comes through the mist.

'What's that melody?' I ask.

'Isn't it the theme from the Wombles?' Wendy's right.

A five-piece band including a clarinettist is here to entertain us. Apparently they're called Tragic Roundabout, are from Brighton and Genevieve is soon besotted by their brand of punk polka cover tunes.

The fun stops abruptly. The convoy's arrived and within minutes the white hats are upon us – grabbing a people's hair and clothes, twisting our fingers and arms into painful positions. There's a young girl near us who's dragged from the line through the mud by the hood of her coat.

We're becoming used to hearing the ensuing screaming. The cries of pain, shouts of frustration and anguish, and desperate pleas for simple humanity are not much more than background noise.

'Camera! He's kneeling on my neck,' is a typical cry above a cheery version of My Way.

We can only hold them off for so long, especially when the police horses come through and trample people. Within the hour the cherry pickers are back in place, elevating the climbers to take out Lee, Spanner and the others who are left. I feel like making a run for the base of the platform and taking out the electrics but there's no way I'd get through and would certainly be arrested.

There's a lot of weeping, comforting and mutual support in amongst the abuse we dish out to the guards.

Wendy, Genevieve and myself walk away from the action trying to find something useful to do. Passing a pile of large, felled trunks Genevieve stops, bends down to read what has been attached to one of them and starts to cry. In a plastic cover is an A4 sheet bearing a photo of the wood in all its previous glory and the words: 'This green and pleasant land that our forefathers fought and died for is worth more than a few minutes in a car.'

'Come on,' says Wendy, rubbing her on the back. 'I think Barb has the temporary answer for this. A litre bottle of Bombay Sapphire. I'm buying.' So we go to the Clocktower to drown our sorrows, and consequently all three of us are not much use the following day. I hang around at Wendy's, have a fantastically bubbly bath, shave off a week's worth of beard, eat home-cooked food, watch trashy movies and snore on the sofa.

I arrive back at Kennet somewhat rejuvenated. As I thought JJ had been arrested on day one at Pixie and was bailed off site on release – but she doesn't give a shit. Kennet is her camp and she'll defend it to the last.

'What's the latest?' I ask breezily.

'Not good. I heard on the radio they went for Snelsmore in the middle of the night. There was only one person in the tunnel and they were inexperienced.'

'Shit,' I exclaim, kicking at the ground. 'Swampy will be livid. He put so much work into that.'

'Any other news?' I ask, putting a couple of logs on the fire.

'Well,' she says suddenly cheering up, 'the boys at Snelsmore aren't very happy with the cops as they had a major hand in taking the tunnel.'

'And?'

'So when they tried to take the trees later in the morning a couple of officers got pelted with latrine bombs.'

'Like pigs in shit you could say.'

Each morning we huddle round the radio waiting on the lowdown from the route monitors, like non-league players listening to the FA Cup draw hoping they won't have to play Man United in the next round.

Then we leap in the van and try to get to the unfortunate camp. There's no real pattern – split sites, half-evictions. The uncertainty is just as big a weapon as the climbers.

Today they're hitting three sites – Granny Ash, what's left of The Chase and Birthday Party. We head down to the first but by the time we arrive the long, thick lines of fluorescent yellow are in place.

By the end of the day we've lost all three – and King Arthur has been arrested for possession of an offensive weapon – his trusty symbolic broadsword. About 40 in all were nicked today including Dom and Eloise. Neither of them were doing anything much to deserve it. The strategy seems to be arrest and process on bail as many people as possible. Another distressing development is for the climbers to cut the top rope of walkways leaving people stranded. They have even got to the point of clipping on to people then cutting the other rope. It's a miracle no-one's been killed.

To coincide with our worst day for a while there's some prick blocking the CB channels with the constant sound of chainsaws and demonic laughter. I think the opposition is really starting to get a kick out of our mounting defeats.

Back at Kennet we sit round a blazing fire sipping on mulled wine. No one's talking – in the flames I see the shapes of bailiffs on platforms, flailing arms, legs kicking to be free, and heads being slammed in cherry-picker doors.

'Did you see the papers today?' says Jane, rocking back and forth while hugging her shins.

'Don't tell me – pandas're on the extinct list. Not shagging enough.'

'Not quite – the climbing community are up in arms about the scabs. Some centres are going to ban them from using their facilities. And to top that, some of the best climbers in the country are coming to help us.'

'Fucking get in!' I say punching the air. 'They can't get here soon enough if you ask me.'

I hear familiar voices approach the camp – Nick and Claire.

'Greetings, kiddiwinks,' says Nick, warming his hands by the fire as soon as he's close enough. 'As Neville Chamberlain would say, I have in my hand a piece of paper. And to go with it is a special mission. Is anyone interested?'

'We've a van ready to take us to the secret rendezvous,' adds Claire.

Knowing these guys as I do it's gonna be good. 'Count me in, mate. Jane?' She pauses, rolls her bottom lip over indecisively then nods and smiles.

'Everyone got gloves? This is a no-fingerprint job. And change into some clothes that don't stink of woodsmoke.' Once we're ready it's into the van and off into the night to the northern end of the route.

'Ok, what is it? I'm dying to know,' says Jane.

'Now that would be telling, my dear.' Nick's determined this is going to be a magical mystery tour.

'It's not too far now. You're gonna love it,' says Claire as we near Chieveley, and the van comes to a standstill in a hotel car park.

'Right,' says Claire, 'simple plan this. You guys get chatting to the night porter like you want to book a room. We'll sneak in and do the rest. It'll all become clear then. Got it?'

'Sounds fine. So we're like Mr and Mrs Smith?' I pucker up as if to kiss Jane.

'Geddof,' she giggles.

'Do I look presentable?' I ask her.

'Just about. And me?'

'Deffo. Are you sure you don't fancy a stretch-out tonight? I think I've got enough in my current account. Des wouldn't mind,' I joke.

We approach the desk. As it's a spotty teenage boy, it's best Jane does the talking. He'll be putty in her hands in seconds.

She leans right in and looks the oik straight in the eyes. 'Can you help me? I'd be so grateful,' she says slowly, winding a tendril of hair in her finger. The poor lad is transfixed. I don't have to do anything apart from not get the giggles as Nick and Claire crawl past the counter. At the crucial point Jane winces and puts her hand up to her eye.

'Ow!'

'Are you ok?' he asks. Fiver says it'll be the stray eyelash routine.

'Can you see anything in there?' Jane leans in further, a couple of inches from his face, adding, 'A stray eyelash perhaps?'

Just as he's about to have a poke around, the entire hotel is filled with the high-pitched woo-woo-woo of the fire alarms. Nick and Claire come bounding down the stairs and it's pretty plain this is our curtain call.

'How did you find out where the climbers were staying?' I ask Claire excitedly on the way back to Kennet.

'The locals on the campaign are like gold dust,' she says. 'Especially if they're at Reading Uni doing a bit of chambermaid work to make ends meet.'

The following day, Wednesday March 6th, we lose Bagnor Lane in the driving snow. It's one-all in terms of serious injuries. A woman broke her leg when a tree was chopped down with her still up it, and one of their chainsaw operators fell and received spinal injuries. Good. He's lucky the saw wasn't switched on or, to quote a cheesy gangster film, there would have been claret everywhere.

I talk to Helen about the risk of injury. It's obvious she's even more set to retire after this than she was at the start. 'I blame Blandy,' she says. 'Have you seen the callous way he gets through the day? People being virtually tortured out of the trees and he stands there eating his sandwiches. Unbelievable.'

I nod ruefully. 'Even if there was a fatality it wouldn't stop the road. There'd be an outcry for a couple of days in the quality press, but I doubt it'd even get on Richard and Judy.'

'Let's just hope no-one dies. No road is worth a life.'

'After some of the crazy shit I've seen here, I think Spanner, Lee Tree and the others deserve a stunt show on TV. It'd be magic. Could be called "Green Round the Gills" or something like that.'

'I think we better finish the evictions unscathed first – then think about their TV careers, don't you?'

Not everyone finishes Thursday injury-free. One of theirs fell out of a tree while clearing off-route and one of ours has a suspected broken ankle after having it stamped on at Skylark. Highlight of the day was the arrival from Sheffield of 'our' professional climbers. Even talking from the ground has had a great effect. Two of the scabs have quit, and Ben Moon, one of only two professional rock climbers in the country, has made it known he'll pay £75 to any of us who can cut off one of 'their' crustie climbers' dreads. We also heard that some naughty people had climbed into the security compound at Tot Hill last night, hot-wired a couple of JCBs and started smashing up the place with them.

I think I'm coming down with a cold or something – not surprising really. Sleep is getting rarer, but even more delicious and seductive when it arrives. But then the freaky dreams start. Thinking you're in an eviction when you're not. Just before waking up you hear the screaming, the chainsaws and then the terrible sound of falling timber – the strain of sinews as the felled trunk falls free of the part still in the earth with a near-human screech, the whoosh of displaced air as it falls and the ensuing crying, wailing and barrage of abuse aimed at Blandy and his men. It's a relief then to find yourself bolt upright and sweating in the treehouse and not on the front line, but there isn't even the option of switching on Radio 4 to lull you back to sleep. There are nicer dreams – well, more satisfying ones, where we capture Blandy, strap him down with a board over him, then put one-kilo blocks of wood sawn from trashed trees on top of him one at a time until he's screaming for mercy. Then I take some sandwiches from a lunch box and calmly eat them until the cries stop. Every time I've had this dream the filling in the sandwich has been different – but the satisfyingly grisly end is always the same.

They've started to evict Gotan – one of our biggest camps. The next two days are relatively uneventful except that they have built a track through to Redding's Copse. Word is they've had to order a cherry picker from the continent as there aren't any big enough over here to reach the top. On Sunday night JJ heard a rustling in the bushes, and on investigating found Sergeant Sully and Barry Norman watching us with infrared night sights. She's lucky she didn't get nicked for breaking her bail conditions. Gotan falls with 28 further arrests, followed by a party at Manic Sha in the evening. The Kennet contingent are jumpy – no-one feels like drinking much and we're back at the camp by ten. It's just as well ...

At 4am I'm woken by the sound of steel bar on steel drum and high-octane yipping. The eviction of Kennet has begun. I pull on trousers, boots and harness in double–quick time then stick my head out into the darkness.

'Tango! Eloise!' I call to my neighbours, who are by now in a similar state of bleary–eyed readiness.

Several trees away JJ is already primed for action, complete with head-mounted torch.

'How's you?' I shout.

'Pissed off,' she replies through cupped hands. 'Looks like they've taken the underwater lock-ons.'

Helen is going from walkway to walkway wishing us all the best and checking we've everything we need. I reply that if we haven't got it by now it wasn't very important.

She smiles weakly, gives me a hug and heads off in the direction of the Mothership, which she intends to defend herself.

Down in the clearing there's the faint rasping of a megaphone. 'This is your formal direction to leave. If you do not vacate the area you will be liable for arrest.'

'Hey Sheriff, you lardy cunt, go fuck yourself!' is the loudest – though not necessarily the best – piece of abuse I hear in response.

I edge across the walkway to confer with Eloise, looking down at the growing sea of yellow-jackets below. 'They've done us. I don't think anyone can get through the cordon.'

'Well, we'll just have to give them what for,' she replies. Inside she's grown ten feet during this campaign.

The cherry picker is positioned next to Dom's tree and the three climbers that are left start to slowly ascend.

'Shit! Where's Ben Moon when you need him?' I say.

Eloise points to the growing crowds below, the other side of the enemy lines. 'He's probably down there, cursing his luck.'

I look down and attempt a rough head count of guards. 'Jesus, there must be what – six hundred down there.'

'And less than twenty of us. Bring it on,' she says. If Tango lets this one go he's a bigger fool than I ever thought he was.

Dom's got his work cut out. He's a very useful climber but on a strictly amateur basis. There's two pros, a couple of guys with chainsaws and two other bailiffs up against him. Fuck.

As they go higher strategic branches are lopped off and Dom is forced to the top of his tree.

We're yipping and clapping like crazy – that's all we can do to help short of relinquish our own position.

He signals to JJ who's in the next tree and she climbs over to provide distraction – but they're not buying it. The higher branches can barely support his weight and with no further options he's forced to resist or give up – like the choice Paulo was given at Claremont.

Suddenly they're upon him – like hounds on an exhausted fox. He's hanging on to the spindly trunk for all he's worth but they've got him. A bailiff brings out a set of kwik-cuffs and applies one to Dom's arm. Fully two hundred yards across the wood I can see the pain all over his face as he's bundled into the bucket and the other cuff applied.

'Yeow, I don't fancy that much,' I say to a transfixed Tango.

'The West Papuans wouldn't stand for it,' he says.

'Well, get them the fuck over here then – and quick,' I reply.

The moment the bucket starts to move, the chainsaw team on the ground sets to work on Dom's tree. He's trussed up like a chicken and couldn't do anything if he tried. There's furtive movement in the crowd, jostling, pushing, trying to create a surge, but there's just too many of them. Can't see anyone getting in front of that blade, but even if they did I don't hold out much hope for that tree – a digger is revving up to smash into it as soon as the trunk is weak enough.

While the cherry picker goes down the climbers are released and go off in search of JJ. She's at a similar level to Dom, but has learnt from his example. She starts to climb high, enticing them into the canopy. Just when you think she has nowhere to go, she attaches a rope then abseils all of 60 feet down and comes to rest on the lower branches.

'Woah! Did you see that? Amazing! That was the coolest mother-fucking thing I've seen at Newbury,' says Eloise jumping manically on a branch.

However, the re-established team of platform and climbers is a potent combination, and within five minutes JJ is cornered with no more means of escape. Maybe because she's a woman, perhaps because they were made to look small earlier, they seem even more brutal than they were with Dom. At the final point of capture it looks as though she's going to fall, and indeed she does, and within five feet the rope takes the slack like a hangman's noose, and she's swinging and weeping – probably very glad to still be alive – as Blandy chews calmly on a sandwich. Her tree is safe for now as they haven't managed to get Gary and Ann out of the lock-on. It doesn't look like our friends from Reclaim The Streets are having a very good time. I can't see properly, but from the noise he's making Gary's being pressure-pointed and as for Ann, I'm sure arms aren't supposed to bend like that.

'Two-nil to them,' I say to my neighbours, 'but it's taken more than 90 minutes so far.' Next it's Izzy and Trev. Same thing again, with the climbers off in pursuit of the next target as the platform descends, and the recently caught prey caged in a waiting riot van.

'I wonder if Trev's on a comedown from last night?' I say.

'Wouldn't surprise me,' says Eloise, 'He lives for those disco biscuits.'

It's a special day so I'm willing to give him the benefit of the doubt, 'There's no evidence he was pilled up last night – and even if he was, so what? It might give him that extra rush he needs.'

Whilst giving them their due, trapping Izzy and Trev isn't going to be the toughest part this eviction. While Trev is slowly but bravely making his way up their tree, Izzy has gingerly moved out onto a walkway. The platform positions itself at the nearest point to the two and releases the climbers. Izzy – all seven stone of her – versus specialised professional athletes. And the amazing thing is there's a smile on the face of one.

'Ooh – can you see that!?' says Eloise. 'He really deserves a smack.' I've never seen her so livid.

There's really no need but the climber cuts the bottom rope and she momentarily falls before the clip and the strength of polyprop saves her from certain death. We can hear the sobbing from here.

The climber signals from the platform to come over and while it's on its way he wobbles the rope once more.

'Where the fuck is the Health and Safety Executive when you need them? He should be fined at the very least,' says Tango furiously.

'I don't think I've seen them once yet,' replies Eloise.

I look over to Trev. He's concerned but he's got troubles of his own. The higher he goes it's more likely a branch will snap and, short of jumping to another tree like a flying squirrel, he ain't gonna get much further.

The bucket's directly underneath Izzy, the climber makes a cursory check this is the case then cuts the other rope and she falls in a heap into the cherry picker.

Eloise is now in tears and I'm not far behind. She screams, 'No one has the right to do that to someone, no matter what they've done! How fucking dare you!'

I look at Tango as if to say 'Are you sure she's gonna be alright with this?' but it's not my call or his.

As Izzy is lowered there's no sign of resistance – just shock and distress. She's what? Twenty – and reduced to this shaking, sobbing heap by the government of her country. There's progress for you.

Down goes her tree and up goes the bucket to collect Trev, who's not going any further.

'What time is it?' I ask. It's noon. I can't believe we've had to endure eight hours of this, and there's plenty more to come.

At ground level Gary's cries worsen – and they're not letting legal support through. Bastards.

'They might as well be torturing him out,' says Tango. 'It's a miracle it hasn't really kicked off down there.'

Gary's cries, screams and tormented appeals for mercy ring hollow through what's left of the most beautiful part of the route. Eventually, he can take no more and succumbs. He clearly needs an ambulance, but there is none – and all he gets is the back of a van like everyone else. Ann's not having a picnic either. She will be lucky to escape this without a broken arm.

'Thank fuck there's only four hours of daylight left. I don't think I could take much more,' I say with a lump in my throat. I start to feel a panic attack coming on. This is all too much to take. I don't want to show it now but I really get the feeling that coming to Newbury was a big mistake.

Tango looks like he's got an idea, 'There's loads of folks down there now. I don't think we'll be done for incitement to riot if we encourage them a bit.'

I can make out some figures in the crowd. There are some fine digger divers amongst them. 'Come on then, what have we got to lose?' There's only us and Helen left and it'll be game over.

We start to shout at the top of our voices: 'Break through the cordon!' 'We need you!' Spanner's below, gets the message, puts a thumb up and starts to gesticulate towards the crowd. Then, like molecules in a physics experiment or little circles in a computerised model, the mass below us starts to move as if it were liquid trying to move through a membrane. The yellow band stretches back and thins, police horses move in from either flank. What was sporadic abuse coming from the sidelines becomes a cacophony of shouting and wailing interspersed with the odd yip of triumph. The Crowd is now its own entity, a creature in itself. Our welfare is no longer its central concern, it has its own temporary destiny to take care of.

'Go on, give it some! You know you want to,' says Eloise, who's cheered up distinctly in the last few minutes.

Even from sixty feet above, you can see the odd person fall in the mêlée, and even hear the associated distinct appeal for help and space.

The forefront of our line is breaking through – and our liquid rabble will soon be free of its rather porous container.

Even the climbers and bailiffs have noticed the mini-insurrection and have stopped what they're doing for now.

'What's with the delay?' I cry, 'Health and Safety? You weren't so worried about that just now.'

The dam is breached, and some of our best sprint off looking for opportunities to climb. A couple of people have reached the Mothership and I'm sure Helen will appreciate the company.

'Is it safe to throw down a rope?' I ask Tango.

'Can't see it doing any harm now. They're not going to step in.'

I attach a purple mid-gauge rope to a karabiner outside my tree-house, tie two prusik loops near the bottom end and let gravity unwind the rest of the coil. As it unfurls, it's as if it takes on more significance than a piece of rope – it's as if it symbolises freedom under duress.

First to reach us is a woman I don't know, and John from Oxford. Both are yipping with extreme glee. We greet them with hugs. The woman introduces herself as Natalie from Cardiff. 'Long time no see, buddy,' I say to John. I know he's been away from actions setting up a research arm of EF! called Corporate Watch but he still feels the need to explain his absence.

'Glad you could make it, guys. We'll try and make your stay here as comfortable as possible.'

Looking back at where the cordon was, it has re-established itself but the cops are looking pretty freaked. Even Blandy has a careworn expression we've not seen thus far in the campaign. A megaphone comes out and the crowd is given an order to disperse.

'That's a bit Fascist isn't it?' says Natalie.

'Depends why they're doing it,' replies Tango. 'They could be making moves to pull out for the day.'

He's right. Within ten minutes the climbers have packed up, the cherry picker reverses out of the clearing and the thick yellow line starts to dribble away.

The occupants of the three remaining treehouses are whooping and cheering like England had won the World Cup. As darkness comes it's a strange feeling. We know with reasonable certainty that we're really gonna get it with both barrels tomorrow, and the euphoria of late victory merged with the emotional roller-coaster we've been on all day reduces our capacity for celebration.

With no cooking equipment available, dinner is reduced to cheese sandwiches – peanut butter for the vegans – and a whacking great carrot cake Wendy made specially.

With Eloise reluctant to use a knife I'd just used to cut cheese, I decide to wind her up a little.

'This dairy-free stuff is all well and good,' I say to her, 'and I can see the reasons why, but where do you draw the line?'

'What do you mean?' she says.

'So do you refuse to eat the by-product of any mammal?'

'Yeah – sure. No yoghurt, no milk, not even honey.'

'How about oral sex then?' I ask. John cracks up and Natalie is stifling the same.

'Not that I want to pry, but I'm guessing ... you know,' I waft my head over at Tango.

'So what's your point?' she asks defensively.

'Well forgive my ignorance if I'm wrong here, but isn't semen – Tango's semen to be exact, the by-product of a mammal?'

She starts to squirm. 'I'm not having this conversation. It's stupid. Is there any alcohol around?'

'You should know, you live next door.' There's just enough red wine for one glass each. 'Sorry there's not more,' I say to our guests. 'Couldn't get the beers in up here as it makes you piss too much.'

'No worries,' says Natalie. 'I'm having a fine time just as we are. Cheers.'

'Here's to today,' toasts Tango. 'May tomorrow be nothing like it.'

Unsurprisingly we're all up bright and early the next day – 4am. Without any radio contact we feel really vulnerable. No sign of them though, the bastards. However, this gives us time for reinforcements and soon after five Bob arrives with a vanload of folks we divide between our trees and the Mothership. Like picking teams in the playground I choose Claire and Nick as well as our beloved quartermaster.

'Nice to see you big man,' I say to Bob. 'It's like trying to stretch out a draw in a cricket match when we've only got a couple of wickets left,' I say. No one really gets it.

'I've got some bad news,' says Bob. 'JJ's been remanded. She's been transferred to Holloway.'

I'm gutted but try not to show it. 'You really know how to brighten our morning, don't you. How is she?'

'The lawyer saw her for five minutes last night. Not much chance of bail though, seeing as she's been charged with breach of her existing conditions.'

We prepare breakfast for old and new guests alike but recent news makes the soya milk taste and even more insipid than usual.

Blandy and the boys roll up about six, as does the crowd and we're back to a similar position as close of play last night except we have four times as many people.

On the upside, they're gonna have more work to do but the sheer number of bodies knocking around can also be a hindrance.

There's twice as many security as yesterday – six, maybe seven hundred. There's no way we can storm the palace gates again. We're on our own.

Also, to add insult to injury there's two cherry pickers.

'How thoughtful of them to get us one each,' says Nick, proudly sporting one of the medals he was given at the rally.

'Is there a strategy?' I ask everyone.

'Don't get caught,' replies Eloise, 'and don't give up.'

I'm not saying I'm built for life in the trees – but Bob really isn't and his 15-minute resistance is more symbolic than actual. Whether it's his age or demeanour they're really quite nice to him. Seeing as he basically lives at the Office getting nicked and bailed isn't gonna make that much difference.

We're trying to keep an eye on progress with the Mothership as well as stay aloof from our pursuers. There's no walkways left, just branches, ingenuity and crossing your fingers.

The climbers are directly below me and Natalie near the cargo net. Whatever supplies we've got left won't be for eating. I grab a tin opener and left-handedly cut the lid off a can of mushroom soup.

I offer it to Natalie. 'Ladies first?'

She takes the tin, aims carefully and empties it all over a nearby climber just as he's in hot pursuit of Eloise.

'Was that fun?' I ask her.

'Got another?'

'No, it's my turn,' I reply in a childish voice.

The other climber for our tree is in the bucket. I'm going to have to wait for a decent shot but it'll be worth it, I'm sure.

'Hey, Natalie. That gives me an idea,' I say, remembering a fireside chat with JJ a couple of weeks ago.

'You're not, are you?' She says as I head back into the treehouse.

'Oh yes. I think it's time,' I say grabbing two half–filled carrier bags full of shit and a good half–gallon of urine.

'I'm glad you girls had a funnel. Gives us more ammunition. Trouble is – it'll be so satisfying to hit them I'll be terrified to miss.'

'Go on, give it here,' she says grabbing the piss barrel and pours at least a pint's worth over the climber she's only just hit with the soup. There's a raucous cheer from the ground as it splashes over his face, and it feels like we're in Jack And The Beanstalk on acid.

'Great shot, you've got some sort of talent for this,' I say as we share a high-five. She bows, playing to the gallery with some finesse.

Our new toys are great but by their very nature not very portable. I'm reluctant to relinquish them, but the guys in the bucket and one we've just hit are no fans of coming near us right now.

'Let's just hope he doesn't take it out on Eloise when he gets hold of her,' says Natalie.

Women have been off my agenda since New Year what with everything going on, but she's not unattractive. If I'm not mistaken there's a cute butt underneath those cargo pants and an infectious grin to match.

Meanwhile, John's been cornered out on a limb by the bucket team and he holds his arms up in mock-surrender. He's got a five-year-old son back in Oxford so must have a higher sense of self-preservation than we do.

'I can't believe how lucky I've been,' I say. 'Nearly a day and a half and they've not really to gone near me. Must be luck of the draw.'

'Or you really smell,' she says with a cheeky wink.

We're up higher than the Mothership and consequently it's taking them longer to shift us than Helen's crew.

It's good news/bad news for Eloise – she's treated quite well but is the first to be taken down by a new tactic. The climber clips onto her, secures a rope to the tree, and abseils down with her attached to his front.

'We're losing numbers – fast,' says Natalie. What shall we do?'

'I don't know – never even built a treehouse 'til ten weeks ago. I s'pose we should split up.'

'Do you want the shit?' she asks.

'Now that wouldn't be very gentlemanly now, would it?'

'No really – you take that, and I'll take the piss.'

I grab the bags trying not to spill them all over me and place them in one coat pocket and the open tin of soup in the other.

'Listen,' I say to Natalie as I start to climb away, 'do you fancy going for a drink once all this is over?'

'I'll think about it,' she says with a smile.

Although my arboreal skills have improved immeasurably this year, I'm still not exactly the King of the Swingers, the jungle VIP. With each new step on a branch you sense both your stability and how pleased that part of the tree is to support your weight. All that as well as looking out for the enemy, trying to pre-empt their next move, and working out your own.

The platform's coming for me now. My luck's run dry but fortunately the bags have not and the climbers were busy elsewhere when I snuck them into my pocket. They're about a dozen feet below me but rising and six feet to the side. I take out the first bag, undo the reef knot holding it all in, and with a combination move of tip and throw, empty the fetid, stinking contents over all three of them. It's a decent shot, and everyone's different varieties of poo have had time to meld into something a bit more viscous than Polyfilla.

There's cheers from below, and I raise my hands in triumph. But the bucket's still coming – and they ain't pleased.

Still, I've done it now, in for a penny in for a pound. By the time I get the second bag out they're grabbing at my boots, and it takes very little skill to get most of it right in the climber's face.

'You disgusting cunt,' he says.

'Couldn't have put it better myself. You're disgusting,' I say in neutral, even tones. Then chuck the soup right over one of the bailiffs.

'Ok, ok,' I say hands aloft, fearful of a beating or worse. 'I give up. I'm coming down.'

I climb in, anxious to stay as far away from the three of them as possible, meekly offering my wrists to be 'cuffed by one of the bailiffs and have my rights read.

As the bucket lowers I peer over the side and see Genevieve with a video camera.

'Woo! Gen!' I shout, 'Are you getting all this?' She nods.

'Good,' I say quietly to the three of them whilst smiling broadly for the lens. 'If you lot so much as lay a fingernail on me I'm gonna sue you big time.' They're as nice as pie after that.

I look up to where Natalie is and give her a double-handed wave. She responds with, 'Nice one, Lester, let's go for that drink in a couple of days, eh?'

'Sure thing. Will do,' I shout, but by now we're only feet from the ground. Platform comes to a rest, ready for my arrest. I'm handed over to a couple of Thames Valley's finest, and shout a loud 'Come on! You've been great!' to the crowd as I'm put in the van.

Compared to the last ten weeks, a night the cells is luxury. There are no draughts, there is conventional plumbing but I do miss the gentle rocking motion of my tree, which barring miracles is now no more. Once asleep, it's some of the best quality shuteye I've ever had.

In the morning I'm bundled into court and – surprise, surprise, am bailed off the entire route. The magistrate asks if I will abide by this, I rise to my full height and clearly state, 'Of course, Your Honour'. Thankfully, the campaign office is not on–route and is where I intend to be until the evictions finish... well, most of the time.

Kennet holds out until the end of that working day. Unsurprisingly, it's Nick and Claire who are last to be apprehended. The Mothership is no more, and neither is my treehouse in all its plain, functional glory. I never did get chance to read that copy of Treasure Island.

'So, Statto,' I say, bounding into the office the day after my release, not sure why I'm so full of the joys of spring, 'What's been happening?'

'Well, someone got pushed off a bike near Skinner's Green Lane by a passing motorist, we lost Castle Wood yesterday, Manic Sha's radio is dead, Pen Wood is surrounded and no-one wants to go on Kilroy tomorrow morning.'

'That's quite an update, but how are you, mate?'

'He's fine,' says Bob. 'Same as he ever is.'

'So what do you want me to work on?' I ask.

'Well. You can ring the local housing office if you like.' says Bob taking me by surprise. Sensing my quizzical look he adds, 'With so many evictions going down, we're increasingly running out of places to put everyone. There's about a dozen staying at Wendy's, using all her hot water. She doesn't mind, bless her, but they've gotta go somewhere.'

'Mmm ... That brings me on to something I was gonna discuss with you. Is there room for me to kip in the office tonight? And the night after?'

'Oh I suppose so, as it's you ... but no bringing back strange women at all hours. Unless you've got one for me too,' says Bob with a smile.

I pick up the phone, ask the lads for the council's number and am certain I'm just about to weird out some housing officer's day.

Strangely, the office isn't as comfortable as a police cell, but then Newbury nick doesn't turn into a crazed nerve centre at 5am every morning. You'd think that with an ever-decreasing number of camps, the campaign would be easier to run. But it isn't. There's a higher injury tally by the day, and we're trying to arrange support for those who've been freaked out. Still, there have been compensations. By what I heard on radio Ben Moon and the other climbers are fantastic assets for the campaign. It all got very personal in the climbing community and they were exchanging punches and kicks high in the air – the kind of duels Vader and Luke Skywalker would have been proud of. When Ben and the others got nicked they were charged with violent disorder – far worse an offence than any of us received.

I go to the Clocktower in the hope of seeing Natalie, but no dice. Fuck knows where she's gone. I've even tried to find her on the campaign database – and yes, privacy-wise I know that's dodgy – but she's not listed anyway.

In the last few days we've lost several camps – Seaside, Babble Brook, Seven Oaks, Heartbreak Hotel and Horseshoe. It's disappointing, but there's one big battle left – to defend the Corsican pine at Reddings Copse. I decide this is too much of a spectacle to miss.

'You're what? Going in disguise? To watch an eviction?'

'Yup.' Bob can't quite believe his ears.

'Are you fucking insane or what?'

'Oh come on, so long as I don't get nicked it'll be fine.'

'Or picked by a snatch squad, or spotted by Sully's goons.'

'Well, I'm sorry, Bob, my mind's made up. I've even bought a dreadlock wig for the occasion.'

'Statto?'

'Yes, Uncle Bob?'

'Have you been dropping naughty things in Lester's tea again?'

'No, I ...' Statto stops in mid-defence to an upraised palm.

'Ok,' says Bob, 'you young 'uns won't be told. At least take a handheld CB in case you hit any bother.'

I give him a hug of reassurance. 'I think that might arouse more suspicion than my wig,' I tell him.

I only have to wait till the following Wednesday. Our monitors have done their job admirably, both slowing down and following the massive convoy to Redding's Copse.

I chat with the guys over the radio. 'What's going to be your opening line? Over.'

'Come and have a go if you think you're tall enough,' is their response.

I hand over the mike to Bob, put on my wig and wait for someone who's going to the eviction to pass by the office. Five minutes later Edna sticks her head round the door and although she doesn't recognise me at first agrees to take me. 'I hope you're gonna go faster than eight miles an hour.' I say.

Reddings Copse has been reduced to Reddings Pine and a few scattered oaks. We park up and mingle, but I try not to say anything for fear of being recognised. Taking a position two lines back in the crowd I fight the feeling of wanting to get involved – trying desperately to convince myself I'm a spectator for the day.

There's three cherry pickers – two regular ones and the gargantuan motherfucker picker they've hired from Europe. They work in unison – the former go for the oaks; the latter makes a start on you-know-what.

Showing both good technique and stout defence our side hold their own for the best part of two hours. I can barely see the guys at the top of the pine, it's so tall.

Things get nasty on the oak when the chainsaw crew starts to cut far too close to an occupied treehouse. I look at the faces around me – composites of horror and fascination – unable to look away. The underhand tactics seem to freak out our team and the oak is cleared somewhat sooner than I would have imagined.

Blandy directs a bulldozer – bucket fully down – to take a run at the oak, which it does. But not with quite the desired effect. The mighty tree twists on its root system and falls 30° shy of where it should have splashed down. It slowly drops with mounting fury straight into the control panel of the monster cherry picker. Like someone scoring a goal from nowhere – there's a momentary silence where we can't quite compute what's just happened. Then we fall about and even news that a bailiff has been injured in the process just makes us laugh even harder. Somebody calls out: 'Didn't you do geometry at school, Blandy?' Another shouts: 'Is that what happens to the angle of your wood when you see the Missus?'

'I'm so glad I came along,' I say to Edna. 'Wouldn't have missed this for the world.'

'This is going to go down a storm at bingo on Friday,' she replies.

Blandy is left with his uneaten sandwiches and a lot of explaining to do. Work is stopped for the day and when I return to the office the radio and phones are red-hot with the story.

Next day in the office it's all back to normal.

Statto gets off the phone and says: 'That was legal support. The person who put the rope around the portaloo has been charged with obstructing an officer in his motion.'

Within seconds Bob's crying with laughter and I get the can't-stop infectious giggles. Statto doesn't quite get it.

Three things aren't quite so funny today – firstly, we lose the appeal on the snails. They'll be translocated to another site, and Rickety Bridge is on full alert. Also, we hear a first-hand account of the pine coming down. At the last moment someone broke through security to try and stop the chainsaw. They got within about six feet before being manhandled to the floor and dragged away. And we have to organise an ambulance off for someone who was pulled out the tree by a rope round their neck. Nice.

Still day after day the trees come down, the tears fall, but tempers are lost, as are the camps. And with a couple of notable exceptions Blandy has not given a solitary shit – not that we've seen anyway.

The next major battle is for Middle Oak camp. At its centre the most majestic example of ancient English tree on the route. None of your Corsican rubbish. This is the real deal. Despite a brave fight much of the camp goes down, but the main tree is still standing.

It's then on to Rickety Bridge – a proper five-day fight. There may be the odd flaky person in most camps, but with Rickety Bridge it's solid talent. More experience, more walkways, more climbing aware-ness and just more balls. There's all sorts to tell – extreme use of techno to freak out the opposition, and from the range of injuries we have to mop up I can only guess there was some extraordinary digger-diving going on.

The other side has their fair share of mishaps as well. A security Land Rover turned over and the driver is in hospital with spinal injuries. The camp eventually succumbs in the fag-end of the month as does virtually all of Mary Hare after similar battles. There's hardly anything left – Camelot's one to look for on your coupons. Apparently King Arthur has written to his fellow monarch at Buckingham Palace requesting her swans be saved along with the camp. Alas too late – Camelot falls on April Fool's Day amid rumours the swans chased Blandy into the river. After seven weeks and many attempts to fell the final tree in Tot Hill they finally succeed the following day. Middle Oak's still standing but there's nothing much left to salvage. Although bail conditions still apply Bob drives Statto and myself down to Tot Hill once we've knocked up a press release marking the fall of the final camp. On our arrival we find Spanner, alone and clearing up debris. He's crying.

'Woah lad, there's no need for that,' says Bob trying to comfort him.

He falls upon Bob's shoulder, sobbing like a child. 'When it was all over,' says Spanner, fighting back a snivel, 'when they felled the last tree the climbers got their wallets out and offered to buy us all drinks down the pub.'

'And did they go?' I ask.

'What do you think? Would you?' he bats back at me. 'Course I wouldn't.'

However, drinks are the order of the day down the Clocktower later on. I've never seen the bar so packed, and Barb seems to be giving most of the drinks away tonight, but with us lot it's not advisable.

Over at one of the far tables I spot Natalie. I catch her eye and she responds with that trademark smile, though I can hardly get through because the pub is completely rammed. There's a festival

atmosphere – a final release from the insane hours, the cruel waiting, abuse, upset and just the general siege mentality we've been
locked into all year. Barb's spinning party tunes and the whole bar
seems to be moving. Maybe put it down to youth, but despite all the
energy we've expended we're still having it. The intro to Fiesta by
the Pogues starts up and a big circle forms; Tango, Eloise, Bob,
Statto, Dom, Jane, Helen, Swampy and a few others I don't know so
well all arm-in-arm. A rough form of can-can involving kicking the
person opposite in the shins starts. As I push past Bob grabs me
and yells: 'Lester, ya basstard. Come and join the dancin'.'

'I'd love to, mate, but I've got important business to attend to over
there,' and point to Natalie who's still smiling in our direction.

'Ok, I'll let you off. But make sure you're up at eleven. Blandy's
holding a press conference at Middle Oak. Pass it on.'

'Will do, boss. I'll be there.' I turn and fight my way to her table.

'I thought we were supposed to go for a drink?' I say finally reaching my destination. It's so packed we're forced closer than normal
social space would allow. I'm not complaining.

'Sorry – I was invited to go to the Gower for a few days after I got
released to recover from it all.'

'It's alright for some.' I say with feigned haughtiness.

'Well – we're in the pub now. What are you having?'

'Dirty thoughts – but I'll have a pint of Dog Bolter as well if that's
ok.'

She winks and heads to the bar. The camps may be dead but it
looks like my luck's changing at least.

As she returns the track ends and the next thing we hear is
Freddie Mercury singing, 'Tonight I'm gonna have myself a very
good time.'

'Oh wow!' I say. 'I love this song. It's ...'

She cuts in with, '... so shit it's brilliant. I think so too. Wanna
dance?'

For the next four minutes we jig around, pogo, roll around on the
floor, crawl through each other's legs and generally get lost in the
moment. As Freddie la-la-las at the end, Dom comes and pours a
pint over my head.

'Sorry, mate, just looked like you needed cooling down there.'

'You're just lucky it wasn't my beer,' I say before grabbing him and
giving him a big kiss.

Once we put each other down I return my attentions to Natalie.
'So how long are you hanging around for?'

'Mmm, not sure. I've put my tent up at the visitor's camp, it's been
a bit like Bosnia there lately. You?'

'I've been kipping in the office since Kennet,' I say with a certain
sense of pride and shame.

'Sounds like you need to rekindle your connection with the great outdoors,' she says, with her big blue eyes looking up at me. 'I'm sure I've got a bottle of sherry knocking around somewhere.'

'I was sold on the idea even before you mentioned the booze. But now I'm definitely in.'

We rejoin the party for half an hour or so – Abba's juxtaposed with Orbital, Don't Look Back In Anger followed by some ear-bleed Gabba. No one really cares about the playlist. Tonight, no-one really cares about anything much.

Tiny dots of sunlight make their way from the centre of the solar system through the polyester of Natalie's tent before joining forces to wake me up. The duvet is blue, warm, and smells deliciously of the naked woman beside me. I don't have much recollection of the latter part of the evening but do remember we stopped at third base as we didn't have any johnnies.

'Morning.' I spoon her, resting 'morning glory' against her inner thigh.

'Oh, it's you,' she says in mock surprise. 'I was expecting the milkman, but you'll certainly do for now.' She turns round and we get lost in kisses, fondling and basically each other for sufficient time to build to a mutually spontaneous climax.

'Shit! What's the time?' I ask in a sudden panic. 'I suppose we'd better get down to Middle Oak for the press conference.'

She clears the hair from her face and sits up. 'Climax or climate? It's a tough choice, but we should do the right thing.'

'Well, I'm all for a bunk-up tonight if you are,' I say reaching for my boxers, then forwards pensively as if listening to what my genitals have to say. 'What's that? Right. My penis just told me to tell you he would very much like that.'

'Tell him I'd very much like that too – as soon as we get some contraception,' she says with a grin. 'I wouldn't wanna get pregnant here. I'd feel obliged to call it some horrific hippy shit name if I did.'

As we arrive at Middle Oak there's the best part of a couple of hundred people representing four 'tribes' for want of a better word. The displaced activists and disgruntled locals make up the lion's share, with half as many pro-road types and around 40 ladies and gentlemen of the press, the remainder being DoT officials, two dozen police and Blandy himself. A plastic banner emblazoned with the DoT logo and proudly saying Roads To Progress is hung in front of the oak from the kind of collapsible stand a software company would use at a trade fair.

A suit, who I assume to be a government press officer, approaches the microphone. 'Good morning, everyone. Today marks the end of the clearance of the route. I'd like to hand over to Sheriff Blandy to say a few words to mark this auspicious occasion.' It would be unfair to say there are no cheers, and it could be where I'm standing but what I mostly hear is a barrage of boos and abuse far beyond any swearing Bernard Manning or Chubby Brown are capable of.

Someone starts singing 'Nick Blandy's no friend, he's a fat earth rapist' to the tune of the chorus of Blowing In The Wind, and within a few repeats we're all singing it, much to Natalie's and my amusement. Another person calls out: 'You've destroyed all this, now fuck off home for your sandwiches.'

Blandy starts to read from a prepared statement over the top of our attempts at comedy. 'Firstly, I would like to thank my bailiffs, security and Her Majesty's Police for executing a difficult operation with efficiency and dignity.'

'They were your hired thugs, plain and simple,' shouts someone, 'you cunt.'

Blandy continues, 'As a concession to the protests it has been decided that Middle Oak should not be felled and is to be a main feature of a roundabout.'

There are some cheers, but mostly disbelief at the man's gall. 'I can't believe he's going to get the credit for that.' Natalie's agog.

'What about the other ten thousand trees, Blandy?' comes a call from behind me, which is ignored.

The Sheriff continues: 'That concludes my statement. Now if any journalists have questions I'd be more than happy to answer them.'

Natalie calls out: 'Has your family disowned you? Are you ashamed?' But Blandy doesn't bite.

One journo asks what Blandy's feelings are towards us and he replies: 'There have been violent, illegal and quite immoral actions carried out by unsavoury elements and this has tarnished the legitimate protests against the road.'

I suppose we didn't expect any better from him, but after the months of pain, anguish and all-round trauma he's put us through, something must have been triggered in our collective psyche. Someone cries out 'Storm the stage!' and without having a meeting or reaching any consensus we're all heading – mostly running – towards Blandy. Not with a view to harm him, more merely to show we are not defeated.

We pile through, past the madly snapping photographers and there are too many of us for the cops to deal with. Even before we take the stage, Blandy has been pulled away and is waddling down the track to the safety of a riot van which, within a minute of him leaving the stage, has revved up and driven away.

We're jumping up and down, excited yet somehow sated. Natalie leaps onto me shouting: 'We did it! We ran the Sheriff out of town!'

We laugh, we make jokes, some sing, others talk to journalists. The DoT banner is ripped down and hung between two mighty branches of Middle Oak as a hammock, and several folks have a celebratory swing within it.

That night, back at the visitor's camp, the locals bring everyone more beer and food than we can possibly consume, then we head off to the nearest unspoilt countryside to watch both a meteor shower and the passing of a comet.

I lie back with Natalie, blankets trapping our shared body heat. Many miles above us cosmic dust overheats and combusts. 'It's as if Mother Nature's putting on a firework display to say thank you.' says Natalie.

'Don't be a such fucking hippy,' I reply with a smirk and a long lingering kiss.

CHAPTER 12

SPRING 1996

Three weeks after Newbury the phone trees ring once more. Mass emails are sent, and there is much licking and sticking of envelopes. However, for once there are no roads to stop, no communities or forests to protect, no corporations to fight and no issues to campaign upon.

My parents forward my invite over to Natalie's house in Cardiff, where I've – brace yourselves – even started looking for a proper job.

A hand-drawn invitation adorned with D-locks, cranes, empty bottles of booze and zonked-out activists around the border reads:

You are cordially invited to Dom's 30th Birthday Party.
Saturday 25th May
Sunny Vale Farm, Lostwithiel, Cornwall
Main party 2pm till Late. Festivities all weekend.
Please note: No one is allowed to call an action this weekend – we deserve some downtime.
Bring friends and a sense of celebration for all we have recently achieved.

'Cornwall? I thought he lived in Manchester?' says Natalie, vigorously rubbing a towel over her newly-washed work hair.

'I think his uncle owns some land down there. It'd be rude not to go,' I say sheepishly, fast learning the tactics needed when living with a woman.

'Of course we're going,' she says, adopting it as her own idea. We breakfast, canoodle on the stairs for a few minutes, then she's off to the wonderful world of youth work leaving me to my own private job club. No Ken Bierce to kick my arse, no resources to blag. Just me, the local paper and a newly-found realisation I can't be an activist on the dole forever. I'm not quite sure what I've been trained to do since university, but hey, I'm looking. There must be some employer out there who'll value the skills I've learnt in the last three years.

We leave for the party on the Friday as soon as Natalie gets back from work. The coach gets us as far as Penzance, and we decide to hitch the rest for the sheer romance of it. We get within striking distance of the farm by dusk, and decide to pitch camp by a stream, build a little fire and just be together.

'I wish I'd known you before Kennet got trashed. We could have done this there – and back to my treehouse,' I say, exploiting my position behind her to tickle her into submission on the ground.

'I wish Kennet hadn't been destroyed in the first place,' she says when she stops squealing for mercy. 'And I wish I had time to still be there.'

I've heard that a few camps remain off-route to try and prevent the contractors building the road. There's been over a thousand arrests but you get the feeling everyone's burnt out and looking to move on, including myself. 'Not sure if I'm ready to return to activism just yet – if at all,' I tell her. 'A straw poll of my head, heart or overdraft would give response "Fuck you".'

'You'll be back to it,' she teases. 'There may be some plan in your head to become a ... what's the latest plan again?'

'Well, last week it was doing teacher training if you remember, but I'd hate the kids, wouldn't I?'

She nods, not knowing what to suggest. 'Activism's in your blood, I don't think the cops have seen the last of you. Now,' she says seductively changing tone, 'I'm thinking you won't feel indecisive about an early night.' We douse the fire with water from the stream, brush teeth and undress as quickly as the space-time continuum allows, then fuck 'til the small hours demand their ration of sleep.

Next morning a bleached blond teen surfer drives us right past the main gate of the farm. We thank him then stride with our tat on our backs through a coppiced glade accompanied by late season cuckoo calls and Natalie goes 'aah' when we see something like a shrew scurry across our path. 'God, isn't it wonderful?' she says, 'should we sack Cardiff and go live on the land?'

'You'd be bored in twenty minutes,' I say with a reassuring hug. 'So would I, and that's why I love you.'

As we reach the farmhouse preparations are well under way. Dom's using his harness to hang bunting, handed up to him by his latest flame. Jane and Des have the glamorous task of digging a shit pit. Eloise and Tango are chilling in the sun, the former holding Kettle Chips up for Kropotkin to eat on his hind legs.

'Well, well,' I say, 'It's like fucking Mr and Mrs round here.'

The birthday boy responds with mock piety. 'You can talk, I'm not living in sin.'

We set up the tent and help with preparation. Natalie raids the recycling bin, grabs all the newspapers she can and makes two six-foot origami palm trees, which she paints brown and green. 'I suppose youth work teaches you something,' I say disguising my girlfriend-related pride.

Before long familiar faces arrive from around the country. Nick and a half-pregnant Claire, JJ and Spanner rejuvenated by a couple of months in southern Spain. Paulo arrives with a stunner in tow, drama student, all tits and teeth but highly decorous nonetheless. Even Helen's coupled up with a quiet fella by the name of George. Colin and Gehan have made the effort to come down from Scotland. There's all the Leeds lot, with the exception of Mark who's still in Brazil. Most of Reclaim The Streets turn up in two vans. In all, by mid-afternoon about 400 activists, friends and partners have made the trip and are ready to have it large.

'Hello Mr Stype.' I hear a familiar voice behind me. It's Bob, clutching a wad of cash, followed by Statto, who's got slightly funkier glasses and haircut than I've seen him wearing before. 'I assume you're up for the all-you-can-drink bar? It's a fiver each – I bought a truckfull from the cash and carry,' continues Bob.

'Does the Pope shit in the woods? Of course I'm in,' I say and hand him a tenner for me and Natalie.

Next to the farmhouse is a big courtyard where Tim, Jane and Des are knocking a bar together. 'I take it that four by two ain't mahogany?' I jest. Jane just sticks out her tongue and continues to hammer away. Across the courtyard is a big barn surrounded by the kind of trees we fought so hard to defend in the winter. Natalie kindly offers to pitch the tent, leaving me to catch up with folks. In the farmhouse kitchen, I spot Beech, my old college football mate-turned-activist, clutching a huge wodge of blankets, which I can only assume contains a baby.

'Hey, how's it going, man?' I ask with a hug careful not to crush the little one.

'Yeah, real sweet. You can see I've been a bit busy lately. This is Meg.' He parts the blankets to reveal firmly shut eyes above a button nose.

'Congratulations,' I say, kinda meaning it.

'Well, all me and the Missus did was have a shag, but thanks anyway.' Then adds an afterthought: 'Oh, did you hear about Sparko?'

'Don't tell me, he would have been here today but he's collecting an MBE for services to the alcohol industry.'

'No,' Beech replies in a serious tone, 'I'm afraid not. He's dead.'

'Oh shit,' I say, feeling guilty. 'Overdose?' Beech nods. It's weird, but despite my dislike of dogs my heart suddenly goes out to poor fucking Strongbow.

On a brighter note there's some lush food being made in the kitchen; grilled aubergine, sun-dried tomato and halloumi stacks, huge vegan chocolate cakes and other vegetarian gourmet delights.

Despite the alluring smells and growing hunger pangs I go in search of Natalie, unsettled by the news of a fallen comrade. I help her put the tat in the tent, and I suggest we zip ourselves inside for an hour or so, wanting our closeness to blot out any feelings of inevitable mortality and decay.

By the time I'm ready to face the world again the party has begun. Techno is coming out of the barn, a fully functioning bar covered with tarps, which look like Newbury veterans, and an array of chaises longues, armchairs and sofas laid out in the courtyard. As I join Eloise at the bar, I see someone's typed up a colourful cocktail menu – minus prices. 'It's great not needing anyone behind the bar,' she says pouring herself a large B52.

'I reckon even the vegans will tuck into that Bailey's once they're twatted enough.' At either end of the bar, optics have been set six feet above the ground, and Nick is encouraging everyone to lie on the floor and have vodka shot into their mouths. 'Come on you two,' he goads us and we comply resulting in cheers and a stinging left eye when the aim is not A1.

Me and Natalie pour a couple of White Russians and head off to the barn to shake our things. Thankfully by the time we arrive the techno has been replaced by the fantastic Lovefool by the Cardigans – and there's loads of folks who weeks before were head-to-head against the state making total prats of themselves singing the chorus in a high-pitch squeal.

Next, to the delight of most, is REM's It's The End Of The World As We Know It. As I look around the dance floor, it's like a little geographical representation of the British Isles. From Scotland to the southwest, relaxed and happy, a whole bunch of my special friends, ragbag revolutionaries, earnest ecologists, some absolute anarchists – so they'd have you believe. Right now they are guests, drinkers, smokers and dancers. The worries of the world fallen from their minds for the evening, or at least some of it. Perhaps we've built walls to add to foundations laid in the '60s. It'll be up to another generation to put the roof on.

'Shall I ask for any tunes?' I ask Natalie.

'Some Roses wouldn't go amiss,' she replies. I go and have a word with Ann behind the decks and after the next fade the drum intro of I Am The Resurrection kicks in to much mutual delight. We throw ourselves around for the full ten minutes, falling into group hugs, jumping up and down and singing the choruses like our lives depended on it.

Sweaty and puffed out, it's back to the bar. Then I plonk down on a saggy sofa in the courtyard next to Helen and George.

'Are you enjoying retirement?' I ask her.

Helen looks round, as if with some guilt, then a smile explodes across her face and she shouts: 'Yes! I fucking love it! Just started training to be a reflexologist.'

'A what?' I ask with genuine ignorance.

As she explains I can see she's transferred the vigour she put into her activism to her new vocation and somehow know she'll be fine.

'Don't you miss it?' Natalie asks.

Barely without thinking time Helen replies: 'Of course. It was the most wonderful, empowering and downright surreal three years of my life. Sometimes, my mind drifts to certain scenarios and I have a good old chuckle. It's like – what the fuck was all that about?'

Just then Tim comes diving over the top of the sofa onto us all. 'Hey, have you ever had alcoholic Dr Pepper? It's the only lager-based cocktail I know,' he says, ripping the top off a bottle of Stella with his teeth. Both curious and skeptical, I alone agree to try one and head off with him to the bar.

Unscrewing the lid off a bottle of cola he says: 'It's quite simple. Half-lager, half-Coke and then,' he says, reaching for the vital ingredient, 'a depth charge of Amaretto.' He drops a shot glass of the almond liqueur into the half pint of base mixture he's already made.

Picking it up I take a sniff, 'Yeah, smells like the real thing,' I say somewhat impressed. And bugger me if it doesn't taste just like it should.

Back at the sofas Dom's arrived. 'Everyone,' he says, 'we're gonna play a little party game now. Pass the parcel, with special accompaniment from Tez,' and there behind him is the troubadour of troublemakers. I sit back down next to Natalie and wave to Tez as he plays a bluegrass tune. Dom passes the parcel to his left and I feel transported back to the kind of party I went to in order to contract chicken pox aged nine. Just as you feel the music's gonna end, Tez plays another little riff, milking the moment for maximum amusement. Finally the parcel rests with Gary. He unwraps the outer layer, and a hash pipe and an eighth falls into his lap.

'Does anyone want this? I don't smoke,' he says and for a couple of minutes the game is disrupted as he is inundated.

I hadn't noticed before but JJ and Spanner are sat right next to me– a sure sign the booze has started to have an effect.

'What are you two up to now?' I ask.

JJ leans forward and says: 'I met some really inspiring people in prison, and we've decided to go into genetics.'

'Oh yeah,' I reply. 'I read something in SchNEWS about all that. Fucking around with fish and rats and shit.'

'... and soya, and corn, and rice and just about anything else,' she says with a sudden seriousness.

'That's great. Lovely to see you and good luck. I'm bursting,' I say pointing to my groin and just making it to the woods before disaster strikes.

Leaning against a tree, sighing with relief I notice Paulo and Trev coming of the woods minus their women.

'Hey dudes, how hangs?' I ask whilst zipping up.

'Woah,' says Paulo, quite unsteady on his feet.

'What have you had?' I ask in a quasi-schoolmasterly tone.

'Nothing he hasn't had,' says Paulo with a snigger.

'Cookies,' says Trev. 'A mate of mine has a grow house and he spun the off-cut skunk in a drum, capturing the pollen, man.'

'They're wicked. Do you want one?' asks Paulo, more off his tits than I've ever seen him.

An overwhelming feeling of what the hell overcomes me and I nod eagerly. Trev opens a flap in his coat, pulls out a Tupperware box, opens it and hands me a cookie.

'We were the bollocks,' says Paulo, picking his nose. 'All over this country, we fucking showed them.'

'Too right,' I say, feeling rather sober compared to these two.

'But is it enough?' asks Trev, pupils the size of dinner plates. 'Is it too late? Are we all fucked? I mean, stopping roads is ok, but what about the fucking planet?'

Nodding sagely I take a big bite on the chocolate cookie. 'I hope it's not too late. I'm gonna have too much fun being angry old wanker around 2050.'

Back at the courtyard the game is continuing and the parcel greatly reduced in size. Tez is having a good stab at the theme from The Deer Hunter then stops as the parcel rests with Natalie. She opens it, and within is a small wooden box with a hinge. I move closer as she parts the two halves revealing a purple silk lining and a wooden ring lying in the middle.

'Wow! It's so beautiful,' she says breathlessly.

'I reckon JJ had a hand in that,' I say turning to the queen of Kennet. She blushes.

I help Natalie put the ring on – making sure it doesn't go on any significant fingers.

Then it's back to the bar and the dancefloor for some groovin' and spinnin' around to Signed, Sealed, Delivered, I'm Yours. Ann plays Sorted For E's and Whizz and the cookie begins to have an effect – the THC crystals morphing my perception of time and reality. Makes the music go with an extra whoosh, and everything's hilarious. The price you pay is to have the short term memory of an elderly goldfish who's licked too many aluminium pans.

I spy Dom catching a breather sitting on a hay bale drinking something green and suddenly feel the need to join him.

'Are you ok?' asks Natalie.

'Nyeagh,' I say wandering off.

Putting one foot in front of the other is not a special move – doing so in a relatively straight line without looking like something further down the primate family tree is another matter. However, I manage to cross the floor without accident or incident and fall onto the nearest empty bale. 'Oi, birthday boy. Nice gig,' I slur, putting my arm round Dom.

'Thanks mate. You look trollied.'

'Sure am. I'm on me 'olidays.'

'Done any daily actions lately?' he asks.

'Hmm ... Not really – I've needed some time to find myself.' I can't tell if the dope is turning me into a philosopher, an arsehole or both.

'Are you gonna carry on?'

'Who fucking knows? Like, what was all that about anyway? Was it just us growing up?'

'Not sure, mate, but it was a lot of fun – most of the time.'

'Yeah – if you take out all the shit bits. Hey, What's that drink?'

'It's a Legspreader. Wanna try?'

I pant like a dog begging for a biscuit and he hands it over. I take a sip and mimic the bird off the food programme on the telly trying to guess the ingredients. 'I'm getting, I'm getting ... I'm getting about ten grand an episode for this shit.'

'Well, if you wanna know it's Midori, Malibu and pineapple juice. I heard an ace joke earlier.'

'Go on,' I say, struggling to focus.

'What sexual position produces the ugliest children?'

'I've absolutely no idea.'

Dom's just about to crack, but before he does says: 'Ask your mum.'

I fall off the side of the bale, giggle uncontrollably 'til I feel tired.

Natalie comes and finds me. 'You're on something aren't you?' she asks cheerily. I smile like a special needs bus. 'Come on, tell me?' Her new tone makes me think I'm in a cot staring up at my mobile and she's going to tickle my tummy.

'Paulo. Trev. Cookie,' is all I can muster, still lying on the ground.

There's a break in the music and Ann announces on the mike: 'And now everyone, Dom would like to say a few words.'

This is met with a cacophony of yips and miscellaneous jungle sounds. My contribution sounds like eeeoooww-aahaaaa-aahaaaa-loolooloo – think a marmoset in labour if you're having trouble working it out. I waggle my hands skywards at Natalie like I really do need lifting out of my cot and she struggles – bless her – to pull me to my feet just as Dom begins.

'It's great to see so many people here today, and I hope you're having a fabulous time. I know it said on the invite that tonight was to celebrate my birthday, but actually there's another reason. In this barn, out in the courtyard, and fuck knows where else are hundreds of some of the most incredible people I've ever met. This party is a small thank-you for all the time, effort, hardship, danger and,' he's lost in the moment, 'well, you know what I'm getting at. So, without further fuss, let's get back to mashing it up – doing to our brain cells what we did to the roads programme. Goodnight.'

The place erupts, feet slam on the floor, the animalistic mating calls intensify and all round the dance floor folks are sharing love. I sweep Natalie into my arms, trying my best to make sure we don't both topple into the dirt.

'Well done you,' I say before going in for a big snog. When we come up for air she says: 'But Newbury was my first campaign – you've done shit loads more than me.'

'That's not the point. You were there – that's all that matters,' I say, momentarily sobering up.

'I think it's booze o'clock,' she replies. 'If you've been on the drugs with the boys I'm playing catch up.'

So it's back to the bar, the cheesy strains of Come On Eileen in the near distance. En route we bump into JJ.

'Spanner's challenged Lee Tree to a prusik and abseil race. Wanna come see?' she asks, just as we hear cries of 'Tequila!' coming from inside the kitchen.

'In a bit,' says Natalie, 'I think that was a sign.' She pulls me towards the farmhouse and the paintstripper liquor of doom.

'Eeees everywaan rrready?' Beech has put his child to bed and is wearing a huge sombrero, a bigger grin and brandishing a cap gun.

'Wait! Two more,' says my special helper-cum-girlfriend. Glasses are found, filled to the brim and dispatched to our hands.

'Rrright. Eeees everywaan rrready theeese time?' shouts Beech again, followed by a big, fat chorus of thirty or so cries of 'yeah!'

'Rreeebaarr, rrreeebaaaarrr, wooooo,' he hollers, repeatedly firing the gun as we all drain our glasses and the foul tasting spirit disappears down our gullets. I gasp. 'That's the last time I ever drink that shit. Jesus.'

In the corner of the room I see Cosmo rolling a joint quite expertly despite the slightly boss eyed thousand-yard stare he's involuntarily adopted. I drag Natalie over to meet an old face. Someone – maybe Cosmo himself – has painted his nose to resemble a penis. On seeing me he points and mumbles 'ittzu' whilst sparking up with the other hand.

'Looking good, fella,' I say giving him a shake, 'lovely to see you.'

'Ah,' Cosmo says, exhaling two lungfuls of smoke. 'But can you really see me? Am I really here?'

'Well, yeah dude, sure you're here – you've just had a shot of tequila and someone's drawn a dick on your nose.' Natalie's picked up a can of lager and stifling her giggles into it.

'Hmm,' he nods sagely. 'Ok, so we're agreed. I'm still on the spaceship with you lot, spinning madly round the sun. But who's driving?'

'Not me buddy, not fucking me.'

'No,' he whispers in all seriousness. 'We're … only the maintenance crew. But there's too many people on board trashing the ship – and it's the only one we've got. They need to be stopped before it's too late.'

'That's deep, man,' I nod, confused and convinced.

He hands me the spliff and I suck for several seconds, try to hold the temporary treasure inside me for as long as I can before blowing the burnt particulates and carbon dioxide molecules out – another minuscule victory for global warming. I turn 180 degrees to face Natalie, but as I do my image of the room continues to slowly spin, and I know a whitey and a chuck-up session is just around the chronological corner. 'I need …' I try to verbalise my imminent plight but the words aren't there.

'What? The toilet? More cookies?' she asks, putting her hand on my shoulder.

Then, moving faster than I ever have past a security guard, and leaping with more urgency than any bulldozer received, I part the path to the sink, plunge my head towards the plug hole and yack up my guts.

'Phoooooowarp,' I wake myself up with the loudest fart I have yet done in Natalie's company. 'Sorry,' I say with three-quarters amusement and the remainder slight shame. We're in a tent – I assume it's ours – no fucking idea how we got here.

'You're forgiven, but only cos it's a special weekend,' she replies, to point out she retains firm reins on my demeanour.

'I feel fucking dreadful. Someone's pumped out all my blood and replaced it with vinegar. Is there any juice left?' I wriggle towards a carton potential life-saving fluid.

'Only if you want hair of the dog. Don't you remember pouring the rest of that quarter bottle of vodka in it about three am?' I recoil as if told of a turd lurking in the orangey goodness.

'How are you feeling?' I ask turning to her, aware my breath is not pristine.

'About the same as you – but I'm not the baby round here,' she replies and receives a double nipple tweak for her insolence.

'That so is domestic violence,' she responds, rolling over to pin me down by the wrists.

I make a four syllable high-pitched squeal similar to Beaker from the Muppets followed by, 'Go tell it to the judge ... and your mum, when she's not busy with all her clients.'

She goes into 'you're-so-not-worth-bothering-with' mode and starts to pack away. The sleep monkeys are hooting excitedly, waggling their dicks through the bars of my cage of consciousness. I turn over and try and sleep it all off.

Next thing I know is the sensation of fabric brushing face and the sudden realisation she's collapsed the tent with me inside. 'Thanks for the alarm call,' I muffle against the polyester, balancing one of the poles sideways across my nose.

She lifts the prone structure from me and peers through the hole. 'Come on, Rip Van Winkle. It's twelve-thirty. We better get a shift on.'

I clamber out to find she's packed my tat. What a girl.

'We've time for some lunch then we'd better make tracks,' she says without judgment.

'I don't think food's a good option right now,' I reply with half open eyes and full-on gut ache.

We pack the tent and wander to the farmhouse to say our goodbyes, but nobody's up.

'Fucking lunch-outs,' I say, 'let's get going.'

There's a breeze which, though not as good as a shower, provides psychological refreshment at least. Back through the woods to the main gate there's no shrew this time – he's probably flat on his back – pissed on the lingering fumes of last night. As we reach the road there's engine noise behind us. It's a couple of newbies in a green and white Bedford truck. We wait and they come to a halt at the junction, a girl winds down the passenger window.

'Do you need a lift?' she asks.

'Yeah, where are you going?' says Natalie.

'There's a chemical plant in South Wales. Some of our mates are planning to ... you know, need-to-know shit. Do you fancy coming along?'

'Sounds fun,' I say, looking Natalie right in the eye. I give a little enthusiastic nod and she's on the same page.

'Ok,' she says with an exasperated smile. 'I suppose I can always ring in sick tomorrow.'

THE END

or maybe not ...